D1058253

Constable's Wedding

Other Five Star Titles
by Laurie Moore:

Constable's Apprehension
Constable's Run
The Wild Orchid Society
The Lady Godiva Murder

Constable's Wedding

Laurie Moore

Five Star • Waterville, Maine

This novel is a work of fiction. Names, characters, places and incidents are either the product of the author's imagination, or, if real, used fictitiously.

First Edition
First Printing: October 2005

Published in 2005 in conjunction with PMA Literary and Film Management, Inc.

Set in 11 pt. Plantin.

Printed in the United States on permanent paper.

Library of Congress Cataloging-in-Publication Data

Moore, Laurie.
Constable's wedding / by Laurie Moore.—1st ed.
p. cm.
ISBN 1-59414-249-1 (hc : alk. paper)
1. Police—Texas—Fort Worth—Fiction. 2. Fort Worth (Tex.) —Fiction. 3. Policewomen—Fiction. 4. Weddings—Fiction. 5. Romanies—Fiction. I. Title.
PS3613.O564C663 2005
813′.6—dc22 2005015978

Dedication

For my daughter Laura, my pride and joy.

Acknowledgments

I wish to thank my editor, Russell Davis, for believing in me, for sticking with my Constable series and guiding me in the right direction; and Hazel Rumney of Five Star, who "discovered" me. For Mary Smith, the Five Star editor of my Fort Worth police mystery series, you are simply the greatest. Without the members of DFWWW who listen to my chapters each Wednesday night and offer their comments, I would not be so inspired. To the Sweet Shop of Fort Worth, a special thank you for supplying the world-class Fudge Love truffles for my book signings. And above all, to my daughter Laura for her constant encouragement and faith in me; I cannot imagine life without you.

Prologue

Judge Ronald Masterson knew just what to do.

He swooped down from the bench with great authority, feeling downright lethal in his flowing, black judicial robe, then swept into chambers, picked up the telephone and buzzed his Court Coordinator over the intercom.

"Get Constable Jinx Porter on the phone. If he's not there, ask for that girl-deputy, Raven. And make it quick. The ship's hit the sand over here."

The old jurist still had the receiver in his hand when a knuckle-rap sounded outside his door.

Two uniformed Sheriff's deputies—one, fanning himself with what appeared to be the unserved Writ Masterson issued that morning; the other, beet-faced and the pulse in his throat throbbing—waited for the go-ahead to enter. Masterson, an imposing figure with white hair and erect carriage, replaced the telephone in its cradle. He pulled off his wire-rim glasses and rubbed the phalanx of wrinkles hooding his eyelids, then reseated the spectacles into the deep pink dents on the bridge of his nose.

The boys from the Sheriff's Office needed to see he meant business.

Ought to thank their lucky stars they weren't going to lock-down for contempt.

Slitty-eyed, he tightened his jaw and looked them over, then waved them in with a downward hand motion aimed at the guest chairs. "Sit."

" 'Afternoon, Judge. Captain said you wanted to see us."

Betcha he did, after I gaveled the phone down in his ear.

Masterson leaned hard against the leather chair back and steepled his fingers. "What happened out at Fleck Standish's house? That Writ commands you to bring him and that child into my courtroom."

The deputy holding the unserved document spoke first. "We did see him, Judge—"

"But there was no sign of the kid." That from the partner.

"—only Mr. Standish said his mother took the girl to the mall and wouldn't be back until this evening. Something about buying clothes for a trip to Disneyland."

Masterson's face burned with primal heat. He addressed them in a low growl. "Deputies, the reason I issued that Writ is because Mr. Standish already ignored a summons. The maternal grandparents filed an intervention for custody on a welfare concern, and it's up to me to decide whether there's anything to it. I can't get both sides of the story if the guy fails to appear. And I can't talk to that girl if she's not here."

Simultaneous head bobs.

Perspiration dotted their foreheads.

The deputy used the Writ to fan his face. Angry red blotches cropped up around his cheeks. "Mr. Standish promised he'd bring her to court Monday morning at nine."

"You believed him?" Masterson kept his voice even and metered. "The grandparents allege he's a devil worshipper. I signed a Temporary Restraining Order last week, forbidding him to hide the kid. Now you're telling me you actually got to see him, and he convinced you he'll come in on his own volition?"

"Well, Judge, I suppose there's a possibility he won't show on Monday and we'll have to go back out and get him—"

"Assuming he sticks around. What's wrong with you

fellas? This heat getting to you?"

"You want us to go out there and wait for the grandmother to bring the kid back?"

The pulse in Masterson's throat throbbed. As a good Christian, he wanted to pull out the Colt Cobra he kept in the bottom drawer and use the butt to hammer the two incompetents into a pink stain. As a good Christian, he wouldn't.

Masterson oozed sarcasm. "Should've entrusted that Writ to Constable Jinx Porter. Or that girl deputy of his—Raven. Maybe sic her on Mr. Standish. Don't think I ever gave those two anything they couldn't handle. And why is that?" He fixed them with his legendary, falcon-eyed stare. "Reckon they're smarter than y'all? I just wonder."

To add to the terror, Masterson leaked a tip. "The Commissioners are talking about taking away the civil section from the Sheriff's Office and giving it to the Constable."

The deputies exchanged *Oh shit* looks.

"If that happens, you two showboats will be up a creek without a paddle. I'll take that Writ now."

Words spilled out in a hyperventilating rush. "We can run back by, Judge. We'll head out right now. If you tell us we can arrest him, we'll lock him up for the weekend and bring him over in jail khakis first thing Monday morning."

With his confidence in the deputies fully eroded, Masterson wheeled the chair back from the desk. He rose, thrust out his arm, palm-up, and let the silence speak for him.

Porter and his girl Raven would bring Fleck Standish in. And anybody else who got in the way, God help them.

The deputy handed over the Writ.

Masterson pointed to the door and they took their cue. "One more thing—"

They halted in their tracks.

"—if Fleck Standish runs with that kid, I'm calling

Channel Eighteen for a press conference. If that happens, you fellas may as well get ready to have your ashes scattered. Matter of fact, I see no reason to sugar-coat it. The last deputy who screwed up this bad is now assigned to the jail—permanently."

Chapter One

In an effort to save money, the sanitation department for the City of Fort Worth had forced plastic garbage cans and recycle bins on its citizens, and every Friday morning at six-thirty, Raven wheeled her trash out to the curb. Channel Eighteen's weatherman had predicted a line of thundershowers, but on this fine June dawn, Raven sucked in a lungful of heavy, unbreathable air that smelled nothing like rain. "Openly Gay José," as she liked to think of the swishy little Hispanic with effeminate hand gestures, wispy moustache and an affected lisp, had a hundred percent rating when it came to forecasting the weather: always wrong.

Her gaze strayed to the Victorian eyesore next door.

The neighbor, Yoruba Groseclose—a cranky old blue-hair with an addiction to Krispy Kremes—hadn't picked up her newspaper.

Might be sick, Raven thought. Old Lady Groseclose doubled as the neighborhood alarm clock each morning, grating metal shavings off the side of her '67 Mercury, backing out of the *porte côchere* in an attempt to get down to the donut shop in time for the first box of sugar-glazed, cardiac arresters. Maybe Miss Groseclose picked up enough to last several days?

Raven briefly considered tromping across the dewy grass and lifting the lion-crested doorknocker, then remembered how the last time she cut through the woman's English garden, the tissue-skinned harpy rattled a three-pronged cane at her.

Still . . . maybe she should brazen it out and do a welfare check.

Her ears pricked to the distant sound of a bleating telephone.

Tommy.

She bolted for the house, inwardly hoping to hear from her fiancé. As she reached the terra cotta porch and flung herself across the threshold of her restored Tuscan villa, the dulcet tone of her answering machine chirped. The smooth, velvety voice of Tommy Greenway filtered out through the speaker. She snatched the receiver from its cradle and spoke in a hyperventilating rush.

"Tommy? Tommy—thank Heaven. Are you all right? Did you rescue Yucatan Jay? What's going on?" A wedge of pressure built behind the bridge of her nose. It radiated past both eyes, sending pinpricks of pain shooting through her head.

"Hi, gorgeous. No time to talk . . ."

He's safe. Thank you, God.

She slumped against the wall. Behind closed lids, she pictured her dark-haired man's peacock-blue irises flickering with that familiar spark—eyes crinkling at the corners; his lean, tawny cheeks plumped from the smile spreading across his face. Tears of relief tracked the blush on her carefully made-up cheeks. She savored his words, searing them into her brain.

". . . I had to call you. Had to tell you how much I love you." Agitation tinged his voice. "I've gotta go."

"My God, Tommy, I've been beside myself with worry. Are y'all okay? When are you coming home?"

"A few more days."

The news jarred her lids open. "A few days?"

"Maybe longer." Heavy breathing. "Look, babe, we're in kind of a jam at the moment . . ."

"A few *days?*" Her voice spiraled upward. "I'm trying to plan our wedding, and you won't be home for a few more days?" She yanked the cordless phone from her ear long enough to treat it like a bottled genie. When no vapor trail seeped out and offered her three wishes, she tucked it into her shoulder and grappled for a pen to scrawl down a callback number.

Tommy had a way of disconnecting at the most inopportune times.

She injected a fresh shot of determination into the conversation. "Now *you* listen to *me,* Thomas Greenway. We're getting married in eight days and I still have to put in a full day's work this whole week. I need help with this wedding. None of the bridesmaids are speaking to each other, the dress alterations are iffy—"

"I'm doing my part." Tommy spoke in a soft, hypnotic voice. "I evac-ed your lame-brain cousin, didn't I? You may not realize it, Raven, but decapitating captives isn't always enough retribution for Shiite Muslims. I don't know if we'll be able to tie the knot on schedule, but at least you won't have to attend Yucatan Jay's memorial service. Not yet, anyway." Uttered in the dispassionate tone of a serial killer. "I'm doing the best I can."

Raven hit a new octave. "A few more days ought to put me in a psychiatric ward."

"I didn't want to say anything, but have you given any thought to mood stabilizers?" Delivered in a harsh whisper.

"You think I should be on Zoloft?"

"Might not hurt to check into it."

She recognized the voice of Yucatan Jay, grousing in the background, distracting her fiancé in an attempt to undermine the conversation. "All right, dumb ass, you said what you had to say—now hang up and let's get the hell outta here."

Raven's startle reflex kicked in. "That's Y-Jay, isn't it?"

"Matter of fact—"

"Oh, shit." Y-Jay. "They found us. Run!"

"I'll always love you, babe."

A blast of automatic gunfire stitched across a hard surface.

Terror snared her in its grip.

"Ohmygod, what's happening?" A dead connection hung between her ears. Trembling, she clutched the phone to her breasts and slid to the floor with the high-pitched zing of ricocheting bullets echoing through her mind.

The old Texas Ranger out in San Angelo said the Standish kid's mother committed suicide. But after the maternal grandparents stormed into the precinct office armed with a family album and a couple of audiotapes, Constable Jinx Porter suspected the kid's father killed her. It didn't particularly surprise Jinx when the couple, his constituents, explained they'd sought custody of five-year-old Magick through a Tarrant County family court, when Fleck Standish refused to let them see the girl; nor that Standish fled with her as soon as the Sheriff's Office served him with custody papers. Now, as Jinx's eyes drifted over the Writ commanding the child's return, the question became: *Where would a practitioner of the satanic and the occult—not to mention a Republic of Texas survivalist with an arsenal of exotic weapons—hide out?*

Probably not Texas.

Evan Rainey, the Hursts' lawyer, braced his arms across the front of his raw silk suit and stared through the bloodshot eyes of a hard drinker. "So, what're you going to do to get Magick back?"

"My job."

Jinx loathed the slicked-up attorney. Rainey was famous

for waiting until Friday afternoons to drop legal cow patties on the precinct. He seemed to time his unpleasant visits to coincide with the throwing of the five o'clock deadbolt, turning a routine court order into a crisis. But Jinx had another reason for despising the Bally-loafered, freshly-manicured, Jaguar owner. Five years before, Rainey'd been a staunch supporter of Jinx's rival opponent for the elected position of Constable.

The attorney's grin angled up in a smirk. Jinx wanted to ball his fist and move the air in front of the shyster's perfect bone structure. But he ignored Rainey's arrogance and addressed the Hursts.

"You have a recent picture?"

Marcy Hurst responded to her husband's elbow nudge by parting the flaps of an oversized leather purse. She fished until she came out with a wallet and thumbed through plastic inserts filled with photos. Pavé diamond rings caught the light from the overhead fluorescents and glittered on her fingers.

She slipped a snapshot of a dark-haired girl out of its sleeve. "Magick's birthday is next week. This picture's about a year old, but she looks pretty much the same. Only he chopped off her curls and now her hair's real short . . . a bad Beatles cut from the sixties. Bo says that no-good snake's trying to make her look like a boy." She paused long enough to glance at her husband, who seemed to be assessing Jinx's ability to find his granddaughter through a piercing squint. "Just before Fleck disappeared with the baby, the neighbor lady said he'd put her in overalls and a T-shirt. That's why Bo says Fleck's turned her into a boy . . . so we can't find her."

Unexpectedly, she covered her face with her hands and leaned against her husband, with her shoulders heaving. The old guy pushed her upright and slung an arm around her.

"Settle down, Marcy. Let's hear the man out."

She peeked through her fingers. "Can you get her back, Constable Porter?"

Jinx pushed the brim of his custom ten-X beaver cowboy hat an inch or so up his forehead, and studied the snapshot of a brunette child with a gamine face.

An angel. In the hands of the devil.

Jinx figured Rainey's afternoon bender started early. The man sat through the drama looking calmer than a tranquilized Doberman. "You on it, or not, Constable? Every minute counts."

Jinx ignored him. Locked gazes with Bo Hurst. Wondered if the Hursts felt bad about turning him down, when he asked to stake a yard sign out in their lawn at election time a few years back. Like Rainey, they'd supported that college kid with no previous law enforcement experience.

He summed up his capabilities in a sentence. "If the girl's alive and living in the United States, I'll find her."

Tension left Marcy Hurst's body in a visible slump.

And that was part of the problem, Jinx thought. Nobody really listened to him.

Not Raven, when he tried to tell her not to marry the psychopath who put the big, pink rock on her ring finger six weeks ago.

Not the District Attorney's Office, when he called across the street to find out why nobody over there wanted to look into the Hursts' case.

Not even his own deputies, when he told them they might have to put in extra hours that weekend, if it appeared they had a righteous kidnapping on their hands.

And now, Marcy Hurst only *thought* she'd heard what he said.

Yes, he said he'd find the kid—what was her name . . .

Magick? And that guarantee happened to be what people in denial automatically seized on. Not reality. Because if she'd paid attention, she would've realized he'd chosen his words carefully.

Like Bo Hurst. Sitting on the edge of his seat, squeezing his wife's hand in a vise grip, trying to keep the quiver out of his chin. The old man had no trouble hearing the gospel according to Jinx Porter. He'd picked up on that carefully-chosen phrase the way it was meant to be received.

If the girl's alive . . .

Tommy might be bleeding to death in a Third World country, but in Fort Worth, Texas, Constable Jinx Porter, Raven's ex-boyfriend and current boss, expected her to stop by his apartment and transport his Siamese cat, Caesar, to the vet.

Numb with terror, Raven came to the heady realization she needed to keep busy. To go to work, fulfill her duties as one of Jinx's deputies and allow the day-to-day insanity at the Tarrant County Courthouse to drive the wild imaginings of tragedy from her mind.

Mechanically, she fell into a routine patrol. She served her court papers by eleven that morning, then swung by her house to see whether Tommy had called back.

Yoruba Groseclose's newspaper still sat baking in the sun, in the exact same spot the carrier tossed it six hours before.

Nothing on the answering machine except the birdlike soprano of Geneva Anjou phoning to remind her of her afternoon appointment at Bridal-Wise Boutique. If she didn't work the fitting in today, the woman announced, the seamstress wouldn't be able to complete the alterations on time.

"You *must* pick up the gown before *Wednesday,* dear. It's

imperative that you do so. And those attendants of yours—honestly, Raven, how can you *stand* being around them? I've never heard such bickering. They're *bridesmonsters,* not bridesmaids. Well, good luck, dear," she chirped, without sounding the least bit like she meant it.

By noon, the weather turned so hot the bushes were following the dogs around.

A little after two-thirty that afternoon, the bottom fell out of the sky, effectively ending Openly Gay José's chance at a shutout for the month.

Raven made her second sweep by the house in the midst of a downpour. Water soaked Miss Groseclose's newspaper. The old Mercury hadn't been moved and the spinster's Siamese cat, Jezebel—looking fat enough to survive the marooning of Admiral Byrd—howled through the wavy glass window like a queen in heat.

Which reminded her.

She still needed to drop Caesar off at the veterinary clinic to have his stitches removed.

Jinx had a lot of nerve, prevailing on her with only eight days left to prepare for her wedding.

"I don't care what you do," he'd said, "long as you serve your court papers in a timely manner." But he seemed to be pulling out all the stops, loading her down with extra work, making certain she didn't have a spare moment to oversee the last-minute details.

She headed for Jinx's apartment at three o'clock, but when she got within a few blocks of the Château Du Roy, she remembered the fitting at Bridal-Wise.

She didn't dare miss it. Lately, she'd adopted the eating habits of a Vietnamese potbelly pig, scarfing down comfort food. On-edge and sick with worry ever since Tommy flew to Sudan to spring her screwball cousin, Yucatan Jay, from capture and incarceration in a high-security prison before the government could behead him for being a spy, she eventually learned Tommy masterminded the jailbreak, and the two managed to escape the scrutiny of border guards. That's when Y-Jay took another assignment. He ended up in the Middle East and got himself locked up masquerading as a Christian preacher—putting in motion a series of catastrophes that made Tommy go back on his word.

"I know I told you I'd quit and I intend to. But I can't leave Y-Jay stranded. They'll kill him."

"Bet he'd leave you if the situation were reversed."

"He wouldn't. This'll be my last job, Rave."

"That's what you said before you went to Sudan."

"This time I promise."

"Swear it. Swear to God that after this is over, you're through."

"I swear. Now come over here . . . let me love you before I go."

Since the general consensus among Shiite Muslims was that decapitation might be too swift; that ransom, physical torture and, ultimately, death for her cousin might fulfill a higher purpose—Tommy headed out on a phone call.

The fitting at Bridal-Wise went great, making it unnecessary for the tailor to take in the two side seams on her wedding gown after all. Before leaving the boutique, she ran a brush through her long, dark curls, and reapplied berry-red gloss to her full lips—Geneva Anjou would never let a customer near a dress unless they'd removed every stitch of makeup and thoroughly washed their hands. Ten minutes ago, she looked like Snow White. Now the stressed face of a desperate woman stared back at her from the shop's full-length mirror. For the hundredth time, Raven replaced Tommy's frightening phone call with a memory from childhood.

"What's wrong, little bit?"

"I'm not going back to kindergarten, Pawpaw. The other kids say you're not my real daddy, you're my granddaddy. And I overheard the principal telling Miss Knippa I don't have a mama."

"Come sit on my lap. It's about time we had us a good, long talk."

Raven closed her eyes. She could almost smell the pipe tobacco clinging to his work shirt. She touched the hairbrush to her cheek and felt the tingle of his whiskers against her skin.

"Tell me what she was like, Pawpaw."

"Prettiest gal in fifty counties. Caused many a car wreck just by walking down Main Street—"

"You're making it up."

"—had every young man within a hunnerd miles weeping like a baby the day she married your daddy, no lie."

"Tell me about him."

"Handsome fella, looked a lot like me. A State Trooper, a wonderful son and a helluva fisherman."

"Why'd they have to die?"

"Lord knows. Not a day goes by I don't ask myself that very question."

"Don't cry, Pawpaw. If you still want, I'll learn to fish. I'll even bait my own hook, if it'll make you happy."

"Out of all the little girls in the world, wonder how I got so lucky?"

Raven opened her lids. Eyes the color of pewter had taken on new vitality and the stress lines in her face relaxed.

"Is something wrong, dear?" Geneva Anjou had slipped

up from behind, unnoticed. "You look so sad."

Wish my grandfather was alive to walk me down the aisle.

"Everything's fine." Raven stuffed the brush back into her makeup bag, pinched some pink into her cheeks and turned to the jittery shop owner. "Actually, I'm relieved the dress won't have to be let out."

"You have to pick it up by Wednesday. You won't forget?"

"Soon as the rain stops."

She left Bridal-Wise in the middle of a gullywasher. If she hurried, she could swing by the house, check for messages and still make it to Jinx's apartment before the vet's office closed.

Uncharitable thoughts turned to Jinx. She suspected he concocted the cat emergency. He'd drummed up a number of unorthodox assignments lately—assignments that made it necessary for them to patrol together—assignments she suspected Jinx manufactured purely for sport. Ever since she'd turned down his last-minute marriage proposal, Jinx Porter had become a master at manipulation, forcing situations that would land them not only in the same zip code, but at the same address.

Well, tough.

No one could blame her because he remained unattached at fifty-five years old. On the Darwinian scale of mate-prospects, Jinx Porter was still a knuckle-dragging monkey on the brink of evolution. Tommy, with his keen wit and narcotic kisses, would make a more evolved life companion.

She rounded the last corner to her Tuscan villa on Astrid Street, made a hard right and whipped into the driveway.

Uh-oh.

Soggy newspaper still out on Miss Groseclose's lawn.

Curtains pulled. No sign of activity inside the haunted house.

Jezebel, braying like a donkey, pawed the window.

Well, hell.

Failure to assist the elderly would be tantamount to pulling the lever on the trap door to Hell.

If the lights weren't on when she got back from the animal hospital, she'd go next door and check on the old battleaxe.

Then she saw it.

The rain-soaked box on her own terra cotta porch tiles.

A gift from Tommy? Another twenty-four-carat gold bracelet from Saudi Arabia? Her cheeks plumped above a smile. After one brief marriage in her twenties, she couldn't believe she'd found the man of her dreams at age thirty-six. For the umpteenth time that day, she glanced at the pink, three-carat, princess-cut diamond from Tiffany's—platinum setting—and tried the groom's name on for effect.

Mrs. Thomas Greenway.

Raven Greenway.

The Greenways. Tommy and Raven.

Elation turned to dread. Until this morning, she hadn't heard from him in five days. What if he didn't call back? He'd drilled it into her how the CIA frowned on agents attracting unpleasant media coverage. If anything went wrong with the ransom drop, Y-Jay and her beloved were on their own.

Please God, watch over Tommy.

As for Yucatan Jay?

She gave the air an aristocratic sniff.

Pawpaw had good reason for rationing her time with Y-Jay. Even if he hadn't been a lawman with the Texas Rangers, Raven figured her grandfather would've seen through the guy's easy smile and penetrating stare. Wise words replayed in her mind.

"I know Yucatan Jay and your Aunt Wren are the only blood

kin left on your mama's side, kiddo, but that little recidivist is bad news."

"Please, Pawpaw, you have to get me an airline ticket to Colorado for Christmas. Y-Jay promised to teach me to ski."

"Last time, you came home with a broken wrist. I warned you not to fall victim to that boy's harebrained schemes."

"Don't go jumping to conclusions, Pawpaw. How could Y-Jay have known my parasail wouldn't open?"

"He packed it, didn't he?"

Raven unlocked her car door, swung a leg out into the drizzle and made a break for the house.

Another mis-delivered package had been left on the porch. Brown paper wrappings with overseas postage—mostly postmarked "Amsterdam" and addressed to her neighbor, Clem Askew—came to her address with increasing frequency. Was the old geezer so addled he couldn't even remember where he lived anymore? She made a mental note to mention this to Clem's wife. Meantime, the neighborly thing would be to walk it across the street and set it near his door. Then she'd check the answering machine and head for the Château.

It took both hands to lift the rain-soaked box.

When she ferried it to her knees, the bottom opened up and the contents spilled out. A canister-like tube rolled across the clay tiles.

What the—?

A penis vacuum pump.

Lovely.

Bold type on the two-hundred-dollar receipt proclaimed: "Seven steps to a bigger penis"; it drifted apart from a thousand foam-packing peanuts, and settled onto a ring of water pooling at her feet. When she leaned over to retrieve it, the invoice disintegrated. Scrunching it into a wad of papier-mâché, she tossed it back into what was left of the box, picked up the plastic gizmo and turned it over in her hand. She wondered what would make anyone in their right mind attach something as scary as "Dr. Wong's magical schlong" to their privates, much less plug the cord into an electrical outlet, but deep down inside, she knew.

The older they get, the more they can't, the weirder they become.

Chapter Two

The Château Du Roy was a hotbed of activity at five o'clock Friday afternoon when Raven wheeled the unmarked patrol car into the parking lot space marked "Future Resident." She barked out a little laugh at the irony—the apartment complex Jinx lived in had been half-empty for more than a year.

The pool hadn't been filled since the maintenance man dove in, ripped the bikini bottoms off the rabbi's wife and suffered a fatal heart attack underwater that left the water contaminated with body wastes. Views were sensational . . . if you wanted to live at hobo junction or listen to a continuous ribbon of screaming ambulances en route to the nearest hospital; and the section the landlord called the Garden Apartments were only called that to make the geriatric set feel better in the event their Alzheimer's cleared up long enough for them to realize their section didn't have a pool.

Raven alighted from the patrol car and did a visual scan of her surroundings. On the second-floor balcony, Agnes Loudermilk, the resident crone, sat chain-smoking in a molded plastic chair, bobbing her head like a Mynah bird. When she gave Raven a half-hearted wave, the loose skin on her arm jiggled.

She picked up her pace. Agnes was famous for inappropriate comments.

The shriveled old woman cupped a hand to her penciled-on prune lips. "Does he have any puzzles?"

"He plays chess." Raven strutted toward the sidewalk with

her eyes firmly averted. Crazy old dement, sitting out in broad daylight dressed in a threadbare chenille bathrobe. Typical Château Du Roy material: misfits, miscreants and misanthropes.

At the base of the stairs, she froze in her tracks.

Inside the courtyard, Glen Lee Spence, the resident transsexual, guzzled umbrella drinks with the Munsch brothers, a couple of drag queens who lived in the apartment beneath Jinx's. Between swigs, Glen Lee, who'd undergone the top half of his sex change operation while serving time in the pen for armed robbery but failed to complete the transformation once he got paroled, tormented the Munsch twins' Scarlet Macaws by tossing popcorn in the direction of their cages. In response, the birds shrieked profanity, flapped their wings and whistled incoming scud noises.

Willing herself into invisibility didn't work.

As soon as Glen Lee glanced her way, he ejected from his lawn chair. "Love the boots, hon. What color is that? Because it looks like you've been stomping grapes." He sidled up beside her and fell into step.

Raven gave him the visual once-over. Glen Lee might be a good one to ask. "Know anything about penis pumps?"

A look of outrage crossed his face. "Have you been going through my stuff?"

"What I want to know is whether they really work."

"To give you a bigger penis?"

"Not me, personally." Said sarcastically.

"Jinx having a little problem in the boudoir?"

"This isn't about Jinx. I just want to know if it works."

"Yes, Raven, it works. It works because your poor willie gets so swollen it plumps up like a ballpark frank. Tell Jinx not to use it."

She picked up her stride, gave the convicted felon a little

finger-wave and ascended the stairs on the strained hope she'd make it to the top without having to answer any wedding questions.

Visiting Jinx Porter at the Château Du Roy took on all the qualities of a bad lay: get in, get on, get out. Today would be no different. She still needed her bridesmaids to show up for their final fittings with Geneva Anjou's alterations lady, to check on whether the florist could get the Birds of Paradise flown in on time and to make sure the printer had corrected the typos on invitations showing the reception at Thistle Hill—otherwise, she'd spend the weekend making seventy-five phone calls giving the correct address to her guests.

The Cinderella wedding she planned since childhood looked more like the ugly stepsister.

Raven kept walking. Halfway up the stairs, Glen Lee shouted through cupped hands. "Raven, we don't know where to go next Saturday. Your invitation hasn't arrived."

Raven played deaf.

It hadn't arrived because she hadn't sent them one.

She reached the second floor landing, strutted to Jinx's door, made a fist and pounded.

Glen Lee wouldn't let it drop. "We are invited, aren't we? Frankly, I'm surprised you didn't want us to be in the wedding party. Gerald and Harold and I were counting on serving champagne to your guests. I have a new red cocktail dress—"

"You can't wear red to her wedding. You'll look like a harlot." Gerald. Spoken in that effeminate slur. Or Harold. It was impossible to tell them apart without being close enough to see the scar Glen Lee put on Gerald's forehead, following a brawl over who had the greater right to a turquoise sequined dress.

"Harlot." One of the Scarlet Macaws seconded the notion.

Raven hauled off and pummeled the door. *Open up.*

Damn Jinx Porter.

She glanced down at the window sill—an architectural design from the fifties—which started a few inches above the floor. A breathtakingly beautiful Seal Point, with his dark mask shimmering like axle grease, stepped into view, had a seat and stared through slitted sapphires. Jinx called him Caesar—a regal name befitting a lanky dictator with fur. He lashed his tail against the wood. His mouth dropped open in a silent meow. With claws extended, he lifted one paw as a subtle reminder not to venture too close.

She didn't hear Jinx's footfalls on the carpet inside, but when the Siamese hunkered down and wiggled his backside against the wood for traction, she sensed him about to let her in. Caesar liked to play "shot-put" whenever Jinx opened the door a sliver.

The deadbolt snicked back. Gray-green eyes peered out through the bottle-thick lenses of his wire-rims.

"Get back, Caesar. I mean it." Jinx and the cat in a contest of wills.

He lowered his voice. "The cat knows he's going to the V-E-T because I got out the carrier. Be careful coming inside. If he gets out, we'll never catch him."

Jinx, who constantly bragged how the Siamese had a four-hundred-word vocabulary, shot the cat a furtive glance. "He hates the V-E-T, and the you-know-who doesn't much like him, either. Last time I took him in for a C-H-E-C-K-U-P, they tacked on a wild animal handling fee. I was in the middle of disputing the bill—might've won, too—but the kitty reached out and slashed the invoice while the girl was holding it. So I paid."

Raven wedged herself sideways into Jinx's living room, while he herded the cat away. Once inside, she shut the door and threw the deadbolt. His new apartment looked exactly like the old apartment before it got firebombed—white walls, threadbare carpet in a boring shade of beige, the same eggshell-colored leather sofa and matching ottoman, Dogs Playing Poker pictures and tons of tall bookcases lining the walls. When she turned around, Jinx was standing in his living room in his Jockey shorts and a V-neck T-shirt. As hard as she tried not to succumb to the gravitational pull, her eyes dipped to his—

Ohforgod'ssake.

She pretended to ignore the bulge behind the cotton flap of his briefs. "Crazy Agnes wants to know if you have any puzzles."

Jinx's jaw dropped. "She did *not* say that."

"She did. I told her you played chess."

Heavy sigh. "Raven, when she asked if I had any puzzles, that's slang for rubbers. Don't even talk to her. She's nuts. Last week, she asked old Mr. Barber if he used to give his mother enemas before she died. He dropped his walking stick and took off like a bat outta hell. When I came up the stairs, she asked if it was hot enough for me."

"So? What's weird about that?"

"She was eyeballing my crotch when she said it."

Cementing Raven's original thoughts about the residents of the Château.

She gave a wary headshake. "Why aren't you dressed? I thought you said you had to check out a house in Arlington."

"Had to grab a quick shower. I'm going out later tonight."

The news stopped her in her tracks. Jinx had a date? Her jaw tightened like a stringed instrument. He'd probably taken up with that skanky chick from the Sheriff's Office again.

Unless . . .

She narrowed her eyes. "Going out" for Jinx Porter usually meant a quick trip to the pharmacy for suppositories and shaving cream. The man was pricking with her. He wanted her to think he'd found her replacement.

Unexpectedly, Caesar streaked across the room, banked off a Lazy-Boy and scaled a seven-foot bookcase. He shaped his taut, muscular body into an egg and glowered from lofty heights. Fur haloed around his normally whippy tail. He rasped, snakelike.

Raven fisted her hip. "Don't hiss at me. I'm doing you a favor."

"It's probably best if you don't agitate him." Jinx glanced around. Settled his gaze on the pet carrier.

Raven read his mind. "Oh, no. You're not making me put him in there. He's yours. You do it."

"I'm running late."

"I don't mind dropping him off at the—

"Don't say it! Don't say—"

"—V-E-T, but I'm getting married in eight days, Jinx Porter, and the last thing I need is scratches on my hands and face."

She couldn't be sure in the gray and white tones of the dimly lit room, but Jinx seemed to pale. His face went slack and a profound sadness dulled the gaze in his slightly asymmetrical eyes.

"Yes," he said without enthusiasm, "well, we can't have you mauled, can we?"

She found the silence discomforting.

"By the way," he added nastily, "you should stock up on Cheetos and beer. I understand Amos is planning a shivaree."

"A what?"

She gave him a blank look. The District Judge of the juvenile court had sentenced Amos, the son of Jinx's other female deputy, Ivy, to four months in the Texas Youth Commission. As far as Raven was concerned, the only thing Amos should be plotting was how to shower without getting stump-broke.

"A shivaree. It's a ritual where friends and relatives congratulate the newlyweds by making lots of noise outside the hotel during the honeymoon. They bang pots and pans, tell crude jokes. You'll hear human screams—some of them may even come from the folks outside your window—"

"That's not funny."

"—and they don't stop until you placate them with food. I suggest Cheetos for Amos. Beer'll work for the rest of us."

"You're not invited on my honeymoon. Neither is anybody else."

"Don't be so sure."

Raven eyed the Siamese. "Let's get him into the carrier. I'll wait until they pull the stitches and bring him back tonight. Call when you get home, so I can drop him back by."

One more order of business remained to be settled. She jammed her hand down the front pocket of her raspberry-colored jeans and fumbled for her key ring. Momentarily, she located the key to his apartment. "I believe this is yours."

His jaw went slack. As if she'd dashed his face with a cold drink.

"Actually, I'd like you to meet me in Arlington," he said, his words even and measured. "So you'll need to drop the cat off at your house and come on out."

"I have last-minute wedding details to attend to. I'm off-duty. You can't make me."

Jinx walked to the bookcase and tried to coax the cat down. "Don't make me have to come up and get you." The cat flared his paw. Claws extended. Caesar slashed the air in front of his face. "You don't fool me, you big baby—"

The Siamese drew blood. Jinx pulled back his hand and nursed the gash on his thumb. The Seal Point backed farther into the corner.

Without further preliminaries, Jinx stalked to the bedroom. Raven heard the closet door hinge creak and wondered what was coming. He padded down the hall and she heard the bathroom door bang against the tile. Jinx returned to the living room with his arms wrapped in Ace bandages, wearing his bulletproof vest.

"You need body armor to handle your cat?" She fought the grin spreading across her face.

Jinx shot her a wicked glare and headed for the kitchen. He returned with potholders, silk-screened to resemble lobster claws, slid over his hands.

That put the olive in the martini. Raven doubled over in a harsh cackle.

"You think it's funny? You try getting him down."

The Indy-500 of cat chases started near the front door. It ended a few minutes later when Jinx extricated the Seal Point from atop a set of shutter doors that sectioned off the dining area.

When he finished crating the pissed-off Siamese, he handed her a signed check with the amount left blank, payable to the animal hospital. Along with a scrap of paper that contained an Arlington address. "Here's where I'll be. And don't dawdle."

"This isn't fair."

Jinx gave her one of his *Just do it* looks. "Fair is something that takes place in Dallas each October." He turned his back on her and went to the bedroom to finish dressing.

And that's why we didn't make it. He's still a back walking away.

Chapter Three

Several blocks from the V-E-T's office, Raven stopped dwelling on Tommy's phone call long enough to glance over at the glowering cat riding shotgun in the passenger seat.

"What're you looking at?" Said dully. "I will not play *Blink* with you. I'm driving."

"Mao."

"You just cursed me, didn't you?"

"Ngow."

"Don't call me that."

"Mack."

"I know what that means. Don't think I haven't had Siamese lessons. I'm personally acquainted with Jezebel, next door. She taught me all the curse words."

"Maaaaaoooooo."

"Stop braying. You act like it's my fault. How about a little music?" She switched on the radio and turned up the volume. A melancholy song filled their shared space. "She's from England. Isn't that pretty? That's Dido. The 'L' is silent."

From the look on Caesar's face, she thought Jinx's cat might've just telepathically suggested she get intimate with a sex toy.

The light turned red. A fat fellow on a Harley pulled up in the next lane, jamming to a tune and singing the lyrics to "Dirty White Boy" like he thought auditions for "American Idol" were being held at the corner of Montgomery Street and Camp Bowie Boulevard. He gave her a grin, exposing a gap where a molar should've been; then tongue-flicked the air and thrust his groin against the bike seat. She did a little eye roll and focused straight ahead. When she gave him a sidelong glance, he had balled up his fist and was tonguing the opening to simulate oral sex.

Pin dick.

The cell phone trilled. The Siamese stuck a paw through the grate.

"I'll get it. I'm pretty sure it's for me." She thumbed the on-button and covered the mouthpiece with her fingertips. "If not, I'll take a message."

Her breath caught at the sound of Tommy's voice.

"Thank God you're alive!" She scanned the area for a safe place to pull over once the light changed. "What happened? Are you all right?" She imagined her cousin the troublemaker, and did a slow burn. "Listen, Tommy, you can't be off globetrotting with Y-Jay. You have to help me plan this wedding. Do you realize we only have eight days? *Eight days.*"

"Calm down, beautiful. You're a competent, capable woman."

"Incompetent?" Y-Jay's rough-textured hectoring filtered through the earpiece. "Dude, that's not nice, calling your fiancée incompetent."

"I didn't call her—*oh, sweet Jesus*—hit the dirt!"

The snare-drum roll of gunfire peppered Raven's ear canal. She sat deathly still, as if she'd just survived electrocution. Every hair on her body stuck straight out.

"Tom, are you hit? Say something." Y-Jay cursed in the background. The rustling noise of a phone hand-off hissed in her ear. Then Y-Jay, calm as a Hindu cow, spoke. "Hi-ya, Raven. How-ya doin'? Listen, we're kinda busy right now. But hey—we'll get back to you real soon, okay? Have a nice day."

The line went dead.

Ohmygod. Her heart tripped in her chest. *They killed him.*

The signal light cycled to green. The guy on the Harley roared off.

Her body turned to lead, effectively rendering her unable to move.

Tires screamed behind her.

On instinct, Raven hunkered her shoulders and scrunched her eyes. The sickening crunch of metal filled the air in a demon's shriek. Raven's world reduced itself to slow motion. Glass exploded. The rear windshield tinkled down like a swift strike across a child's xylophone. The back of her head slammed against the headrest. A flash of white momentarily blinded her. The impact from the rear-end collision propelled her into the intersection and sent the cat carrier airborne. With her mouth agape, she watched it collide with the glove compartment, then bounce back against the passenger seat, before coming to rest on the floorboard.

The Siamese let out a string of cat profanity, speeding Raven's world back into real time.

She grabbed the plastic kennel by its handle and hoisted it onto the seat. The seal point forced one paw through the metal grate and extended his claws.

Raven applied a universal theory of behavior. As long as he's yowling, he's alive.

Unlike Tommy and Y-Jay, who were probably dead by now.

She had no way of knowing their fate. No way to call them back. She'd probably hear about it on CNN: two Americans murdered by Arab insurgents. Government agents would put their own spin on it.

Ohgod, please don't let this be happening. He said he'd quit. He promised it'd be his last job.

The rest of her thoughts tumbled out in a wail. "I can't take any more of this."

Door ajar, she bailed out, favoring her neck.

Traffic ground to a standstill. Two guys from McDonalds ran over to a late-model pickup and helped a withered, bronze-skinned lady out of the cab. A flush of bright yellow birds escaped, airborne. The woman flailed her arms and screamed at them in an unknown tongue.

Raven's eyes went wide. She recognized resident evil on sight. To a normal person, the woman of indeterminate age and oily, Mediterranean skin, wearing a thin, cotton housedress might be mistaken for someone who relied on charity. But Raven knew Sabina Balogh. The sister of Ivan, Prince of the Gypsies—the same Ivan Balogh who put out a contract hit on her three years ago—wanted to do Raven in. That whole tribe did.

She regained her composure and strutted over to Ivan's sister with confidence in her step, prepared to demand the old gypsy's driver's license and proof of insurance. Six feet from the black-haired woman with the enlarged right eye, she halted in her tracks. A putrefied, decomposing-body odor swirled inside the cab of the truck, triggering a memory from childhood. Raven recognized the one-of-a-kind smell of *bacala* and her nose involuntarily snapped shut in self-defense.

Sabina Balogh eyed the princess-cut diamond on Raven's finger. Her mouth curled up in a smirk. She crooked a gnarled, nicotine-stained finger. Blood-red lips parted into an ugly gash, exposing a set of decayed teeth that jutted up from her gums like uneven gravestones.

"You'll not marry. I curse you!"

Raven wanted to laugh. To tell the pinched-face parasite to pack a lunch and stand in line when it came to bad luck. But she kept her thoughts sealed in the airtight Tupperware of her mind. When dealing with the Baloghs, the less said, the better. Her eyes flickered to a sign on a wire cage inside the bed of the truck, printed in childish scrawl: *Canaries for sale—$5.00.*

Probably headed for the Mexican flea market.

For no particular reason, Sabina Balogh rushed her. Executing a chimpanzee broad jump, the gypsy latched on to Raven and encircled misshapen fingers around her neck. The women fell to the pavement, enveloped in the foul odor of dried, salted cod and feathers.

The distant wail of sirens pierced the air.

Sabina possessed freakish strength.

Incredible pressure bulged Raven's eyeballs. The jaundiced-skin crone maintained super-human energy, hanging on like a Florida chad on the presidential ballot. Raven meshed her fingers together and formed a teepee-like wedge with her arms, then forced upward to break the stranglehold.

So much for police academy training.

Next time she took a self-defense class, she'd tell the instructors how that trick wouldn't work with a body on top of you, squeezing out your tonsils like the last smidgen of toothpaste from its tube. About the time vivid colors turned into a brown blur and Raven figured she was in trouble for real, a squad car rolled up. A patrolman bailed out and peeled the gypsy off of her.

A second officer rushed over. His face scrunched into a hideous mask of disgust and he yanked away his outstretched hand, leaving Raven to hoist herself up off the ground.

The officer took several steps backward. "What'd you roll in?" He fanned the air in front of his nose. "Smells like Eau de Outhouse."

Raven's jaw tightened. "Don't get smart with me. The only thing in the toilet is my life. That's Sabina Balogh over there." She pointed to the shrunken, hook-nosed crone. Judging by the animated hand gestures, the gypsy princess was spewing misinformation about how the collision occurred.

The officer blinked. Clearly, the Balogh name meant nothing.

"Where've you been? Are you new to the force?" Raven took it upon herself to educate him. "Are you even familiar with gypsies? The Balogh tribe? Family of thieves and cutthroats? Snake-oil sellers? Lots of high-end cars on their properties, none with matching VINs? Did you just get here?"

He gave her a blank look.

"Oh, for God's sake. They're scam artists." Words came out in a hyperventilating rush. "Check out that cage. Those weren't canaries. They dye pigeons yellow and sell them at flea markets. They run one-nine-hundred numbers out of their houses and do palm readings while their kids sneak in and pick the pockets of desperate, unsuspecting customers. That phone-sex commercial on late-night TV?" Raven jabbed a finger in Sabina Balogh's direction. "You're not talking to a hot babe when you dial that number—you're talking to her or one of her hook-nosed daughters. I wouldn't be surprised if they operated a chop shop. Find me a vehicle identification number on any of their automobiles that matches another VIN on the same car, I'll eat this nasty-smelling shirt."

A loud commotion erupted behind her. An eerie cry cut through thick, stifling air. Her shoulders involuntarily hunched at the rusty hinge shriek. Raven and the patrolman whipped around. Thirty feet away, Sabina Balogh swiped the air in front of the investigating officer's face. The scrawny gyppo hauled off and gave him a swift kick in the shin with her pointy-toed shoe. While Raven stood in a mind-numbing stupor, the backup officer took off in the direction of his partner.

In seconds, the skirmish was over.

It took both officers to snap the hooks on Sabina Balogh. Each wrapped a vise-grip hand around an olive arm in an effort to escort her to the patrol car. Raven suspected the gypsy queen affected an acute limp in order to garner the sympathy of gawkers gathering on the corner near the fast-food chain.

Without warning, Sabina Balogh's leg fell off.

A collective gasp eclipsed the steady white noise of passing traffic. Princess Sabina let out a squawk, then dropped, dead weight, to the ground—forcing The Blue to carry her and her emancipated, artificial leg to the blue-and-white.

Shouts of "Police brutality!" erupted from the onlookers.

An unidentified bystander lobbed a half-eaten Egg McMuffin through the air, grazing one officer's head. A third patrol car wheeled onto the scene. A go-cup, filled with brown liquid and hurled on the breeze, splattered the side of the cruiser. The patrolman bailed out and gave chase to a couple of juveniles.

Reeking of *bacala,* Raven moved toward the unruly crowd. "Show's over. Move along."

Onlookers dispersed with amazing speed, leaving her to sniff her shirt and wonder if the odor of *bacala* could be packaged in an aerosol container as an alternative to pepper spray.

She trotted back to the unmarked Chevy. The afternoon sun had seared through the clouds, and she needed to roll down the windows so Caesar's brain wouldn't fry. For a landlocked cat whose entire universe revolved around a two-bedroom apartment at the Château Du Roy, the rotten odor of *bacala*'s putrefaction would be the Holy Grail of smells.

She expected the Siamese to fall in love with her.

Then she saw it.

The gaping door to the patrol car.

Her heart skipped. She looked inside and felt her jaw unhinge. The wire mesh gate on the cat carrier hung open, leaving an empty cavity where she last saw the Seal Point. Caesar enjoyed playing "lay in wait," a predator-skills game he'd mastered as a kitten. Once, he stayed awake for three days after catching a mouse in Jinx's apartment, patrolling the living room and secreting himself on a bookshelf until he'd flushed out its mate.

She leaned into the car's interior, half expecting to find the cat cowering in the back floorboard.

Her heart fluttered.

Maybe he'd taken refuge beneath the seat?

She gave the headrest a sharp pat, hoping to flush him out—and almost passed out from shock.

The three-carat pink diamond ring was missing.

Worse, so was Jinx's Siamese.

Across the street, skulking through a patch of grass on the un-mowed, vacant lot, Caesar peered through myopic eyes. He hadn't planned to leave the cat carrier but when the baby pigeons flew out in a flapping yellow mass, the noise frightened him. When he stood on hind legs, looked over the front seat and peered past the shattered back windshield to the huge amber cloud ascending, he never intended to investigate. But when that fabulous, unworldly scent of—he didn't recognize it, but it made every hair on his body halo with excitement—he had to check it out.

That's when he struck out on his own.

The girl fell to the ground with the old woman on top of her. He watched from a distance, fascinated by the colorful smear of clothes. Amazed by the amount of dust shimmering up from the pavement, and by the air—suddenly filled with the heavenly aroma of wonderment—he reveled in the glory of each savory breath.

Caesar lashed the ground with his long, whippy tail. On impact, it stirred up a tiny dirt devil that settled a light coating over his sable coat. He pulled his attention from the fracas long enough to groom himself. Since he was a kitten, back when his mother cuffed him and his brothers and sisters around, he made cleanliness a fetish. When he looked up, a shot of fear went through him.

The girl was gone.

How inconvenient!

What about my dinner?

Where's my bowl?

My nap?

How dare she leave me!

Chapter Four

A block from the Arlington address Fleck Standish shared with his mother, Jinx and three of his five deputies rolled up to the curb. Dell Teague and Mickey Van Slycke arrived as a two-man unit, leaving Jinx's only full-time female deputy, Ivy, in the other unmarked car.

No one wanted to ride with Ivy. The only thing famed serial killers Henry Lee Lucas and Ottis Toole carried around in their car that Ivy didn't have was a severed head. She lived out of the front seat and used the back for storage. Ate chili dogs for breakfast and turned the passenger floorboard into a compost heap. Kept the stereo tuned to an AM station that featured a four-hour talk show hosted by a crackpot with a mug-shot for domestic violence, and questionable credentials. Put more dents in her police Chevy than the Cinco de Mayo hailstorm of 1995. Jinx yin-yanged his patrol unit even with Dell's, leaving Ivy to stare from pale-lashed, unblinking amphibian eyes. She shrugged, *Oh well,* parked her squad car and walked over for a quick briefing.

Jinx felt certain she'd left her navy windbreaker with CONSTABLE silk-screened in large yellow letters elsewhere, since she wore one of her polyester pant suits in a color more suited to working air traffic control at DFW. Ivy treated routine procedure like an unsolvable algebraic equation: gassing up the vehicle, leaving her .38 in the ladies' restroom, being the Joe DiMaggio of Tarrant County for at-fault collisions—the nitwit had locks on those skills. If the government ever designed a peacekeeping mission for the Middle East using law enforcement officers to implement their programs, Jinx thought Ivy might make the perfect weapon of mass destruction.

Ivy gave a slow blink. "Now what do we do?" Sniffling, she swiped her bulbous nose with the back of her hand. "It may not occur to you, Jinx, but I actually have a life outside of work."

Jinx slid Dell and Mickey a sideways glance. The men shed their hired-killer image long enough to snigger like a couple of cartoon dogs.

"It's like this." Jinx held up the Writ and used it as a directional pointer. "The girl and her father lived in that trailer park across the street. They're probably long gone. But just in case they're not, we're going inside and have a little sit-to with the paternal grandmother."

Dell and Mickey perked up. Once inside, Jinx expected them to toss the place like a salad, looking for bodies—or clues that would lead them to bodies.

"Ivy, Dell, cover the back." Dell scowled. Mickey reacted with coltish enthusiasm. "Mickey, you and I take the front. Everyone wearing their bulletproof vests?"

Dell and Mickey fisted their chests with the bravado of a gorilla. Ivy said, "Sure," but refused to make eye contact.

Armed to the gizzards, they descended on the trailer in less than a minute.

Jinx and Mickey flanked the door. Jinx stepped off to one side and wielded his fist against the frame. Both strained to listen. An audible click snapped near the knob, followed by the hiss of a chain sliding along its track. The door opened a sliver.

Jinx took it as an invitation; the two barged in with holsters unsnapped, and came face to face with a woman ugly enough to haunt a house. An unbearable stench hit him like a baseball bat to the nose.

"Top o' the mornin' to you, Mrs. Standish." He flapped the Writ in her face. "Where's your son?"

"I dunno."

"You're under arrest."

He spun her around. Demonstrated his Olympic speed-cuffing technique. Sat her on a ratty, threadbare couch.

"What're you picking on me for?"

"Interference with child custody."

She snorted. "That's a bald-face lie."

"Tell it to the judge."

"You can't arrest me. I haven't done anything."

"Button it."

He ordered her to stay put while Mickey unlatched the back door. Dell and Ivy burst inside.

Once Jinx's eyes adjusted to the light, the room came into sharp focus.

This must be how it felt to wake up in a garbage dump.

Stacks of newspapers cropped up to form a maze. Piles of musty clothes littered the linoleum pathway leading into a narrow hallway, along with grease-soaked sacks from fast-food dives. Animal feces formed pyramids beyond the open door of a bathroom, and Jinx recognized the small, white casings that crunched underfoot as roach larvae. The whole house smelled of death and decay. Mentally thanking his lucky stars for not eating a quick burger on the way out, Jinx wondered how long it would take to crave food again.

With Ivy posted in the cramped, roach-infested living room guarding Fleck Standish's mother, Jinx and the deputies executed their search like a well-choreographed ballet.

"Look inside everything. If it's big enough to stuff a little kid inside, open it up. Empty out all the drawers.

Take the clothes out of the closets."

Mickey and Dell practically wet themselves with excitement. Dell fixed Jinx with the hardened stare of a cold-blooded killer. Aqua eyes glinted beneath the Resistol, dipped low on his forehead.

"What about this jewelry box?"

Mickey chimed in. "How 'bout shoe boxes?"

Jinx gave them the green light. "If a kid's severed finger will fit in it, open it."

When they returned, empty-handed, Ivy was reciting a recipe for mock-chicken salad to a captive audience.

Jinx stepped into the hall, pulled out his hand-held and ran a warrant check on Venita Standish.

Momentarily, the dispatcher radioed back with the return information.

No hits.

Jinx sauntered up and towered over the woman. The last remnants of sun shone through the dusty mini-blinds, striping her face with a pale yellow light. For a few seconds, he stared, studying her sharp facial features and a nose that could slice cold butter; memorizing the slope of her forehead, her posture and the choppy home-cut of oily brown hair streaked with gray. Five-foot-six. One eighty-five, give or take, with a body as frumpy and worn as the threadbare, tan housecoat she had on. Gimlet eyes behind hooded, puffy lids; a stub of pale lashes; with a mouth pressed into a thin, crimson thread. He made another run at Venita Standish.

"You've got one last chance to come clean. Where's your son?"

"I dunno."

"I'm locking you up."

"You'll never make it stick."

"You can beat the rap, but you can't beat the ride."

A silhouette appeared in the front doorway, back-lit by the glow of the street lamps. Instinctively, Jinx's hand moved to the butt of his Smith & Wesson.

"Knock-knock." The sultry voice hinted of a smoker's rasp.

Female. Broad-shouldered. Curvy. Palms up, hands aloft in surrender.

"Halt." Jinx. "Identify yourself."

"Can I come in?"

"Why not? Everybody else in town's here." Venita Standish.

"Don't move." Jinx again. "Who're you?"

"Sigrid Pierson."

She moved into the light, revealing her white-blonde hair and Scandinavian ancestry. A Viking goddess in skin-tight pants that accentuated the contours of her thighs and beyond. Halfway back up her body, Jinx's eyes settled on her killer rack, and he found himself talking to the breasts of Evan Rainey's investigator. Once he checked ID, he allowed the gumshoe to question Venita Standish, and made his way into the kitchen.

An ominous crunch sounded underfoot.

Jinx flicked on the light switch.

Roaches skittered for cover.

He felt his gorge rise and headed for the cabinets. Canned goods seemed to move on their own. Bugs dropped onto the countertop, before Jinx could slam the cupboard shut.

He headed for the icebox, a sixties model with rounded edges and a lever for a handle, still working despite its grinding compressor.

Opened the door.

Sensed the invisible stench coming at him even before it hit his nostrils. Blood ran down the inside walls of the refrigerator. Yellowish bones with hunks of meat clinging to them lay visible through their plastic bags.

Jinx yelled for Ivy. She scurried into the kitchen with her thumb mashing the off-button of her cell phone.

"Get a box out of the trunk of my car, load up this stuff and tag it as evidence."

"Evidence of what?"

"I don't know. Maybe murder. Just do it." He peered out the kitchen window and spotted several black plastic garbage sacks, burgeoning to capacity, on the easement next to the curb. He sauntered outdoors, went to the trunk of his vehicle, dug out a pair of latex gloves and wandered over to investigate. As he snapped on the gloves and opened the first bag, Venita Standish tuned up screaming.

"Get away from there. That's my trash. You can't touch my trash."

"Mine now. Abandoned property."

Jinx watched the blob through the screen door, wrangling against the grip of Rainey's private-eye. Dell's sturdy German form materialized behind her. He jerked Standish's mother up on tiptoes and whisked her deeper into the bowels of the trailer.

Jinx went back to the Dumpster dive. Sifting through the rubbish, he learned a lot more about Standish's dietary habits than he cared. Then he came to a bag of used cat litter. Ammonia fumes hit his nose and blistered his eyes. Then he saw it.

Jerked his hand away and took a step backward.

Raked his forearm across the perspiration dotting his forehead, and yelled for Ivy.

"Get Raven on the horn and tell her to get out here, *pronto*. And don't come telling me you can't locate her, or swear to God, you'll be the one out here helping me sift through these trash bags."

★ ★ ★ ★ ★

Until she located the seal point, Raven made up her mind not to take Jinx's phone calls. So when an unfamiliar number popped up on the digital display of her wireless, she pressed the talk-button, thinking it might be the flower vendor calling about the Birds of Paradise, and answered with a cheery hello.

"It's Ivy." Said in a monotone.

Ivy.

Proving, once again, that a village was being deprived of its idiot.

Raven did a little eye roll. She couldn't stand Ivy—or that monster-boy of hers—but Ivy had backed her into a corner a few weeks ago, demanding in front of the deputies and Dixie, the part-time secretary, to know why she hadn't been asked to be a bridesmaid when everyone else had. "Everyone" being Dixie and Georgia, the other part-time secretary, and Cézanne Martin, a Fort Worth homicide detective Raven befriended three months before, when a paroled convict tried to kill Jinx and ended up on the business end of a bullet. So Raven had concocted a flimsy excuse.

"I didn't figure you'd want to."

"Izzat so?"

"I thought you were going to be on vacation."

"Oh yeah? Well I'm not. So what day are you getting married?"

"What day are you going to be on vacation?"

Noodle-spined, Raven buckled under Ivy's gimlet-eyed stare. Asked her to be an attendant, then spent the next three weeks kicking herself. Since Ivy still hadn't picked up her dress from Bridal-Wise, Raven figured the call might be a feeble attempt to foist the job off on her.

Wrong.

"Jinx says get out here right away. We're in Arlington." Ivy gave her the address.

"I can't. Tell him there's been an emergency." Raven thought fast. She didn't want to admit the cat was gone.

"What kind of emergency?" Ivy, suspicious and unconvinced.

She could mention the wreck—

"I . . ."

—but then Jinx would wonder if it happened before, or after, she dropped the cat off.

". . . see, what happened is . . . there's this missing seven-year-old . . ."

It wasn't a complete lie. Just because she didn't clarify which species.

"Uh-huh. Quit making excuses and get your ass out here."

"Okay, but I think something bad happened to my neighbor. She's old and lives by herself . . ."

"Old, schmold. I'm getting Jinx. Tell it to him."

"No, no, no. Don't do that."

"So you're on the way out?" Ivy, sounding smug.

"I'm on the way." Raven hit the off-button, slid her cell phone back into its case and resumed the conversation she'd started with the huge, black jail matron on the other side of the booking desk.

"You want us to *what?*" The woman, a meaty, mal-humored deputy sheriff who'd introduced herself as Emma-Jewel Houston, stared out from under penciled-on eyebrows. Gold chains the size of jump ropes hung from her neck.

"Put her in a room without a toilet, give her a bucket and feed her Ex-Lax."

"Girl—" Emma-Jewel drawled out the word. She

scooched her chair closer to the government-issue gray desk and rested her double chin in her palms. The polyester fabric of her short-sleeved shirt rode up her arms, exposing a Biggie Smalls tattoo on one beefy bicep. "You outta your mind? We ain't gonna stand around watchin' somebody take a crap, even if she did swallow a two-carat diamond."

"Three. Three carats," Raven said, "and you don't have to be there when she does her business. You could monitor it on closed-circuit TV."

"Mmm-mmm-mmm." The jail matron shook her head. "I *could.* Don't mean I *will.*"

Raven glanced around the room. She felt sorry for Emma-Jewel Houston. The thermostat on the A/C must've been set on the high eighties, and the hotbed of activity taking place at the booking desk only added to the staleness of the air. A scraggly man, waiting for the booking officer to complete his paperwork, reeked of rancid wine and excrement. And the crack whore propped against the wall, wobbling on stiletto heels while a deputy did a brisk pat-down, stank of cigarettes and sex.

Raven stepped off to one side and fanned the air in front of her nose.

Deputy Houston shook her head. Gave her a rueful smile. "Girl, that's you you're smellin'. What the hell's that stench?"

"Dead fish."

"You oughta cover yourself in Saran Wrap, 'cause you look like leftovers."

She locked Deputy Houston in her gaze. "Look, I'm asking for a little professional courtesy, okay? I'd do it for you—"

"Keep it on the down-low, sugar."

"Okay, you *have* to help me because—" Raven's chin

quivered "—I don't have anybody else."

"Girl, I wouldn't do it if that rock was *mine*." Deputy Houston pushed back from the desk, opened a drawer and pulled out a Mr. Goodbar. She broke it into sections while it was still in the wrapper, then held it in front of her and danced it through the air. "Want some?"

Raven shook her head. Weighed her options. She could pull rank. Ask for a supervisor. But there was no love lost between the Sheriff's Office and the Constable's Office. A light bulb idea went off in her head.

"Emma-Jewel . . . may I call you Emma-Jewel?" Not waiting for an answer, she rushed on. "Hear me out?"

"Girl, I'm listenin' but I ain't promisin' nothing." Lounging against the chair back, Emma-Jewel braced her arms across her ample bosom. Relaxed humor played in her face. "You actin' like we got a Scatological Division here at the SO. This is the three-to-eleven shift. This ain't Turd Watch."

Raven cupped a hand to her mouth. She lowered her voice to a whisper. "Don't you people have a new-hire you can pawn this off on? Better still, an officer on disciplinary review? *He* could do the vigil."

Emma-Jewel's eyes widened to the size of jawbreakers. "You askin' do we have a troublemaker?" Glossed, hot pink lips split into a grin. "Girl, everybody working in this hellhole's here on account of they pissed somebody off."

"Even you?"

" 'Specially me. Stepped on a judge's toes and now I'm stuck here in Purgatory 'til the next dumb bastard's sent down here to do penance."

"So can't you find a problem child you could post at a TV monitor, give him a pair of latex gloves and have him call you when the deed's done?"

Muffled chuckles filled the air like an Uzi with a silencer. "That boy—he's in deep doo-doo anyway. Might be kinda fun." She pulled a hand-held radio out of the side pouch on her Sam Browne belt, put it inches from her mouth and let her thumb hover just above the talk-button. "Since he's always pullin' shit, maybe he oughta get to play in it."

Raven gave her the thumbs-up. "I can't thank you enough. Call me when you've got my ring."

"Oh, girl, you gonna thank me all right. You gonna thank me big-time."

She already knew she was in so much trouble she couldn't dig her way out with a backhoe and a front-end loader.

Now she wondered whether she'd inadvertently hocked her soul.

Chapter Five

The sun dipped below the horizon, leaving a cloudbank dripping down the sky in shades of melted taffy. To complete the Norman Rockwell image, Jinx Porter stood in front of a broken-down trailer with his bald head glistening and a scowl on his face.

Raven's heartbeat thudded in her throat. Jinx loved that cat. He might just kill her.

She opted not to break the news right away.

He stepped off the curb and strolled up. She shoved the gearshift into Park, and powered down the driver's window.

Jinx braced his palms against her door. "We've got a custodial interference on our hands. The guy split and his mother won't talk. Ivy hauled her downtown where, hopefully, she won't be able to make bond before I get her in front of Judge Masterson Monday morning."

"Why am I here?"

"You have to see this." His hands slid from the window to the door handle. Raven killed the engine, tucked a flashlight into the waistband of her jeans and waited for Jinx to step aside and let her out. Together they walked toward the house.

Jinx took a short detour. "Over here."

"Garbage?" She halted in her tracks. "You expect me to sift through somebody's garbage? What the hell's wrong with you? I just had my nails done. I'm getting married in eight days."

Jinx faced off with her. "It has to be you."

"Why? You want to punish me?"

"Because you're our resident ritualistic crimes expert."

It was true. She'd gained a reputation in the law enforcement community after she conned Jinx into paying for three forty-hour schools. It wasn't the topic that excited her as much as the fact that two of the conferences were held in Hawaii. Except for the times Ivy went off her meds, Raven caused more car wrecks romping around in a bikini than Ivy ever dreamed of.

Jinx handed her a fresh pair of latex gloves. As she slipped them on, a leggy woman with bottled-blonde hair sashayed out from behind the trailer. The spray-paint quality of her jeans accentuated her contours, and her tank top rode up above her waistband enough to show the glint of a belly ring.

Hoochie. Rhymed with coochie. Which is what Jinx seemed to have fixed in the crosshairs of his scope.

He had a ready explanation. "Rainey's private investigator. I hear she's good at skip-tracing."

The woman cast a devious stare in Jinx's direction.

Raven felt a fire in her cheeks. "Maybe she ought to try to find her underwear. If those pants fit any tighter, they'd violate the obscenity laws."

"Really?" Said with mock innocence. "I hadn't noticed. That slingshot she's wearing looks a little snug, though."

The hair on the back of Raven's neck stuck straight out. Jinx had turned ogling women into a spectator sport. She didn't like to think of him replacing her with a curvy blonde. Especially one with huge . . . *doe eyes* . . . and lashes the length of palm fronds.

Rainey's girl angled across the yard with Mickey and Dell orbiting her like Mars's moons.

"Hi. I'm Sigrid."

"Raven." She ignored the outstretched hand and cut her

eyes to Jinx. His gaze dipped to the woman's belly-button ring protruding out from the low-slung waistband of her Saran Wrap pants.

"Show me what you found," she said archly, and stomped off.

He caught up with her at the trash bags, stuck in his hand and pulled out a picture.

Raven sucked air. "What else?"

"You recognize this?"

A baphomet.

"It's the Goat of Mendes. Having sex with a virgin."

Jinx nodded knowingly. "Take a look at this." He handed her an envelope with a February date stamp, and a return address in Fort Worth. The letter inside had been ripped in half, but the hasty scrawl could still be read in the glow of the mercury vapor street lamps.

You're invited to the full moon ritual at my house. Bring Magick.

"Magick? Black magic, white magic, Houdini magic?"

"That's the kid's name."

Rainey's PI sidled up to Jinx and whipped out a photograph. Raven couldn't be sure, but she thought Sigrid Pierson grazed her breast against Jinx's arm.

Slut puppy.

"This is Magick, the missing child."

The evening light was fading fast, and Raven squinted to see. "She's just a baby."

Jinx shook his head. "That's an old picture. The kid's birthday's next week."

Just in time for summer solstice.

Raven pulled out her flashlight and shined it on the photo. "What else do you have?"

Jinx ran down the items for her: child pornography, letters

from known Wiccans, an ID card from a supremacy group that bestowed upon him "the right to kill niggers." Articles on child incest. Satanism. And marital aids of various dimensions and shapes.

The inventory chilled her to the core. "Anything else?"

A slow nod. "I need you to help me go through the rest of these bags."

No sense in arguing. Seventy-five phone calls to her wedding guests, notifying them of the printer's mistake on the invitations, could be done in the morning.

Partway through the second bag, Raven let out a squeal of disgust. "Oh, for God's sake. What kind of asshole throws his used condoms in the trash?" But she was talking to herself. Jinx had migrated a few yards down the sidewalk and was acting chummy with Rainey's private eye. Raven shot him a withering glare. He shoved his business card in the woman's hand and sauntered over.

"Problems?"

"Men are gross."

"That's not what you used to say."

"Zip it. Why am I the only one up to my armpits in trash?"

"Because you're the only one who knows what to look for."

She pulled out a paper, creased into quarters, and unfolded it. "Hold this." She shoved her flashlight at him and held the diagram up to the light for inspection.

Sick.

"Is the suspect married?"

"Wife's dead."

"Foul play?"

"Supposedly suicide. I don't buy it."

Smelling of scented bath soap, Jinx did a subtle lean over her shoulder for a better look. His breath warmed the back of her neck, and she took surprising comfort in his presence.

Raven swallowed hard. "It's a blueprint. Showing how to disembowel a human, and section him into little pieces to be devoured." She drew in a quick breath. "You said she's having a birthday? How old will she be?"

"Six."

"Oh, no." Clues spun in Raven's head. "When did the mother die?"

"A few weeks after the kid was born. Why do you ask?"

In order to raise the child, he had to get the wife out of the picture.

Raven's skin tingled. "You've gotta find her, Jinx."

"Did you just pull into town? Why in hell do you think we're out here?" A rhetorical question.

"That's not what I meant." Tears blistered behind Raven's eyeballs. "Six is the magic age. He's got to do it before she turns six."

"Do what?"

Panic crept into her voice. "Don't you get it? The summer solstice? A virgin sacrifice. The guy's a devil worshipper."

"Are you saying he's planning to rape her?"

Her voice warbled with the effort of speech. "Worse. I think he intends to kill her."

Caesar knew he was too old to be lost. In cat years, he was middle-aged, like his owner. He should've been back at the Château Du Roy, curled in the warm hollow Jinx made when he sat up in bed and wiped the sleep from his eyes.

He didn't mean to lose his way; he'd only planned to enjoy a quick game of *Bluff* with the girl. He and Jinx played it each morning. The way it worked: five out of seventeen tries, he'd slink past Jinx's foot—positioned between him and the door. He'd trot ten steps and look back over one shoulder. Jinx always said the same thing. "You're bluffing—get back here." Not angry. It was all part of the game.

He'd lead Jinx on a chase, skulking rat-like along the balcony, hunkering close to the wall. If he made it down the steps without Jinx catching him, he'd reward himself by writhing in the low spot where dirt collected after a good rain, and he never strayed past the base of the stairs. Then Jinx would cart him back upstairs and toss him inside the apartment, where he would spend the remainder of the morning getting the dirt off himself so he'd have a nice, gleaming coat by the time Jinx stopped in during the afternoon for a pet check.

Indignance mounted.

He couldn't believe the girl would leave him.

Maybe she thought he was a bad kitty.

But when the cat jail flew off the seat and hit the floor, and the mesh door swung open, he followed the girl out of the car. He didn't expect a flock of yellow birds to fly out of the bad woman's truck, and the commotion startled him. For a seven-year-old who could trace his roots back to the Royal Family of Siam, he sure felt like a bad kitty, sitting all by himself, waiting for traffic to slow.

A raggedy orange tom with a torn ear and thick coat strutted past. A deep yowl vibrated in Caesar's throat, a determined warning calculated to frighten the big orange furball invading his space. A Siamese was nothing to screw around with, not unless you wanted to spend the rest of your life stumbling around with a glass eye and white cane.

Caesar hunkered low and breasted the ground. The old tom was twice his size. Caesar decided not to show himself. Without warning, the tomcat streaked toward the street.

A horn blasted.

Followed by a sickening thud.

Caesar raised himself up. The orange tom lay still in the roadway.

Looking much flatter next to the car.

Caesar's heart thumped.

He's gonna be mad when he gets up.

What if he comes after me?

But the cat didn't move.

Caesar missed Jinx.

He even missed the girl.

He didn't want to end up twisted and red.

Must get home.

Must find Jinx.

Must not cross road.

Chapter Six

While Ivy transported Venita Standish downtown to the sally port to process her in at the booking desk of the county jail, Dell and Mickey heaved trash bags into the trunk of Jinx's unmarked patrol car and called it a night. Standing beneath the blue glow of the street lamp, with Sigrid Pierson lurking nearby, Jinx turned to Raven.

"We need a place to paw through the rest of these bags. Room to spread out. Unless you've got a better idea, I say we go back to the office and use the entire first floor." When she didn't chime in with a resounding *Okay by me,* he said, "It's not like people can come and go as they please. If anyone comes to the door, we can wave them off."

Rainey's sleuth piped up. "Thought you said we'd go out for a drink."

"First things first."

Raven sniffed. "You're such a jerk, Jinx." She stalked off to her patrol unit, chagrined to hear him trotting up behind her.

"Why're you mad at me?"

She whipped around and pointed her finger inches from his face. "You think you'll make me jealous, trying to get it on in front of me with your long-legged little friend? I'm getting married in eight days, Jinx Porter. I could care less if you bring that rubber-band-wearing skank down to the office, clear off a desk and boff her right in front of me."

"Now that's an idea . . ."

"Don't you dare bring her downtown. If you do, I'm outta there."

"You'd walk out on a little kid in the middle of an investigation??"

That sucked the wind out. "Suit yourself. Bring her along. I don't care." She keyed open the door, collapsed into the driver's seat, slammed the car shut and hit the electric door locks.

She couldn't imagine why Jinx gave the window a little knuckle rap. But she slid the window halfway down and got missile lock on him. "What?"

He spoke in a tender voice. "She's not coming downtown. I don't want her there."

Okay.

Relief massaged her shoulders. Fury cooled.

"So I'll meet you downtown."

Fine.

He swatted the door and stepped away from the car. She fired up the engine, flipped on the headlights and wrenched the Chevy into gear.

Watching from her rearview mirror as Jinx receded into a two-inch Weebil, an interesting thought occurred.

What'd I just do? I'm sending mixed messages.

What if he thinks I'm flirting?

Why should I care who he beds down with?

Stupid man. He still thinks he can win me back.

She's still hot for me.

Tommy Greenway may be AWOL, but I'm not.

And until she says, "I do," there's still a chance she'll come to her senses.

Jinx gave Sigrid Pierson the bum's rush and headed to the station.

Raven was waiting at the loading dock when he pulled into the rear parking lot of the building the Constable's Office shared with the Sheriff's Office. Half-expecting her to help him unload the Standishes' garbage and carry it inside the building, Jinx got a surprise.

"I'm not taking that in. I just had my nails done. I'm getting—"

"—married in eight days," Jinx chimed in unison. "I heard you the first ten times."

They went about the business of sorting through the debris in silence, with the rustle of paper and dust shimmering up from the disturbance, and an occasional sigh as the only movements. After an uneventful search through a bag that consisted mostly of old clothes, Raven's head snapped up.

She fisted a handful of torn photo remnants with one hand, and removed a paper, badly crinkled and yellow with age, with the other. "How'd she die?"

"Who? The girl's mother? The old Texas Ranger I talked to said she had post-partum depression. That she ingested some kind of poison."

"I don't think so." Breathless.

Jinx walked over and did a subtle lean-in. She handed him a list of chemicals Standish had purchased almost six years ago to the day. "He poisoned her."

"I agree." Raven unfurled her fingers. "Picture pieces. We need a flat surface to work on. And some tape."

Jinx made a beeline for the outer door of the Constable's Office and keyed the deadbolt. He returned with a tape dispenser and a small end table the secretary used as a stand for potted plants. Together, they reassembled the pieces like a jigsaw puzzle. When they finished matching edges, Jinx dropped in the final pieces. A mousy woman in a gauzy wedding gown stared back at them through the same gamine features as the missing child's.

"It's her. Gotta be." Jinx.

In reverse order, Raven reassembled the pieces face down, then taped the back of the photo. Water-spotted, with bleeding blue ink in one corner, she made out the words and recited them aloud.

"Emily Hurst Standish, on her wedding day."

Followed by the date.

"This is creepy," she said with a shudder.

"So you'll help me?"

In a voice soft with resignation, Raven gave in. "I'll help as much as I can, since I'm—"

"*Getting married in eight days*—I know. Only now it's seven." He pointed to the hall clock.

Five after midnight.

The lines in Jinx's face relaxed.

Raven gave a deep sigh. It was the least she could do, considering she'd wrecked his life and he didn't even know it yet.

He reached out for her hand and she didn't pull away.

"Honey, look . . ." He massaged her naked ring finger.

A firewall went up in her head. "Don't call me that, Jinx. Don't use terms of endearment on me anymore. It isn't proper."

He tightened his grip. "You think I'm coming on to you?" His tone went strident. "I called you *honey* after the Bobby Goldsboro song: 'She was always young at heart, kind of dumb and kind of smart;' that's you, honey."

Smart-ass.

Raven jerked free of his grasp. "I'm leaving. I need a shower—"

"I wasn't going to say anything about that, but you stink. I had to stay upwind of you at the trailer park. We all did."

Raven torqued her jaw. Her eyes darted about, in a room heavy with memories. She'd experienced one of the best sexual encounters of her life bent over a cleared space on Jinx's desk. The image simultaneously brought tears to her eyes and made her want to laugh. "Maybe if you didn't take such delight in insulting me, we'd still be together."

"Hey—I'm not the one screwing everything up by getting married."

"Don't blame me because the relationship failed. I'm not the one who paraded hundreds of women through our lives."

"Don't exaggerate." He gave her a dismissive flick of the wrist. "It's more like a dozen."

Jinx showed symptoms of *lie-arrhea.* Raven's gut sank. "I thought there were only three."

"A baker's dozen."

He acted like it didn't bother him, but she wasn't the one who carried on with Loose-Wheel Lucille, the lush from the corner apartment. And she wasn't the one who circled Personals ads, looking for one-night stands.

"All right, for the hundredth time, I'm sorry."

"I hate you," she said, halfway to hyperventilating.

"Remember, there's a thin line between love and hate."

"To avoid any misunderstanding, I feel compelled to make the distinction. I hate you."

"And just so you know, *I* feel compelled to inform *you* that the opposite of love isn't hate. It's indifference."

She stared at him through the silence.

A drop of sweat trickled down her back into her bikinis.

"I am sorry, Raven." His expression softened. "For everything. I wish I could take it back. I don't know why I'm fucked up, but I've had a lot of time to think about it and I'm pretty sure it has something to do with my dysfunctional family."

Unnerved by his bluntness, she bit her lip to keep from agreeing.

"You did the greatest thing anyone's ever done for me. As long as I live, I'll never forget that."

"By being your girlfriend?" On occasion, Jinx just flat choked her up. She clamped her teeth together to still the quiver in her chin.

"No. I'm talking about Caesar. If you hadn't given him to me, I'd be all alone. He's the best thing that ever happened to me."

She wanted to ball up her fist and slug him. And then it erupted. Five years of frustration, capped off by the final insult.

"The cat's gone, Jinx."

Sigrid Pierson was sitting on the steps at the loading dock when Raven stormed out of the old Criminal Courts Building. She glanced over, her blue eyes wide-awake, even though it was getting close to one in the morning. Sucking on the filter of her cigarette until the tip glowed bright red, she blew out a contrail and stubbed what was left out on the concrete.

The unexpected presence of Rainey's employee reinforced Raven's suspicions: there would never be a shortage of victims out there, eager to drink the Jinx Porter Kool-Aid. She gave the woman a bland smile and waited for the smoke to clear before wedging herself between those skin-tight pants and the handrail.

"So how do you like working for Evan Rainey?"

"The fringe benefits aren't bad." The girl seemed a bit resentful. "Is he still inside?"

Raven gave the door an over-the-shoulder glance. "Who? Jinx?" She tried to make her voice light and convincing. "He had to make a couple of phone calls. That's what happens when you juggle too many women. You have to keep them from finding out about each other. I think he's breaking a date with his girlfriend so he can go out with you."

With her face tilted up to the overhead bug light, Rainey's investigator looked jaundiced.

"He has a girlfriend?"

"Several, really. It's difficult to keep them from finding out about each other . . . the guys usually take turns making excuses for him when the ladies call. Except for the time the county health department phoned, wanting the names of all the women he'd slept with in the past three months. Something about venereal disease, and they had to find all the victims. I'd be lynched if I told you the whole story." She mimed a smile. "But you should go out with him. He's all better now. I think."

Looking anxious and vaguely resentful, Sigrid Pierson stood. Her whole body seemed to sigh as she brushed the dust off the seat of her tourniquet-tight pants. "Gotta get."

"See-ya." Raven told herself she only did it to keep Sigrid Pierson's butt out of a sling, but the devil within goaded her. Jinx wasn't the only one suffering from an occasional bout of lie-arrhea. "Hey, wait a minute."

Halfway down the steps, the pseudo-sleuth turned on one heel. "What's up?"

"Nothing really," Raven said with a smile. "It's just . . . well, I'm getting married soon . . . and you know how it is . . . we girls need to stick together. So I asked Jinx what he thought my fiancé would like for a wedding present. He said I should ask you for the name of the surgeon who did your boobs, so I could get a set just like them."

Chapter Seven

Jinx was locking the exterior door when Rainey's investigator peeled out of the parking lot, so Raven figured he didn't glimpse the woman jamming a stiff middle finger up at the rearview mirror as she sped out the drive.

Should she feel bad?

Maybe a little.

Did she?

Not hardly.

She considered it her *croix de guerre,* keeping a member of the sisterhood from pouring her energy down an empty hole.

With a pocketful of change jingling, Jinx met her at the loading dock. After the yelling died down, they agreed to retrace Raven's steps one last time, looking for the Siamese before going their separate ways.

At nine o'clock Saturday morning, functioning on five hours of sleep, Raven awakened to the persistent sound of Cézanne Martin, Fort Worth's premier homicide detective, repeatedly stabbing her doorbell.

She slid back the security chain and unlocked a series of deadbolts Dell installed for her three months before. The wedding shower Cézanne planned, with a guest list that included the office freaks, didn't start for another six hours. Now that the ace detective arrived early, they could start trimming circles of netting, and cutting ribbon to tie up rice bags. When the time was right, she would swear her to secrecy before relating details of Tommy's terrifying phone calls.

Yawning into the sleeve of her silk PJs, Raven opened the door to her grim-faced maid of honor. A braying Siamese struggled in Cézanne's clutches.

"Caesar! You found him." Elation fizzled at the sight of her friend holding the wrong cat, immobile, by the scruff of the neck. "That's Jezebel," she said dully.

"You don't mind if we come in, do you?" Cézanne pushed past with the screaming queen in tow. Beyond the front porch, police officers, dressed in the summer uniform of shorts and short-sleeved shirts, swarmed around Yoruba Groseclose's house.

Raven leaned far enough out the front door to see five squad cars and the ME's wagon.

"What the—?" She turned to Cézanne for an explanation, but her friend had wandered off into the kitchen. A cabinet door slammed shut. Running water hissed from the faucet.

Raven closed the door and toggled the bolts. Padded quickly into the kitchen where Jezebel stood happily lapping from a soup bowl placed near Cézanne's feet.

"Old lady Groseclose finally died?"

Cézanne's normally breathtaking face hardened. Periwinkle blue eyes narrowed into the shrewd glint of an ocular lie detector. Full, pouty lips thinned into immobility. She butted her slim hips against the kitchen countertop. Braced her arms across model-like breasts and regarded Raven with suspicion. Arched a brow and stared coolly into the depths of Raven's gray eyes.

"Where were *you* night before last?"

"Ohgod. Please tell me she died of natural causes."

"Pretty natural . . ." Cézanne nodded, ". . . if natural means having your head caved in with a blunt object."

Raven moved toward the breakfast nook at a zombie-like pace. Under the weight of bad news, she slumped heavily into a chair and stared at some point in the distance. "Somebody killed old lady Groseclose?"

"Anything you'd like to get off your chest?"

Raven snapped her head in Cézanne's direction. "Don't start with me. I'm getting married in eight—seven days—and I can't take any more drama in my life right now. What're you doing?"

Cézanne opened a cabinet door and selected a crystal stem. She headed for the refrigerator and set the icemaker on "Crushed." Gears ground, sending tiny ice shards past the lip of the glass. "What do you want in this?" No response. "Great. You get water."

Unexpectedly, Raven wanted to cry. To bury her head in her hands and rend the air with a guts-out scream. She cast her mind back to the previous morning, to the soggy newspaper and the awful gut-gnawing that persisted throughout the day. Should've checked on the elderly woman. Should've called the fire department, maybe had them axe down the front door. Should've—

All at once, she did cry. "I'm a horrible person. What if I could've saved her? How long has she been dead?" The question earned her a blank stare. "She was always so mean to me . . . still, I should've checked on her. Now she's dead and there's a killer on the loose."

Cézanne slid into the chair next to her, set the glass on the table and lopped a slender arm around Raven's shoulders.

"It'll be okay." Cézanne patted her back. "We'll find him."

Raven came up for air. "How do you know it's a *him?*"

"How many women do you know who smoke cigars? Not those sweet Cubans. The ones nasty enough to choke a goat."

Investigator skills kicked in. "What have you learned so far?"

"It's not my case. Sid Klevenhagen and Teddy Vaughn are working it. I dropped by because I recognized your street when the dispatcher put it out over the radio."

"But you have an idea what happened, don't you?"

Cézanne shrugged. Her easy demeanor turned abruptly professional. "You know I can't tell you that. But keep your doors locked. In the meantime—" she jostled Raven's shoulder and gave her a sly wink "—you get to look after the cat. Won't that be fun?"

"Wait. I can't take Jezebel in. I don't even like cats. I lost Jinx's Siamese yesterday."

Cézanne's eyes lit up. "Terrific. Give him this one. Maybe he won't know the difference."

He'll know.

"I don't have cat food. And there's no time to buy any."

"Look at her. She's a porker. She can stand to miss a meal." Her mouth split into a grin, making Raven wonder where she ever found the confidence to invite one of Fort Worth's most beautiful women to be her attendant. If Tommy'd met Cézanne first . . .

Oh, God bless. I'm turning into the Firestone tire of self-confidence.

"Please, Zan, don't make me feel bad. I don't want a cat."

The detective dragged out a long sigh. "I guess I could haul her to the animal shelter . . . of course, if no one wants her, they'll gas her."

"Why don't *you* take her?"

"Me?" Cézanne rocked her head back and laughed at the ceiling. "Perhaps you've forgotten. Deuteronomy brought her dog."

Of course.

Deuteronomy Devilrow—Duty, for short—the skinny black teenager Cézanne let live at her house so the kid could attend summer school. She hailed from deep East Texas and claimed to be a direct descendant of the Shreveport Devereaus, even after Senator Jean Lafitte Devereau called a press conference and issued a blanket denial that his ancestors held slaves. The front page article in the *Shreveport Times*—calculated to coincide with his re-election—quoted him as saying his great-great-great grandfather, Jean Robespierre Devereau, couldn't have bedded his children's mammy. So Deuteronomy Devilrow carried a laminated copy of a yellowed newspaper article with her, and routinely whipped it out in an effort to inject a little blue into her bloodline.

Raven's attention returned to the cat. She gave Jezebel the once-over. "She's huge. How much do you think she eats?"

"Feed her table scraps until you can get to the store."

"I'm not sure Tommy likes cats. How long would I have to keep her?"

"A few days. Until we locate Miss Groseclose's next-of-kin. Maybe one of her relatives will take her."

Raven gave her a glum nod. "A few days. No more."

"It's a nice thing you're doing. Now come on. Let's get you dressed and go pick up that gorgeous gown."

In the privacy of her bathroom, Raven took inventory of herself in front of the mirror. A tiny zit the size of a pinhead showed up on her chin. Pewter eyes that usually gave her face an exotic quality seemed dull in the marquis-like vanity lights, and the pale pink in her English complexion appeared blotchy. While she traded her PJs for a pair of seafoam green clamdiggers and white strappy sandals, the phone rang. The Caller-ID flashed "Out of Area."

She grabbed it, willing herself to hear Tommy on the line.

Jinx.

"Be ready in ten minutes. Venita Standish made bond. I'm coming by and we're going back out to arrest her again."

Raven thought fast. Slipped into the Guatemalan accent of the housekeeper.

"Missy Raven no here. Missy Raven getting married in seven days. *Siete días.*"

"Nice try, Raven. I know it's you."

"Missy Raven *no está aquí. Está comprando su—*"

Jittery, she drummed her fingers against her side.

What's Spanish for wedding gown?

Ah, screw it.

"—Missy Raven go to buy the wedding gown. *Adiós señor. Hasta luego*. Bye-bye."

Thus exhausting her foreign language vocabulary.

Except for Siamese.

Now cat-speak, she was getting proficient at. Especially now that she'd undertaken a Berlitz course taught by Jezebel.

After Raven hung up on him, Jinx headed out the apartment door. Agnes Loudermilk had commandeered a plastic lawn chair from the courtyard and seated herself at the edge of the balcony. From her perch overlooking the street, she hurled insults at Mr. Barber down below.

"Did you used to give your old mama enemas?"

Barber, whose ninety-five-year-old mother expired the previous month, pivoted on one foot, injected a bit of spring into his gait and took off in the opposite direction. Before Jinx could duck back inside, Agnes bobbed her head in his direction.

"Is he gay?"

"Who? Mr. Barber? No, he's not gay."

"How would you know? Unless maybe you came onto him and he turned you down . . ." Agnes stomped her foot and jabbed her finger into the air as if she found herself howlingly funny.

"I'm outta here."

"Is something wrong with your leg?"

Jinx picked up speed. Thundered down the stairs and angled off in the direction of the parking lot.

Her laughter climbed to a hysterical pitch. "Is it bigger than a peanut? I've seen 'em bigger than that before."

Jinx couldn't peel out fast enough. Blending into the traffic with the snout of the patrol car pointed toward Arlington, he turned the stereo on talk-radio and boosted the sound up.

If Agnes Loudermilk happened to be the most brazen crackpot in town, Venita Standish had to be the stupidest woman in the world.

Jinx never expected the ex–school teacher to open the door to his hammering knock late Saturday morning, but she did.

"Ron Masterson sends his regards."

She fixed him with a bovine stare, as if the gears in her head had ground to a complete stop trying to figure out what key position Ronald Masterson played in the ongoing custody dispute.

"Where's your son?"

"I dunno."

"You're under arrest." He latched onto her wrist, spun her around and clicked on the cuffs.

"You can't charge me again." She twisted her head in an attempt to communicate with him over-the-shoulder. "You already arrested me for that."

"New day, new offense."

"But I haven't even had my coffee."

"That's okay. A few more days' worth of green baloney and stale bread ought to loosen your tongue."

He paraded her out the door, to the delight of onlookers, and stuffed her in the back seat of the patrol car.

"Aren't you gonna lock my door? What if someone breaks in?"

"By all means. We wouldn't want anyone to steal all this high-dollar stuff." Delivered with a sarcastic bite.

"Aren't you gonna read me my rights?"

Jinx glared. "Let me guess. You watch a lot of TV: 'Miami Vice' and 'Hawaii Five-O' re-runs? Well let me set you straight, Ms. Standish. I don't have to read you your rights because I'm not asking any questions. But if you don't get in the back seat and button it, I might just give you a fat lip."

For good measure, he carried a roll of yellow, Day-Glo crime scene tape up the wobbly front steps, twisted the lock button on the knob and pulled the door to, then affixed bands of CRIME SCENE plastic across the entrance into a big "X."

Strolling back to the patrol car, he announced to no one in particular, "If anybody's conscience bothers them . . . if you know the whereabouts of this missing girl, call the Constable's Office and ask for Jinx Porter—*or Raven.*"

Chapter Eight

A few minutes after ten that morning, Raven and Cézanne swung by the detective's house to pick up Deuteronomy Devilrow. Raven honked once and a black girl around sixteen came out the door, gave a quick wave and fumbled with the keys before locking up. She stood tall and willowy sauntering across the lawn, and wore her hair fashioned in a short, straight style. As she climbed into the back seat, her sleeves rode up her thin arms, making her seem unusually fragile. But the wide, toothy grin hinted of a rural toughness, and brought an effervescence of instant cheer into their midst. Behind almond-shaped eyes that tilted at the corners, raw intelligence blazed.

By way of introduction, Cézanne sliced a hand through the air. "This is Deuteronomy Devilrow, descendant of the Shreveport Devereaus."

Raven locked eyes in the rearview mirror and did a backward finger wiggle.

"I expect you's the bride. You look like a bride, all happy. Can I see yo' hand . . . just for a second. I need to check something." She reached over the seat.

"Give it up, Duty, you're not telling fortunes." Cézanne gave her the eye but the teenager grabbed Raven's hand and twisted it, palm up, in an over-the-shoulder grasp. "She thinks she has second sight," Cézanne added in a stage whisper.

"Yep, you gonna make a beautiful bride. Gonna have six kids, too. Three boys, three girls. I have names picked out for mine; if you wanna use 'em I could let you have 'em and get me new ones. It would be my wedding gift to you."

Raven tried to wriggle free of the strange girl's grip. Duty held fast. "Just one problem, though. Hmmmm, this is pretty serious."

"Duty, don't start."

"Your beau, he's worried about—"

"I mean it, Deuteronomy."

"—he's worried about whether you have too much to do before the wedding. That's where I come in. I could help you do stuff. My gramma Corinthia, she say idle hands is the devil's work. I seen the devil once. Sittin' at the foot of my bed. Miz Zan don't believe me, but it's true."

Cézanne moved closer and lowered her voice. "Sorry, I should've muzzled her."

The girl's words faded into a buzz.

As Raven pulled into traffic, Cézanne glared past the headrest and Duty abruptly went quiet.

At Bridal-Wise, the three walked into a room heavily scented with the sweet smell of exotic perfumes worn by would-be brides looking for one-of-a-kind designer gowns. Dresses hung from racks mounted against the walls and, in an anteroom, stacks of shoe boxes eclipsed a Grecian mural. The proprietor, Geneva Anjou, a petite lady with birdlike bone structure and a beak to match, intercepted them at the entry. She wore her brown hair swept away from her face and pinned at the sides and, when she ushered them inside with a whirlwind of cheer, unruly curls dropped down past her shoulders and flounced about like coils of springs.

She spoke in a librarian's voice, with her back to a door marked EMPLOYEES ONLY, as if she didn't want the male occupant seated behind the desk, his head bent in concentration above paperwork, to overhear. "Thank goodness you arrived early. My alterations lady leaves at noon. If the hem's too long, there's still time to make the adjustment. You understand you *must* have your gown out of here by Wednesday?" She grasped Raven's hand in a pleading gesture. "It's *imperative* that you pick it up before we close. And your bridesmaids, where are they?"

Raven glanced around. "They were supposed to meet us."

Geneva Anjou seemed on the verge of panic. "I told them yesterday to take possession of their dresses before Wednesday. *Wednesday.* But that Ivy woman said she had to go out of town. Something about her son being locked up in the reformatory. And those other two ladies—Dixie and Georgia—need my alterations lady to let their dresses out at the waist. Your friend Shiloh's the only one who's followed through."

It figured.

Except for the cost of the gown, Shiloh Willette had been tickled pink to accept the invitation to be matron of honor, not that she and her husband Kenny had discretionary income to spend on such foo-foo things. Shiloh, too, had gotten caught up in the Oster blender of Jinx Porter's life, and married him. Seven years later, their dancing German Shepard slipped its chain and Shiloh trailed the family pet down the unlikely footpath to a neighbor's house. Upon hearing passionate screams coming from the bedroom, she upended a metal trashcan. One look through the window and she packed Jinx's bags. He ended up at the Château Du Roy—where he'd lived ever since—leaving Shiloh free to find Kenny one Saturday night at Stagecoach, where he two-stepped his way into her heart.

It was enough that Shiloh had befriended her through that horrible incident with Loose-Wheel Lucille, the lush from the corner apartment at the Château Du Roy, back when she stumbled in on Lucille waxing Jinx's carrot. For the next two years, Shiloh encouraged her to unload Jinx Porter like a dump truck at a landfill, and seek out someone worthy of her devotion.

Shiloh was a true friend. But the other women?

Georgia, who'd been on a weight loss program called *Starving for Jesus,* apparently hadn't been.

And Dixie? She endorsed the French fry and bacon-double-greaseburger diet. The woman had slow metabolism and a caboose wider than a piano bench. If Dixie ever hauled ass, she'd need a moving van to do it.

As for Ivy . . . truth be known, Ivy was the consummate X-factor. Raven inwardly wished a raging case of strep throat on the office hypochondriac.

She gave Geneva Anjou a wary headshake and a weak apology for the confusion.

Duty wandered across the carpet to a rack of dresses that had been rolled into view.

"Miz Zan, come see. This the most beautiful dress I ever laid eyes on."

"In a minute." Cézanne cut her eyes to Geneva Anjou. "What about my gown? Did the seamstress finish taking in the sides?"

"Yours is ready. We'll bring it out and you can slip it on. I'll be back with yours, too, Raven. I'm sure you'd like your friends to see it." The tiny woman hurried to the back of the shop on invisible vapors of energy.

Across the room, Duty tuned up giddy with delight. "Come see what I found. Tangerine gowns!" All eyes moved in a collective shift.

She stood near a rack of floor-length gowns, clutching a piece of skirt from the most hideous women's apparel Raven had ever seen: a shiny, polyester, floor-length, box-pleated hoop skirt in the shape of a bell, with a fitted bodice boned with bustier stays. A low-cut, button-up, devil dress with cap sleeves, each with its own gauzy, chiffon train that draped down the arm and hung to the wrists in shiny, see-through orange net.

The friends exchanged *Ooooh, ick* looks and migrated to what could only be described as the Ugly Dress Rack.

It was orange. Not the fun tangerine-orange or the juicy naval-orange color of ripened fruit, but a burnt-orange, flame-retardant parachute material that looked as if it had survived the fires of Hell. A shade that, instead of enhancing the skin tone, made a person look dead for a month.

"This the most beautiful thing I ever saw in my life. Look, Miz Zan."

"It's so bright, you could suntan under it."

"Can I try it on? This my size. I'm a four. I would like to slip this on and see if I don't look like Cinderella."

Cinderella? Maybe after the fairy tale princess committed mass murder and went straight to the devil.

The hideous attire looked like prom doings, if the social event were held in a crackling inferno. Fashioned out of Day-Glo fabric that shimmered like embers, it ignited visions of paratroopers drifting into Hell.

Cézanne lifted one transparent sleeve to the light. "What would you call this? Abscess orange?"

Duty, a tall, reed-thin girl with skin the color and smoothness of pale brown marble, affected a serious pout. "I think they's pretty." Luminous maroon eyes blinked.

"They're frightful." Raven grimaced. "This could scare small children. It's like rotten pumpkin soaked in iodine. Without the flies buzzing around it."

"*Halloween* meets *Nightmare on Elm Street.*" Cézanne, with her point well taken.

"The last time I saw anything this scary was when my grandfather carved jack-o-lanterns that looked like the FBI's Ten Most Wanted."

"I don't know whatchoo talkin' about. We don't have no TV back home in Weeping Mary—" Duty broke her gaze and turned her attention back to the dress "—but I was thinkin' if they can't get yo' bridesmaids' dresses let out for the fat ones on time, you could take these. They got all different sizes, all the way up to Thirty-Woman's."

Raven mumbled, "Kill me now."

Cézanne whispered, "Or kill *them*. . . ."

They were still doubled over in the throes of laughter when Geneva Anjou came out of an anteroom hoisting an unwieldy garment bag overhead. It was stuffed to capacity.

Duty toed the mauve carpet. With her head cocked in a coy tilt, she lifted a handful of orange fabric. " 'Scuse me, but could I try this on?"

"No-no-no, dear. Those are rentals—for poor people. You should check our sale room in back for odd sizes." The shopkeeper smiled at Cézanne. "You'd want her to have something nice."

Translation: expensive.

Cézanne wandered away, took one look at the markdowns and scowled at the price tags. She re-entered the main room shaking her head. "No way. Not with a gun to my head and the hammer cocked."

The tailor glided in, gently cradling the maid of honor's dress as though a baby rested in her arms. Cézanne gave the tucks in the side seams a tentative inspection. The alterations lady unzipped the low-slung back and slid the gown off its hanger.

Duty unhanded the orange cloth. Stared through wondrous eyes at the slinky silk. "Miz Zan, that's about the most beautiful dress I ever did see. It matches yo' eyes. Like looking at dawn on a hanger."

"Periwinkle blue," said the owner. "That's the color. But the designer gave it a name. It's called *Rapture*."

"Rat shit?" Duty, momentarily distracted with a swirl of bugle beads, stared in disbelief.

Geneva Anjou paled. "Rapture," she enunciated.

Duty dodged Cézanne's glare with a downcast look and a soft-spoken, "Oh."

Cézanne and the seamstress slipped out of sight, into a nearby dressing room.

The proprietor hung the enormous garment bag on a wall hook. She unzipped the casing and released Raven's wedding dress.

Duty sucked air.

A fitted corset with long princess sleeves, a sweetheart neckline, and hand-beaded, embroidered silk laced up the sides. Tiny hand-sewn pearls encrusted the edges, which dipped a few inches over the low-riding waistband of the skirt in uneven points. That the bodice resembled the leaves from the tight part of a rose was not lost on Raven. The skirt flowered out below in the softest, most beautiful lace she'd ever seen, falling over folds of duchess satin, gathered up to make six billowy scallops, each one rising a foot off the floor, with the individual splashes secured at every crevice by a two-toned, blush-pink satin rose.

Duty spoke for them both. "If Miz Zan's dress is *Rapture,* this must be *Heaven*." She blinked back tears.

Raven took pity. Slipped an arm around the teenager's waist and gave her a quick squeeze. "Don't cry. Why're you crying?"

" 'Cause this the most beautiful dress I ever did see." Duty leaned in. Lifted a tentative hand and snatched it back at the last second as if awaiting permission to touch.

"Are your hands clean?"

Enthusiastic nod.

"One quick feel."

With reverence, Duty caressed a satin rose with her fingertips. Her hand dropped to her side and she turned to Raven in complete earnest. "If I was ever to get married, I'd want a dress just like this. I wouldn't care if I had to live in a rundown shack the rest of my life. But just for one day, I could be a real, honest-to-goodness princess." Her voice went dreamy. "I could live on that memory. That I could."

Abruptly, Duty shook off the fantasy. "You love Tommy? Is he yo' prince?"

"He's wonderful." Spoken softly, to the toes of her Bally flats.

"He treat you good?" Duty stared through the squinty eyes of a sage.

"I want to have his babies. I never wanted children before." Her eyes misted.

"I have a brother; when he was little, my momma made me change his diapers. Smelled so bad it 'bout melted my eyebrows. You sure this man's the one?"

"Absolutely."

"When did you know? At what exact point?"

As soon as I shot him and he didn't die.

"Why the inquisition?"

"No particular reason. It's just that Miz Zan said you used to be girlfriend-boyfriend with Mista Jinx Porter."

Raven's eyes widened.

Duty mounted a quick save. "I know Mista Jinx. He saved Miz Zan's life a couple of times. We like him."

"That was a long time ago. Tommy's my prince. Jinx is a toad. Toads don't get married, they just give you warts and screw up your life." A tear bubbled along the rim of Raven's eye. The shopkeeper pulled the gown away in a protective yank, guarding it from the saline damage of borderline hysteria.

"I'm sorry, Miz Raven. I didn't mean to make you sad. I wouldn't like to put a curse on Mista Porter, but I can if it'll make you stop makin' those spooky sounds."

"I'm not crying because of him. I'm happy with my life . . . or rather the way my life will be when Tommy comes back."

In a feeble attempt to change the subject, Duty stroked Raven's arm and made an important observation. "What kind of flowers you gonna carry in your bouquet? You gonna get roses like the ones in yo' dress? Maybe little tea roses? Tyler got a lot of roses. Tyler close to Weeping Mary, where I come from. Tyler the rose capital of the world."

Raven gave an abrupt sniffle. Duty'd just given her a verbal face smack.

Roses.

She'd forgotten to order the bouquet.

"Noooooooooo." She crumpled to the floor with her head in her hands, making marine animal noises.

Cézanne burst forth from the dressing room. "What the hell just happened?" she asked of the room at large. On instinct, she shot Duty a withering glare. "Did you mention Jinx Porter? I'm sorry, Raven, I never should've mentioned anything to her about Jinx."

Clearly frightened, Duty cut her eyes to Raven, still seated, yoga-style, on the floor.

She thinks I'm going to out *her.*

Without glancing up, Raven shook her head no.

"Calm yourself, Miz Zan. It's an emotional time. I'll make a little spell, it'll all be over in a jiffy." She raised her hands in front of her face and did a little finger dance through the air.

Cézanne grabbed her wrists and arrested the hocus-pocus in mid flight. "No Voodoo. We talked about that. Whatever you did, tell Raven you're sorry."

Raven looked up. Momentarily composed, she covered for Duty. "She didn't do anything. I forgot to order the flowers for my bouquet. This has to be perfect, and everything's going wrong. And I'm getting married in seven days—*seven days*—" her voice spiraled up until only a Weimaraner could hear it.

Cézanne stooped to offer comfort. An audible rip came from the trumpet skirt, casting a pall of silence over the room. For several seconds, everyone held their arrested breath.

Raven tuned up again.

Geneva Anjou knelt beside her. "No, no, no, don't cry. We can repair the split. My alterations lady's a wizard. She can fix anything."

Raven unburied her face. The seamstress didn't appear physically imposing, but she had the discipline of a drill sergeant. It showed in her beady eyes and in the defiant way her jaw jutted forward.

"Can you mend it?"

A determined nod.

"See? I told you so." Geneva Anjou helped her to her feet, gushing, "Isn't Cézanne just lovely?"

The man seated at the desk beyond the door marked EMPLOYEES ONLY made a beeline for the shop owner. He pulled her aside, and rattled a handful of papers at her. They spoke in hushed tones, with the kind of facial stress and wringing hand gestures that suggested bad news. As quickly as he popped into view, he retreated into the cramped office.

Cézanne pirouetted, pulling the fishtail train along in a graceful arc. "Other than my butt sticking out, what do y'all think?"

"Miz Zan, you the prettiest lady I ever laid eyes on." Duty caught her *faux pas* and amended it. "Maybe not as pretty as Miz Raven's gonna be in her dress, but it's her wedding. And she gets to be queen for a day, right? So you don't mind takin' a back seat?"

"We know what you mean," Raven said with a touch of fondness. She could see why her friend had fallen victim to the strange girl. Why she let her move into her home and enrolled her in summer school. Why she hoped Duty would involve herself in the police chapter of Explorer Scouts and follow in her footsteps one day. Why she'd started to treat the teenager more like a daughter than a serious lapse in judgment.

No, she was glad Cézanne brought Duty along for the experience. The girl had posed a few clarifying questions.

She did *love Tommy.*

Believe it or not, Jinx was *history.*

And that Voodoo thing?

Never could tell when that might come in handy.

But Dell . . . nobody'd mentioned Dell.

For a fleeting second, she latched onto a memory, and held it until it shattered at the sound of the shopkeeper's voice.

"Come, Raven, let's get you into your beautiful gown."

Chapter Nine

After booking Venita Standish into the county jail around eleven thirty, Jinx headed for Raven's house. He didn't care if she was getting married in seven days or seven minutes, she'd by God better help him search for that cat.

Once they finished, he'd take her to that hamburger joint in the next county—a secret he and Dell kept from the rest of the staff. Raven loved adventure, especially when it carried the allure of spontaneity.

He'd get her out into the countryside.

Maybe feign car trouble on their way back from lunch.

Or spend the rest of the afternoon guilting her into helping him look for Caesar.

And later that night, if he caught her in the right mood, he'd try to talk some sense into her.

Raven didn't need a spook for a husband. CIA agents were sociopaths and loners. Tommy Greenway didn't need a wife. And Raven sure as hell didn't need him.

She wanted the security of marriage and the promise of a family.

Jinx could give her both.

He drew strength and resolve from a comment Raven herself once made, after she found those bikini panties stuffed under the floorboard of the passenger seat of his car—and discovered the truth about his brief encounter in the gentlemen's club parking lot with the Baldwin sisters. They'd had a huge blowout and she stomped out, vowing never to return.

But when she finally came back to him after a three-month absence, she'd put the hopeless affair into perspective.

Why would you even look at another woman, Jinx? You don't stop loving a person just because you're mad at them.

Raven exited the fitting room with strains of classical music presiding over the din. Prospective brides gathered with attendants of all sizes and shapes, giving the appearance of a sorority meeting at the "I Felta Thigh" house.

To her right, a stringy-haired waif who looked as if she'd dressed from the rag bin lifted the price tag on a gown. She drew in a sharp intake of air. One glance at the rough-hewn teenager's tattered jeans, and Geneva Anjou spoke of the benefits of renting the bridesmaids' gowns and ushered her straight to the Ugly Dress Rack.

To the left, Cézanne appeared to be wood-shedding Duty.

Probably warning her not to bring up the topic of Jinx.

For all anyone cared, Raven could've been wallpaper. She walked toward the mirror with the hem of her gown whispering along the floor. A collective gasp filled the room. For a moment, onlookers ceased to breathe.

Hushed murmurs of "gorgeous" and "ravishing" filled their shared space. Mothers of the bride teared-up and a few fathers, no doubt dragged into Bridal-Wise against their will, got misty-eyed and relaxed amidst the chaos of fittings.

Cézanne, re-dressed in her linen slacks and pullover, turned around. Duty brushed past her. She made her way to the center of the room and pulled off a little curtsy.

"Cinderella in the flesh. Please, may I be in yo' wedding? Please, please, please?" Duty's hands fused together, prayer-like. "I could sing. I gotta good voice."

"Deuteronomy!" Piqued, Cézanne strode over and buttonholed the girl by the elbow.

"I could buy a dress. I have money. I earned it keeping house for Miz Zan."

"Stop it right now."

"Miz Raven, I would be so grateful if you would give me this one day."

Raven felt the heat of a blush. "I'm sorry, Duty. There's no time. Everything's in place."

"Pleeeeeaaaaasssssseee?"

Cézanne's irritation evaporated. "Maybe you have something she could do? The rice bags?"

"Whatchoo mean, rice bags?" Duty, intrigued.

Raven thought fast. If she let Duty hand out rice bags at the reception, that'd make her feel important. Not to mention, keeping her distracted and out of the way.

"I think passing rice bags out would be a wonderful idea." Raven smiled big. She caught her reflection in floor-to-ceiling mirror. An electric chill traveled the length of her body, prickling the hair beneath the lacy, fingerless gloves peeking out from under the princess sleeves of her corset.

Look at me, Pawpaw.

This is what Tommy will see.

Even with this zit I'm beautiful.

Duty, still in a curtsy, gave the gown a squinty-eyed glare and dropped another verbal bomb. "Is that a grease stain on yo' dress?"

The alterations lady identified the dark speck on the gown as sewing machine oil and promised to spot clean it to perfection over the weekend. But that meant picking up the gown on Monday, leaving Raven to spend the rest of the weekend wondering if the stain would come out.

Back home, she said good-bye to Cézanne and Duty, and went inside with an eager swoop down on the answering machine.

No blinking message light.

No word from Tommy.

Her stomach fluttered.

She remembered Jezebel and did a cursory walk-through of the house.

No cat.

What the hell? The old girl was probably skittish, hiding under the bureau, or lowboy, or even the bed. An open can of cat food should flush her out. Raven went to the kitchen and composed a quick grocery list.

She'd no sooner locked the front door when Jinx wheeled the patrol car into her driveway.

"Great," she said through a fake smile. "Just what I needed." She glanced skyward and wondered if God might be pricking with her.

Jinx alighted the vehicle. "Top of the mornin'."

"What do you want? I'm in a hurry."

"In a hurry to help me look for Caesar, you mean."

She stared, open-mouthed. Halfway to *How dare you?* guilt set in. "I'll give you an hour. No more. I'm sorry-sorry-sorry about your cat, Jinx, but I'm getting—"

"Married in seven days—" they said in stereo.

"Yes, I'm so glad you reminded me—"

"That's right, Jinx Porter. I still have wedding details to take care of."

"—otherwise, I might've actually forgotten."

He stepped up onto the porch, past a thick coil of vines climbing up a concrete pillar. Sunlight cast ivy-shaped shadows on his face. "That cat's all I've got."

Her protests lost effect. "All right," she huffed. "Two

hours. That's all I can spare."

"Three."

"Fine. Three. Don't bother me the rest of the weekend. Deal?"

"All right."

"Say it. Repeat after me: 'I swear I won't bother you for the rest of the weekend.' "

"I swear I won't bother you about the cat for the rest of the weekend."

But when she climbed into the passenger seat of the idling Chevy, she wondered. Jinx was a master at word play.

He slid behind the wheel with the makings of a smile forming. "Show me exactly where you were when the cat escaped."

They drove to the intersection of University, where Seventh Street and Bailey converged like spokes on a wagon wheel, and Camp Bowie Boulevard began as a bumpy, brick road.

As Jinx waited for the light to change, Raven said, "I was eastbound on Camp Bowie, in front of the McDonald's, like it says in my report. You can probably still see tire marks where Sabina Balogh plowed into me."

Jinx overshot the intersection at Camp Bowie and Montgomery, and made a mid-block U-turn. The last remnants of taillights and broken glass had been swept to the curb.

He pointed to skid marks, smeared into the bricks. "There's your point of impact. Which way do you think he went?"

"Probably south. I can't imagine he'd cross against the traffic."

Jinx swallowed hard. On instinct, Raven tried to raise his comfort level.

"If Caesar'd been hit by a car, I'd have noticed."

He nodded.

She injected a lilt in her voice. "I say we try the Will Rogers complex. They always have parties over there. He probably smelled food."

Jinx made a hard right, whipped into the fast food drive-in and out the other side. No cat. Caesar was a finicky eater.

They checked the area around Will Rogers, including the exhibition hall. Still no cat.

Jinx filled in the vacuum of silence.

"I've got a surprise." His face cracked into a grin. "New lunch experience."

Raven noted the time on her watch. "Long as I'm back in two hours. Where're we going?"

"On an adventure."

She regarded him with suspicion. "Where?"

"Don't ask. I'm about to give you the gift of calm. If you start bullying me for answers, you'll blow it."

She stole a glance at the gas gauge. With less than a quarter tank, he couldn't exactly spirit her across the state line.

On the way out of town, Jinx related details from the morning's experience with Venita Standish. Once he had her 'cuffed and stuffed, she tuned up her caterwauling about not getting her Miranda rights.

He spoke directly to the windshield. "It was all I could do to keep from dough-popping her." His hands tightened around the steering wheel in a white-knuckled grip. "Masterson said to arrest her every time she bonds out. If she cools her hocks in jail a few weeks at a time, she'll eventually tell us where they went."

Unless it's too late.

The Fort Worth skyline receded into Raven's side mirror. They rode into the oak-dotted countryside, on a road parallel to a long expanse of train tracks. Raven sat wordlessly, staring off into a freshly-plowed field. Sections of farmland rolled by like a huge patchwork quilt made with squares of various shades of yellow, brown and green. Steam rose from the blacktop, distorting images in the car's path. She adjusted the A/C vent to blow directly on her face. Shielding her eyes against the glare of the sun, she couldn't remember the last time she'd gotten a decent night's sleep.

She wished she could break out a picture of Tommy. She suspected his refusal to be photographed stemmed from some secret, ten-commandment, CIA Standard Operating Procedure manual. *Thou Shalt Have No Likeness of Thine Image Made.*

So she'd come to do the next best thing: when she wanted to see Tommy, she shut her eyes and let herself remember his gaze, of a blue so deep you could swan-dive into it and never hit bottom. Glittery, peacock-feather irises that shimmered with laughter, or clouded over like stormy skies, depending on his mood. Of dark, glossy hair that framed a *GQ* face, and white, even teeth that looked like they belonged on a celebrity. Of the tan, six-foot frame he kept in perfect shape—

—absolutely perfect—lean and firm like a Greek statue, only with its pecker unadulterated.

Lulled by the drone of Jinx's voice, she closed her lids.

An image of Tommy appeared.

Physically, she sat curled up in the patrol car with her head resting against the glass, but in her mind, she was back home saying good-bye to the man she loved. Her stomach rolled over with the reality of his departure. He'd promised not to take another mission, but Yucatan Jay had gotten himself into another scrape—assassinating a dictator was a two-man job, and Equatorial Guinea wasn't a place to putz around.

From the moment Tommy got the assignment, he launched into survival mode, implementing a strict, no-sex policy until his return. While awaiting orders from his Commander in Chief, he paced the floor and focused on distant points in space, formulating a plan to liberate Y-Jay from his captors.

"Don't cry, Rave. I hate it when you cry."

"What if you don't come back? What if you die in some Third-World country where they cut off your head and hoist it up on a pole as a warning to others?"

"Then think of me fondly and go about doing whatever you were doing before I came along."

"Fondly? You move like a ghost through other people's lives and expect them not to be changed?"

"It's my last job. Soon as I locate Y-Jay and bring him in, I'm quitting."

Among his gear, Tommy packed an array of lightweight clothing, a government-issue windbreaker from the Department of Defense, with DOD Translator silk-screened on the left panel where a breast pocket should've been, insect spray and a small wooden box he went out of his way to ensure she never snooped through.

At the front door, while exchanging good-byes, she tried to put on a stoic front. Crybabies irritated him. A façade of remote, cool detachment would show him her inner strength.

He fixed her with his azure gaze. Studied her through eyes that were level and unyielding.

"I've worked hard to shield you from my business, Raven."

She shook her head, slow on the uptake.

"One day you might get a stranger knocking at the door. Don't let him in. If he tells you I'm dead, don't swallow it."

Chills snaked over her body, leaving her suddenly cold. Her heart raced. Her lips trembled. He gripped her shoulders and gave them a gentle shake.

"Listen to me, Raven. He wants to hurt you. To get back at me."

The room blurred.

"Uncle Jack—if Uncle Jack shows up on your doorstep and says I'm dead, maybe *you can believe it. Or the President."*

"What?"

"Oh, sure, I bitch about him being a micromanager, but we're pretty tight. He's a good guy. You can trust him."

This isn't happening.

He pressed his lips against hers, powerful and insistent. She latched onto the curve of one muscular arm and hung on for dear life.

"Tommy, don't go."

His name was a husky cry against her mouth. She scrunched her eyes. Tried to pretend this wasn't happening, and tasted salt.

"I want you to keep a gun near the door—one of the small ones—what am I saying? You probably have one duct-taped to the silk ficus."

His cheeks plumped, crinkling his skin as if she'd done him proud.

She could've kissed him forever; but his hand fisted in her hair, snapping her head far enough back to make serious eye contact.

"If it's the President, you can believe him. But only if it's him."

"You're scaring me."

"Pay attention, Rave. If he tells you I'm dead, then it's true. But make him show ID. Don't let him in unless you're sure it's really him, understand?"

"Please don't leave me this way."

She clutched his hands and slid them under her shirt—a cheap ploy that proved as effective as nailing Jell-O to a tree.

When she let go, his fingers seemed to disintegrate. She clamped them tight. Massaged them against her nipples, showing him what to do. This time, he didn't resist. He cupped her breasts on his own volition; not squeezing, but not pulling back, either. Her eyes fluttered with euphoria.

Convincing him to break his no-sex rule would be like asking for unicorns and getting a My Pretty Pony with a toothpick impaled in its head.

In a brazen move, she took his hand and slid it into her panties.

Their eyes met, and he smiled.

"You're right. It'd be cruel to leave you like this."

A mournful wail yanked Raven out of the bedroom, into the present. She roused to the groan of a freight train and blinked her surroundings into focus.

As usual, Jinx was still talking. "So I figure on Monday, I'll subpoena for the phone records. Maybe see if Fleck Standish phoned that old harpy. Or if Venita Standish contacted him. And I want to visit the witch—"

"Wiccan."

"—who sent him that invitation to the full moon ritual."

She managed an unenthusiastic nod. Squinted into the sun in an attempt to make out a road sign in the distance.

"Because of his wife's death, the kid receives a Social Security survivor benefits check each month, made payable to Standish. If his mother doesn't fess up soon, I'll sic the postal inspector on it and we can dog their mail. That might be a good job for Ivy. Stupid people do well at mindless activities."

Jinx exited the freeway and cut through the small town of Decatur. He picked up a back road near the old courthouse square, where farmland played out and trees grew in thick, lush stands.

The cell phone in Raven's purse shrilled. She retrieved it on the third ring. Pressed the talk-button and greeted her caller.

Emma-Jewel Houston.

"Girl, are you ready for this?"

"Did you get my ring back?"

"Good news, bad news. I'm sittin' here wearin' it. That's the good news. Bad news is, my finger swole up so tight I can't get it off."

"That's okay. I have bolt cutters in the trunk."

"Girl, you don't wanna go cuttin' on this beautiful diamond with bolt cutters."

"I wouldn't dream of it. They're for your finger."

Emma-Jewel let out a belly laugh. "Girl, you crazy. Come on down before three and I'll give it back."

Raven hung up and heaved a deep, elated sigh. "They retrieved my diamond."

Jinx gave her a brittle smile. "When I try to visualize the little bride and groom on your wedding cake, I see Beelzebub and Barbie."

The dig drew fire from Raven.

"That's okay, I used to try to visualize you and Loose-Wheel Lucille." Without warning, her mind replayed that horrible afternoon when she walked into his apartment and discovered Loose-Wheel Lucille performing CPR on Jinx's alter-ego. She tried to fight off the shocking memory by watching him now, all starched and pressed and smelling of soap; but like a resistant strain of Asian clap, the image came back twice as strong. She remembered how she watched in stricken silence as the toothless old crone revived him for another go-round . . . and effectively canceled out her existence. She'd come so close to killing him that day, it paralyzed her with fear. Seething with unresolved emotion, she smacked her forehead. "Oh—that's right—what am I saying? I was *there,* so I got to see it *in person.*"

"You don't have to get smart."

"There you were: like Abaddon and one of his minor demons, frolicking in the imaginary *Hotel California* of your queen-size bed, looking like hell and playing like the Devil." She set her jaw. Blinked her lashes so fast she could've almost levitated off the seat. "How well I remember."

Jinx checked the rearview mirror. He slowed at a crossing, flipped on his turn signal and made a hard left, down a dusty, two-lane, farm road, past several greenhouses full of hanging baskets in vivid colors. A wooden sign popped up in the distance where the lanes forked. Jinx turned off to the right and killed the engine in front of a dilapidated grocery store with rusty screens and flaking paint.

The vision took her breath away.

He'd put her smack-dab in the middle of a Norman Rockwell painting, where two old, yellow, porch dogs slept in the shade of a weathered oak church pew. Raven stared long and hard, watching for the rise and fall of their chests. The retriever-mix with the pink leather nose might be dead. Before she could call Jinx's attention to the expired canine, an ear twitched, sending a couple of horseflies into orbit.

"How come you never told me about this place?"

"This is my own little piece of Heaven. Hope you believe in time travel." He gave the area a furtive scan, then set his jaw.

"What's wrong?"

"Nothing."

But she knew by the way his expression hardened, whatever he'd come expecting to find wasn't here.

He opened the screen door, gripped the embossed tin knob to a second set of doors and gave it a twist. Raven stepped inside, and the screen slapped shut behind them.

Activity faltered when they entered. Old men in faded overalls and gimme caps watched through shrewd eyes. Middle-aged men in hardhats, with their names stitched across oval patches on the fronts of their uniform shirts, gave them blank stares. For a moment she halted in place, barely breathing, as if they'd somehow interrupted a meeting of the Fraternal Order of White-Tailed Deer.

The gentle whir of an evaporative cooler hummed through their collective silence.

Feeling conspicuous, she gave everyone a little finger-wave.

In a domino effect, men touched their caps, some momentarily removing them, others taking them off and hooking them over their chair backs. More than a handful gave her toothy grins. Then they went back to their meals, their heads bent in concentration.

The air held the permanent scent of hamburgers, onion rings and French fries, like an ancient piece of furniture that had developed its satiny patina from centuries of hand-polishing. Two elderly women, with hairnets and spatulas, hunkered over a grill, sharing a laugh. Raven inventoried the room in a glance. Glass bottles of pop, beaded in sweat, glistened in the cooler. Staple goods, washing powder and tissue paper lined a back shelf, along with pyramids of canned beans and ravioli. A freezer filled with ice cream sandwiches, Nutty Buddies and Mr. Goodbars hummed against one wall, its compressor periodically groaning on and off.

Jinx stepped up to the counter. His gaze drifted over the menu board. One of the old fry cooks shuffled over and slapped her order book on the counter. She whisked a pen from her apron pocket and looked up expectantly.

"Double-meat cheeseburger and fries for me." Jinx turned

to Raven and cocked an eyebrow.

The woman printed Jinx's order in crude shorthand, then pointed the pen at her.

"Hamburger, no onions, and a bag of barbeque potato chips."

"Cut mine, too."

Each selected a soda from the cooler—his, a Big Orange; hers, a Big Red—and seated themselves at a butcher block table. The only thing lacking was a bunch of old-timers, playing a mean game of dominoes.

Raven smiled across the clutter of spices centered between them. Being with Jinx was fun again. Like the early years, before Loose-Wheel Lucille and the Baldwin sisters. Before she found the blonde pubic hair on her side of the bed, and called the number on the Personals ad he left sitting out on the coffee table. "This is so cool. How'd you find this place?"

"My grandmother used to bring me when I was little."

"I didn't know you had a grandmother." He gave her an exasperated face-scrunch and she amended the observation. "I just meant you never mentioned your grandparents. We only know about your parents and your sister." The whole office took turns poking fun at them—except for Georgia. Jinx himself used the word *dysfunctional,* when referring to his family. When chastised by the secretary, he apologized and admitted he'd misspoken; that using the D-word to describe the people who raised him would be unfair since, in truth, they were *totally-fucking-dysfunctional.* Georgia, on the other hand, considered them well-bred. She advanced a conspiracy theory: that the Porter dynasty's real firstborn had been switched at birth, the result of a cruel social experiment, and that the real Jinx Porter grew up to be an entrepreneur like his father. She suggested Donald Trump could actually be a Porter, since he looked more like Jinx's parents than Jinx—especially since Donald Trump had more class than to rent a two-bedroom hellhole at the Château Du Roy.

Raven caught herself smiling at the memory.

"I decided not to tell anybody about the grocery. Didn't want the atmosphere spoiled by success. Only thing different about this place is they don't sell gas anymore. Take a look at the pumps when we leave. One's for ethyl."

"Thanks, Jinx." She relaxed against the ladder-back chair. Tension flowed out of her shoulders. "Thank you for bringing me here."

One of the apricot-haired fry cooks padded over with their order. Raven stuck her nose into the steam rising off the grilled meat patty. On first bite, she let out a low, primal moan.

"Careful." Jinx peeled back a corner of grease-dotted tissue. "Sounds like that'll get you a public lewdness charge."

They ate in relative silence, in the way of seasoned law enforcement officers—at the corner table with their backs to the walls, with an occasional eye scan designed to thwart any stick-ups.

Raven's first inkling of something amiss occurred when the husks of people around them stopped eating.

A shadow fell across the table, enough to make her hunch involuntarily.

Dell.

He loomed above her, having moved in without her knowing it.

"Mind if I sit?" The brooding German slid a chair across the rough-hewn floor and straddled it.

"Thought you said nobody else knew about this place." Raven to Jinx.

"Just me and Dell."

Without explanation, Dell, who'd achieved fame in the

law enforcement community for his terse, economical language, said, "Sorry I'm late. Couldn't be helped." He removed his Resistol. Hair the color of flax shined bright under the incandescent light of a naked bulb. Aqua eyes cut to Raven. "How're the wedding plans coming?"

Raven sensed he didn't really want an answer. Her decision to marry Tommy had a crushing impact on him. He'd already declined to stand up for her as a groomsman.

"How can I do that when I want you myself?"

"Nothing's going right." She watched Dell's response. Waited for his lips to angle up in a smile. They didn't.

"Maybe you ought to postpone it."

She turned toward him, not sure how to respond. Realization washed over her. She narrowed her eyes. For no reason other than instinct, she shifted her attention to Jinx.

"Is this an intervention?" If they'd set out to discourage her from getting married, it had the opposite effect. She slapped the half-eaten burger into the plastic basket. Grabbed a napkin and wiped the grease off her fingers. Glared at Jinx and coined new expletives in her head. "You brought me here to debrief me?"

"I agree with Dell. Why don't you back off . . . give this a little more time? What's the hurry? You don't even know this guy."

"Better than I know *you* two bum steers."

Jinx gave a derisive grunt. "Raven, you're on a blind date with a ticking time bomb. Everybody sees it but you." He stared at her with a look of censure.

"I thought y'all were my friends."

"We are." In unison.

Locals got up to pay. Gave the trio wide berth on the way to the cash register.

Jinx reached for the salt shaker. "Lower your voice. We

wouldn't be here if we didn't care about you."

"Care about me?" Words exploded from her mouth. "Is this the way you care about a friend? Drive out to the boondocks and start in on me like I'm some sort of Moonie convert-held-captive?" She pushed back from the table, scraping the chair legs against the floor. Dell brought his hand down on her shoulder, forcing her back into the seat.

Raven stared, betrayed. Dell's circuits were wired differently from other men she'd known. "How could you do this? I expect rotten treatment from Jinx . . . but you? Can't even be straightforward with me . . . you have to Texas-two-step around the problem." She wound up in a normal tone of voice.

"It should be one of us, Raven."

For a second, she thought she was having a synaptic misfire.

Jinx seized the reins. "What he means is, if you're gonna do this, you should pick me or Dell. Frankly, I think it should be me. No offense, Dell, but Raven and I are a better match."

Ironic, coming from a man with a deep-seated fear of a life-binding contract. And to think she and Jinx might actually still be together if he hadn't turned ogling women into a spectator sport.

It took a moment to sort through the hurling confusion.

Fellow rivals.

Got together, mapped out a strategy.

Better for a member of the home team to win than an out-of-towner.

She gave them the slow blink of ultimate distrust. "You people slay me. I want to go home."

Jinx dropped the last remnants of burger into the basket. Within the invisible force-field of their gazes, he and Dell exchanged a few seconds of non-verbal communication that bordered on telepathy.

"All right," Jinx said. "I'll drive you back to town."

"You think I'm riding with you? You tricked me." She shot him a look of utter disgust and turned her attention to Dell. "You're not much better, but I don't think anybody else'll give me a ride into Fort Worth, so tag—you're it."

She tossed her shredded napkin onto the table and stalked out fuming. The screen door sucked shut behind her, leaving her alone with the pink-nosed retriever. He raised his head an inch and offered a "woof," before relaxing back onto the warped boards of the porch. With purpose in her step, she plodded the dirt road toward Dell's car, muttering curses along the way.

"They don't even know Tommy."

A thought that originated from a breaking heart, to the tip of her tongue.

She appealed to the sky. "What gives them the right to screw with my life?"

But her mind imagined the lowering of railroad crossing arms, flashing red lights and the clang of warning bells . . . and a soft, steady mantra from the spirit world that could've been the voice of God.

Get off the track.

You're about to get hit by a train.

Chapter Ten

Raven figured Dell knew better than to prick with her on the drive back to Fort Worth, so when he tried to strike up a conversation as soon as they hit the highway, she turned her face to the window and ignored him.

"You can't blame us," he said softly.

Oh, no?

"If it was Ivy getting married, we'd start an office pool to see how long it'd take the victim to run screaming into the night. With you, it's different."

She caught herself nodding and stopped.

"I suppose it's possible to love somebody you've only known a couple of months."

It is.

"But you're a sharp cookie, Raven. You don't just go jumping off into something like marriage without putting a decent amount of thought into it."

I have.

"It's the biological clock ticking, isn't it? You think you're getting too old to have kids, and if you don't do it now, you'll lose out."

This time he went too far. She rotated her head, *Exorcist*-like, in his direction and clamped her jaw shut to keep from responding.

Dell persisted. "Does he even want children?"

She turned away. Watched the scenery sliding by, and wondered. It wasn't as if they'd picked the topic apart. Oh, sure, she asked Tommy if he liked babies. He said, "Certainly . . . if they're someone else's." But that's the way he teased. It was just him trying to get her goat . . . wasn't it?

Lost in thought, she touched a fingernail to her lip. "What about you? You're over forty. Would you want more children?"

"I could see it happening, if the right woman came along."

She riveted her head in his direction, suspicious of his answer. The week before, she'd overheard him telling Mickey he was glad his kids were grown and out of the house. That if the girl—a newlywed—got pregnant, she could find some other dumb ass to baby-sit now that he'd finally gotten rid of that energy-sucking vampire of a wife of his. That he may've had to turn over the house to his ex—and it's true, she'd gotten all the good stuff while he'd gotten stuck with the debt—but now that Judge Masterson applied the tourniquet that effectively cut off the blood-siphoners in his life, now that the ingrate ex could no longer spend him into the poorhouse, some of the old judge's detractors seemed to think the property division was unfair. But Dell knew better: Judge Masterson had let him walk away with the grand prize—and now Jinx's deputy had the remote control all to himself.

With his eyes shaded from the afternoon glare, Dell set the cruise control ten miles over the speed limit. Fence posts went by in a smear.

Raven's lids grew heavy. She patted a small yawn. Fought against dozing, but when her chin dipped forward with a snap, she reflexively jerked her head back.

"Don't read anything into this." She un-clicked the passenger restraint, dropped over onto the seat and used Dell's thigh as a pillow. "I need a power nap. Wake me in twenty minutes."

She shut her eyes and let herself remember, fixing

Tommy's hungry expression in her mind. As she drifted off to sleep, her face tingled from Dell's fingertips stroking the hair back from her cheek.

Tommy used to do that—used to smooth the curls that way.

"Mmmmmm. That's so nice."

"Take your nap, poor tired baby." Dell faded into the distance.

Iridescent spheres of blue and red floated in her head. On some level, she recognized the slip into bonds of slumber. Tension drained from her shoulders. She teetered on the brink of sleep, sensing the memory of that final hour before the flight to D.C. would consume the last vestiges of consciousness.

Tommy stood in the doorway, saying good-bye.

She tried to entice him to make love one last time. Slid his hands under her shirt and cupped them to her breasts.

"Please don't leave me this way," she murmured, vaguely aware she'd spoken aloud.

"I'm not going anywhere." The words belonged to Dell.

But she heard Tommy's voice in her head.

"You're right. It'd be cruel to leave you like this."

They'd adjourned to the bedroom with her practically pulling him up the stairs.

Heartsick, she unbuttoned her shirt—Tommy's shirt, actually—an old flannel she'd rescued from the dirty clothes bin that morning, with sleeves that fell to the second knuckle, and the lingering mix of Arm & Hammer and testosterone permeating the cloth. Stepping out of her bikinis, she moved to his side. With a sense of desperation, she tugged at his fatigues until they ended up on the floor in the rest of the clothes pile.

He assaulted her mouth with narcotic kisses. The hard,

thrusting shaft grazing the flat of her belly excited her. She melted into the muscular wrap of his embrace. Gripped by a heightened sense of promise, she relaxed into a dreamy calm and waited for him to sweep her onto the dangerous shoals of his lovemaking.

He cast his eyes downward.

"Come on, baby. Give Big Tom some sugar."

She sank to her knees, knowing what he expected and aiming to please.

Live in the moment. Don't think about the bad things that can happen once he boards that aircraft.

Halfway to a flawless performance, he gasped as if she'd scorched him. Unexpectedly, he pulled her to her feet, searching her face with the tenderest of looks.

"I love you so much, Raven."

Together, they crashed onto the mattress, their nude bodies writhing against the sheets, pillowed in the fresh scent of fabric softener.

His tongue forged its way into the juncture of her thighs. He made it perfect for her, applying the right amount of pressure to all the right places, and didn't let up until he'd left her hot, damp and trembling. When the sensation wore off, she realized this must be how it felt to survive electrocution—and she could see herself sticking her finger in that light socket everyday for the rest of her life.

He feathered his fingertips across her breasts. Moved beside her and smoothed her hair away from her face. Called her name as he sank himself deeply into her softness. After a few strategically-guided strokes, her eyes rolled back in her head. When his breath quickened, she unsealed her lids, peeked beyond the fuzzy veil of mascaraed lashes and caught him staring.

"I know what you want, you little temptress."

He pushed himself into her, hard, and went for the sweet spot beneath her jawbone. Rolled off and pulled her on top, where she impaled herself on him. Gripped her waist and rocked her until she moaned . . . cried out . . . collapsed against his chest with a violent shudder.

Like taking a hit from a high-voltage wire.

Fried in fireworks.

And then it was over.

Tommy left.

Please come back to me. Undamaged—with all your fingers and toes, and your head screwed on straight.

Dell's foot hit the brake, violently jarring her back into consciousness.

"Busted." He uttered an uncharacteristic expletive.

She jumped at the sound of his voice. Reflexively, Raven grappled to sit upright, but he forced her back down in the seat.

"Stay put. It's DPS." He'd piqued the attention of a State Trooper behind the wheel of a black-and-white, concealed in the tall grass of the easement, with the radar aimed at oncoming traffic. "Wouldn't want 'em to get the wrong idea."

Raven sat up anyway. The squad car lunged onto the on-ramp like a panther running down its prey. Dell hit the toggle switch to the emergency strobes recessed in the Chevy's front grillwork and back dashboard. They whooshed up even with the traffic unit, just as highway patrolman activated his overheads. Dell gave the driver a curt nod and got a dirty look. The DPS officer patted the air in a downward motion and mouthed, "Slow down."

Dell pulled into the fast lane and checked his speed. "I swear, these fellows'll give their grandmothers a ticket . . ."

Raven's attention flickered to the side mirror. The trooper

pulled a U-turn, bounced over the median and repositioned himself for the next speeder.

She heaved a sigh. "Way to go, leadfoot."

"Are you crying?"

She touched her fingers to her cheek and they came away wet. "Of course not. Must be pollen in the air." But she knew better.

A mile up the road, Dell killed the lights and punched the accelerator. "I need to stop by the station before running you home."

She arched a brow.

"Jinx thinks sooner or later one of the neighbors'll drop a dime on Fleck Standish. He wants the answering machine checked for tips that'll help us find that little girl."

"Let's hope it's sooner."

Making the extra stop didn't faze her. She could use the time to trot across the street and get her ring from Emma-Jewel Houston. "Let me out at the jail."

Dell completed a mid-block U-turn, and curbed the vehicle in front of a coral-bricked, multi-story building with Tarrant County Corrections chiseled into the stone above the portico. If things worked out, she could meet him at the Constable's Office, return home, then dash off to the Kimball Museum where Cézanne was hosting her bridal shower, all in under an hour.

She found Emma-Jewel Houston reclining in her chair with her feet propped on the desk. Her heart did a little tap dance when the jail matron stuck out her hand and gave the pink diamond an admiring glance.

"Girl, you gotta believe this was the craziest thing I ever did." The jailer gave her a toothy grin.

After dispossessing Deputy Houston of the ring, Raven inspected the stone for damage. Finding it in mint condition, she slid it onto her finger and held it to the light. A rainbow of colors danced over the facets. "If there's anything I can ever do for you—anything—please ask."

Maroon eyes crinkled at the corners.

Uh-oh.

Something dead up the creek.

Raven's stomach went squishy.

"Girl, when you gettin' married?"

"Next Saturday." Her eyes went wide. She'd blurted out the truth, when instinct told her to lie.

"Ain't that a hoot?" The deputy spanked her knee, laughing *Hee-hee-hee*. "It happens I'm free that day, so thank you very much for asking, *I would love to sing at your wedding*. Gimme a list of songs you like; I'll pick my favorite and buff up on it by Saturday."

Raven rattled off a few titles by The Cranberries, and made a mental note to put out a BOLO on Emma-Jewel Houston for the ushers to enforce, should she actually show up at the church. Confidence restored, she headed back to the precinct.

The cowbell rigged above the office door clanged out her arrival. Dell poked his head out of the copy room just as the phone bleated.

He jutted his chin. "You mind? I'm expecting a call-back. One of Standish's neighbors thinks he killed that teenage couple Arlington found murdered a couple of months ago. Told her I'd come out and take a statement. She's supposed to agree on a time with her husband, and call back."

Mickey's desk was closest to the copy room. Raven flopped in his chair and took the call with her ring hand out-stretched, at eye level.

The voice of a hysterical female asking for Jinx vibrated through the earpiece.

Probably one of his barflies, pissed off that he stood her up.

"Jinx isn't in. It's Saturday."

But the woman on the other end of the line wasn't one of Jinx's floozies. Her name was Dorretha Bright, and her story went like this: her six-year-old son, Cedric, had supervised visitation at a county-operated facility on Ben Street. Her ex-husband, Joe, snatched the boy and ran.

"Did you call the police?"

"The shelter called and a patrolman came out. But I need Constable Porter. He knows Joe . . . knows how to get through to him, maybe talk him into surrendering . . . gimme back my son."

"I'll have him call you."

"Please, baby, please. Cedric's all I have. Joe says if he can't have him, neither can I. Joe says he's gonna kill my baby, only Constable Porter won't let that happen."

Raven took down the number, along with a few extra details. Vehicle description. Car tags. Joe Bright's DOB, so they could run a warrant check, and his DL number, to get a current picture.

She ran, head-first, into Dell, as he was flicking off the light switch on his way out of the copy room. A handful of papers drifted to the floor, with the upturned pages of Fleck Standish's driver's license picture leering at her from several directions.

She looked at Dell and said, "Sorry, my mistake."

For a few seconds, they stood locked in the electric charge of each other's stare.

She bent to pick up his papers but he pulled her back up.

"I love you," he mouthed without sound.

Raven's heart fluttered. She was doing her best not to lip-read. He hooked an arm around her neck and pulled her close. His heart pounded against her ear. She listened to the whoosh of blood coursing through his body as he pressed a kiss into her hair and drew her farther into the room's darkness.

His velvet-soft mouth against her lips turned high-voltage.

"We shouldn't be here," she whispered.

"I know." He repeated it to her neck.

She curled her fingers into his shirt. Drew him closer, knowing she shouldn't. Her breast skimmed his arm, sending a shot of heat down her torso. He slid a hand around each side and hauled her up under her arms. Lifted her, on tiptoes, and sat her on top of the copier. He'd already unfastened a couple of buttons. Fingered one nipple like he was pinching out a candle wick—not at all similar to Jinx's idea of foreplay: where he treated her nipples like they were radio knobs to be dialed from 88.7 to 1580 in three quick twists.

Dell was licking the salt off the curves of her bare skin when the cogs in her brain seemed to get a fresh squirt of lubricant.

"I'm getting married in seven days." Delivered in a desperate pant.

"I know."

Next thing she knew, he unzipped her capri pants. A hand-held vibrator seemed inferior when compared to Dell's finger, especially once he brought her to the point of making mewling kitten sounds.

The last of her resolve tanked.

Her heart beat so fast it echoed in her ears. She slumped against the wall in surrender, eager to test his expertise in body cavity searches. After two moves, she gave him an *A-plus*.

The cowbell jangled in the front office.

Her brain's startle-reflex engaged.

Busted.

Dell zipped his fly. He stepped out into the hallway, pulling the door closed behind him.

In a panic, Raven buttoned her shirt. She listened through thin walls.

"Jinx. Urgent message. Joe Bright kidnapped his son. Says he's going to kill him. The boy's mama says you're the only one who can reason with him, and to call her right away."

Jinx's footfalls grew faint.

Seconds later, Dell opened the door and signaled a clear coast. Raven couldn't clear out fast enough. At the patrol car, she discovered in her haste she'd mismatched her shirt buttons.

What's wrong with me? I bought a ticket aboard the Concorde to Hell.

While mating buttons with the appropriate holes, she vowed not to dwell on the encounter. But once he met her in the parking lot, the regrettable interlude sneaked into conversation.

"Look, Dell . . . I'm not sure how . . . things got out of hand . . ." She knew the rest of her lines by heart. "What we did back there, that can never happen again."

Intense, aqua eyes peered from beneath the Resistol brim riding low on his forehead. Without words, he entered the vehicle and thumbed open the electric door lock. Raven let herself into the passenger side, turned the stereo to talk radio, anxious for its distraction.

In less than twenty minutes, she needed to dress for her bridal shower.

Dell's kiss sneaked into her thoughts. She shivered.

Lord help her. Maybe what she *really* needed was a different kind of shower.

A damned cold one.

★★★★★

After Caesar witnessed the death of the orange tom, sixty-five hundred years of cat domestication began to unravel.

Forced to live outside of the Château Du Roy, preservation instincts came into play.

For a few seconds, he felt like scratching the girl.

He'd done it once before, when he was little, the first day the girl brought him home to live with the man. He wanted to show the man the tricks he'd learned at his first house. But when he ran up the curtains, the girl pried him off.

He didn't like the way she screamed when he clawed her. The way she cried *Jinx,* and showed the man the long, red gash in her hand. For a second, he wanted to bite her, too. But Jinx called him *bad kitty,* and there was something cold and speculative in his gray-green eyes. That's when he knew he'd have to put up with the girl to be able to live with Jinx. He didn't want Jinx to give him *that* look again.

And he wanted to go home, even if Jinx called him *bad kitty* and spanked him.

Should've been in bed with a full stomach, not having to hunt for his own food. Street mice moved fast. Not like the practice mice at the Château. Word got around the Château after his first two catches. Jinx carried them out of the apartment for everyone to see. Threw them over the balcony, into the courtyard next to the *flaming fairy's* apartment, as a warning to other mice.

Thinking of mice, raw hunger set in.

Enough to make contact with other humans.

Bad girl.

Tired. Hungry.

Hate you guys.

Chapter Eleven

With emotions still flaring, Raven arrived at the Kimball Museum, in the heart of Fort Worth's Cultural district. She spied Georgia's car in one of the disabled parking spaces; a blue wheelchair tag hung from her rearview mirror. Ivy parked her old rattletrap in a disabled space, too, only Ivy didn't have a tag. Must've figured mental incompetence excused her.

Cézanne was a pal, offering to host the bridal shower at the museum's restaurant. The guests would love the clean, Spartan atmosphere and first-class fare.

Inside the glass doors, her cell phone went off. A guard shot her a menacing look, and she ducked back outside and took the call beneath the portico. As soon as the digital display registered "Out of Area" against the tiny screen, her heart stumbled into an erratic rhythm.

"Hello? Tommy?" The caller's response came in the form of heavy breaths. "Is that you? Say something." Whisper soft, the sound of her name reached her ear. She collapsed on the nearest bench.

"Can't talk now. Love you." Delivered in the faintest murmur.

Shouts of angry foreigners in the background blurred her concentration.

"I love you, Tommy. Please come home."

"Soon."

All at once, she was listening to dead air.

She stared at the bronze at the Kimball's entrance, then

across the street to the Modern Museum, where a rusty sculpture of twisted metal towered above the ground like the Jolly Green Giant's castoff orange licorice stick.

At least he's still alive.

Thank you, God.

Inside, she ascended the travertine marble steps, lightheaded with relief. She arrived at the second floor gallery where three reserved tables had been cordoned off from the rest of the dining area. Raven checked out the surroundings. On one table, stacks of boxes with elegant wrappings formed a Pisa-like tower. Party guests flocked around the other two.

Cézanne, dressed in a lilac linen skirt and matching jacket, glided over to embrace her. Concern lined her face. Before Raven could ask, Duty sidled up looking mature for her age, dressed in what appeared to be one of Cézanne's classic Chanel suits.

"Thank goodness yo' here, Miz Raven."

"Why? What's wrong?"

Cézanne had the look of someone who's realized too late that she's parked on an incline and forgotten to set the emergency brake, or has seated volatile personalities too close together.

"We may have to call in the Fire Department to hose these women down."

"Looks to me like they're making an effort to behave."

"You're only saying that because you weren't here earlier."

Georgia and Dixie were huddled together, their shoulders heaving with silent laughter. Georgia wore her processed blonde bob cut short, without the usual brassy wiglet. Her hair had thinned considerably over the past year, with patches of pink scalp visible between wisps of hair. She'd dropped some weight, too.

Mass is neither created nor destroyed, it merely changes shape.

Whatever Georgia sweated off during workouts at the "Y" must've glommed on Dixie.

Curly red hair framed Dixie's face. Absorbed in an animated conversation, she nodded with such vigor that ringlets bounced over her forehead like flaming Slinkys. The atrium's sunlight brought out coppery highlights, which in turn, complemented the colors in her tiger-print dress. Piercing blue eyes glittered behind alabaster skin like lakes on a moonscape, and brown lip-liner outlined her crimson lips.

Raven gave a little finger-wave to the two secretaries, then exchanged hellos with the ladies from the civil courts building and a couple of brain-deads from the Administration Office who'd invited themselves upon hearing news of a shower. Several female sheriff's deputies seized the opportunity to dress in feminine clothes, and Judge Masterson's court reporter showed up looking like an haute couture runway model.

She settled her gaze on Ivy. Taser-styled, wheat-colored "do." Frumpy polyester pantsuit in the shade and sheen of a Tootsie Roll. Matching clodhoppers and a huge handbag that could double as an airport carry-on. She looked like the Mummy of mutants, with a thick piece of gauze wrapped around her fingertips, clear up her arm, past the elbow.

Raven moved in for a closer inspection. "What happened to you?"

"I missed firearms qualifications. Jinx sent me out to the range for night-firing after I booked Venita Standish."

Ivy couldn't hit water, falling out of a boat.

"There aren't enough lights at the pistol range," Ivy went on in her irritating prattle. "I'm telling you people the God's honest truth—that place is so dark a mole couldn't find its ass with a directional pointer and a spotlight. And the range master stores the bullets in those army-green cartridge containers, with nothing but a hand-marked, paper label on the metal box to distinguish the caliber. So I'm out in the middle of no-fucking-where, groping for shells in the dark. Long story short, I loaded the cylinder of my .38 with .45 ammo and stove-piped the barrel. *Stove-piped it!* I'm pretty sure I have a good lawsuit."

Cézanne put her lips to Raven's ear. "If stupidity ever goes to forty dollars a barrel, I want the drilling rights to her brain."

Raven laughed until she gasped for breath.

Dixie piped up in a raging soprano. "I think suing the county's a good idea. I'm thinking about doing it myself."

Georgia's interest peaked. She pulled a small notepad and pen out of her purse, and slid her colleague a sideways glance.

Dixie tuned up like a piccolo. "It's Jinx. He's an energy vampire. He'll suck out your energy and use your head as a trash can. He yelled at me yesterday for letting that pissant Evan Rainey sneak in at five o'clock. It's not my fault the guards didn't lock the front doors."

Raven caught herself nodding. An Arab could come in with a stinger missile over his shoulder and the guards would be hunched over the crossword puzzle.

"He said if he had to stay late, I had to stay late." Red blotches cropped up on Dixie's cheeks.

"Men are swine." Georgia turned to Raven. "Honey, are you sure you want to get married? A slave never builds his master stronger chains."

"Love slave," Duty said through a giggle. Cézanne elbowed her into silence.

Shiloh Willette slipped up from behind and grabbed Raven at the waist.

Delft-blue eyes hardened. "I couldn't help overhearing—" Jinx's ex handed her an envelope. "—you ask me, men are like a nice omelet. They start out as eggs and it's up to women to beat the shit outta them until they're decent to have breakfast with." Jinx's ex, at the top of her game. She gave her head a good toss. Coffee-colored hair skimmed her shoulders and cascaded down her back.

Raven made eye contact with Dixie. "Remember to pick up your dress before Wednesday."

"I'll get it as soon as the seams have been let out."

"Mine fits," Georgia bragged. "The alterations lady sewed elastic into the waistband, so it's got some give to it. Maybe you should have her do that with yours."

Dixie snorted. "I'm not worried. Even if mine ends up being a little snug, I can work out between now and next Saturday."

Ivy gave a derisive grunt. She turned to the girl seated next to her. Played like she intended her words to be confidential, but spoke so loud a deaf person could've picked up vibrations.

"Work out? Ha! The only way Dixie'll get any exercise is if her husband straps a cheesecake to his ass and runs around the house."

"I heard that, sister." Dixie balled her fist and shook it. "You're just mad because you can't get a man."

"That's a load of crap, and you know it."

"Ha!" Dixie said, to no one in particular. "Ivy's vibrator gets so hot she has to use a potholder to hang onto it."

Ivy came up out of her chair. "I oughta box your jaws."

Georgia yelled, "Ladies, y'all don't cause a scene. Ivy, settle down."

"Don't worry about me, Georgia, I can take care of myself," Dixie gave the air a haughty sniff. To Ivy, she said, "If you weren't off your meds, I'd clobber you."

"I'm not on medication."

"Sister, that's pretty damned obvious."

"Shut up."

"I'm not talking to you. I'm talking to the rest of your personalities. The voices in your head ought to be counseling you." Dixie flashed a stiff middle finger.

An elderly couple seated at the next table got up and moved.

"Have you checked out your ass in a mirror lately?" Dixie cackled. "You're so fat you smoke turkeys after sex."

"At least I'm having sex."

"You don't know that I'm *not* having sex."

"Yeah? Well if you are, you probably have to put twinkle lights around it, so your husband can find it."

Dixie coughed up a mouthful of tea. Her face flamed. "If I were you, I wouldn't be talking. In case nobody told you, your ass has gotten big enough to use as a helipad."

Ivy rocketed to her feet. Georgia caught her wrist with a two-handed grab and hung on. "I know what you're thinking, you two-ton, Brillo-headed—"

"If you know what I'm thinking, then why aren't you running for dear life?"

Duty, who'd been in and out of the conversation, unexpectedly demonstrated her powers of clairvoyance. "I know what's going on inside both yo' minds: *You can run but you can't hide.*"

"That's not what I'm thinking." Ivy, still trying to wriggle free, fixed Dixie with a murderous look. "I'm thinking you can run but you'll just die tired."

People at other tables stopped what they were doing and stared.

Raven leaned within whispering distance of Cézanne. "What on Earth was I thinking when I decided to put these heifers in my wedding? These people shouldn't be allowed in public unsupervised."

Cézanne called a halt to the insults. Rounded up the guests and shepherded them in the direction of the food.

Everyone took turns bad-mouthing Evan Rainey on the short walk to the buffet.

They dined on cream of asparagus soup, nibbled chicken salad sandwiches and forked Quiche Lorraine along with bite-sized chunks of fresh fruit. After the first cups of coffee were poured, Cézanne nodded at Duty.

The girl stood, glanced around uncertainly and smoothed the front of her skirt. She addressed the women in the spirit of a game show host. "Miz Raven gonna open presents now. I'm gonna write down whatchoo people gave her, but I don't know yo' names. So lemme know who you are, or you ain't gonna get a thank-you note." She dropped into her seat and spoke in a loud whisper. "Did I do good?"

Raven opened boxes of crystal, picture frames and linens; and from Cézanne, a place setting of the china pattern she picked out with Tommy before he took off for the Middle East. Shiloh's envelope contained a gift certificate to a five-star restaurant in downtown Fort Worth, a contribution the Willettes could ill-afford.

Misty-eyed, Raven embraced her matron of honor. "I think you and I should go—just us girls."

"Nope. Take your man out for a night on the town and let us know if you get lucky."

She thought of Tommy, and her chest tightened.

Where the hell can he be?

If Yucatan Jay gets him hurt, or killed—

No, no, no.

Can't think about that now.

Down to the final gift, Raven picked up a festive paper

bag, with matching tissue poking out of the top. She noted the card, addressed in Ivy's psychotic scrawl.

She un-layered the wrapping.

Blinked hard.

Then blinked again. "Just what I always wanted." She forced a smile and inwardly reminded herself to keep a light, convincing tone.

The White Trash Cookbook.

With feigned interest, she flipped through the pages and landed on a recipe for possum.

Lovely.

"How thoughtful, Ivy. I'll think of you every time I use it."

Chapter Twelve

The envelope that contained Standish's invitation to the Wiccans' spring ritual showed a Fort Worth address near a wooded area off Loop 820, not far from the trailer park. Once Jinx ran an Internet search on the location using the county's property tax database, he identified the owner.

When he pulled the patrol car into the drive of the two-story brick townhouse, he didn't have a copy of the woman's driver's license photo with him for comparison purposes. He hadn't expected her to be attractive. Whenever he raised his expectations, life had a way of kneeing him in the groin. Kind of like asking for a life-like, life-sized Barbie and getting your brother's used blow-up doll with the hair painted school bus yellow. Yet he knew, on instinct, the dark-haired woman with the alabaster skin had to be Lyrica Prudhomme.

He delivered his opening salvo with characteristic bluntness.

"You don't look like a witch."

"Wiccan." Bright green eyes danced, as if she knew the punch line, and made him the joke. Full, pouty lips parted to reveal even, white teeth. A bolt pierced her tongue; a tiny silver ring threaded through one eyebrow glinted in the light, and when she moved, smells of incense and lavender oil drifted up Jinx's nostrils. He gave her gothic outfit the once-over.

"Come in, you're letting the cool air escape."

Not bad-looking for a woman nearing fifty. Maybe even

pretty. With supple skin and firm breasts behind the gossamer fabric of her top, and a face free from the ravages of cigarette smoke or leathery lines from summers at South Padre, yet way too frail to mistake for a beauty. And the way she stood back from the door and waved him in seemed a bit too casual, as if she'd been expecting him, and made him uneasy in her presence.

With a sweep of the eyes, he inventoried the room.

She'd decorated her home with furniture that leaned toward the clean lines of Danish modern. Near the fireplace, several large pillows still carried body indentations; and on the bookshelves, between stacks of best-selling hardcovers and the classics, were birds' nests, crystals and jagged pieces of quartz. Long vines of ivy hung from a section of driftwood on the top shelf, and wound across small hooks placed at two-foot intervals, that kept it from drooping over the book titles. A copy of the *Faerie Grimoire*, sandwiched into a row of cookbooks, might have escaped notice, had Raven not prepped him on what to look for. His gaze stopped on a handful of bleached bones, encircled by river pebbles.

"May I offer you a cup of green tea, Constable?" She continued to smile, but her eyes mocked him with a coolness that kept him unsettled.

He gathered she divined his identity, not with magical powers or witchcraft, but from the police antenna and chrome spotlight on the unmarked Chevy parked out front.

"Nothing for me, thanks." Should've brought Raven along. When it came to predicting women, Raven had the intuition of a Jewish mother, the instincts of a feline and the impulses of a skeptic. "I'm here about this." He waved a copy of Standish's invitation in Lyrica Prudhomme's face.

She gave it a dismissive glance. "What about it?"

"What goes on at these things?"

Away from the harsh glare of the sun, her pupils dilated, forming dark, fathomless pools surrounded by luminous green rings. He'd seen eyes like that before on people who were stoned. But unlike a pothead, Lyrica Prudhomme appeared to have complete control of her faculties.

"Would you like to sit, Constable . . . I don't believe you gave your name?"

"Jinx Porter. I'll stand. You were saying?"

She had a musical laugh. "Ah, Mr. Porter . . . that's just it. I don't believe I did say."

Irritation mounted. "Why don't you tell me now?"

"In time."

The eyes seemed to evaluate him. To be focused on piercing his composure. Nipples turned hard enough to cut glass beneath the diaphanous voile of her strange black costume. She glided toward one of the pillows and seated herself on the floor with bare legs splayed in the "Welcome Sailor" position, and her body hunched over; clasped hands, resting in her lap, formed a barrier to what lay hidden beneath the sheer folds of her skirt.

"You want to find out if I'm acquainted with Fleck Standish."

"I think we've established that." Caustic responses seemed in order. "I want to know why you'd ask him to bring a child to a ritual that's more obviously suited to adults."

"Says you."

"Why don't *you* say?"

She licked her lips, letting her tongue deliberately linger before it snaked back inside her shimmering mouth. "Most children are born with scary social inclinations. Magick's a sweet little girl. No trouble at all. She plays quietly, and doesn't exercise proprietary rights she doesn't have by disturbing my possessions or getting underfoot. Why shouldn't he bring her?"

"Because it was midnight. She should've been in bed."

"Not everyone goes to sleep when the sun goes down. I'll bet once upon a time *you* even worked the graveyard shift." She moved her hands to her sides and sat erect. When she did so, the silky skirt rode up her thighs.

Jinx did his best not to look. He failed miserably. "So what goes on at these little soirées?"

She struck an awkward pose, pulling one leg against her body enough to rest her chin on her knee. Glanced over the room, seemingly oblivious to the fact that he could see straight up her dress.

His groin throbbed.

Lyrica Prudhomme made unabashed eye contact. She patted the closest pillow. "Sure you won't join me?"

"You people dance naked in the moonlight at these shindigs?"

A rueful smile crossed her lips. She straightened. Transparent fabric slid over her bent knee and down her thigh, where it gathered softly in her lap.

Lyrica Prudhomme wore no panties.

Offering Jinx a clear view of her genitalia, almost up to her tonsils, halfway to Kansas City.

A high-voltage sexual current traveled the length of his body. "Your skin is showing."

"Is that bothersome? Bodies are beautiful, would you agree?"

"Some are, some aren't. I can take it, if you can."

"You have a nice body . . ." She locked him in her emerald gaze. "What I can see of it." Her attention drifted down his shirt and settled on his fly. "I could take care of that for you . . ." She traced the line of her mouth with an ebony-lacquered fingernail.

"And I could take care of *you.*" Angry. "If you paraded that little girl around naked at your party, that's a crime."

"Not necessarily." Green eyes narrowed into slits. Lyrica Prudhomme rose with the grace of a dancer. Moved toward him as if on a whisper. "It's not for sexual gratification, Mr. Porter," she said in a low, sensual voice. "That *would* be a crime. What you're speaking of is part of our religion."

She unlaced the tie holding her sheer top closed, and simply walked out of it. It fell away, revealing the small, perfect breasts of a ballerina.

A vial of blood dangled from a chain around her neck.

"Put your clothes back on, Ms. Prudhomme. I'm not gonna play mind games with you."

"You think this is a game?" She moved within several feet of him. "Maybe it's not your mind I care to play with."

"Stay where you are."

"You're afraid I'll hurt you?" Her voice itself, bewitching.

"Keep your hands where I can see them."

She did. Kept them right on the sheer folds of silk in her skirt and peeled herself like a ripe peach. "You can see my hands now, can't you Mr. Porter? There's no place to hide them. I have no weapons—at least not any you can see." She extended her hands, palms up, until they were inches from his buckle.

And the Smith & Wesson six-shooter strapped to his belt.

He grabbed her wrists and pinned them together. Slim fingers turned as pale as her bare breasts.

"You're in my home, Mr. Porter. What're you going to do now?" Laughter glittered behind her eyes. Sensual lips tilted up in a smirk. "You want to know what went on that night? Why don't I show you? We could re-enact it."

Words came out in a methodical cadence. Hidden sexuality revealed itself in her tone, mesmerizing him into a mind-numbing stupor. He tightened his grip around her bloodless hands. For an instant, he wanted to haul her up on tiptoes. To simultaneously slap her into silence while ravaging the living daylights out of her. To let her take him to her bed and strip him naked. To hear her beg him to perform certain indignities on her, then have her return the favor.

His fingers whitened against her skin.

She should've flinched. Should've shrunk from his strength. Should've cried out in pain.

Instead, she wove a spell of double entendres, spoken in a beguiling tone.

"Don't make it hard on yourself, Mr. Porter. Big lawman like you doesn't need to rely on brute strength to take me down. What do I have you could possibly want?" She teased him with her eyes. "What could I possibly do to help you find what you're really looking for? Is that fear I see? Ah . . . Mr. Porter, what are you afraid of? Not me, I hope. I couldn't hurt you. Why . . . just look at me—"

Her voice went deep and forbidding as she held him in her gaze.

"—feel free to look at every inch of me," she said with a terrible intensity. "Do I have what you want?"

A tremble started in his knees.

"I can't harm you. Not physically. Unless you want me to." The melody of her words taunted him. "Why don't you just take what you need and go? Big, strong man like you—is it because you've thought twice now that you're in my home, persecuting me for my religion? Because the only leg you have to stand on is the one hanging between the two that should've carried you out of here ten minutes ago, as soon as you figured out you were out of your league? Is it because you don't have the guts to do what you wish you could do, now that you can't figure out how to browbeat the information out of me?"

Words rang, obscene, in his ears. Remote, cool detachment swam behind the depths of her eyes. She appealed to the darkest part of him. To that raw, animal side he saved for whores like the Baldwin sisters and women from the Personals ads, a caveman desire left over from the Stone Age that hadn't been bred out of the Porter men.

He wanted to—

His breath went shallow.

He wanted to—

His heart raced.

He wanted to knock the living daylights out of her.

Should've brought Raven along.

Raven.

That broke the spell.

He shoved Lyrica Prudhomme away with such violence she sprawled across the floor, legs splayed, into the pillows next to the fireplace.

Bent over at the waist and sucking air, she lifted her head enough to deride him with a musical laugh. "Do come back, Mr. Porter. I'd love to see more of you."

"Next time you see me, I'll have a warrant." But what he meant was, *I'll have Raven with me.*

Later, at the Château Du Roy, after he finished his computer work for the night and climbed into bed, he replayed the rest of the day's events in his head.

He'd left Lyrica Prudhomme's townhouse with his pulse throbbing in his throat, and a blue smoke trail boiling out of the Chevy's tailpipe. Worse, when he arrived at Raven's place to tell her about it, she gave him that skeptical squint and acted put out that he showed up without calling.

How was he supposed to know she'd have a house full of

women sitting around, swilling wine and trimming net for rice bags?

"Hello Jinx. Just in time. Here's a spool of ribbon. Make yourself useful."

"I don't have time to participate in your pre-nuptial bullshit."

"If you don't want to make rice bags, then I have seventy-five phone calls that have to be made."

"You're not turning me into one of your bridesmonsters."

"This isn't Wallow City and you're not the Mayor. If you can't wait 'til the party's over to pester me for information, then at least tend bar. There're drunken women here who need fresh drinks."

"I'm not here to lighten your workload; I'm here to lighten mine."

At which time she hustled him upstairs to the attic and told him if he wanted to pick through her carton of ritualistic crimes material, he could haul it down to her study and educate himself on what he was dealing with. Otherwise, she'd said, he should make himself useful and join the rice-bagging assembly line downstairs.

In the end, she helped him carry the cardboard box into the study, where he spent over two hours pawing through files. Found the Goat of Mendes and other eerie writings by Aliester Crowley, California's "Night Stalker" Richard Ramirez, and Anton LaVey, who Raven dismissed as a circus figure.

He was sitting at Raven's desk with his head bent in concentration when Deuteronomy Devilrow came upstairs with a glass-bottled Coke and a couple of finger sandwiches with barely enough chicken salad inside to satisfy his hunger. The girl gave him a sad look and asked if he wanted her to cast a spell on Fleck Standish. He shook his head in a no motion, but told her if she had one that might keep a little girl alive a bit longer, she should go ahead and use it.

"I got a Voodoo spell my gramma Corinthia taught me, could help you get over Miz Raven."

"By all means, cast it."

"Might oughta hold out a little longer, though."

"Why?"

"Poor Mista Jinx. Don'tchoo fret. Lotta things can happen in a week."

Then she looked at him slitty-eyed. He turned his back on her and felt a mosquito sting on his scalp. He massaged the barbed spot until the pang disappeared; when he turned around, he caught Duty with one hand hidden behind her back.

"Did you just pull my hair out?"

"Sorry, Mista Jinx. I thought it was loose. Sho' 'nuff looked that way to me."

Before the hen party shifted into high gear and the women adjourned poolside, he took the unguided tour through Raven's house, nosing through bedrooms and closets for signs of the competition. At the rear bedroom, he looked out the French doors to the balcony, scanning for Raven. Judge Masterson's secretary and a woman from the Commissioners' court were splashing in the Jacuzzi like a couple of human swizzle sticks in a giant-sized Blue Lagoon. Then Raven padded into view wearing a string bikini, and set a tray of umbrella drinks on a bistro table. Dripping bodies, oiled to a fine luster, climbed out of the pool and jiggled over to the hooch. Dixie and Ivy, looking like watermelons with legs, killed any chance of conjuring up beach-harem fantasies.

He slipped into Raven's bedroom for a quick peek. She had a miniature version of the Sistine Chapel painted on her bathroom ceiling, and an oval window of stained glass that cast colorful spots on the carpet when the sun hit it. He studied her bed—a king—decorated to a fare-thee-well with expensive linens and inviting pillows, and wondered how many times Tommy Greenway had made himself at home, and taken his deputy to bed.

Time got away. He ended up lingering long enough to get caught.

Raven walked in, her cheeks ablush with laughter and spirits. She headed for the bathroom closet and pulled out a beach towel. When she turned and saw him, her smile wilted.

"What're you doing, Jinx? The guest bathroom's down the hall."

He pulled her close and she let him. Pushed the bedroom door to, took off his wire-rims and mashed the tiredness out of his eyes before putting them back on.

He stared into irises as big and gray as musket balls. "You have to help. It took you weeks to learn all that stuff. We don't have that kind of time."

She set her jaw. Her chin went hard, as if she expected him to scam her. But the wine must've short-circuited her poker face because he detected a flicker of concern in her eyes.

"Now that Joe Bright's threatening to kill Cedric, we've got two child abductions to deal with." He ran it down for her in angry, abbreviated strokes. "Want to know the hell of it? The TV stations only care about one of these cases—the black kid gets an Amber Alert while the white kid gets a media carnival—how jaded is that? Joe Bright's every bit as deadly as Fleck Standish. So I know you're getting married in seven days, but I'm asking you to stop what you're doing long enough to—"

He'd almost blown it. Almost said—*work me into your life*—but he made a quick save at the last second and finished the thought the way he'd intended.

"—help out when I ask you to."

Raven's face went soft. She batted heavy, gunpowdery lashes and said, "Okay." Not in a dejected tone as he expected, but in the way of a true friend. As if she'd given her word and aimed to keep it.

"I'll take on the Bright case, Jinx. If he's calling the mama from a pay phone every five minutes, they're probably still in Fort Worth. And if you need me to help on the Standish case, I'll do that, too."

Later, in the privacy of his own bedroom, he analyzed Raven's next disturbing move.

After he'd thanked her, she put out her arms. They'd embraced in a quick, platonic, Great-to-see-you-let's-do-lunch hug that left a world of hurt constricting his chest and shortening his breath. But the choppy squeeze fizzled, replaced by an unexpected move on her part: not out of character for Raven-the-woman, but definitely off-kilter for Raven-the-bride. She relaxed in his embrace and even nuzzled his chest when he leaned in to inhale the fragrance of her hair.

The high-energy sexual tension he'd experienced earlier with Lyrica Prudhomme began to build with Raven—until her words left him with a case of limp dick.

"Jinx, there's something you can do for me . . ."

"There's something you can do for me, too."

"Seriously. I don't have anyone to give me away. I'd like it to be you."

"You don't want to pull at that thread. Ask Dell. He probably has a cable of masochism running through him."

"Please?"

"I'm not walking you down the gangplank, Raven. Don't ask me again."

* * * * *

Around midnight, he returned home to the disturbing sight of Agnes Loudermilk, sitting on the balcony like a Biblical scourge. She wore a flimsy robe, and as she rocked against the molded plastic chair back, Jinx could see the outline of her jiggly old mammaries dangling from her chest like a couple of empty light sockets. The woman was keeping vampire hours.

Or waiting up for him.

She took a long pull on her cigarette. "Did I ever tell you I used to work for the County?"

"Don't believe you did." He gave the area a furtive glance. All alone. He picked up his gait.

"Got hired on as a typist." Smoke poured from her mouth. Shrewd eyes tracked his movements.

"I see."

"Worked with a bunch of other women in a big room. Slowest one typed seventy words a minute. Not me, though. The fella who hired me didn't care about my typing skills. He knew I was just a huntin' pecker." Agnes let out a maniacal cackle. She slapped her knee, and when she rocked back in her chair and her feet came up off the decking, he had a bird's eye view of her privates.

Once he deadbolted the door behind him, he settled into a chair and turned on the computer. On the scant hope he'd find useful information to track Fleck Standish, he entered an Internet search for Wiccan cults. An interesting discovery provided renewed motivation.

He stumbled upon a Wiccan chat room.

Around one in the morning, when his energy played out and his head pounded from eyestrain, he logged off the computer. By two, he stopped placing so much emphasis on Raven marrying in six days, and started thinking more in terms of: *six days to win her back.*

Jinx rubbed his bloodshot eyeballs. Reached over and turned out the night lamp next to the bed. In the pitch-black room without the low-humming purr of Caesar-the-Siamese to comfort him, his mind replayed the encounter with Lyrica Prudhomme.

Deep down, the witch hit a nerve.

He knew it.

She knew it.

If he hadn't left when he did, Lyrica Prudhomme might've peeled off more than his clothes. She might've layered right down to his basic instincts, then sauntered down to the District Attorney's Office and filed an official oppression charge against him.

He closed his eyes.

Waited for sleep to descend—

—and inhaled the fragile scent of Lyrica Prudhomme's lavender.

Jinx sat bolt-upright.

Impossible.

No way she can work her magic on me from across town.

She has no power over me.

Did she plant a suggestion in my head?

His heart pounded. He spent the next few seconds reassuring himself that this denizen of the unseen world hadn't invaded the sanctuary of his home—that she hadn't slipped, ghost-like, through the sheetrock. The scent of her perfume must've lingered on his clothes, stirred to his nostrils by the A/C.

He'd gripped her wrists, and transferred the smell of lavender oil to his skin. He sniffed his hands. Good; that explained the scent.

The memory of her face invaded the darkness. He mashed

his lids until blue comets streaked across the inside of his skull. They disintegrated, replaced by embers of orange in the witch's green eyes, glowing the way they had as he cut off her circulation.

He envisioned her lips . . . fleshy . . . berry-stained . . . inches away from his. They mouthed words without sound. As if to entice him close enough to hear.

He'd wanted to kiss her—not in the loving way he wanted to kiss Raven in her bedroom—but with savage brutality.

Lyrica Prudhomme *knew* it.

And she played him like a Vegas card cheat.

Stupid Jinx.

He'd been the first to break eye contact.

He settled back into the pillow and conjured an image of Lyrica Prudhomme on his own. This new scenario would play out differently. In the fantasy, instead of sending her sprawling across the floor, he threaded his fingers into her thick mass of hair, and pulled her lips to his. He could almost feel her hot tongue probing his mouth, flicking itself against his lips in anticipation.

With nothing but the dark and the soothing rush of cool air from the A/C vents, he took his hand to himself . . .

. . . spent the next few minutes reliving the most erotic moments of the witch's sick, sexual seduction . . .

. . . then surrendered to sleep, more unfulfilled than ever, still haunted by thoughts of losing Raven.

Chapter Thirteen

Sunday morning, Raven heaved herself out of bed and wandered downstairs to see if she could find anything in the refrigerator that didn't have a layer of tundra on it. Still groggy with sleep, she resorted to the freezer for something that would take less than ten minutes to prepare.

As she coaxed a toasted strudel toward the front of the oven with a fork, the doorbell chimed. She didn't expect company. Cézanne and Duty weren't coming over to help make phone calls until three that afternoon. With the stove ajar, she scraped her breakfast onto a plate, placed it on the countertop, then cinched her kimono.

Before she could answer, the uninvited guest pounded on the door. She scampered through the living room and stared out through the peephole.

Clem Askew, watery-eyed and fidgeting, stood on the mat with his brow furrowed. He wore a threadbare sweater thrown over his shoulders, and had what appeared to be a blob of oatmeal crusting the front of his haphazardly-buttoned shirt.

"Mr. Askew. What's wrong?"

Her neighbor's voice quivered with age and fright. "There's a strange woman in my house and she won't leave."

Raven stuck her head out and looked the length of her porch. The blue glow of the street lamps galvanized the lawns with a dewy sheen. No sign of traffic, too early for church. She clutched the lapels of her robe and stepped, barefooted, onto the welcome mat.

"Where's Mrs. Askew?"

"Who?"

"Your wife."

"I'm not married."

Raven blinked. She'd attended their fiftieth anniversary at the Elk's Club reception hall. Met their three sons and most of the grandkids.

She chose her words carefully. "This strange woman . . . what's she like?"

"A bottle of wine and a man with a hard dick."

She wasn't clear whether he'd seized the opportunity to say something raunchy, or if he'd misunderstood. But since his eyes gleamed and an unexpected leer spread over his face, she felt pretty certain she had a dirty old man on her front porch. "That's not what I meant. Describe her."

"About your height." He raised a hand to shoulder level. "Skinny and hunched over, with a face like a washboard. And her hair's white. She's mean, too."

He'd just described his wife, Lola, the sweetest lady on the block. With dozens of wrinkles fishnetting her face, and parchment skin that tanned to a golden brown during summer months spent weeding flowerbeds. She baked cookies and treats for the neighbor kids, and toted a load of books on gardening into the house each week after walking to the library, dragging a red Western Flyer wagon behind her like a tail. Yellow flowers that looked good on Monday disappeared at the following week, replaced with bright pink botanicals or other festive colors, depending on her mood and inclination. Every now and then, the elderly woman shared a secret family recipe.

"Let's see . . . oh! Here you go, Raven. I can let you copy this one."

"Why's it called 'Engagement Chicken'?"

"Fix it for your beau, and he'll get you that ring."

Raven dusted the memory away like a cobweb. Mr. Askew must've said something. His lip trembled and his eyes were rimmed red.

"I told her to get out of my house. Ordered her off my property." With a shaky finger, Askew pointed across the street. "She won't go. Called me an old fool and hit me on the arm with a fly swatter."

He peeled his shirtsleeve halfway up and gestured to a non-existent injury.

"Give me a minute to change clothes. I'll go talk to her."

She stepped back inside. Pushed the door until it clicked shut. Skedaddled upstairs and was hiking up a pair of jeans when Clem Askew walked in on her, bare-breasted. He'd somehow followed without her hearing. She grabbed the kimono and clutched it to her chest.

"I'll be down in a minute."

"Hi, girlie. You want some?" The confusion in his eyes had cleared. With a shaky hand, he went for his fly.

"What're you doing?"

"You want some?"

The awful sound of his zipper snagging along its track catapulted her into action.

She rent the air with a yell. "Don't do it."

Grabbed the phone.

Pressed speed-dial.

His eyes gleamed stubbornly. He groped through the fabric of his blue boxers, whipped out his wrinkled appendage and massaged it.

A quavering voice warbled a hello.

"Mrs. Askew? This is Raven. Your husband wandered

over, confused, and he's followed me upstairs into the bedroom. I think he's about to disrobe and I wondered if you could come get him."

The old man stopped in mid-stroke. "Izzat the po-lice?"

Raven kept her voice carefully modulated, enough to conceal her anger. "It's your wife. Says she's on her way over with pinking shears to cut that thing off."

"You called my wife?" He fixed her with a wounded look.

"Like I said, she's on the way."

The front door banged open.

"Clem!"

The charging rhino roar of Lola Askew pierced the second floor. Footfalls stormed the hardwoods.

"I'd quit jerkin' the gherkin before your wife sees you, if I were you," Raven said, tossing the phone onto the bed and shrugging back into her kimono.

"Clem! Are you up there?"

Back went the fire hose . . . or Vienna sausage, in the neighbor's case. Up went the zipper. Clem Askew turned his back on her and ambled out to head off his wife.

Raven didn't bother to follow. She hurried to the bedroom door, slammed it shut and threw the deadbolt, listening to pounding swats glancing off bare flesh.

Jinx arrived at Raven's half-expecting to find her sleeping in, so it surprised him to see an old man bolting out her front door at the crack of dawn with his hands shielding his head in self-defense. An old woman followed close behind, taking swings with a rolled-up newspaper.

He wheeled the patrol car into the driveway and jammed it into Park. Raven appeared at the front door, breasts heaving, with her mouth rounded into an "O."

"Kind of old, even for you, Raven." Jinx angled over to the

porch. "A real man would've gone out the second-floor window."

"Not that I owe you an explanation, but I'm pretty sure my neighbor's in the early stages of Alzheimer's." She felt her blood rise. "Why're you here?"

"Mrs. Bright called. She heard from Joe again this morning."

"Could she tell where he was calling from?"

"Pay phone."

Raven exercised the last of her patience. "No, Jinx. Did she hear any background noise?"

"Ask her yourself. We're picking her up in a few minutes. Are you wearing that?"

He stared at her chest and she remembered she hadn't had time to put on a bra.

"Stop ogling me. I'll give you three hours, tops."

"Unless we catch him."

"Unless we catch him," she repeated, as if by saying the words, she'd made him enter into a binding contract. "I'm getting married—"

"—in six days," they said in unison.

"—and I have to make seventy-five phone calls today. Those are the same seventy-five phone calls I would've made yesterday if you and Dell hadn't planned your Moonie intervention."

She left him downstairs while she finished dressing. When she returned wearing a cotton pullover in a pale mint green that brought out the tan in her skin tone, he was sitting on a chair holding a fractious Siamese against her will.

"When did you get a cat?"

Jezebel screamed. Jinx tightened his grip.

"Yesterday. You want her?"

"No. I want my own cat back."

"Well, you can have this one. She belonged to Miss Groseclose, next door. I only took her because the police haven't been able to reach her next of kin."

Jezebel's paw flared. Where claws should've been, tufts of fur stuck out.

"You can't turn this animal outdoors. She can't defend herself."

"No? This cat doesn't need claws. If you ever get to hear her when she's really pissed-off and claim you're not scared, you're a pathological liar." She slid onto the sofa next to him and slipped on one shoe.

Jezebel hissed.

"Remind me to get cat food before we come back. Although she could stand to miss a meal."

"You think this cat's fat?"

"She's a frickin' elephant."

"Raven, it's pregnant."

"What?" She gave the Siamese a dumb stare, then made up her mind to confine Jezebel to the laundry room until she could get her over to the V-E-T and make sure. She didn't trust Jinx, who knew nothing about women and probably less about female cats. But she knew better than to get in a debate over it.

Ten minutes later, after Jezebel had been watered, and left with a saucer of Cheerios and whole milk, and an old towel to sleep on, Raven and Jinx headed for Mrs. Bright's house on Fort Worth's east side. Within twenty minutes, they exited the Poly Freeway and rolled up in front of a modest brick tract house from the fifties.

Dorretha Bright, a well-groomed woman with a statuesque figure and a worried look lining her face, burst out of the front door and hurried to the street.

"Thank God you're here, Constable." She leaned in for a

look into the passenger seat. "Howdy-do?"

"This is Raven. She's helping out on your son's case."

"Let me grab my purse and lock the door. Won't take but a minute."

"Do you have a picture of your son, and your ex-husband?" Raven called out after her.

Cedric Bright's mother returned with both, as well as a brown paper bag filled with Milky Way bars, Cheetos, beef jerky and glass-bottled Cokes. Raven took the photo and studied her subjects against the light.

Cedric Bright. Six years old, with buzzed-off hair and a gap-tooth grin. Wearing a Stars jersey and Nikes.

Joe Bright. Forty-something, with buzzed-off hair, ears that stuck out from his head like side mirrors, wearing a Stars jersey.

Raven twisted in her seat. "When was this taken?"

"Four or five months ago. That's how they look."

"What was Cedric wearing when you dropped him off at the Ben Street facility?"

"A Stars jersey and blue jeans. His running shoes. The kind with flashing red lights built into the soles."

"Did you give a description to the police?"

"Yessum, I did. And they put out an Amber Alert. That's it."

She handed Jinx the snapshot and he gave it the once-over, then dangled it over the seat until Dorretha Bright took it from him.

Raven said, "I'll need a copy of that picture. It'd help if you'd take it to the one-hour photo place this afternoon."

Dorretha nodded.

Jinx checked his watch. "It's a few minutes after eight. If Joe's still in Fort Worth, he's probably taking Cedric to breakfast. Unless he can cook."

That drew a *harrumph* from the back seat. "Joe never lifted a finger around the house. Only thing Joe can cook is microwave popcorn, and half the time he burns it."

"Where might he take your son to eat?"

Dorretha rattled off the usual places: fast food burger joints and convenience stores with short-order grills. An occasional stop at a rundown barbeque shack over in Stop Six, and covered-dish suppers at the Missionary Baptist Church.

"I think we can rule that last one out," Jinx said.

With little encouragement, Raven got Mrs. Bright to recount the latest phone call.

It came in around seven that morning. Awakened her from a dead sleep. Considering she'd ended her telephone vigil around two hours earlier and had dozed off with the telephone book open and the Blue Pages of governmental listings pressed to her chest, it took a moment for her brain's startle reflex to engage. She missed part of Joe's tirade in the time it took to drag the phone to her ear. The sound of his voice made her come alive, though, especially when he told her for the umpteenth time, "You never gonna see dis boy again."

Raven opened her purse and took out her sunglasses. She slipped them on while Jinx squinted fiercely and shielded his eyes with the sun visor.

"Did you hear any background noise?"

Dorretha Bright, who'd removed her seat belt to hunker closer to the front seat, shook her head.

"You must've heard something. A church bell. A horn honk. Water running. Airplanes?"

"I don't remember anything like that."

They rode through the East side, with Cedric's mother pointing out landmarks.

He went to school there. That's our church. His friend LeShaun's house on the corner. His gramma Beulah's. His other gramma Cecelia's. The house where his Cub Scout leader lives with his wife. The house his Cub Scout leader stays at with his mistress.

When the three hours they promised Mrs. Bright were up, Raven left her with instructions.

Sweet-talk Joe into putting the kid on the phone.

Ask Cedric questions likely to elicit answers that wouldn't rile his father, or tip him off and cause him to do the unforgivable.

Get a tape recorder and a supply of tapes, plus a suction-cup attachment, and hook it to the telephone. Then wait for the next phone call.

"Let us know when you hear from him again."

"You think the FBI will join in the search, Constable?"

He slid Raven a sideways glance. "I don't know that they're not already looking for him."

But the two lawdogs knew the truth.

Unless they had proof Joe Bright crossed the State line with the boy, there wasn't a Chinaman's chance anyone besides them would be looking for him.

It was a domestic.

They were black.

In short, except for Cedric's mother, the Constable's Office and maybe a couple of Fort Worth officers from the East Sector, nobody much gave a damn.

Chapter Fourteen

Instead of heading west on Interstate 30, Jinx took Loop 820 to a mixed neighborhood near the Woodhaven area.

Raven stiffened against the seat back. "Where're we going? You said three hours. I'm getting married—"

He rocked his head from side to side and mouthed the inevitable.

"—in six days." She tried to shape her anger into just the right words. "You promised. You said unless we caught Joe Bright . . ." Her voice trailed off. She slumped in her seat and rested her head against the passenger window. It'd be a snowy day in July before she ever climbed into a car with him again. Or Dell.

Jinx floored the Chevy. "I need you to do something with me."

"*For* you, you mean."

"Fine. I need you to do something for me."

"I hate you." Tears of fury gathered behind her eyeballs and converted themselves into a splitting headache. "What do you want?"

"There's this woman . . ."

"Not my problem. Get a prescription for Viagra."

". . . this Wiccan woman over on the east side, near the Arlington city limit."

Raven lifted her head from the glass, twisted in the seat and pulled her sunshades down enough to peer over the tops. "What does that have to do with me?"

"I think she may know where the missing girl is."

Raven ripped the glasses the rest of the way off. She sat perfectly still with her internal loran engaged, waiting to catch him in a fib.

"I went out to see her yesterday; I think she tried to put a spell on me."

"That's ridiculous."

"I know how it sounds."

She sat wordlessly staring off into space, with an occasional glimpse across the seat to make sure his face didn't crack into a grin. Jinx was good at seeking out unsuspecting victims to be the butt of his jokes. "Okay, I'll bite. Elvira-of-the-Dark put a hex on you. What makes you say that . . . your dick fall off?"

"Not a hex. A spell." He turned off the interstate and aimed the Chevy at a pair of brick columns flanking the entrance to a residential neighborhood where property values jumped a thousand dollars a mile, the farther they drove from Dorretha Bright's house. "My dick didn't fall off. But it does itch."

"Well, don't look at me." She rolled her eyes and tried not to speculate how it got that way. When the gut-cramping moment passed, she said, "I doubt it's a spell. You probably got too close to that skip-tracing skank Evan Rainey has on the payroll. The one with cellophane pants."

"Sigrid Pierson."

"Exactly. Tell *her* about it."

"I didn't sleep with her. I didn't sleep with anybody."

Raven was thinking, *Well that's gotta be a first,* when Jinx began a thumbnail sketch of the encounter with Lyrica Prudhomme. He turned down a tree-lined street, curbed the vehicle and cut the engine. Powered down the windows for ventilation. Twisted in the seat until they were face to face.

"I want you to have a look around her townhouse. She's got these books on a shelf . . . birds' nests and other weird shit . . . I don't know what to look for. I told her next time I came back, I'd have a warrant."

Raven arched an eyebrow. "Do you?"

"I don't. But I do have a subpoena for her to be at docket call tomorrow. Ron Masterson signed it at six thirty this morning."

She gave him a *Good lick!* grin of approval, then proceeded to gnaw the inside of her bottom lip. "I'm not sure I'll do you any good."

"All I'm asking is that you go inside. Maybe snoop around while I'm talking to her."

"I can do that. I'm a good snoop."

"Best I ever saw," Jinx deadpanned.

She suspected he meant the time he caught her rummaging through his things at the Château Du Roy, rifling through drawers without permission, leafing through file cabinets on a quest for incriminating evidence linking him to other women.

And Jinx must've come to the heady realization that his snide remark torpedoed any cooperation he might've otherwise gotten out of her, because he barely restrained a sigh.

By the time Jinx pointed out Lyrica Prudhomme's townhouse and disengaged the Chevy's door locks, Raven had lapsed into a full sulk.

"You don't kick a mule in the tail when he's working, Jinx."

"What's that supposed to mean?"

She shot him a wicked glare. "You already wrangled my assistance; you don't get to insult me on top of everything."

"I didn't insult you. I paid you a compliment."

"It's fine if *I* call me a snoop." Her lip protruded into a pout. "It's not fine when *you* do it."

"I only meant you excel when it comes to nosing around. Come on."

"No."

"What?" He gave her a slow blink.

"You heard me. You're on your own." She turned the back of her head to him and folded her arms across her middle.

Furious, Jinx grabbed his Stetson from the back seat and alighted the patrol car. He slammed the door, smashed the hat onto his head and strode to the front door with Judge Masterson's subpoena wedged into his waistband at the small of his back. He leaned on the doorbell, once, twice, three times, then repeated it for effect until the deadbolt snicked back.

The door opened a sliver, held tight by a chain. One green orb peered out from under a sparse eyebrow, lightly penciled-in with dark brown liner. At the instant of recognition, skin crinkled at the corner of her eye.

She greeted him in a low, breathy voice. "Hello, Constable. I've been thinking about you, and now you're here. Who says telepathy doesn't work?" The Wiccan slid the chain along its track. Using the door as a shield, she backed away, opening it barely enough to allow him inside. "You must've brought that warrant." A long strand of hair slid over one shoulder and fell to her waist. She closed the door behind him. Full, sensual lips angled up in a smirk.

Her presence sucked the air out of him.

"Ms. Prudhomme. Nice to see you . . ."

Naked except for a cluster of gold bangle bracelets riding up the elbow of each arm.

"You here to arrest me? Because I'd like an opportunity to dress before you parade me out to the street in handcuffs."

Eyes like green fire taunted him.

"You'd like that, wouldn't you?" He didn't wait for an answer. "No, I'm not here to arrest you—yet. But I do have a couple of questions I want answered."

She tossed her head, flinging tresses of silky black hair back over her shoulder, then padded, barefoot, deeper into the house.

Three long strides and Jinx cut her off. "Where do you think you're going?"

"To my bedroom. To put clothes on." She wet her lips. The glint of her tongue bolt caught the light. "Do you need to frisk me first?"

She made what he considered a half-hearted attempt to slip past. He grabbed her arm, digging his fingers in hard enough to make her hunch involuntarily. A whiff of lavender oil snaked up his nose.

"I'm not letting you out of my sight."

"Follow me then."

He thought better of it . . . how it would look if Raven suddenly decided to get off her duff and do her job . . . how damning it would be to find him in Lyrica Prudhomme's bedroom, with a crow-bar hard-on and a naked witch with nipples so firm she could make a living chiseling names into granite headstones.

He relaxed his grip.

She eased her arm away. Stared through perceptive green pools.

He could hear himself breathing.

Hell, he could hear his heart trying to jackhammer a hole through his chest from the inside out.

His eyes locked on her small, firm breasts and he sensed that she'd rouged them with lipstick or blush to give them extra color.

Lyrica Prudhomme spoke in a velvet voice.

"You're so tense, Mr. Porter," she said, and Jinx reminded himself that she didn't actually give a rat about him. The seductive tone was just another mind fuck to keep him from dragging out of her what he really came for: *Where the Sam Hill is that kid?*

"You did it, didn't you?" She gave him a smug nod.

"Did what?"

"Fantasized what it would be like to make love to me."

The air thinned.

She lifted a shellacked fingernail to her mouth. Thrust it between her lips. Pulled it out, wet with saliva, and touched it to the thumb-sized bruise forming on her arm. She repeated the gesture, slower, as if she intended to simulate what it might be like to let her perform oral sex on him.

The hedonistic move made Jinx's pulse stall.

"You're wondering if I'm capable of hurting you."

"Oh, you're capable all right."

She clasped her hands, prayer-like, and offered them up. "Hold me like you did yesterday. You can walk me, backwards, into the bedroom, and watch while I dress. *Or not.*"

His blood pressure moved into the red zone. It was if she'd issued a command. His hand closed firmly around her wrists.

"Good," she said in a whisper.

Not good.

Not a game.

You're not going to play me.

He tightened his grip until she winced.

She closed her eyes. Sucked in a shallow breath. "Not too tight."

He was the one in charge, not Lyrica Prudhomme.

He inflicted a brutal squeeze. Her eyelids popped open in astonishment and her face went pasty-white.

"Walk backwards," he said through gritted teeth. In seconds, they were standing in the hall. "Which way?"

Her eyes cut to the right. He steered her down a long hallway, where he knew her room would be.

A few feet from the closed door, she stopped with such abruptness Jinx walked her into the wood. For several seconds, their bodies pressed together with such force that a gasp left her throat before she could squelch it. Inches from her lips, Jinx detected the smell of mint on her breath.

She pulled her arms in tight enough for his fingers to skim her breast. Her mouth went slack. Her eyes flickered. "I thought about you last night."

He fumbled for the doorknob with his free hand, and grazed her hip. Hot skin pressed against his thumb. A chill lanced his heart.

"You should've come back." Her voice dissolved to a whisper. "I would've let you in. *I'll let you in now.*"

His patience slipped away. He twisted the knob and felt the first licks of genuine fear. Upon opening the latch, his stomach went hollow. Overwhelmed by the strong scent of herbs, he waited a few seconds for his senses to clear. The room must've had a separate thermostat from the rest of the house. The temperature seemed more suited to a morgue.

Lyrica Prudhomme fixed him with an emotionless stare. "We both want the same thing, Mr. Porter."

"And what might that be?"

"You need me." Relaxed humor played across her face. "And I need you."

Paused in the doorway, he took stock of the room. Just off center, a ceiling fan whirred above a king-sized bed. With the covers thrown back and a fresh indentation in the black, satin sheets, it appeared he'd awakened her from the crypt. In the dimly lit hallway, he made out folds of fabric falling from the ceiling, and knew where the windows were. But the room seemed unusually dark, as if she'd covered the panes with aluminum foil to prevent daylight from seeping in; and he knew, without asking, she was a day sleeper.

"Where's the light switch?"

"Wired to the ceiling fan. Mr. Porter, my hands are going numb."

"Where's the nearest light?"

"Across the room, on the far side of the bed."

He backed her into the room, relaxing his grip only slightly. "This is fucked-up, not having lamps."

"I prefer candles. More erotic, don't you think?"

He steered her past the bed to the far side of the room. Reached for the switch to the night light with his grip still firmly encircling her wrists.

"Please don't turn that on."

Jinx's fingers tingled from blood loss. He hauled Lyrica Prudhomme close and spoke inches from her face. "I'm going to release you in a few seconds. But if you so much as look at me funny, I'll dough-pop you and slam you face-down on the floor. Understand?"

She nodded.

He unhanded her, on guard as she rubbed one wrist, then the other, working the feeling back into her hands. He bent low, fumbling beneath the lampshade.

"Why don't you take off your shirt?"

"No."

No switch.

"I could give you a back rub. You're so tense. This is a terrible job you have, Mr. Porter."

"Where the hell's the switch?"

"Midway down the cord. It falls behind the night table. I'll get it for you."

At the first sign of movement, he blocked her with his body.

He reached off to one side and yanked one of two chains dangling from the fan, flooding the room with light. Against the wall, opposite the bed, was an altar, covered with a silky black cloth. A bell sat atop the table runner, along with a quartz crystal and what appeared to be sheathed daggers. Above the altar hung the bleached skull of an axis deer with an herb garland strung between the antlers. Dried rosebuds poked out from holes where eyes had once been.

When he looked back at Lyrica Prudhomme, he noted her furtive glance toward the nightstand. He tracked her gaze.

Knife.

A long, copper-blade knife, with intricate scrollwork carved into the bone handle and etchings along the blade, glinted from the table's flat surface.

Jinx snatched it up. "This what you were after?"

The witch shook her head. "They're all over the house. If I wanted to hurt you, I would've gotten the silver one next to the fireplace yesterday."

"You have knives all over the house?"

"Not knives. *Athanes*. Made of copper and other elements. For religious services."

"Like the ones you use to sacrifice little girls?"

The woman's eyes went wide. She gathered her long mane to one side and twisted it into a loose rope, before coiling it behind her head. "I'm going to get a couple of hair pins from my dresser," she said, taking a slow step backward. She fished her painted talon into a ceramic dish and came out with a couple of V-shaped wire fasteners.

When she reached for a drawer handle, Jinx commanded a halt.

In two strides, he opened it himself, pulled a tank top off

the top of the stack and pitched it at her. Behind louvered doors that turned out to be a walk-in closet, he found a gauzy skirt, yanked it off the hanger and stood guard over her while she dressed.

She was pulling the skirt up over her hips when he noticed a visible change in her face.

Giving him the skin-crawling feeling they weren't alone.

"And just what the hell is *this?*" came a voice from behind, and to the right.

With a sinking gut, he turned at the sound of Raven's call.

Chapter Fifteen

"Never would've happened if you'd done what I told you." Mired in an atmosphere charged with hostility, Jinx hit the entrance ramp to the freeway and floor-boarded the Chevy. "I blame you."

"You liked it. I could see it in your face. If your tongue dropped out any farther, you could've noosed your neck with it." Raven flexed her fingers into a fist. "Jerk."

"Why do you care?"

"I don't," she lied, feeling suddenly colder. "Besides, she's old."

"She's in great shape."

"*I'm* in great shape."

"But she's not walking the gangplank in six days."

"Stop saying that." Angry thoughts vibrated off the top of her head. "I hate you."

Dumb bastard hasn't changed a bit. Probably thinks a hard-on counts as personal growth.

Scenery flew by in a colorful smear. She needed a cup of coffee, a couple of aspirin and a bigger gun.

Closing her eyes to vanquish the sight of Jinx's torquing jaw didn't help. His image popped up behind her lids, staring at her with the sort of baffled expression a bank robber confronted by a gun-toting granny might have. How did he expect her to respond, when he was standing close enough to skim the nipples of a naked suspect?

"What do you want, Raven?"

"I only want what we went out there for—information." Big, fat whopper. What she *really* wanted was to see scissors sticking out of the side of his head.

"That's all I was doing."

Pretty ballsy reply, considering she'd caught him cozying up to a naked woman.

But during her unguided tour through the townhouse on the way to find Jinx, she'd stumbled into Lyrica Prudhomme's study. And right there on the computer monitor, an instant message to *Sorceress* from *Blademaker* flashed onscreen.

"Are you planning to see her again?"

"What if I do? I have an ongoing investigation. I may have to."

"No, you don't. I got her computer password and her instant message ID. Now we can get into her chat room."

"We?"

"You're not going back out there without me, Jinx Porter."

"Jealous?"

Ha! The word exploded in her head like a cannon blast. "It's for your own safety. The last thing you need right now is a DOJ investigation." The Department of Justice loved burning cops. "You don't want to be the cop who discovers that the breeze mussing your hair comes from a wrecking ball." She wound up in a normal tone of voice. "What does Fleck Standish do for a living?"

"He makes knives. And lives off his dead wife's Social Security benefits."

Blademaker.

Raven experienced a lightheaded rush. "He communicated with her." Jinx corkscrewed an eyebrow. "Fleck Standish is sending her instant messages. She calls herself Sorceress. I saw one from Blademaker on her computer. She knows where he is."

"Why should she help him?"

"Honestly, Jinx, you're so stupid when it comes to women. We're a treacherous lot. That's what we do best—manipulate men. Nobody can filter through a smokescreen like another woman. Next time, I'll talk to her."

"Sounds like you don't trust me anywhere near her. Wonder why that is?"

Raven tightened her jaw. Went into a pout. Her concern had nothing to do with Jinx. This was about protecting the badge.

They needed the services of a computer geek. A program monkey like—

Amos.

Ivy's miscreant son could help. The juvenile court judge had sentenced him to ninety days in the Texas Youth Commission. Amos ought to be released any minute.

She glanced out the window. Considered bringing up the idea of using the thirteen-year-old to hack into Lyrica Prudhomme's computer and nose around, then thought better of it. Introducing Amos into the conversation would be enough to send Jinx straight to the liquor store.

Jinx took the Montgomery Street exit and turned in to drive to McDonald's. He powered down the windows and slowed to a crawl.

"Caesar," he called.

"Jinx, he's not going to stay around a fast food joint."

"Why not?"

"Because he's a picky eater. If you really want to do some good, we should go drive through Trinity Park and see if he's taken up with the feral cats."

Jinx whipped the car, hard right, onto Lancaster and punched the accelerator.

"What're you doing?"

"Driving over to Trinity Park."

Leaving her to ask herself, *Why'd I say anything? This'll just prolong the agony.*

Caesar awakened from his dream, twitching. Jinx and the girl had been calling his name. It sounded so real, he sat up and blinked. He couldn't be sure, but the distant rumble of an engine reminded him of Jinx's car—he pricked up his ears and listened. He wandered toward the sound. Nearby, a squirrel tormented a dog on a leash. An unexpected breeze blew in and the air around Caesar came alive with smells. He knew these scents, but he didn't know the names for them. But he'd smelled them before at the Château Du Roy, when the people rolled their grills into the courtyard and made fires. He stretched out his front paws and shook the tiredness from his elongated body, then arched himself into a horseshoe.

Where's Jinx?

Where's home?

Where's the girl?

Chapter Sixteen

Sigrid Pierson sat on a barstool in the Ancient Mariner, the neighborhood tavern—a cop pub owned by a couple of retired PD officers that catered to law enforcement and Assistant DAs. She was flirting with the bartender and sucking down drinks when Jinx walked in Sunday night and straddled the seat next to hers. He got the barkeep's attention by slapping a fifty on the counter.

He made a finger gesture in the PI's direction. "Set 'em up."

Rainey's little tin star didn't seem to mind swilling free highballs, but when he said, "How's it going?" in an effort to make conversation, she gave him the dickless leper treatment. The new pick-up line he tried out on her went over like a Led Zepplin, but two "Down the rat holes" later, he managed to talk her into a quick game of pool. By the time the place thinned out around one o'clock, he had her slamming back shot glasses, and wincing at the burn. When last call rolled around, management bellowed into the loudspeaker with their trademark poem:

"Last call for alkey-hol.

"Hotel, motel—we don't care.

"You don't have to go home, but you can't stay here."

Jinx steered her to an empty booth in the corner and ordered doubles.

He knew a sure thing.

For one thing, Rainey's PI had on a pair of red, stiletto-heeled, do-me pumps. For another, she'd encased herself into a tube top the width of a rubber band. Sun-tanned breasts glistened under the harsh glow of the Mariner's fake Tiffany lamps. Perspiration dotted her upper lip, and when she tugged the cardboard coaster out from beneath her drink to fan herself, she knocked over the glass.

"Did you canvass the neighbors?" Jinx asked.

"Most o' them," she said, her tongue thick, and her speech slurred. "The people on either side of Venita Standish's trailer don't wanna get involved. They're scared of the Standishes, but others think Fleck Standish killed those two lovers the Arlington police found in the woods behind the trailer park a couple months back."

The bartender delivered fresh drinks to the table. Halfway back to his station, he turned, exchanged looks with Jinx and shook his head.

She raised her glass, *Salud,* then clinked tumblers with him. "Cheers to beers and queers."

"Bottoms up." Jinx belted one back. "Did you pass on the neighbors' information to APD?"

Sigrid snorted. "Sure did." She burped against the back of her hand. "The lead detective said, 'We dunno who did it, but we know who didn't do it—and Standish didn't do it.' "

Jinx saw red. "The only way you know who didn't do it is if you know who did it."

He felt a nudge and realized Rainey's investigator had sandwiched his boot between her dirk-heeled snakeskins.

"Wanna go someplace quiet?" Blue eyes coolly narrowed.

"What'd you have in mind?"

"You'll see. C'mon."

She slid out of the booth and wobbled toward the cash register with her mini-skirt riding up in back. He paid the tab while she air-kissed the bartender, then held open the door and watched her reel across the parking lot on shaky legs. She angled over to a Dodge pickup, crashed into the fender, then hooked an arm over the tailgate for balance.

"Here's my ride." She hiccoughed, lowering her shadowed eyelids to half-mast. "I'm plastered."

No shit, Nancy Drew.

"You're too hammered to drive. I'll run you home. You can come back for the truck when you're not plowed under."

"Thassa great idea."

She let go of the tailgate, pitched forward and melted into his arms. He hauled her up by her armpits and propped her against the truck's bumper. She caught him staring.

Her cheeks flushed bright beneath the sodium vapor lamps. With the skill of a forklift operator, she cupped her hands to her breasts, lifting them inches from his chin. "So . . . you like my boobs?"

"Nice." He gave the parking lot a furtive once-over, scanning for lookie-loos.

She unhanded herself. Implants sprang into place. "I wanna kiss you now."

Zeroing-in, she missed his mouth and planted a sloppy liplock on his chin. Realizing the mistake, she unsuctioned her lips and giggled. Her head lolled to one side and her eyes rolled back into her head.

"Mmmmm," she said, as if he'd passed the taste test. The corners of her mouth tipped and her eyes momentarily crossed. "Mmmmmm—you smell good. Whadda you have on?"

A hard-on, but I didn't think you could smell it.

He steadied her shoulders in his grip. "Sit still. I'll bring the car around."

Without prompting, Rainey's PI condensed her life story to fit the four-mile drive home, and delivered it like a books-on-tape version of a cheesy romance novel. Five times engaged, three sour marriages, a stint in the military right out of high school. The inadvertent disclosure of a kid she put up for adoption in her twenties, the by-product of a weekend liaison. An affair with a sixty-year-old man who paid her way through school long enough to help her procure an investigator's license. Two bankruptcies, one in her twenties, another in her thirties. And a handful of one-night stands, including a bisexual encounter with a lesbian stripper she met when they both danced topless at a scuzzy bar in unincorporated Whiskey Flats.

He wondered how she'd made it to age thirty-nine without producers of the "Jerry Springer Show" beating her door down.

"I only did the girl thing to pay the rent. Then Buck showed up—"

The old geezer.

"—and rescued me." Abruptly, she slid her hand from his knee, up his leg. "Know what I'd like?"

He shook his head and mentally tried out a couple of variations on the same theme: himself, Sigrid wearing nothing but those shoes, a porn star with auburn hair and a strap-on, a five pound can of Crisco and . . .

. . . *Lyrica Prudhomme?*

The image hit him like a harpoon to the brain.

Where the hell'd that come from?

He hardened his jaw. Lyrica Prudhomme should be jailed.

He shrugged off the brazen fantasy but the image returned clearer than ever: the witch, on her knees, looking up at him through compelling eyes, taunting him with seductive insults. Jinx's heart tripped. No telling why she'd invaded his thoughts. It wasn't as if they had chemistry. They had no respect for each other. Their philosophies differed radically.

The woman infuriated him. Clouded his thoughts and made his tongue thicken when she came near. Wasn't even that attractive with her underdeveloped body and fat lips . . . fleshy lips . . . berry-stained lips that sent a shot of ice up his spine and a firebolt to his groin when he looked at them . . . thought of them closing around his . . .

Lyrica Prudhomme *should* be in jail; not roaming, unescorted, inside his head, prying locks off the Pandora's box full of secrets he stored in his mind. Lyrica Prudhomme *would* be in jail, as soon as he figured out a charge he could make stick.

"I'll tell you what I'd like . . ." With her flammable breath close to igniting, Sigrid Pierson cozied up beside him and purred. "I'd like to see you buck naked except for your cowboy boots."

"Is that right?" The woman made him want to bend her over the trunk and do her right there.

"You got any tattoos?"

"No." He grimaced. Ink-infused needle jabs? Thanks, but no thanks.

"I used to date a homicide detective . . ." she gave him a cagey look, ". . . had FWPD tattooed on his dick . . ."

Jinx pretended to meditate over her comment.

". . . when it got aroused and swelled up, it spelled out Fort Worth Police Department Homicide Unit."

He jerked the steering wheel, hard left, to avoid sideswiping the car in the next lane.

They ended up at a two-bedroom crackerbox in Dell Teague's neighborhood, where frame houses tended to have a homogenous look, allowing for color variations in the painted exteriors. But Sigrid Pierson's place turned into a cliché. It had a generous amount of gingerbread cutwork applied to the mitered edges, and a white picket fence with a tight spring attached to the front gate that sounded like a sprung rat trap when it banged shut behind him.

Inside the door, he took stock of his surroundings. Punched-silver mirrors, edged in Mexican tiles, hung on the walls next to watercolor flamingos, matted in metal frames. From his place on a rush mat, the motel Tropicana motif that began in the living room seemed to extend to the kitchen and beyond.

She owned a flat-screen, high-definition TV mounted prominently on a wall painted bright turquoise, with surround-sound speakers concealed behind the fake palms and banana trees in the corners. An overstuffed sofa took up most of one wall, along with a wooden barrel-half that had been transformed into a coffee table by turning it upside down.

All this place needed was a six-toed cat and an iguana stomping around.

"Bathroom's thattaway if you need to drain the radiator." She slung her arm out in a wide crescent, gesturing to a bright yellow bedroom that had been converted into a study. The Caribbean motif continued clear up the walls, to the blades of ceiling fan—which were little more than oval wicker paddles sculpted to look like fan palms. A rattan entertainment center made of cut bamboo and cane held her computer in one corner, and she'd arranged her file cabinets against the only wall without windows. Camera equipment littered the floor, as if it had been abandoned in haste on a mad dash to the can.

The lipstick-pink bathroom had opposing pocket doors. Jinx suspected the one he didn't enter through opened into Sigrid's bedroom. When he heard the rustle of fabric on the other side, he was sure. Above the toilet hung an oil painting with Sigrid Pierson's name printed in the lower right-hand corner. He decided she had a modicum of artistic talent when he recognized the subject as Fabio. Whether her female friends enjoyed urinating with a guy looking over their shoulder, he didn't know; but using himself as a barometer, he was willing to make book that the thrill didn't extend to any men who stumbled into her lair. He switched off the light and exited through her study.

The buzz from the booze wore off.

Stalled in the living room, he wondered if he should turn on CNN. Viewing their good-looking brunette commentator life-sized, instead of compressed to a twenty-seven-inch screen, might be fun. Or porn stars on Pay TV. Fleshy lips doing unwholesome things to big pricks . . . now *that* carried an allure. Or . . .

. . . talk her into setting up that camera equipment. Maybe get her to videotape herself showing him what she liked, then pop it into the VCR . . . play it back on the big screen TV while he bent her across the barrel coffee table and put it to her.

Rainey's investigator called his name.

He followed the sound of her voice through the kitchen, a long, narrow space with red Formica countertops, a small four-burner stove and an undersized refrigerator. He would've welcomed a cold beer, but the sight of dirty dishes stacked high in the sink discouraged him.

He arrived at the door to her dimly-lit bedroom, where she sat in the middle of a queen-sized four-poster, with the sheets pulled up around her chin. With a lusty gaze, and a pat on the mattress, she invited him into the sack. He apparently didn't move fast enough, because she threw back the covers for encouragement. The sight of her breasts—more like double-D feedbags—took his breath away. She heaved herself out of bed, took a couple of Bambi-like footsteps, and unbuttoned his shirt. In her haste, the last button pinged onto the floor and ricocheted off the baseboard.

He removed his boots, fished in his pocket for a tin of Copenhagen, stepped out of his slacks and let her tug off his briefs. She sighed in approval, then pulled him onto the mattress, barely allowing enough time to set the smokeless tobacco onto the night table.

Chivalry was about to pay off big.

She guided his hand between her legs.

Showed him what to do with his finger, then groaned when he removed it.

Jinx executed orders with his eyes. Even though soused, Sigrid Pierson got the picture.

Me first. Then you.

The big Swede positioned herself at the foot of the bed. Worked her tongue up his inner thighs, where he unexpectedly became aware of a new erogenous zone. She plied him with playful bites, then engulfed his erection with an eager mouth.

Sinking deeper into the pillows, he afforded himself a decent view, watching her descend on him with the ravenous appetite of a carnivore.

Rainey's employee had a dynamite repertoire, which she ruined by breaking stride to utter suggestive comments or ask questions.

"Do you like that?"

Jinx grunted. He wanted to tell her if he didn't, he'd let her know. Otherwise, get back to work.

"What about when I do this?"

He stared at the ceiling. Duct tape would be nice—to stick over her mouth. But then she couldn't do what she did so well, with her tongue temporarily disabled. Her constant need for reassurance reminded him of Loose-Wheel Lucille. That was the trouble with women like Sigrid Pierson and the Baldwin sisters. Incessant babbling spoiled the mood. He closed his eyes and wondered how long it would take before Sigrid Pierson dug out the Trojans and handed him one.

With any luck, he'd finish before that happened, then *Adiós, chica.*

Rainey's sex-crazed tin star must've thought he was taking too long, because she stopped in mid-stroke and let out a sigh of impatience.

"What if I slather baby oil on my breasts . . . would you slide it between them?"

"Do we need all this talk?"

For a while, thank God, she shut up. Without all the yammering to break the mood, he could call up a memory and pretend this was Raven he was about to slide into. He closed his eyes and felt the electric current building in his groin.

Beautiful Raven.

Gorgeous Raven.

Perfect Raven.

Gimme another chance. This time I'll treat you better.

I do love you . . . do love you . . . do . . . love . . . you . . .

"I love you." Raspy words exploded from Rainey's amateur sleuth, detonating the fragile mirage playing out in Jinx's head.

His eyes snapped open in horror.

"Jiminy Christmas." Disgusted, he half-swore. She couldn't hear his mind screaming, *Good Lord, what the hell's wrong with you? Take it back!* She was too busy shoving him off her, scrambling out from beneath him.

Enough of this crap. Thank God it's done.

That's the problem with crazy women—never know when they're gonna start purchasing drugstore greeting cards from the stalker section of Hallmark, and send them to you.

In his mind, the card he expected to get from Rainey's squeeze read, *"Thinking of you and remembering the good times we had."*

He reached for the snuff.

Next thing he knew, the big blonde mounted him like a broncobuster. Parted herself with her fingers, and guided him inside. Dug her heels into his legs and rode him like a bronco at the Mesquite Rodeo. Best he could tell she stayed on the full eight seconds before timing out with a guttural moan, and collapsing in a damp heap beside him.

Her lips were smeared scarlet. Make-up had rubbed off, giving her mouth the faint outline of a happy clown.

Unfulfilled, he considered returning the favor—maybe with a little extra incentive she'd get her second wind and finish what she started. He glanced past heaving breasts. The leering grin of Evan Rainey stared at him from a wooden picture frame on the nightstand. Jinx came to a conclusion: if she had as many dicks sticking out of her as she'd had stuck in her, she'd look like a porcupine.

He slid off her passion-rumpled sheets. Left the private eye in a snarl of hair and sweat, and the bed looking like a crime scene.

On the way home to the Château Du Roy, Jinx took a detour that placed him on Venita Standish's rickety porch. He pounded the doorjamb with his Mag-lite. Footsteps trundled through the house. On the other side of the door, he heard the jagged cough of a heavy smoker.

The raspy, three-pack-a-day voice of Magick's paternal grandmother called out. "Who is it?"

"Constable Jinx Porter. Open up."

The chain slid away. The bolt snapped. Venita Standish stood inside the crummy trailer, cinching the tie on her terrycloth robe.

She scrunched her eyes in an effort to blink away the slumber. "It's three in the morning. What do you want?"

"Where's your son?"

"I dunno."

He reached for the handcuffs resting in the small of his back. "You're under arrest. Turn around and put your hands behind your back." When she took too long, he latched onto her wrist, spun her around and snapped on the cuffs, click-click.

"Why're you doing this? I only got released six hours ago."

"New day, new offense. Suck it up."

"What do you want from me?" Said in a whimper.

"Not a damned thing."

But what he really wanted was what he couldn't have: to gain legal entry into the house, hit the Play button on Venita Standish's answering machine and listen to the messages behind the pulsing red light.

Chapter Seventeen

Early Monday morning, before Raven had a chance to hop in the shower and dress for work, the phone rang. Caller-ID showed an out-of-area contact.

She snatched up the receiver, said a breathless hello and spent the next ten seconds panting fear into the mouthpiece.

"Rave?" Tommy's voice sounded faint and distant.

Her heart did a little tap dance. "Ohmygod, what's happening to you? Tell Y-Jay I'm gonna kill him."

"Raven, listen. Everything's going to work out fine."

"No it isn't," came the taunt from Y-Jay, "because you can't stay off the fucking phone. Every time you get on the fucking phone—"

"Don't listen to him, babe." Tommy. "He's just pissed because he doesn't have anyone to call."

"—they locate us with their transponders. Now hang up before they kill us both."

Raven's stomach went hollow. "Who's after you? Where are you? What's going on?"

Unexpectedly, she found herself talking to her deranged cousin.

"Hello, Raven," Yucatan Jay said in the same sweet conman tone he'd once used to coax her into jumping off the cliff behind his house with a homemade hang-glider strapped to her back. "Sorry to cut in, love, but your fiancé keeps endangering our lives so he can reassure you we're fine." His tone degenerated into the condescending lout she remembered seeing off at the train station, when Uncle Jack and Aunt Wren sent him off to reform school. "Stop being neurotic. Get some Prozac and take it."

"Put Tommy back on the line."

"I will not."

"You will, too."

"Will not. Now you listen to me and listen good. Tell the man you love him; that you don't need to hear from him every day, and—" staccato shouts of angry foreigners broke out in the background, "—sorry, love. Catch you later."

The rustle of fabric suggested Y-Jay had stuffed the phone in his pocket. A faint conversation unmeant for her ears took place between her cousin and fiancé.

"What's wrong with you, Tom? I'm the one who takes unnecessary risks, not you."

"I can't help it. She's scared. And I love her."

"Enough to get us both killed?"

"Look who's talking: *Hey, Pot, this is Kettle!* I wouldn't even be here if you hadn't gotten your ass in a crack." The background buzz of a propeller grew louder. "Look. There he is. Think we can make it to the tarmac?"

"Dunno. How's your foot?"

"Hurts like hell."

"I say screw the tail-dragger. Let's make a run for the border." Y-Jay.

"Are you crazy?"

"Can't be more than a thousand yards."

"Only a *thousand yards,* moron?"

"The pilot's about to touch down. Let's decide."

From her end, Raven imagined she heard two fists striking two open palms, three times: *rock, paper, scissors.* She rolled her eyes and experienced a wave of faintness.

"Ha. I win." Yucatan Jay. "We go for the airstrip."

"Okay, Forrest. *Run like the wind.*"

The signal cut out in a hail of gunfire.

Raven slumped to the floor like a cartoon cutout. She smashed her hands against her temples and pressed until blue stars danced in front of her eyes.

He's coming back to me in a box.

Time suspended.

Her pager shrilled out, jarring her from the trance.

Dorretha Bright's number popped up on the digital display. A quick phone call to Cedric's mother took her mind off Tommy's peril and set the rest of the day's pace.

Joe Bright had inflicted another one of his torture-calls on her, making the latest contact while drunk or hopped up. No big surprise when he threatened to kill Cedric for the gazillionth time.

"Did you talk to your son?"

"I got the whole thing on tape. Can you please come over and help me look around?"

Now that the seventy-five phone calls had been returned, Raven thought of the flower shop, and how she needed to swing by and order a bouquet; and to check on the special order of Birds of Paradise, to make certain they'd arrive by Friday night, before the rehearsal dinner. And to pick up her fairy tale gown from Bridal Wise.

"I'll be right out."

She telephoned Jinx to let him know she'd be late, and got his voice mail.

Poor guy. Probably still snoozing after spending half the night looking for the Siamese.

Thirty minutes later, the tires on Raven's unmarked patrol car crunched over Mrs. Bright's gravel driveway. The front door banged open and Dorretha Bright bounded down the steps with a cordless phone in her hands. She'd dressed quickly, and miscalculated, since she started buttoning her shirt on the wrong button. With an animated hand gesture, the lady pointed to the receiver and mouthed her ex-husband's name.

Raven shut off the engine. She took great care exiting the vehicle without undue noise, while Cedric's mother tried to reason with her ex.

"I don't know why you wanna be this way, Joe. Haven't I always done right by you?" Long pause. "Joe, honey, if you'd just lemme talk to him—"

Raven held up two fingers. Danced like a Rottweiler pulling against its chain. "Two minutes," she mouthed without sound, then flashed all five. "Ask for five."

"—lemme have five minutes with him, so's I know he's all right. Two, then. I'm not tricking you, Joe. I just wanna know, has my baby had enough to eat?"

The distraught mother stood rigid, frozen in fear, with her fingers paling against the hard plastic cordless. She covered the mouthpiece and whispered, "He's getting my baby. What do I say?"

"Ask him what he had for breakfast. Ask where he ate. Ask what he's having for lunch. Ask him—"

The woman waved her off. "Cedric? My child!" She collapsed to her knees, to the rocky earth beneath the sun-scorched lawn. Tears ran down her cheeks in rivulets. She made an effort to inject a lilt into her tone. "Did you eat breakfast?"

She glanced up at Raven and nodded. "What'd you eat?" Long pause. "At the Burger-Doodle?" She locked eyes with Raven and did a quick head bob. "Whatchoo gonna have for lunch? Another cheeseburger? Fries, too? Mmmmm, that sounds good. Did you walk or did your daddy drive you? You walked? Walking's good exercise. Where you gonna eat dinner?"

Her eyes widened in astonishment, as if she'd touched an ice cube and gotten burned.

"Joe!" She recovered in an instant, filling her voice with false cheer. "Thank you for feeding him good. Listen, baby, he likes to snack on animal cookies. Maybe you could get him some." Another long pause. "They don't have them at convenience stores, Joe. You have to buy them in a regular grocery store. Can you get him a box of animal crackers and maybe some white grape juice? Cedric likes purple grape juice, Joe, but it's real hard to get outta his clothes, so get him the white stuff, okay?"

Sun bathed Dorretha Bright's skin in its gold light. She shielded her eyes from its glare, and sank one hip onto the ground.

"When you gonna call again, Joe?" She winced, pulling the phone away from her ear. An angry male voice vibrated through the earpiece. "I'm only asking so I can be here, Joe. I have to pay bills and I don't want to miss your call. I know you don't believe me, but I've missed you, Joe. I've missed both my boys."

She stared up at Raven, crestfallen. Pulled the phone from her ear and thumbed the off-button.

"What did he say?"

"He said he's still gonna kill Cedric. And he told me to go fuck myself."

Raven helped her up off the ground. She dusted her britches off and fisted tears from her eyes. Together, they reviewed what they knew so far: Cedric ate a cheeseburger for breakfast, and planned to have another for lunch. Burger-Doodle was their nickname for the boy's favorite fast food restaurant. Since the burger places were a locally-owned chain found only in Fort Worth and Arlington, Raven knew Joe Bright and his son were still in the area. And the boy said they walked to their destination, which meant they were either staying in a motel near the burger place, or that Joe rented an apartment. According to Dorretha Bright, none of Joe's friends would put him up after pulling this type of caper. And if the man actually bought his son the animal cookies and white grape juice, he'd have to find it at the grocery store.

So, the only thing left to do was to listen to Dorretha's audiotape and hope for background noises to give a clue to Cedric's whereabouts; get the telephone book out and locate the nearest Burger-Doodle; drive over, show the employees a picture of Joe and Cedric; if they found any witnesses, then check out any apartments and motels within walking distance.

No big deal.

Talk about bad odds.

Kind of like asking for mermaids and getting a handful of minnows.

At nine o'clock, when Venita Standish took the witness stand in Judge Masterson's court and testified, under oath, that she didn't know the whereabouts of her son and granddaughter, Masterson and Jinx adjourned to judge's chambers.

Masterson shrugged out of his judicial robe and hooked it over a brass peg mounted behind the door. "What do you want out of this, Constable? Even if I jail her on a contempt charge, you still may not be able to find the girl in time."

Point well taken.

"Here's what would make me happy, Judge. If you'll lock her up for the time being, and order her to give us a deposition, that might help."

"She has to have notice. I'm afraid it'll take longer than you've got, if Raven's ideas are true."

"Just lock her up, Judge. I'll go to the District Attorney's Office and file on Venita Standish and her son for Interference with Child Custody."

Masterson liked the idea enough to remand Venita Standish into the custody of the Sheriff's Office for three days for contempt of court, while Jinx followed through with a visit to the Intake Division at the Tarrant County Justice Center.

He had a bit of problem parking. The usual spaces allotted for police cars were clogged with wreckers, towing a string of unauthorized vehicles from the area designated for law enforcement. When he walked through the metal detectors and greeted security, he found out what started the mess.

Raven.

According to a couple of bailiffs in-the-know, gypsies from all over the United States had descended on Fort Worth to protest Sabina Balogh's arrest and unusually high bail.

Jinx took the elevator to the basement, to the intake unit of the District Attorney's Office.

The Assistant DA in charge didn't register any enthusiasm when Jinx brought up the subject of filing criminal charges against Fleck Standish.

"You want to get a warrant for Interference with Child Custody?" In a doom-filled baritone, the ADA, a bespectacled man in his early sixties, sat back in his chair like an overfed rat. With his shirt sleeves ringed in sweat, the prosecutor looked him dead in the eye and delivered the rest of his opinion in an odd cadence. "Constable, you're going to cause a bunch of shit—"

Merrily, merrily, merrily, merrily, life is but a dream.

Dumb bastard.

Jinx Porter doesn't run from trouble.

"—and I do mean a bunch of shit, filing a criminal case."

"You think I care? Shit's my middle name. I live in it."

The prosecutor rubbed a hand over a sparse, neatly trimmed goatee, and expelled a ragged sigh. "Did I tell you? I'm set to retire in six months."

"Congratulations. About that warrant . . ."

"How come weird shit never happens to other people, Jinx? It only happens to you. Why is that?"

"I'm a shit magnet." *And I'm in your office, looking at you across the desk. Since we're the only ones here and I'm the magnet, what does that make you?* "Do I get the warrant or not?"

"This is your way of getting it listed in TCIC/NCIC, isn't it?"

Having a Teletype routed to the Texas Crime Information Center and the National Crime Information Center would allow local and state law enforcement officers to access the information, as well as encourage the FBI to take an interest. Not that Jinx wanted the Feds poking their noses in, but with the clock ticking, he needed all the help he could get. Including the television stations. Channel Eighteen would be good, especially that ass-wipe news reporter, Garlon Harrier. Once Harrier got on the scent of a good scoop, he was like a pit bull with his jaws locked tight . . . have to put a bullet in him to get him to let go.

"So if I file it, will you take the case or not?"

"Six months, Jinx. After this, I don't want to see you around here until the day of my retirement party."

Fair enough.

Next stop?

An exclusive interview with Channel Eighteen's Garlon Harrier.

Entering the Constable's Office, Raven passed Ivy and Jinx's chief deputy, Gilbert Fuentes, ricocheting off each other in an attempt to be first out the door.

She sent Dell a wobbly smile. "What gives with those two?"

"Jinx gave them the afternoon off."

"Why?" She headed for Ivy's desk and tossed a handful of notes on the blotter. There was work to be done and they could've used two extra minds. Make that one and a half. Compared to Ivy, a drooling socialite looked like a scholar.

"He had them out searching for Caesar over the weekend, so they're taking comp time."

Raven put Mickey and Dell to work cross-referencing burger joints with area motels and apartments within reasonable walking distance, while she spent the better part of the afternoon making a series of unsuccessful attempts to hack into Lyrica Prudhomme's computer.

Around three, Dell walked over with a list of possibles. Seven of the top fifteen had grocery stores within a six-block radius. "Want to check out a couple of these before we go home?"

"I'll do them tonight. I need to swing by the florist's and I still have to pick up my dress."

"Let me go with you."

"Dell . . ."

The cowbell clanged above the glass door, and everyone except Dixie glanced over to see who'd come in.

Jinx.

Eyes the color of nickels coolly narrowed. "Well, Raven, once again you've managed to stir up a hornet's nest."

She cast her vision to the floor, feeling suddenly flushed and a little bit guilty. Her eyes shifted to Dell, who conveniently looked at Mickey.

"I'm speaking of the gypsies. They're descending on this city like the Mongolian hoards."

She didn't have to ask. Jinx ran it down for her with

remote, cool detachment. "Gyps set up camp in front of every county building downtown. We'll be lucky if they don't strip the faucets out of the bathrooms." Dismissing her with his eyes, he slid a letter from an envelope and shook it open. "I found this stuck under my windshield."

Dixie stopped typing. "Okay, I'll bite. What is it? Ransom note? Going out of business sale?"

"It seems we have an Internet hacker. Says he's following the Standish case. That cultists are using chat rooms to stay in touch and shuffle Standish from place to place. Says the girl's still alive."

"Good. Sounds like he wants to help." Dixie again, hunkering over the keyboard.

"Not good," Jinx snapped. "I finished an interview with Channel Eighteen. The evening broadcast won't air for another two hours."

Without taking her eyes off the monitor screen, Dixie said, "So?"

"So how'd he know what's going on, unless he's involved?"

The phone bleated. Dixie swept up the receiver. "Constable Jinx Porter's office, may I help you?"

Raven twisted her engagement ring so the diamond faced her palm. She offered up an explanation. "Could be one of Standish's neighbors. I think those people know a lot more than they're telling."

"Don't think so. You haven't met the neighbors. I smell a rat."

She moved uneasily under his intent regard. "For God's sake, Jinx, if you've got somebody who wants to help, let them. I've tried all afternoon and I can't figure out how to get myself into Lyrica Prudhomme's chat room."

Worry lined Jinx's face. "Look, Raven, whoever wrote the

note's only offering their services if they can deal with you."

"Me? Why me?"

Dixie bosomed the telephone receiver. Interrupted the lively discussion with her *don't kill the messenger* grimace. "Jinx, Agents Longley and Hough, from the FBI, want to talk to you."

Raven stiffened. Longley and Hough almost arrested her three months before, back when she first met Tommy—after he forced her at gunpoint to accompany him to the bank to exchange U.S. currency for Canadian gold Maple Leaf coins. The FBI got her picture off a mounted camera; after that, trying to get them to lose interest in her was like trying to shake two pit bulls off her ankle. Nothing good could come out of a call from Longley and Hough.

Dixie arched an eyebrow. "They saw the Teletype on TCIC/NCIC and want to you to let them know if you locate Standish or the girl."

The contours of his face went hard. By the looks of everyone in the office, they were all thinking the same thing—the glory hogs only wanted to be involved long enough to steal their thunder.

Jinx said, "Tell 'em I said, 'Go fish.' "

Dixie grinned big. The woman loved telling people how the cow ate the cabbage. She put the receiver to her ear and addressed them in her piping soprano. "Constable Porter says when we want you, we'll ask for you."

Jinx's eyes shifted to Raven. "By the way, when we set up the meeting with the computer hacker, you're supposed to wear a provocative dress."

The man at the flower shop promised the Birds of Paradise would arrive on an upcoming flight and be ready for pick-up by Friday noon. Floral arrangements could be assembled in time for the rehearsal dinner, then transported to the First United Methodist Church for Saturday's wedding. Relieved, Raven turned her attention to a loose-leaf binder filled with nosegay prototypes and selected a bouquet of white roses and baby's breath, with a touch of purple statis to complement the bridesmaids' dresses.

Events fell into place until Raven discovered she couldn't fit her wedding gown into the BMW without crushing it. Out of ideas, she called Dell to meet her at Bridal-Wise.

"Like trying to push a polar bear through a transom," he said when he saw how much room the skirt took up. "Should've brought my pickup."

"Just figure out a way to get it into the back seat without smashing it, can you?"

With a bit of wrangling, they fit the stiff petticoat and yards of silk fabric between the floorboard and rear dash. The garment bag billowed up over the headrests like a huge marshmallow, obscuring the back windshield.

Raven followed Dell to the house. Unable to see into the front compartment of the big Chevy, she gauged his irritation from stolen glimpses into his side mirror. Ten minutes later, Dell pulled over to the curb enough to allow her to precede him into the driveway. As he wheeled in behind her, the first drops of rain splattered across the windshield.

Threatening clouds hung overhead. She hopped out of the BMW and bolted toward Dell's vehicle. Fretting in the passenger seat over whether or not to make a break for the house, she calculated their chance of success. About the time she decided to make a run for it, raindrops pelted the hood.

In seconds, the bottom fell out of the sky.

"What now?"

"We have to wait. Water spots will stain it."

"The clothes bag should protect it."

"I don't want to take any chances."

They sat in front of the house watching sheets of rain cascade over the glass. When the windows fogged up, Dell turned on the defroster.

"About the other day . . ." He fixed her with his aqua stare.

"I don't want to talk about it."

"It's because I'm not good enough for you," he said softly.

Not at all. If anything, I'm not good enough for you.

"I never meant to hurt you." She rested her hand on his knee. "It's not like I set out to fall in love with the guy. At first, I hated him."

Her initial confrontation with Tommy had almost induced a stroke. She'd grown up watching Hitchcock reruns, and the gruesome shower scene in *Psycho* left her with a particularly grim impression. Stumbling upon an intruder in the house could do that to a half-naked person. When he didn't die after she shot him, she spent the next two days plotting ways to kill him. Being handcuffed to the bed while a terrorist made himself at home had a way of putting grisly ideas into her head. Entertaining cruel fantasies made the time go by faster, but they grew more violent the longer he stuck around. She couldn't place the exact moment she'd fallen into the blue sweep of his gaze, but the night she thought he died for real filled her with unexpected sadness. And when she found him alive, she'd given herself over to him whole hog.

Seconds of silence turned into minutes, measured by the slapping of wiper blades against the glass.

Dell turned on the stereo. A country tune filtered out into their shared space. The cowboy's plaintive baritone resonated over the airwaves, telling the listener how he'd bought a one-way ticket to relationship Hell, now that the woman he loved had run off with the Devil.

As suddenly as it started, the rain tapered off. The last of the sun broke through, backlighting the clouds in a butterscotch swirl. To the east, a rainbow arced across the sky.

Dell looked her way. "Ready to brave it?"

"Yes, but make sure you lift it high enough. Don't even let it skim the ground."

"Anything you want."

She felt pretty certain he wasn't talking about the dress. "Be my friend, Dell. That's what I want. I need that more than ever."

Once inside, she trailed him upstairs, eyeballing the bottom of the garment bag. At the door to her bedroom, he scanned the area for a place to hook the hanger.

"Where do you want it?"

"Lay it across the bed for now. I haven't cleared out enough closet space to accommodate it."

Positioned across the spread, it looked like the body bag for the carnival fat man.

Dell had another take on the matter. "Kind of reminds me of a huge cocoon with a beautiful butterfly waiting to be released."

The description surprised her. Each time she considered he might not be refined enough for her, he came up with observations of sheer poetry.

"Can I see it?"

She almost said no. Modeling the dress she would wear to marry another man might pain him. And Dell must've tapped into the thoughts back-flipping through her brain, because he said, "I really want to see what you picked out."

Her skin tingled in inverse proportion to the lowering of the zipper. He helped her gather the crisp folds of silk and soft panels of lace, freeing them from the confines of their plastic wrapper.

"I bet you look like a princess."

"It's so tight in the waist, I'll be coughing blood."

His stony exterior cracked. The makings of a grin angled up one side of the brooding German's face.

"The lady at the store got impatient with me. She said my screams were scaring off the other customers." She found Dell's smile intoxicating. It felt like old times, before outside pressures took their toll on the relationship. "I have to lay off desserts between now and Saturday, or I'll never get it fastened."

"Limit yourself to rabbit food."

"It's all this cake my bridesmaids feed me at these wedding showers. I've been eating like a hog."

"I think you're gorgeous." He slipped a hand beneath the back of her hair and grazed the nape of her neck.

She should've pulled away when he massaged his fingertips into her skin. But she closed her eyes, letting the warm shiver radiate up her head and down her weary back. Unexpectedly, Dell touched a finger to her chin. Tilted her face. Parted his mouth and sucked her into the swirling vortex of his charm.

His lips grazed her ear. "One last time?"

Tiny hairs pricked her shirtsleeves. She already knew what to expect, based on their last clandestine encounter three months before: the way he called her name with great tenderness, then uttered it again as a rasping cry against her mouth. In the confined space of the Teletype room, her body had betrayed her. She sank into his embrace and responded to his brawny, unrefined cowboy moves when she should've given him the gate.

She loved Tommy.

And yet every bit of surface area Dell Teague touched on her body cried out for more. He was a real Ponce de Leon with the door to the Teletype room closed, exploring the contours and hollows of her body. Unlike Jinx, when he locked up one Friday evening five years ago, Dell hadn't cleared the desk and tugged off her silk panties and narrow-legged jeans with the skill of a caveman; his oversized hands worked more like erasers, making the fabric of her Capri pants disintegrate as he slid his fingers past the button on her waistband, down the smooth curve of her hips, inviting himself into the warm softness of her body. A regrettable lapse in judgment that returned with a vengeance each morning just before dawn.

An involuntary shudder broke the spell. "I can't."

"Don't marry him, Raven." He moved in to kiss her, soft at first, then harder. Gathered her to him and moved past her lips to her ear, then down her neck. She sank against the bed, onto the only spot her wedding gown didn't occupy. Inertia kept her from getting up.

Shouldn't be doing this.

If I cheat, I'm no better than Jinx.

Going to Hell in a hand basket.

And I don't even need a basket.

Lightheaded from Dell's kisses, Raven mistook the first chirp of the cell phone for an internal alarm going off in her head. The second unmistakable shrill brought her upright and scrambling, grappling for her purse, digging for her wireless. Ignoring Dell's irritated sigh, she thumbed the on-button, swept it to her ear and choked out a breathless hello.

"Hi babe. Can't talk long. Just letting you know I'm in Dallas—"

"Tommy?" She brought a finger to her mouth, *Shhhhhh*. "Did you say Dallas?" Surely she'd misheard him. She stuck a finger in her free ear. "*Dallas, Texas?* Where in Dallas?" Jarred by her shriek, Dell buckled his belt. "I'll come get you right now."

"That's just it. I can't see you while I'm here."

"What do you mean you can't see me?" Anger blurred her euphoria. "Why not?" Her voice climbed in volume and pitch. Jezebel, who'd concealed herself under the bed, slinked out and headed for the hall. "Let me get this straight . . . you called to say you're thirty miles away and you can't see me?" She unplugged her finger and stared at Dell with the same kind of dazed confusion a survivor stumbling out of a train wreck might have.

"We have to stay in hiding. The Libyans are still after Y-Jay."

"Libyans? But I thought—" Fury filled every pore. Her tone dropped to a lethal calm. "Is he there with you?"

"Who, Y-Jay?"

"No. Brad-fucking-Pitt. Of course Y-Jay. Put the bastard on the phone."

"She wants to talk to you." The man of her dreams passed the phone to the jerk of her nightmares.

"Hi-ya, cuz. Long time no see. What's up?"

"I've decided to kill you."

Dell's eyes went wide. Without bothering to tuck in his shirt, he zipped his Wranglers and backed toward the landing.

"I just thought you should know," she said, building on her wrath. "It's the sportsmanlike thing to do."

"It's sportsmanlike to kill me?"

"To warn you. I plan to accomplish what no one else seems to be able to do—kill you deader than a wedge. Just so you know."

Paused in the hallway, Dell kept her in the trajectory of his gaze. Wary-eyed, he followed Jezebel's lead, taking the first of thirteen steps down to the living room.

"You don't mean it," Y-Jay said.

"I do. I do mean it."

"Well that's a fine how-do-you-do. You do realize you're acting unbelievably spoiled, don't you?"

"I'm sorry. From now on, I'll try to act more believably spoiled."

"Sarcasm doesn't become you."

"No?" This triggered an eye roll on her part. She faked concern. "I'm sorry. It's just that I use caustic humor to insulate me from disappointment caused by people I truly care about."

"There you go again, sarcastic as shit."

"Let me ask you something—" she'd thought of a way to kill him but hadn't figured out how to dispose of the body "—how much do you weigh?"

"One seventy, one eighty. I dunno." He muffled the phone and started a conversation with Tommy. "Hey—do I look fat to you?"

"No, man. You look fine. Why? Do I look fat?"

"No, dude, not at all."

Typical locker room high-fiving.

Raven shouted into the mouthpiece. "Listen, you crazy son of a bitch, get back on the phone, I'm talking to you."

"Yeah. Where were we? Oh, right. One seventy-five. Why? You need my measurements in order to reserve a tux?"

"No. I need to know how many cinder blocks to pick up, for when I sink your cold, dead body in the middle of Lake Worth."

He lowered his voice in an aside meant for Tommy. "Man, she's bitchy. Sure you wanna get married?"

After a minute of discussion, the phone was returned to Tommy. "Listen, babe, we should be home in a few days."

"A few days? I'm trying to plan a wedding and you won't be home for a few more days? Now you listen to me, Tommy Greenway. . . ."

Y-Jay's shrill froze the words in her throat.

"That's them behind us. Floor it!"

In a command voice meant for Y-Jay, Tommy yelled, "Hang on, buddy."

"Is that a bridge?" Y-Jay's panic thundered all the way down to her ear drum. " 'Cause you can't go over that. Dude—what the fuck you doin'? Those are barricades."

She couldn't be sure if the wail of sirens originated inside her mind or had filtered through the receiver. But a crystal clear visual of Tommy with a white-knuckled grip on the steering wheel of a rental . . . government . . . stolen . . . car flashed into mind and stayed there.

Her cousin came back on the line.

The presence of Yucatan Jay always added a new level of terror to the equation.

"You sure you wanna marry this guy, Rave?" Words came out low and lethal. "Holy 'molé. This bridge isn't finished. Is that . . . ? Oh crap, it is, isn't it? Dude, we can't swim. . . ."

Raven intercepted Dell downstairs, beached on the leather sofa in front of the television.

He clutched the TV remote, pressing the channel selector as if dry-firing a revolver. He stopped scrolling when a "Breaking News" caption flashed onto the screen. Silhouetted against the backdrop of a car gurgling beneath the inky surface of Lake Ray Hubbard, Channel Eighteen's swarthy reporter, Garlon Harrier, spoke into the mike. A wayward lock of greasy black hair cut across his forehead like a scythe.

Grim-faced, Harrier addressed his viewers. "Dallas Police say the chase began when this bullet-riddled Pontiac—"

The cameraman panned to a beat-up, circa seventies Bonneville, where uniformed officers had three bearded men of indeterminate race bent face-down across the hood, in handcuffs.

"—fired on the sinking Volkswagen Beetle."

Zoom-in for a close-up of the VW, bobbing in the water like a float from the Jolly Green Giant's fishing reel.

Raven turned toward the kitchen.

Dell, basking in the blue flicker of late afternoon TV, upped the volume. "Don't you want to see this?"

"Not without alcohol speeding through my system." She glided a dozen steps to the refrigerator.

"It's like watching a jumper swan dive off an overpass. There's nothing you can do about it, but you can't pull your eyes away. You really oughta follow this."

She reached for an unopened bottle of Dom Perignon chilling on the bottom shelf, stripped the foil and popped the cork. Bubbles effervesced over the lip, geysering onto the granite countertop.

"If they identify a guy named Yucatan Jay among the dead, I'll pour one for you, too, and we'll celebrate."

He craned his neck to see past the dining room.

She figured he must've noticed that her face had numbed into the flat affect of a mental patient, because his next comment came out more subdued. "This isn't the man you're going to marry, is it?"

Padding back into the living room with a crystal stem in one hand and a chokehold on the neck of the champagne bottle, Raven thrust the glass out in a silent offering. He declined with a headshake. She set it on the coffee table, took a long draw from the upturned bottle, then crumpled, unladylike, into the leather wingback. Half a bottle later, her head pitched to one side.

Thick-tongued, she spoke to the lamp. "They're gonna kill 'em both."

"They? Who's they?"

"I dunno. You think he tells me stuff?"

"Doesn't he?"

She answered by way of guzzling more bubbly. "I thought I knew him," she told the silk lampshade airily, "but I dunno him at all. He's a maniac. They both are. Brothers to the Gates of Hell." She honored them with a palsied salute.

Thoughts of Tommy's survival fragmented inside her head.

If the President showed up, she wanted to be good and drunk.

Chapter Eighteen

Tuesday morning, Dorretha Bright received back-to-back phone calls from Cedric's father.

When Raven arrived at her house armed with the pared-down list of burger joints, the distraught mother barreled down the porch steps dressed and ready for the hunt.

"I think we ought to start with these seven." Raven showed her the locations.

"You're in charge." Cedric's mother held up a micro-cassette recorder. Her thumb hovered above the Play button. "You ready to hear the tape?"

She nodded.

As the car idled in the driveway, Dorretha played a recording of Joe Bright's latest threats. Her ex sounded as if he were on the verge of a psychotic break, but her son must've had a genius IQ. It was as if he knew authorities needed fresh clues to find him, and he did his part without tipping off his crazed father.

"This morning I ate a burger and fries. But I also got a milkshake 'cause I was good. Last night, Daddy said if I went straight to bed instead of watching the airplanes take off, I could have a chocolate shake for breakfast."

"That's wonderful. Do you have your own room?"

"Uh-huh."

"What can you see from your window?"

"Burger-Doodle."

In the second phone call, Joe Bright extracted an insane

trade from his ex-wife: take her own life so that Cedric could live. As soon as he saw her obituary in the paper, he'd turn the boy over to their pastor. Dorretha reminded him suicide was a sin, but that she'd think real hard on it and have an answer next time he called back. Before Joe severed the connection, she persuaded him to let her talk to Cedric one more time.

"Has he taken you to swim? The weather's awful hot."

"If I'm good, I can go this afternoon. I like the swimming pool. Someday I'm gonna be a lifeguard just like Darius."

"Who's Darius?"

"The lifeguard at the pool."

Raven rattled the page of burger locations at Cedric's mother. "What do we know so far—that he can see airplanes taking off, right? Out of these seven possibles, three are near DFW. One's close to Meacham Airport. And none near Alliance Airport. I say we eliminate Meacham first."

Cedric's mother agreed.

Raven reached beneath the driver's seat and pulled out a phone book. "I want you to call every public swimming pool run by the city and ask them if they have any lifeguards named Darius. Write down the name of the person you talk to, and the phone number. Unless Darius works at an apartment complex, I think your husband's taking him to swim at one of the parks."

"What about Joe saying I had to kill myself to spare Cedric?"

"Jinx has friends at the newspaper. Maybe we could get them to run a fake obituary in tomorrow's paper."

"They do that?"

"I have no idea."

Dorretha Bright kept busy making phone calls while Raven headed for the north side of town. Cedric's mother hit one dead end after another.

When they arrived at the first burger joint, Raven groaned. The boarded-up windows were tantamount to an invitation for rival gangs to tag the brick exterior with their colors, graffiti and slogans. The distraught woman red-penned the address off the list.

Raven pointed the snout of the big Chevy toward Loop 820.

By ten o'clock, she knew they needed reinforcements and radioed Dell. The second burger joint had three apartments within walking distance, so pulling a deputy off the street would make shorter work of casing the places.

Before they could finalize their plans, Jinx intervened. He'd set up a meeting with the Internet hacker and wanted her to break off the search and return to the office.

Dorretha Bright ended her last phone call. Tension lined her face. "What's wrong?"

"That's like asking how many grains of sand there are."

"What can I do to help?"

"Do you pray?"

Mid-morning, Raven sauntered through the door of the precinct office, heralded by the cowbell clanging overhead. It surprised her to see Dixie lounging in Georgia's chair. The two women had arranged a time-sharing plan wherein Georgia worked mornings and Dixie afternoons, yet it was Dixie seated behind the desk with an open magazine.

Alarmed, Raven said, "Georgia's not sick, is she?"

"We struck a deal." Dixie set the magazine on the blotter, opened the top desk drawer and pulled out a cellophane of coconut Sno-Balls. "Thanks to your wedding, she's back on the *Starving for Jesus* diet; I offered to come in a few hours early every day this week, so she can swim laps at the 'Y.' "

A nice, unselfish thing to do and Raven said so.

The secretary snorted. "Not really. Georgia hocked her soul. Now that she's obligated to me, I'll see to it she babysits my juvenile delinquent while I play Bingo the next four Thursdays. If you'd ever met the little thug, you'd know we're not talking about an even trade." She tore the wrapper off the Sno-Balls, picked one up and examined it against the light. "Last time I bought a package of these out of the vending machine, it had ants."

She stuffed the whole thing into her mouth and returned her attention to the high-gloss magazine. It lay face-open to an article: *How to make your man scream in bed.*

Raven leaned closer. Not that she and Tommy needed any help in the boudoir—the man must've been born with some sort of internal loran that gave him the ability to steer it to port in the dark. Still, she tried to read upside down.

"Don't bother. I could've written better advice." Dixie listed to one side and retrieved a powder compact from her purse. "Want to make your man scream in bed? Set fire to the mattress." She snapped open the plastic case and scrutinized her reflection. Her tongue moved over her lips like a wet mop, eliminating the last of the coconut evidence.

Nearby, Jinx sat at Mickey's desk fielding a phone call. He gave Raven the once-over, followed by a disappointed headshake. "Swear to God, Tarrant County's nothing but an insane asylum without locked doors," he said, making a big production of slamming down the telephone in a county employee's ear before they did it to him.

"Problems with the auditor's office?" Dixie said directly to the mirror. She traced the edge of her lip liner with a copper-tipped finger, then snapped the compact shut and fixed Jinx with a bovine stare. "When're you going to learn that the auditor's office is like the IRS? When you have a problem with the IRS, you don't want to bury your head in the sand because the IRS owns the beach. Same thing with the auditor. If you want money for a fleet of new cars, you've gotta do some serious sucking up."

"It wasn't the auditor's office. Looks like I'm gonna have to take Ivy's Taser away."

"You authorized Ivy to carry a stun-gun?" Raven's voice shot up in alarm. "What's wrong with you?"

"She asked if it'd be all right after she had the altercation with that toilet-brush-wielding schizophrenic last month. Apparently she didn't understand the it was to be used on prisoners, not to move to the head of the license tag line."

"I can see where that might be a gray area," Dixie deadpanned.

He shifted his glare from Dixie to Raven. "Where's the sexy dress?" He gave the powder blue linen slacks and matching shirt a dim once-over. "The hacker wants to see you in something provocative. Only way that's gonna happen is if you trade that top for a wet T-shirt."

Raven flat-ironed the deal. What could he do . . . give her a bruising disciplinary review for not being a team player? Fat-lotta-good that threat would do. She'd become immunized to his tyranny the minute Tommy said she could quit work, and make little Tommys.

"I'm wearing this. Get over it."

With a world-weary expression riding on his face, Jinx stalked back to his office.

At wit's end, she placed her arm on Ivy's desk and rested her head on it. Physically, she was sitting at Ivy's desk, but in her mind, she was a world away, reliving that Colorado afternoon when Tommy nibbled his way down her naked body and pushed his tongue past the tender folds of her skin. She could almost taste his salty kiss when he came up for air, before he guided himself into her deeply . . . thoroughly . . .

with a heat and passion she hadn't felt since . . .

Dell.

. . . when he took his mouth to her and sucked the memory of Jinx Porter right out of her head—for the moment anyway.

She had no inkling how long she'd dozed, only that she sensed a sudden drop in cabin pressure. She roused herself, half-expecting to see oxygen masks descend from the ceiling.

Shadows fell across the desk. From her lopsided angle face-down on the blotter with drool seeping out from one corner of her mouth, she viewed the interloper in stages—the scuffed toes of his sneakers, an electronic monitor strapped to one fat, hairy ankle, furry shins with scars on his dimpled knees, and finally, camouflage fatigues that had been butchered into shorts. A hole-y, FU UK T-shirt showed off his full complement of tattoos, including the one of Anna Nicole Smith he could make belly dance by flexing his muscle.

She tilted her face.

Amos.

Shoving food into his mouth like a chili-cheese coney through a woodchipper.

The last time Raven saw Ivy's Ritalin-ingesting son, he was hotfooting it down the fire escape, out the emergency door of Our Lady of Mercy, after he copped a feel under her hospital gown.

A juvenile judge had sentenced the teenaged lummox to shock probation in the Texas Youth Commission for his part in the Odie "Straight-Eight" Oliver melee, and it looked like he'd been released to serve the remaining nine months deferred adjudication in the free world. He'd packed on at least twenty pounds. Jail food and indolence tended to do that to an inmate. Even kiddie jail.

Now, here he was, with his face still pimply and one ear pierced—probably to externally flaunt his sexuality. When she couldn't recall if it was the left ear or the right ear that meant gayness, she remembered this was Amos, and gayness be damned, everything he did was just plain fucked-up.

While the rest of the deputies were getting over their collective shock, Jinx strolled in from the back office sipping a Coca-Cola. He took one look at Amos and carbonated water spewed out his nose.

"What're you doing here?" He cut his eyes at Raven, and they exchanged frown-encrypted messages. *Wasn't he issued a criminal trespass warning to keep him out of this office?*

"Don't holler at me, dude, you're the one set up this meeting." He wiped his hands over the front of his "T."

"What meeting?" His eyes thinned into slits. Realization dawned. "*You're* the hacker?"

Amos mimed a grin. Slitted eyes swiveled in their sockets. "Hey. What's up, Raven?"

Jinx's neck veins plumped. "Where's your mother?"

"Draining the radiator, dude." Amos pointed to the bathroom.

The top of Jinx's head turned redder than a Kojak light. Made it hard to tell whether he'd been out in the sun without a hat or if Amos caused his blood pressure to shoot into the danger zone.

But Amos' much-deserved reputation as a junior hacker, breaking into the county's mainframe and wreaking havoc on the constables' arrest stats, took precedence in an investigation with a child's life at stake.

Raven felt her cheeks blaze and realized she was staring. An idea flashed into mind. "How easy would it be to hack into someone's computer if you had a name from an instant message and knew the owner's Internet provider?"

"Fifth Amendment, dudette. Right to remain silent."

She rolled her chair away from the desk. Ivy would be

coming out of her second office soon, and she needed to strike a deal with Amos before his mother could queer it.

"This isn't a set-up. We need help with a case."

Amos spoke directly to her breasts. "What's in it for me?"

In an effort to redirect his focus, she made a "V" with her fingers and pointed them at her eyes. "Focus up here, *Eric Cartman*. What do you want?"

"I hear you're getting married."

Fist to hip. "Maybe. What's it to you?"

"I wanna be in your wedding."

Like that's gonna happen.

"All the spots are taken. Sorry. But I'll buy you a music CD if you want. Or a DVD movie."

"I like Freddie Kruger. Do you have a ring-bearer?"

"Too old."

"Head usher?"

"Got one."

"Groomsman?"

Not no, but hell no.

"Forget it. We'll treat you to the all-you-can-eat buffet out of the petty cash fund."

"Can I watch you get dressed?"

"Dream on, you little extortionist."

Amos braced his arms across his chest in a standoff. "Then what do I get out of it?"

Raven thought hard. What did she have that Amos wanted, that she'd be willing to give? In an instant, she came up with the answer.

"If you help us, there's a chance I might actually be able to like you someday."

Ivy wandered in from the bathroom, hitching up her slacks. "Looks like a football huddle out here. What's all this about?"

Jinx scowled. "It's about stuffing eight pounds of crap in a five-pound bag, that's what it's about."

He stared at Raven as if she might be the weirdest exhibit floating around in the jar at *Ripley's Believe It or Not!* They exchanged guarded looks, then adjourned to the hall as if by mutual agreement.

Conversation took place behind the glass, eyes alternately flickering between Amos and each other with the speed of a Stars game.

"Have you lost your mind?" Jinx groused. "We don't negotiate with terrorists. That, and the fact we'd probably be parties to committing a federal crime. That's all we need—Longley and Hough, charging us with criminal enterprise under the Ricco statute. Or mail fraud. Mail fraud's the easiest charge in the world to make. The biggest gangsters in American history went to the clink on mail fraud."

She sensed him wimping out.

"You're gonna run this by the DA, aren't you?" She held up her hand without giving him a chance to dissuade her with more talk of doing time in the federal pokey. "Today's Tuesday. Magick's birthday is Thursday, and so is summer solstice. If I'm right, and Fleck Standish plans to offer her as a satanic sacrifice, we can't fiddle-fart around for a mamby-pamby ruling."

"Don't you remember what you learned, day one, in the police academy? *Fruits of the crime, tools of the crime?* We should at least ask for a clarifying opinion."

"I admit this looks like a plum, dropped in our laps."

"Plum?" His voice went strident. "This isn't a plum, it's a stinking watermelon suppository about to get jammed up my butt. Any more of these so-called plums and we're likely to get indicted. Besides, if it ever came out in court that we did this—hacked into her computer—we'd lose that evidence as fruit of the crime."

"For God's sake, Jinx, there's no time to run it by the DA's Office." Not that he wasn't right, of course, but attempting to keep the fruits of the crime secret would be like trying to flush an elephant down the toilet. Maybe they couldn't make a criminal case stick against Fleck Standish if anything shady about the investigation came out in court, but all things being equal, preventing Magick's death made good reason to skirt procedure. "You know how prosecutors are. First they'll analyze the crap out of it; then they'll call the Attorney General's Office for a ruling. Only they'll get that stupid recorded phone menu that'll keep them orbiting the cosmic phone system for hours—possibly days; and assuming they do get through and speak to a live body, then the AG'll have to call John Edward or James Van Praagh or Sylvia Browne to channel the spirits of Dear Abby and Ann Landers for an opinion." Fury expended, her shoulders slumped. "I say we do it."

"What we'll *do* is day-for-day life sentences."

Raven thumbed at the door. "Look at him in there with his feet propped up on the desk—we're dealing with the poster boy for the failure of the probation system."

"Amos'll use an entrapment defense and get off scot-free."

"No dice. Amos approached you; you didn't approach him. All we're doing is giving the kid a venue to commit the crime."

"So you admit it's a crime?"

She didn't trust herself to speak.

For the longest time, he stood still and mute, with the dumbfounded look of someone who'd staggered into the ER, poleaxed. "Well, fuck it," he finally said, pressing the wrinkles out of his forehead with a firm hand. "Let's see what Ivy's hulking recidivist can do."

It turned out Lyrica Prudhomme didn't have a firewall.

By four o'clock, they were in.

"Waddaya know?" Amos shoved a sausage finger at the computer screen. "See the little smiley face?" He pointed out the tiny yellow icon while everyone except his mother looked on. Ivy had commandeered Jinx's office and was calling lawyers to get the jump on defending the Ricco charge. "Blademaker's online. Let's see if he—"

Up popped up an instant message.

"—has anything to say."

Blademaker: We're here. How's the heat?

Raven stared at the pulsing cursor. "I don't think he means the climate. He's talking about The Heat. He wants to know if the cops are after him."

She scooted up even with Amos and hip-checked him by proxy with the upholstered arm of her chair. He inched aside, and she sat with her fingertips hovering above the keyboard. "Do I have to type in *Sorceress* anywhere?"

"No, babe, you *are* Sorceress. The way this works: it's like you're sitting in the woman's house, using her computer. You *are* her."

Her heart skipped. "So I can say pretty much what I want and he'll think it's her?" she said, double-checking the terms.

"Yeah. You smell good enough to eat. What's that perfume you're wearing?"

"Back off."

"How about a ride on the baloney pony?"

Dell, who usually acted as her first line of defense, slipped into view. He towered over Amos, shrinking him with a scowl.

"You make one more lewd comment to her again, I'll snatch you up and jail you so fast your tattoos will have to catch a cab to meet you there."

Amos did everything but roll over and play dead.

Raven's fingers swarmed over the keyboard. She typed: *Pretty uncomfortable here, but nothing I can't handle. U need money?*

Blademaker: U got some?

Raven typed, *How much U need?*

Blademaker: How much U got?

She looked to Jinx for help. The petty cash fund never contained over fifty dollars. Coffee money. Filters. Bottled water that sent huge bubbles gurgling up every time they filled the disposable white cone cups. Air freshener for the bathroom. The occasional get-well, get-your-ass-back-to-work card. And rarest of all—sympathy cards. Nobody at the county much gave a damn about anybody else. Like filing income taxes, the only way out for some employees was death or disease.

"Try to find out where he's headed," Jinx said, more to the computer monitor than to the deputies. "Tell him you have a thousand dollars. That you'll wire it to him. See if he'll give us an address."

He said *us*.

Raven smiled inwardly. So he planned to take the fall with her.

She typed, *Have 1000 on me. Where R U?*

Blademaker: Where I said I'd be.

"That bitch!" Jinx. With outrage on his face and blood in his eye. "She knew all along."

Raven fought the smirk angling up her face. "I'm not saying anything," she said, prolonging the agony in a singsong, *told-you-so* voice.

A disconcerting thought jolted her. She jerked her fingers from the keyboard as if she'd been scorched. "Uh-oh. He backed me into a corner. I can't very well say I forgot. Think, Jinx. What do I do? What do I tell him?"

"Why not give him your cellular number?" Amos. Lazily picking at a scab on his knee, looking bored.

Everyone looked over in a collective shift and gave Ivy's son the hairy eyeball.

"Brilliant." Jinx.

Raven's stomach went hollow. She did a panicky review of their options. The last thing she wanted was Fleck Standish calling her. Probably couldn't pull the wool over his eyes, anyway, since she hadn't spent enough time with Lyrica Prudhomme to get down the proper speech inflections. Without a firm grip on the true nature of that relationship, it would be hard to pass herself off as the Wiccan.

"Waddaya have to lose?" Amos said. "Tell him not to call the house 'cause you're afraid the phone's tapped. Have him call the wireless if he needs anything."

Jinx gave her the green light.

She typed, *Best not call house N case of more heat. Here's a safe number, 24-7.* She pounded out the ten-digit number, moved the cursor to the Send box and clicked.

The instant message to Standish shifted upward, into the conversation box.

A minute went by.

Raven's heart pounded, triple time. "Busted," she whispered, as if by not announcing her fear too loudly, they might get a reprieve.

"Ask how Magick is. Ask him where to wire the money. Tell him you lost the address if you have to." Jinx's voice went strident. "Just do it."

Raven stabbed out a new message: *How's M?*

Blademaker: Ready for her BD.

Sorceress: Need location to send $.

Blademaker: Do wire X-fer.

Sorceress: Where 2?

Activity faltered.

Answer me, she commanded him telepathically. To her colleagues, she said, "Swear to God, I may stroke out if he doesn't respond."

Blademaker: I'll get back 2 U.

For effect, Raven typed: *Doorbell. Looks like the heat's on. Call tonight w/ info. How long B 4 I C U?*

Blademaker: I'll send you a pic when I'm N Canada.

A red message popped up on the screen. Blademaker had logged off.

"Wow," Jinx said. "That was close. Now all we have to do is wait 'til he calls you with an address, or a bank account number. Soon as we know what town he's in, we can contact the nearest agency and put him under surveillance."

But Raven wasn't listening. Chills swarmed her arms, as if an ant farm staked a claim to her body.

Only Jinx seemed to notice. "What's wrong?"

She carefully modulated her voice to conceal her worst fear. "This had better work."

"It will."

"No, Jinx." Her mouth trembled with the effort of speech. "Didn't you read what he wrote?"

Jinx blinked. Oblivious.

"He didn't say he'd send her a picture when *they're* in Canada . . . he said he'd send her a picture when *he* got to Canada. Singular, not plural." Her voice dissolved to a whisper. "And the reason Magick won't be with him is because she'll be dead."

Chapter Nineteen

By six o'clock Tuesday evening, Raven had done enough running around to drive a lizard crazy. She rounded the corner to her house with thoughts of a quick dip in the pool and a pint of Ben and Jerry's on her mind. But when she saw Cézanne and Duty parked at the curb, she remembered they still had place cards to make for her wedding guests. God forbid Ivy should find herself seated at the dinner table next to Dixie and Georgia. Be like tossing a grenade in a henhouse.

While the women sat at the table with calligraphy pens, hand-lettering blank card stock, Duty brushed Jezebel with a pet comb.

"What's wrong with yo' cat?"

Tufts of fur came out like cheap cotton batting pulling apart.

"It's not my cat."

Cézanne's eyes glittered *Yeah, right,* but Raven ignored her. She poised her pen above the next card, and appraised Duty through slitted eyes.

"You really know Voodoo?"

Cézanne went stiff. "We don't like to talk about that."

But Duty perked up. Let go of the cat and beamed. "I know Voodoo, that I do. I can cast a curse that'll make the *pop* go out of a man's weasel—can make it retract so deep it'll look like a turtle head," she gamely informed them.

Cézanne fought the beginnings of a smile.

"Couple o' hand moves . . . a little spell . . . I can make him pee razor blades." She sat cross-legged on the floor, looking pleased with herself, as if she'd done it a hundred times and refined it into an art form. "Not *real* razor blades. But them feeling it is about the same as them doing it."

Raven nodded. Maybe Duty really could whip up a hex that would take the angle right out of a man so fast it'd leave him cross-eyed. "That's scary," she said in barely more than a whisper.

Her mind went through a series of mental gymnastics. Put the whammy on Joe Bright . . . put the double-whammy on Standish. Maybe even throw in a little hocus-pocus to disable Lyrica Prudhomme.

Cézanne's words came down like the final curtain. "She can't practice Voodoo if she lives with me."

Duty held up a finger. Wagged it at no one in particular. Spoke to some invisible presence on the ceiling.

"I never liked the use of that word 'practice.' Ain't no practice to it. I can do it and that's that. 'Practice' makes it sound like I'm no good . . . like I haven't refined my craft; and my gramma Corinthia saw to it we Devilrows are the best at Voodoo in this here state. Maybe second only to Marie Laveau, back in Louisiana."

"Marie Laveau's dead," said Cézanne.

"That's whatchoo think." With a pout of defensiveness, she turned to Raven and brightened. "Anyway, I ain't practicing. I'm doin' it for real."

"*Practicing* is merely an expression of speech that describes one's calling," Cézanne explained. "Like a practicing attorney. Or a doctor practicing medicine."

"They use *practicing* to describe doctors and lawyers 'cause half of 'em don't know what they're doin'. How come they's the only ones needin' malpractice insurance?"

"Do you realize how obnoxious you sound?"

"I'm a kid. That's how I'm s'posed to be." Duty jutted her chin at Raven. "Me?—I could make a spell for you. Whose dick you want to rot off?" Her eyes took on a speculative gleam.

Cézanne slapped her pen down on the placemat. "I said no Voodoo. And I'm in charge."

"Maybe I got a little somethin' for you, Miz Zan," Duty scolded, then grinned and winked to show she didn't mean it. She got up from the floor, moved to Raven's side and slung a thin arm around her shoulders. "But let's talk about you. Whatchoo need me to do? Want me to have somebody killed?"

Cézanne called a halt to the discussion. "Don't you go making work for me. We haven't solved the murder next door yet."

Duty gave her a dismissive hand wave. "You'll know by Friday."

"That sounds a bit optimistic, since we don't have a single lead. What you really ought to be putting your energy into is cleaning your room."

"You got that cigar. Oughta test it for DNA. And about my room—what do I look like? Napoleon's mule? Can't we get a maid?"

"You're supposed to be the maid."

"I'm way too talented to be used as a domestic. . . . Woman as successful as you oughta have a housekeeper to clean for both of us." She stifled a yawn with the back of her hand. "Whatchoo want five days before yo' wedding, Miz Raven? Say the word and I'll give it to you as a gift."

What she really wanted was for Joe Bright to pee razors, have to go to the ER and give Cedric the opportunity to escape. For Fleck Standish's pecker to fall off so he'd have to form a search party to find it, and Magick would turn six before he knew what day it was. And Jinx . . . now that was a tough one. Maybe just make Jinx's dick droop for the next couple of weeks . . . enough for him to deny the feminine wiles of undeserving women such as Sigrid Pierson and Lyrica Prudhomme.

"Ouch!" Raven's scalp smarted with a sting.

"Something wrong, Miz Raven?"

"You pulled my hair." She mashed her fingers against the barb of pain, then gathered her long tresses and repositioned them.

"Really? Sorry, Miz Raven, I sho' 'nuff didn't mean to."

The girl gazed down in maroon-eyed innocence. With her hand hidden behind her back and a strange smile tipping up at the corners, she breezed out of sight.

Cézanne mouthed, "Uh-oh."

Raven arched an eyebrow, *Now what?*

"I don't like it," the maid of honor continued in a half-whisper, half-lip sync. "She's up to no good."

"Don't be so hard on her. I'm sure she didn't intend—"

"You don't know her like I do," Cézanne hissed. "I've seen her bend spoons using sheer concentration. One minute they're sterling silver eating utensils. Next minute—" she crooked her finger downward "—it's like a man coming off Viagra."

The detective moved in closer. She grasped Raven's arm in a confidential squeeze and lowered her voice to a conspiratorial whisper. "Once, I made the mistake of confiding in her. Told her my secretary embarrassed me in front of the Chief. The next day the woman was standing in front of the PD waiting to cross the street. When the light changed, she stepped off the curb and her skirt fell off. Walked right out of it. Got halfway through the crosswalk before she noticed the horn honks and finger-pointing were for her." Periwinkle eyes sparked. "That's right—Deuteronomy. She'd swiped a pencil from my secretary's desk and snapped it in half. Don't ask me how she does it. I don't want to know and I don't want to be an accomplice."

Raven debunked the story as coincidence and superstition.

"No, no, no. See, that's what she wants you to think. Then you let your guard down and *Wham!* you're calling in sick because your left testicle's swelled up to the size of a grapefruit. It happened to one of my guys. He poked fun at her when she told him not to fly to Jamaica. You won't believe this, but the plane crashed on takeoff. If he hadn't been home with his nuts on ice, he'd have died in that crash."

Abruptly, Raven's stomach clenched. "Where's the cat?"

They exchanged awkward looks. She pushed back from the table and broke for the kitchen. Empty bowl. No cat.

Cézanne called out from the dining room. "What's wrong?"

"Jinx thinks Jezebel may be about to have kittens." She rushed into the hall, to a downstairs bedroom with Berber carpet. Got on all fours and looked under the bed. No Jezebel. Saw the second guest bedroom was closed and headed for the stairs.

At the top of the landing, she glanced down into the dining room and saw Duty clutching her head like she was experiencing the Godzilla of all migraines.

"What's wrong?"

"Uh . . . you about to find out," the girl said in a far-away voice.

Raven dashed into her bedroom, where she'd hooked the gown over the ledge above the doorjamb to her closet.

Only the gown wasn't hanging.

It was on the floor.

Defiled by Jezebel, who couldn't have cared less. Nesting in the middle of it, licking the bloody coat of kitten number three.

Once Channel Eighteen aired Garlon Harrier's interview exclusive with Jinx, the phone lines opened up and crackpots started phoning in tips.

One call stood out from the others.

A representative of the Mueller Institute, a church-based group that tracked satanic cults, had information that might prove helpful. The United States was dotted with deadly cults: dabblers in Satanism as well as serious practitioners. The Mueller Institute had powerful people in their organization: senators and legislators whose children had been kidnapped or murdered by satanic cults; men and women with more cash than leaves on trees; even an alleged member of the Mafia. They'd be happy to help in any way—just say the word, and they'd spring into action—provided they knew Standish's general location.

Around five o'clock Tuesday afternoon, Jinx headed home for a quick bite. He'd planned to microwave a couple of leftover barbequed pork ribs and pop the top on a glass-bottled Coca-Cola, but when he angled into a parking space near the front lawn, the sight of Agnes Loudermilk took his appetite away.

Before he'd left the Château Du Roy that morning, he stuck his head out the apartment door and looked the length of the balcony. All clear. As he tiptoed across the decking to the stairs, Agnes's form took shape in the dark. Enveloped in the vapors of cigarette smoke, she'd positioned herself at the point of the L-shaped balcony, the welded, mitered edge Jinx thought of as the Crow's Nest. Her son sat in the chair next to hers with his wide-set eyes intent on the stream of cars down below. When Jinx realized he couldn't creep past unnoticed, he did what any man would do: bounded down the steps like a scalded ape.

Agnes's eyes slewed around.

She rattled a tin can at him.

"Nuts?" Her mouth split into a diabolical grin.

Before he could tell her they played hell with diverticulitis, she said, "I love 'em. Gobble 'em up whenever I can," and fell into a fit of laughter. The boy, as Jinx liked to think of him even though they were probably close to the same age, shot her a quick glance and said, "Oh, Mama, put a lid on it."

Now twelve hours later, the chain-smoking hag paced back and forth along the balcony looking like one of the three witches of *Macbeth*, with her rag-tag bathrobe skimming the deck and her pleated face enveloped in a gray haze. A stale breeze sent the fabric aflutter; a flap of cloth caught on the wrought-iron railing, revealing varicose veins as plump as garden hoses. When she faded around the corner, Jinx actually thought he could climb the stairs unnoticed.

Halfway to the top, his stomach rolled over.

Agnes floated into view. Flyaway gray hair snaked around her head like Medusa's serpents. She headed for the railing with a predatory glint in her eyes.

For several seconds, she leered. As a precaution, he glanced down to check his fly. When he made eye contact again, she addressed him in the sultry tone of a vixen.

"I've looked in the glass and seen you at the computer . . ."

Agnes Loudermilk, a window peeper? A disturbing thought to say the least.

". . . I've seen you sitting around in your 'Looms before, so I want to ask you a question about sex perverts."

"Excuse me?" He stiffened, wondering where this was all going.

"Isn't there a list of sex perverts on the computer? I thought there was a way to check."

He gave her a wary nod. "There's a database."

"Good, because I think I'd like to look one or two of 'em up. How many do you we have living here?"

He looked her dead in the eye. "Only one that I know of."

"There's a couple of dildos around here I've been watching." Agnes took one last pull on her cigarette and flicked the butt over the railing. She shook another one out of the pack, took a lighter from her pocket and fired it up. "There's an old boy next to you, walks with his hand in his pocket and it isn't even cold. And that son of mine? They say he's got to register the rest of his life. He didn't know how old that girl was."

"Statutory rape is a strict liability offense."

"Whatever that means." Agnes took a long drag, letting the smoke snake out through her nose.

"It means it doesn't matter whether he knew how old she was. It's like speeding. You either are or you aren't. They're either legal or they're not."

Agnes looked him over, squinty-eyed. "Is it hot enough for you?"

Jinx took a couple more steps. "Yeah. I suppose it got pretty hot today."

From his place on the stairs, he could see straight through her robe thanks to the raw, heartless rays of the afternoon sun. It appeared Agnes Loudermilk had strayed from her apartment without underpants. Apparently Mr. Barber, paralyzed with fear, also noticed there was nothing covering the waterfront. He stood anchored on the sidewalk, entranced, staring up with his face molded into a grotesque caricature of itself.

Agnes let out a maniacal laugh. "Did you get any relief?"

She doubled over and swatted her knee. Drew up her leg and reared back in a rollicking chuckle. Almost induced a couple of heart attacks with her brazen, earthy shamelessness.

He sensed the conversation heading in an unseemly direction and trotted up the remaining steps. At the top of the landing, he groped his pocket for the key chain.

"Can you feel 'em?" she called out after him. "Are they still there?"

Jinx picked up his stride. After a quick fumble, he shook out his house key and jammed it into the lock.

"Didja get any on your hands?"

As he hustled inside, he heard her going after Mr. Barber. "Whatsa matter with you? How come you're walking funny? Is it binding? You got a case of spoonleg? You know what that is, don'tcha? You pee and the last spoonful goes down your leg."

Jinx closed off the rest of Agnes's indignities with the slamming of the door.

Inside the apartment, he flipped through the Yellow Pages. Once he made a list of commercial airliners operating out of DFW Airport, he enlisted the help of a DFW Police Sergeant. By seven o'clock that evening, all flights had been checked. Fleck Standish's name didn't appear on the passenger list for any of the carriers departing DFW, and no one could recall seeing a man traveling with a young girl.

He faxed a copy of Judge Masterson's Writ to a reservation agent at Dallas Love Field. If Standish had booked a flight on Southwest Airlines, he'd know about it soon enough. Before making a last-ditch drive to Meacham Airport to see if Standish had chartered a plane, he decided to check out the Greyhound Bus Station.

The bus station was located across from the Convention Center in downtown Fort Worth, where winos dotted the landscape. Inside the building, bewildered travelers from an incoming bus headed for pay phones and restrooms. Jinx sauntered up to the ticket counter with a copy of Fleck Standish's driver's license picture in hand. None of the employees admitted to seeing Standish, but the regular clerk was in the back office eating. If Jinx didn't mind waiting, someone would fetch him.

"Fine by me." The Coca-Cola he chug-a-lugged back at the Château Du Roy seemed to go right through him. With a "Be right back," he excused himself to the restroom.

The place had emptied out, except for a closed door to one of the stalls. Instead of glimpsing a pair of trousers bunched around the ankles, Jinx's eyes riveted on a pair of women's heels, pointed toward the commode.

At first glance, he thought he'd stumbled in on a female prostitute giving sexual favors. Or a male prostitute transvestite—a gump.

He felt the small of his back for the handcuffs looped through his belt. Pulled out his badge and waited to see who and how many came out. A loud flush echoed off the walls. As the door swung open, Jinx flashed his shield.

"Jinx!" The crow-in-heat screech reverberated through the room.

The female turned out to be Glen Lee Spence.

It was an "Ah-ha" moment.

Rouged and girdled, Glen Lee minced out with one hand crammed down the front of his skirt in a struggle to pull up his pantyhose. He tossed his head and his ponytail fell down his back in a strawberry blond cascade. Chartreuse platform shoes strapped tight around his ankles gave him trouble, and he ended up leaning against the metal door while he regained his balance. His low-riding, black vinyl skirt, held snug above his hips by a chain-link belt, shimmered with the remnants of sex. Naturally thin lips, made to appear fuller with the use of dark liner, were smeared crimson.

"What the hell are you doing? And don't try to tell me you have legitimate business here." Jinx stomped over with arrest on his mind. Without preliminary, he banged open the stall door, half-expecting to find someone cowering inside.

Empty.

Glen Lee used his haughty voice, the one he treated residents of the Château Du Roy to when he and the Munsch brothers fought over evening gowns in the courtyard. "Last time I checked, this was a public place. I am the public."

A scraggly-headed young man about twenty or so poked his head inside the door as if he were looking for someone. His easy smile, meant for Glen Lee, faded as soon as he saw the stainless steel handcuffs dangling loosely from Jinx's fingertips.

When he didn't high-tail it out of there, Jinx yelled, "Take a hike."

Alone with Glen Lee, Jinx scowled. "I oughta arrest you."

"For what? I only came in here to drain the lizard."

"Bullshit. You came here trolling for gays. Aren't you supposed to be HIV-positive? What you're doing is a felony."

"Taking a piss is a felony?" Glen Lee batted his luxuriously mascaraed lashes. "Really, Jinx. Get a life."

"Knowingly having sex with someone when you have AIDS is a felony."

"I'm not here to have sex."

"No?"

"No. That's just your evil mind working overtime. Besides, Jinx, you may not know it, but ever since I got my boobs, I don't even think about sex any more. Like most females, I am beyond that."

"Obviously you never met Agnes Loudermilk."

"That dried-up old crab cake?" Glen Lee flip-flopped his wrist to make a point. "Honey, if I were you, I'd avoid that nasty thing like the plague." As if he could read minds, he glanced down at his red-lacquered talons and assumed a superior tone. "You can't arrest me, Jinx. I haven't done anything."

"Only because I stumbled in before you could actually commit a crime. I might not be able to arrest you this time, but I can damned sure make life uncomfortable for you."

"Maybe we can make a deal."

"I don't negotiate with terrorists. How often do you come down here—tell the truth."

"I'm offended. You think I'd lie to you." Glen Lee gave the stale air a self-righteous sniff. "I may be a convicted robber, but I am not a liar."

"Answer the stinking question."

"Once or twice a week. Coming to the bus station isn't a crime."

"Coming *at* the bus station is."

"There you go again thinking I'm . . . how did you say? . . . trolling for sex? Not that it's any of your business, Jinx, but I'm here to pick up a package."

Jinx's eyes coolly narrowed. "What kind of package?"

"Don't bother calling in the drug dogs. I came here to pick up a dress to wear to Raven's wedding next Saturday."

A laughable thought. "You're invited to Raven's wedding?"

"I'm sure she meant to invite us, Jinx," he said, including the Munsch brothers in on the deal. "We just haven't received our invitations yet. It's the damned post office. They lose things. For all I know, my invitation's floating around in the Dead Letter Office."

"You're not invited to Raven's wedding. Besides—"

words rushed out before he could rein them in, "—Raven's not getting married."

"Not getting married?" Glen Lee went into a swoon. "Poor baby. What happened? Did they break up? She's probably a wreck."

Jinx did some serious backpedaling. "They didn't break up. As far as I know, the wedding's still on. But that doesn't mean she'll go through with it. I know Raven. Once she gets a gutful, it's over."

Glen Lee responded with a harsh lecture. Jinx had no right talking about Raven that way—after all she'd done for him. Besides, if he hadn't taken up with Loose-Wheel Lucille, they'd probably still be together. "If you don't like what you see, Jinx, take a good, hard look in the mirror and do something about it." Abruptly, he changed the subject. "So I'm free to go?"

"You're free to go. But I'm warning the employees about you."

"Listen, Jinx, I was thinking . . . since you're here, could you wait for me to claim my package and give me a ride home?"

"Absolutely not."

"But it's a rough neighborhood once the sun goes down. I could get rolled."

"Occupational hazard." As the dejected transsexual swished toward the door on wobbly feet, a powerful thought occurred to Jinx. "Wait a minute. Come back here."

Glen Lee whipped around. Steadied himself against a sink. "Are you giving me a ride, after all?"

"No."

"What?" Hand to hip, he vamped a pose. "You gonna read me my rights?"

"What is it with you people?" Jinx thought back to Venita

Standish asking the same thing. "Do you just sit around all day watching cop shows?"

"What do you want, Jinx? Unlike you, I have a life. And at the moment, I have a package to pick up."

"When's the last time you came down here?"

Glen Lee regarded him with a squint. "Friday evening. What's it to you?"

On a whim, Jinx strode over and showed him Standish's photo. "Ever seen this man?"

The transsexual leaned in for a closer look. He reached for the flyer and held it up to the light, studying the details through an intense gaze. "Yeah, I remember him." Blue eyes, heavily shadowed, glittered under the fluorescents.

Poker-faced, Jinx reclaimed the picture. "What time did you see him?"

Glen Lee stared at a distant point in space. He put a glossy fingernail to one corner of his lips and pressed a dent into his skin. "Four o'clock. Maybe five. I just know it was before six. I have to be home by six." Smoothing a stray hair from his face, he appealed to Jinx in earnest. "You won't say anything about this to Gerald and Harold, will you? Because they think I'm independently wealthy, and if they knew I got my ball gowns from a thrift store in New Jersey, I'd never live it down."

The disclosure baffled him. "That's what you're bothered about? You're a convicted armed robber, you're HIV-positive and you're worried the Munsch brothers might find out you buy secondhand clothes?"

"I am not HIV-positive." Veins plumped up near the drag queen's temples. "I only made up that story when I got my boobs and my estrogen level changed. To discourage unattractive men from stalking me. As for my conviction, I never pulled a gun on that store detective—it was lipstick. How many times do I have to say it? I don't care what he testified to."

Yeah, yeah, yeah. Heard it all before.

Indignance be damned, Glen Lee might hold the crowbar to breaking the Standish case wide open. "I'll keep your secret, but you need to do something for me."

"Oh?" Mistrust tinged his voice. He noticed one breast about to do a Janet Jackson and stuffed it back under his tank top. "And just what do I need to do for you?"

Jinx didn't like his tone. Smokin' mad, he fought the urge to take a swing. To knock those estrogen-enlarged breasts onto the chest of some flat chick, and that downy blond chin halfway up his nostrils.

He rattled the flyer. "Was he alone?"

"Really, Jinx, you don't have to get huffy."

A couple of west Texas cowboys strutted in, and Glen Lee tried to get their attention by shimmy-shaking his tits. Honestly, the freak didn't have the sense God gave a billy goat.

Jinx badged them. "It's a guy."

One of them asked if Jinx wanted them to help beat him up.

"Scram." Glen Lee's voice dropped an octave. "Can't you see we're talking business?"

They left without using the facility.

He regained his feminine side. "No, Jinx. He was not alone. He was traveling with a little girl about yea-high." He measured a distance where his hand came even with the bolt piercing his belly button.

Eyewitness accounts didn't always pan out. Jinx decided to test Glen Lee's story.

"Was she wearing a dress? A frilly pink dress with puffy sleeves and a butt bow in back, with ruffles on the bottom and lace on the collar?"

Glen Lee fanned off the notion with hand wave. "No, silly. She was dressed in overalls with a striped, short sleeve shirt. With her hair cut short like a boy's. But he was with a little girl."

"How can you be sure the kid wasn't a boy?"

"Really, Jinx. I have a discerning eye for men." He glanced around, restless. "So does that help?"

"Where'd you see them?"

"He brought her in here. Well, dragged her, more like. She looked scared. And he slapped her hard across the face when she tried to pull away."

The air thinned.

"How do you know? Did you see it?"

"I was—" Glen Lee dummied up, "—can you arrest me if I tell you?"

"I don't want to know what you were doing. I only want to know what you saw."

"Then let's just say I was in one of the stalls helping out an elderly gentleman who was having a little prostate trouble. I know you don't believe me, but it's true. I am a very compassionate person. Don't look at me like that. I am *not* a liar."

"Focus."

"I heard her whimpering. Heard him slap her and stuck my head out the door. She had a handprint across her face but she wasn't crying. Her eyes got big and so did his. They didn't think anyone else was in here."

Jinx was halfway to hyperventilating. "Did he say anything?"

"He called her 'Buddy,' but I don't think that was her real name."

"Why not? What else did you hear?"

"Before they saw me, he said something about magic. Then again, maybe I heard wrong. It made no sense."

But to Jinx, it made perfect sense.

"Here. Rough neighborhood." He pulled out his wallet and handed Glen Lee a twenty. "Take a cab home."

"Hey, you two fags." A burly black bus driver walked in with his cap perched jauntily on his head and a cell phone in hand. "This is a family place. You can't be doing that shit in here. Take your act on the road, or I'm calling the cops."

Chapter Twenty

When Jinx pressed Raven's doorbell later that night, he half-expected to arrive at Wedding Central.

Instead, Cézanne Martin yanked open the door and jammed a fist against her hip. He glanced over the detective's shoulder at an inconsolable Raven—collapsed on a crimson Persian rug in the middle of the living room floor with Duty in attendance.

In a soft, hypnotic voice, the police detective treated him to the *Reader's Digest* condensed version of the pregnant Siamese and the soiled wedding gown.

Raven came up for air long enough to moan like a wounded harp seal. "I'll bet that makes you giddy, Jinx Porter. My dress is rat-fucked, my fiancé's AWOL and I'm getting married—"

Everyone chimed in. "—in five days."

Writhing on the floor with her head buried in her hands, Jinx didn't hear the ravings of a madwoman or dwell on the blotchy, mascara-tracks hardening on the face of a woman in the throes of a conniption fit. His ex had enough talent in her little finger to put the world to bed; yet here she was wallowing in self-pity, with remnants of tissue paper stuck to her nose. Fresh tears cut a track down her cheeks. And when she placed her head in her palms, massaging what had become an obvious headache, he felt a stab of pain brought on by her misery.

Duty pushed her upright, propping her back against the

leather wingback. For a few seconds, she sat helpless, de-clawed by events, then rolled away and assumed a corpse-like position on the rug. He couldn't recall ever seeing her this puffy-eyed and vulnerable before.

"Anybody got any chalk? Maybe we should draw a little outline around her."

Levity bombed.

"Let's get her off the floor," he said quietly. Cézanne and Duty grabbed one arm. He took the other. They hoisted her up and deposited her into the leather wingback.

Duty looked him over. "You should see 'em, Mista Jinx. They's three of 'em, all white. But Miz Zan says they get their black masks and tails and the feet turn dark in about six weeks. I hear you been missin' a cat. Maybe you oughta take a look at one of these."

Thoughts of Caesar, roaming around scared—or worse—put a golf-ball-sized lump in his throat.

"Later." He pulled Cézanne aside, dug out his wallet, parted the flap and palmed off a hundred-dollar bill. "Call my chief deputy, Gilbert Fuentes. His brother owns a dry-cleaners. Take the dress over there tonight and get him to start working on it." He fished a stack of business cards out of his shirt pocket and thumbed through them until he found what he was looking for. "Here's the number. Do it now, before she strokes out on us."

"You think he can restore it to its original condition?"

"Gil's brother can take the spots off a Dalmatian. Just do it."

Cézanne glided over to Raven. "Don't fret, honey. Duty and I can have the dress fixed."

Raven shook her head. "It's ruined."

"We don't know that yet. But we have to act before those stains set in."

"My life sucks," she said dully, then listed to one side and tuned up keening.

Jinx and Cézanne were exchanging pity glances when Duty let out a scream. No one had even noticed her leave the room.

"Miz Zan, Miz Raven. Come see what I found."

Raven roused herself from her grief. "Are there more?"

Cézanne cupped a hand to her mouth. "First things first. Duty—get a box and move the cat and her kittens off the dress."

"So we can kill them?" Raven frowned through her confusion.

Jinx shot her a look of censure.

"I already moved 'em, Miz Zan. They's in the bathtub on some towels."

"Good," Raven mumbled. "We can drown them. I hear it's painless."

Duty yelled, "I heard that, Miz Raven. We ain't killin' no cats today. Mista Jinx, he need a cat and I'm thinking o' taking one, and with you getting the first pick, all we need to know is who's gonna get Jezebel."

Jinx jutted his chin at the front door. *Take that fricking dress and get outta here,* he commanded telepathically.

"Come down, Duty, we need to leave."

"No, Miz Zan. I got the answer to Miz Raven's problem."

They exchanged *What now?* looks.

"Has anybody seen my gun?" Raven's eyes darted over the room.

"You're plotting to shoot the cat?" Jinx.

"No. You, for thinking 'told you so' about fat Jezebel."

Cézanne drew in a sharp intake of air. She cocked her head in the direction of the stairs and listened with great intensity. "Oh, no. Deuteronomy found your computer. I forgot to warn you. Never let that kid near a computer. I could tell you stories. . . ."

"It's on Ebay," Duty yelled from the study. "The auction ends in twenty minutes."

"What's on Ebay?" Cézanne to Duty.

"Miz Raven's wedding dress."

"Oh good grief." Cézanne looked past lavender-shaded eyelids with an *Is she stark-raving mad?* expression. "I told that girl to stay off Internet auctions. They don't police unscrupulous sellers. I should know. I got ripped off by a psychopath named Dawn from Medina, Ohio to the tune of five hundred bucks. I thought I was buying Haviland Limoges, but it turned out she didn't even own the stuff. Just went to an antique shop and photographed a set of dinnerware. I had hell getting her to send the dishes and, when Ebay finally suspended her after she ripped off sixty other honest buyers, she mailed me a box of china that looked like it'd been dropped from an airplane." Raven's eyes widened. "It'd been broken into so many pieces, it was unidentifiable except for a single hallmark fragment that was still readable. And let me tell you, sweetie, representing inferior merchandise as the real thing is fraud." She wound up in a normal tone of voice. "Really. The cow should be in prison."

"I'm gonna put in a bid," Duty shouted.

The women bounced off each other in their scramble upstairs. Jinx caught up with them in the study.

The teenager sat at the computer, hands hovering above the keyboard. "Here it is."

She spoke in reverent, hushed tones, as if raising her voice would make the image on the screen disintegrate.

"You're ordering me a wedding gown off the Internet?" Raven said, beyond the point of good manners. "Ohmygod, this is so ghetto."

Inwardly, Jinx seconded the notion. He tried to imagine her throwing a ghetto wedding. Like asking for an Incredible Hulk doll and getting your sister's Ken painted green.

Duty gave them the rundown. "It's not just any dress—it's a Vera Wang, so I thought you'd approve. The auction ends in twenty minutes."

"The last thing we need is you wearing a bogus designer gown that comes unraveled the moment you step on the chapel train." Cézanne appealed to the cop part of Raven's personality.

"Miz Zan, you so jaded. You got to have faith."

"Just because it says Vera Wang on the label doesn't mean it's not a fake." Cézanne's gaze strayed to the monitor.

Bewitched, the friends moved in for a closer look.

"It's the wedding dress Angelique wore in 'Mes Amis.' "

Jinx, soaking up every word, felt suddenly out of place. As if he'd stumbled onto a ship's deck of women admirals speaking in a code that could only be deciphered by people without Y-chromosomes.

Duty seemed to be the only one who noticed. "Really, Mista Jinx, you should get out more. 'Mes Amis' is the most popular sitcom on TV today." With her hand on the mouse, she moved the pointer just-so, then clicked on the photo of a wedding gown and enlarged it so that it filled the monitor's screen.

"It's pink," Raven whispered.

"*Ice* pink. It'll match yo' ring."

She studied the picture. The dress had a boned bodice cut in a "V," with a pleat of blush pink satin to conceal peek-a-boo cleavage. Iridescent, pink bugle beads, hand-sewn to form tiny tea roses, covered the front. The left side of the hem had been gathered up to the thigh; the right side had been bunched to the knee, with a shimmer of matching silk beneath it that fell to the floor.

With a click of the cursor, Duty called up a back view of the dress.

Satin-covered buttons, spaced at half-inch intervals, went down below the waist of the rich, gathered skirt.

Duty, impressive in her game show hostess imitation, pointed to a line in the description. "It's a size ten, but it says it's been altered to fit a size eight. It also states it's in mint condition."

Cézanne's eyes narrowed into slits. "It's pink. Pink isn't a color for a wedding dress."

"It's a color meant for a contemporary, high-fashion woman who's not afraid to be daring. That's you, Miz Raven," Duty said. "Whatchoo think, Mista Jinx?"

"Looks like the chest plate for a gay gladiator. Did a glitter factory blow up on it? Reminds me of Pepto-Bismol with sequins."

"Bugle beads." Cézanne gave a heavy eye roll. "Can it, Jinx. Things're bad enough without you stirring the pot. And Duty, if you really want to help, you should try to find an exact copy of Raven's dress." With put-on sweetness, she gripped Raven's arms and spoke in the low, soothing voice of a good psychiatrist. "Honey, I know this looks like the end of the world, but we'll figure it out."

"Miz Raven, you don't strike me as the kind of woman to shy away from convention, but if you don't want it . . ." She moved the cursor to close out the page.

"Wait!" Raven took a cleansing breath. She addressed her comments to the pink gown, as if it was alive and they had reached an understanding. "I do like it."

"See? She likes it." Duty touched Raven's arm. "Not just anybody could wear this dress."

"Let it go, Duty." Cézanne.

"No . . . say more stuff like that." Raven's words came out slow and soft, as if she'd fallen under a spell.

Duty perfected her salesmanship abilities. "As I was about to say, not just anyone could wear such a dress. It would take a woman of powerful confidence and . . . elegance . . . yes, elegance. And in this dress, you would turn every head in the room. Not just because you the star of your own show, but because nobody in that room could ever get away with wearing such a beautiful, dramatic creation. It takes a confident woman to wear a dress as pretty as her face."

"Oh, give it up." Cézanne oozed sarcasm. "What we need's a good drycleaner."

Still mesmerized, Raven head-bobbed a zombie's nod. "You're right. It wouldn't hurt to have a back-up dress."

"Oh for God's sake. Getting another wedding gown is like ordering multiple coffins. Duty, shut that thing off."

"But I need a dress now," Raven said dreamily.

"Me and Miz Zan can go get it. We can take a road trip." The girl looked past Raven's shoulder to her guardian, recessed in the shadows and shaking her head. "It's in Oklahoma City. We can be up there and back by tomorrow night."

Raven gave her maid of honor a slow eye blink. "You'd do that for me?"

"You really want it?"

From the halting way the detective spoke, Jinx sensed she'd gotten caught up in the euphoria of the moment. He cracked a thin smile. Deuteronomy Devilrow should have her own television show, fleecing millions of gullible followers out of their hard-earned savings. A televangelist on Sunday morning programming. Or one of those hucksters on the shopping network.

A veritable Pied Piper on a PCP kind of experience no sane man should have to witness, let alone take part in.

The bid jumped to twelve hundred dollars.

Raven's heart raced. "This is crazy."

"No guts, no glory." Duty.

But Raven waffled, unconvinced. "That's a lot of money. What if something's wrong with it?"

"We'll call you." Duty's maroon eyes widened expectantly.

Jinx stood perplexed. He didn't understand women—especially not these women. And yet they seemed to be resolving the conflict without any more hissy fits.

Raven pulled up a chair and slid in beside the girl. "It might even be more beautiful than my other gown."

"So, is that a yes?" Cézanne said. "Because if it is, you should make sure you're wearing Victoria's Secret underneath for when the skirt falls off."

Duty sat with her hands poised above the keys. "How much you wanna pay?"

"Bid fifty dollars more."

The teenager gave her a dedicated eye blink. "Miz Raven, you gotta be serious. We're runnin' out of time. Bid like you mean it."

She gnawed her thumbnail. "Okay. Raise it five hundred dollars."

Duty gave her an enthusiastic nod, one with the potential to cause spinal injury—and sat idly by.

"Aren't you going to type in the bid?"

"Calm yourself. You lookin' at the Ebay queen. I'm everybody's nightmare." She beamed knowingly. "I'm what they call an ambush bidder."

Raven took a series of shallow breaths. "I can't afford to lose this dress."

Duty checked the time. She waited for the minute hand on

her watch to make another revolution.

"Oh, for God's sake. Just put it down and be done with it. You're making us crazy."

"Patience, Miz Zan. Everything has its own time. And I have the patience of Job." Duty placed the bid.

The computer returned an automatic response. Outbid. The price jumped another hundred.

Thirty seconds left on the clock.

"Whatchoo wanna do?"

"Two thousand," Raven shrieked. "Type two thousand."

"That's what I like. A woman of conviction."

Jinx thought the only thing that required conviction was the person selling the dress, for scamming people into paying money for something sight-unseen.

"I'll put twenty-five hundred," said Duty, "just to be sure."

"Pretty free with my money, aren't you?"

"Fifteen seconds." Duty's hands fluttered above the keyboard like a couple of giant moths. "You want it or not?"

"I want it!"

Cézanne's emotions flared. "Hurry, we're almost out of time." In a moment of panic, she let out what sounded like a battle cry. "Remember Dawn from Medina, Ohio. This is exactly how I got ripped off. Did you check the feedback people left for this person? Dawn had sixty negative feedback entries. *Sixty in a row*. Don't do it."

Duty entered the bid.

The auction closed.

Raven won the dress.

It wasn't that Jinx was unassailably indifferent to her plight. Upon cool reflection, he wondered why he'd tried to help her out with the king of drycleaners.

Downstairs, a cell phone chirped.

The flush of color drained from Raven's face. "Uh-oh, what if it's Fleck Standish? I forgot to change the phone message." They barreled downstairs in a collective herd.

She barely had time to tap the on-button.

"Hello?" She gave Jinx a big head bob. He put a finger to his lips as a warning to Duty. "No, I'm just out of breath. Had to run for the phone. And I'm catching a cold." She invented a little coughing fit for effect, in case he suspected a trap. "I'm sorry . . . you'll have to do most of the talking."

Jinx mimed applause. If Standish thought Lyrica Prudhomme sounded different, now he had a plausible explanation.

Raven played charades with them. She crimped her fingers to suggest a pen and scrawled across the air for a writing pad. Duty lunged for the dining table while Raven made little grunts of understanding into the phone.

"Go ahead," she said when Duty supplied her with a calligraphy pen and card. "More than a thousand?" She screwed up her face and mouthed, *What do I say?*

Jinx held up five splayed fingers.

Five thousand. You can wire him five grand without any trouble.

"I can send five. What's the number?"

She made a weird hand gesture only Duty could interpret. The girl turned her back to them; Raven slapped the card against Duty's shoulder and used her as a writing surface.

"Let me repeat that. What town is it in? Oh. How's it spelled?"

Gray eyes took on a silvery shimmer beneath the glow of the crystal chandelier. She finished scribbling and shoved the card at Jinx.

Below a series of numbers, she wrote: Saline County, Nebraska.

Jinx worried she might give up too much information, or blurt out questions that Lyrica Prudhomme should already know the answers to. He enacted a pantomime designed to cut short the conversation by slicing a hand across his throat to indicate an absolute ending.

Raven nodded. She held up one finger.

"How's Magick?" She gave a little head nod. "Can I speak to her?"

Jinx gave his head a violent shake. Bad enough trying to convince one person she was Lyrica-the-witch. But two? Mighty risky.

"Wait—the doorbell. I think the cops are back. They are," she said enthusiastically. "No, not the bozos from the Sheriff's Office. It's the Constable."

Whatever Standish said after that made Raven double over with laughter. For a few seconds, Jinx worried she'd tip the cretin off. Raven had a distinctive laugh. Lyrica Prudhomme's didn't even come close. If the witch had a laugh like wind chimes—thin, contrived and musical—Raven's pealed out like a bell—throaty, honest and from the gut.

She faked another coughing spasm. "I have to go. I'll do it tomorrow morning at nine."

But Fleck Standish kept her on the line. Her eyes went wide. Her mouth rounded into an "O."

"Sounds good. They're pounding on the door. Good-bye."

She severed the connection. Jinx's heart raced. For several seconds, nobody spoke. Raven side-stepped to the nearest chair and flopped down in it.

"He's somewhere in Saline County. That's all I know. He says Magick's fine . . . that he told her she's getting a Barbie doll for her birthday." Raven's eyes misted. "He said she doesn't know."

"Doesn't know what?"

"That she's going to see her mother." She burst into tears. "I was right." Red-eyed and runny-nosed, she bolted over and threw her arms around Jinx's neck. "I'm sorry about the wedding gown. Sorry about giving you a bad time. I'm sorry-sorry-sorry I've been so selfish these last few days." Remorse turned to concern. "What if we can't find her in time?" She fisted her eyes. Stood there infuriated, with a threat hotwired to her tongue. "I want to go out to that witch's house—"

"Wiccan."

"—and you can hold her while I wring it out of her. Swear to God, Jinx, I want to kill her."

"I could have her killed. That I could do." Duty glanced at Cézanne, who kept quiet.

"Lyrica Prudhomme, Fleck Standish, Joe Bright and all the other rat-bastards out there that hurt kids . . . I'd like to do them in."

"If we was to work something out, I might could give you the first killin' free, but the others I'd need to charge for."

"You're not going out to Ms. Prudhomme's," Jinx said with conviction. "You're going to cart that wedding dress over to Gilbert's brother, and while you're out, take another look around for my cat."

He left without telling her why he'd come by in the first place: that he'd already found out Fleck Standish bought a bus ticket to Nebraska. That FBI agent Longley and his partner had seen the latest teletype he'd sent out over the wire, notifying Nebraska law enforcement agents Standish might still be in their state. That Longley called to say thanks for the tip, and that the feds would be looking into it now that Magick's whereabouts had narrowed. That the Standish case had become more than a kidnapping—it had turned into a horse race—a matter of personal pride. And that he had no intention of reining in his efforts so the FBI could gallop in and take over his investigation like white knights on silver steeds.

Because he knew if he did manage to find the girl alive, he'd need Raven to accompany him to Nebraska to bring her home.

Wedding or no wedding.

That's just how the mule chomped the apple.

His ex had enough on her mind right now. And judging by her reaction to Standish's phone call, if he gave her a few more hours to mull it over, she'd probably volunteer to go up there herself.

Raven loved kids.

Almost made him wish he had one with her.

Chapter Twenty-One

For Raven, Wednesday went by in a blur of activity.

Dorretha Bright heard from Joe again. A thirty-second conversation with Cedric produced a valuable lead that enabled the Constable's Office to narrow the scope of their search. The Burger-Doodle had a movie theater across from it. If Cedric behaved, Joe promised to take him to a Disney movie.

Only three screens in town were playing Disney shows; only one was across the highway from Cedric's favorite burger chain. With a .38 strapped to her belt and a hand-held radio at her side, Raven wheeled the patrol car into the parking lot, and the two women entered the restaurant.

At the register, Raven asked for a manager. A pimply-faced kid with hair plastered down under a hairnet approached the counter.

He wiped his hands with a cup towel. "You have a complaint? Because we already set mouse traps and got lids to cover the grease vats."

Raven slid the picture of Joe and Cedric from a folder. "Recognize these people?"

"You're not from the Health Department?"

"Constable's Office." She badged him. "Have you ever seen them?"

"Did they sue us? Because I'm pretty sure we paid 'em off." His eyes went wide. "Not that we're admitting liability. You have papers? Because those are supposed to go to our lawyer. We have a guy on retainer that handles all our lawsuits."

Raven cut her eyes to Cedric's mother. Future reference: *might want to pick another eatery.*

"I need to know if you or any of the people who work for you ever saw these two people."

"Why? What'd they do?"

"The boy's missing. They eat at your food chain."

Food chain. Where she herself seemed to occupy the bottom rung.

"I don't know 'em."

Dorretha's face sagged.

"But I've been in training the last two weeks. I left Pablo in charge."

"Get him."

Raven expected a clone of the manager. She got an older man of Mexican descent, early fifties, with silvering hair that protruded beneath a paper cap.

He had that bewildered *What?* look going for him. He said, *"¿Qué?"* and the boy rattled off a string of Tex-Mex.

"Great," Dorretha said, world-weary, and standing at the fringe of an unstable cliff, staring into the chasm of sheer panic. Raven suspected they were thinking simultaneous thoughts: language barrier.

Pablo craned his head for a closer look.

"Sí. Estaban aquí esta mañana."

Dorretha Bright didn't understand Spanish, but she understood the vigorous head bob. Tears rimmed her eyes, sluicing down her cheeks in rivulets. Her lips trembled, and she clawed her throat in such a way that Raven thought the two men would hurdle over the countertop to perform the Heimlich maneuver.

Pablo pointed toward the door, wagging a thick finger as

he spoke. The boy translated.

"He says they come in once or twice a day. The man orders three burgers and two fries. The boy gets milk. The man drinks water."

Raven's heart picked up its pace. "Ask him what kind of car they have."

Pablo apparently understood more English than he let on. He shook his head and said, *"No carro. Siempre andan."* He walked his fingers through the air in a pantomime, then pointed to an apartment complex across the street and rattled off more information in his native tongue.

Building on her impatience, Raven broke in. "Do they live in those apartments?" She anticipated the answer from the universal, palms-up shoulder shrug. "He doesn't know. But they come from that direction."

Dorretha's voice wavered. "How does my son look?"

She got a headshake reply.

Raven pulled out her business card. Wrote her cell number on the back of it and instructed them to call if Joe and Cedric returned.

Outside, she pulled out her hand-held radio and keyed the mike. She called for Jinx, gave him a rundown and asked him to meet them. The radio squawked. Jinx's answer came over the airwaves. He was still at the office interviewing a witness in the Standish case. It'd be another half-hour before he could shake free.

"Don't do anything until I get there."

"Ten-four." She slid the handy-talkie back into its leather pouch.

Cedric's mother had other ideas. Panic filled her voice. "We need to go over *now*. Please. Joe's crazy. Who knows what he'll do?"

Raven sensed the woman's desperation, but they had to

assume Joe Bright was armed. Common sense told her to wait for backup. If he was hell-bent on trading bullets, she wanted the advantage of more firepower.

Meantime, other clues needed checking out. For one thing, they couldn't be sure Joe and Cedric were renting at the Cannonglade Apartments. If one of the residents gave them sanctuary, they'd need the manager's help to find out who was hiding them out.

"We're going over there, Mrs. Bright. We can't just go busting in doors. We need to pin down their location."

It took all of two minutes to hide the car. Raven parked it in one of the stalls at an adjacent car wash.

Joe Bright wouldn't know her on sight but if he and Cedric occupied one of the apartments overlooking the car wash, they would recognize Dorretha and run—or worse, create a hostage situation where everybody loses. "Do you have a scarf, or something to cover your head?"

"I have sunglasses."

"Put them on." She checked her watch. It'd be at least twenty minutes before Jinx arrived. She looked past the headrest, into the back seat, for the throw-down jacket she carried with her during summer months. In case she had to make an appearance, *incognito,* the blazer would conceal the gun holstered at her waist. She shrugged into the lightweight cotton fabric before stepping out of the patrol car, then engaged the electric door locks.

They headed toward the apartment, Dorretha with her head ducked and Raven with hers held high.

When they arrived at the office, Dorretha's cell phone trilled out.

She checked the display. Panic flashed in her eyes. "Oh, Lord. It's him."

Raven pointed her to the bathroom and buttonholed the

manager, a young brunette with hair strained back from her face in a chignon. The bun didn't make her look older. Neither did the oversized glasses Raven suspected had non-prescription lenses; but the pinstripe suit added a few years, putting the girl's age at thirty, tops.

The manager introduced herself as Fran and glided toward the mini-blinds. She twisted the rod until the slats slanted down and striped her face with slivers of sunlight, then pointed across the courtyard swimming pool to a door near the corner. "He moved in two weeks ago. He said he recently got custody of his son, so I suggested he might be happier in a two-bedroom."

"Have you seen the boy today?"

"They just came home. I know because he came by the office to tell me a crazy woman was trying to kill him, and to take his name off the mailbox immediately. That was about five minutes before you got here."

A guts-out scream rocked the walls.

Dorretha staggered out of the bathroom hyperventilating. She sliced the air with the cell phone like a totally deranged throat-slasher. "Today's the day. He's gonna do it when Cedric takes his nap. He's gonna cut his throat. Raven, if you don't get over there now, I'll go myself."

Talking Dorretha out of storming the apartment would be about as effective as removing a tattoo with spit.

Raven followed Dorretha's eyes to the wall clock. "What time does your boy take his nap?"

"Now."

"I need a passkey."

The manager seemed slow on the uptake. Nice-and-cordial wasn't working. Raven held up her fingers, one-two-three. "Lead, follow or get out of the way."

The girl stood slack-jawed. The climate of helpfulness

had changed for the worse.

Building on her irritation, Raven shouted, "Now."

"Okay. But I want you to know I'm calling the cops."

"Great idea. Call nine-one-one, call in the National Guard, call whomever you want. Just don't interfere in police business unless you want three hots and a cot."

As extra incentive, she pressed an elbow against the strap on her holster. The snap-release gave an audible click.

Properly motivated, the girl moved around to the safety of her desk. She rifled through the top drawer and tossed a key ring in their direction. Raven caught it mid-air.

The two women headed out the door, leaving the young lady with her cordless, stabbing out numbers on the keypad.

Dorretha ducked back inside.

Sprinting off in the direction of Joe Bright's apartment, Raven caught the tail-end of Dorretha's threat.

"Bitch, you got no idea what I'm capable of, so don't even think about warning him."

For Jinx, Wednesday brought the Constable's Office one step closer to finding Magick.

The night before, he'd teletyped a BOLO to Nebraska for the Saline County Sheriff to be on the lookout for Fleck Standish and the girl. Now, a tip from the Mueller Institute confirmed satanic activity in Saline County. When Raven called for backup, he had just hung up with Nebraskan authorities.

Standish didn't show up at the bank.

Jinx wanted to be the first to tell Raven he'd purchased a plane ticket to Lincoln . . . and that she'd be along for the ride. Which would make her about as happy as a lobster in a steam bath.

He settled his Stetson low on his forehead and headed out

to the parking lot. The police radio crackled to life. Dell had heard the information exchange between them and called *en route*.

With a lead foot and a shot-glass of luck, he'd beat the brooding German to her location.

By saving the boy, he'd save the girl.

May the best man win.

And the best man for Raven wasn't Dell.

Chapter Twenty-Two

The piercing laugh track of a sitcom penetrated the walls of Joe Bright's apartment. The place had a creepy feel, with the curtains drawn and the TV blaring louder than the rap music vibrating out from the stereo's jumbo speakers. With her snubnose drawn and positioned at her thigh, Raven rapped on a spot near the doorframe, hard enough to bruise her knuckles. She sensed movement behind the steel door and watched the peephole darken. Muscles tensed along her back. Thoughts of survival disintegrated inside her head. Taking deep intakes of air had a dizzying effect. It creeped her out, having his attention fixed on her—like being caught in the crosshairs of his scope. If he opened up with gun pointed in her face, an orange flash from a muzzle blast might be the last thing she'd ever see.

She gave the eyeball a little finger-wave and held her breath.

The deadbolt clicked back.

The door opened with a yank.

It snapped to a halt as the slack went out of the short length of chain.

Half of a man's face came into view. A network of wrinkles bracketed one glaring brown eye, as cold and indifferent as staring into a gun barrel.

She felt the first licks of genuine fear.

"Hi. I'm your neighbor." *Can't see his hands.* "My phone's out and I was wondering if you—"

"No."

"You don't understand. It's an emergency—"

"Fuck off." His voice brimmed with hatred.

"Please. I don't need to come in. If you could just dial the number and hand me the phone—"

—then I could snap on a handcuff—

"Get the fuck outta here before I bash your skull in."

She jammed her boot through the open sliver. The crush of metal against her instep sent a shot of pain up her leg. Yellow dots danced in front of her eyes. Instinct programmed her to shoot the chain. In the split second she raised her .38, an eerie shriek rended the courtyard. *Dorretha Bright . . . human battering ram . . .* burst forth.

Cedric's mother crashed her shoulder into the door, knocking Raven aside like a cast-off rag doll. Her revolver clattered to the sidewalk. It twirled several revolutions before stopping. The chain popped free from its guard, sending Joe Bright reeling backward, flat-nosed by the door. Dorretha delivered a haymaker to the orbital bone.

The first blow floored him.

Raven grappled for the Smith.

She limped inside to the sight of Cedric's father, proned-out on the floor with his ex-wife straddling him. He tried to shield his face from Dorretha's blows but her arms moved like pistons, dispensing a series of corkscrew punches to his jaw. Raven watched, thunderstruck, as the woman's corporate image degenerated into that of a ghetto street fighter.

A rash of inventive new expletives erupted from her mouth. "Kill myself? I'll kill you, *muh-fuh.*" Flashes of gold arced in the light. Dorretha wore rings on all of her fingers. "Take my son away from me? Be kinda hard if the getaway car's a wheelchair, *muh-fuh.*"

It was like watching a Pay Per View prizefight between a

middleweight and a flyweight. Madison Square Garden had nothing on these two—the Kilkenny brawl taking place on the carpet needed a ref.

Definitely a one-sided match.

Probably ought to pull Mrs. Bright off, now that his face had the look of freshly-ground meat.

"Hey, slugger—ease off."

"This is for me." She peppered her tormentor with a quick succession of blows. "This is for Cedric." She sledge-hammered with a wicked left.

Aw, what the hell. Settle his hash.

Dorretha K.O.'d him with a right hook.

The bedroom door opened a sliver. The wide-eyed face of a little boy peered out.

"Mama?"

Dorretha Bright froze in mid-strike. "My baby!"

Raven moved in on Joe Bright with her pistol leveled at his head. She didn't have to worry about him coming after them. Dorretha delivered a crushing kick to the stones as soon as she rolled off. The TV sitcom laugh track went off, followed by canned applause. Cedric sprinted out and his mother swept him into a protective embrace.

Raven swallowed the lump in her throat. Every now and again, the job just flat choked her up.

Downtown, the Channel Eighteen crew had showed up for an exclusive interview. She stumbled into the office with that "just laid" look, feeling the full effect of her injuries. Seeing Garlon Harrier with his outstretched mike and greasy hair that parted under its own weight, she forced a smile and gave a little finger-wave.

"How'd you get that limp?" Harrier shoved the mike in her face. A dark lock of hair separated from the rest, cutting across his forehead with a pendulum swing.

"Stuck my foot in the door."

"And that shiner?"

She touched her throbbing cheek, wincing at the pain.

Realization dawned on the reporter. "Haven't I seen you before?"

"I don't think so."

"I have." He put his finger to his throat and made an invisible slice. The cameraman turned off the directional light and hoisted the camera off his shoulder. "I *have* seen you."

"A case of mistaken identity."

He gave her a vehement headshake. "No, your picture was found in a car full of Libyans after a police chase ended at Lake Ray Hubbard."

Raven swallowed hard. "I'm sure I don't know what you're talking about."

"Why would they have your picture?"

She couldn't recall what explanation she stammered through, only that he didn't buy it. Fixing him with the look of practiced innocence, she said, "So whatever happened to the two guys in the VW Beetle?"

"They dragged the lake for them. Sent in divers, actually. But they didn't recover any bodies."

Raven spent the next ten minutes in the office bathroom, forming cold compresses out of stacks of paper towels soaked in water. In the foyer, Garlon Harrier shouted variations of, "How'd she know how many men were in that car?" If what the reporter said was true, Tommy and Yucatan Jay had practically led a cell of terrorists to her front door. She couldn't remember the last time she ended the workday with a bigger headache, and was still incubating in the calamity when Jinx barged in.

She addressed his reflection through the mirror.

"Can I have a little privacy?" She moved in closer to the

glass, barely grazing her fingertips across the swollen tissue around her eye. Teardrops shot out like automatic gunfire. They slid over the purple egg plumping up near her cheek, and she suspected they were both thinking, *Wedding pictures.*

"Are you crying?" He propped himself against the doorjamb. "Cops don't cry."

"Merely the kind of involuntary reaction you'd expect when you get your tear ducts smashed." She made eye contact through the mirror and oozed sarcasm. "Oh, right. I guess you wouldn't know. Reptiles don't have tear ducts."

"So I'm a snake?"

"Where were you?" Her lower lip stuck protruded. "Undercover with Rainey's skip-tracer? If you'd gotten to my location faster, none of this would've happened. Now look at me: I've got a black eye, and I think my foot has a hairline fracture. I'm going by the ER on my way home. Probably have to cut my boot off, and this is only the second time I've worn them."

Jinx took a deep breath and held it.

Raven narrowed her good eye. "What?"

"How do you feel about Rabbit Rangers?" When her forehead lined in confusion, he said, "Game Wardens?"

"Why—did you pick one out for me to marry?"

"Just want to hear your take on them, that's all."

She returned her attention to her bruise and daubed at it with the compress. "I suppose they're underrated. They generally work alone," she said, ticking off reasons not to be one, "they know every violator they contact will have a weapon—but that could be a good thing, too, because if you know they have one, you'll be more careful—and they work out in the boondocks without a backup for miles."

Her good eyebrow arched.

Like me. Today. Out there without any help.

"You had backup. We probably ought to hire Dorretha, though. She makes a helluva battering ram."

"I'm glad you're enjoying yourself at our expense." She consulted the mirror. "Only way I'm gonna get rid of this purple moose by Saturday is if I hire a mortuary to do my make-up."

"Assuming you're back by Saturday."

Raven whipped around. "Now what?"

"We're catching a flight to Lincoln, Nebraska in less than two hours. That's what I came to tell you, Pod-nah. You're coming with me."

Chapter Twenty-Three

Arguing with Jinx did no good. In the end, Raven occupied the seat next to his on the flight up to the Nebraska capital. Arlon Deavers, Sheriff of Saline County, met them at the airport and filled them in. On the ride to the station, the burly man talked with a jaw packed full of Red Man. When he rolled down the window and arced out a stream of brown spit, Raven, seated in the back, involuntarily ducked.

"Game Warden found them," he said, with an occasional glance in the rearview mirror. "Rolled up on them in a stolen car and arrested the whole lot of them."

Jinx already knew the story, and had told it to her on the plane ride north: Standish befriended a security guard in his early twenties at the bus station. The man took him home, where the three of them stayed in a room at his parents' house the next few days. His mother thought Standish was traveling with a little boy, but suspected the child's appearance had been changed. For one thing, the kid's hair had been dyed black and parted down the middle. For another, Standish refused her offer to wash his "son's" clothes. And when the homeowners met the kid, she asked for a hot dog, confiding to the lady of the house that she hadn't eaten in two days.

According to Deavers, the security guard's mother wasn't allowed inside her son's room, a corner bedroom on the second floor of the frame house. But when he and Fleck Standish and the kid stole the family car, the worm turned.

She rifled through Standish's duffle bag and hit pay dirt.

Standish's bag had porn, cult material and a subpoena TCSO served ordering him to bring Magick to court. The lady'd already reported the car stolen; once she read the subpoena, she called the Sheriff. By that time, the Game Warden had already arrested the men for auto theft

Since Standish refused to identify himself, they were holding him as a John Doe. Once the Sheriff and the Game Warden put two and two together, they booked him for Interference with Child Custody.

"Just like it says." Sheriff Deavers made eye contact with Raven and rattled Jinx's Teletype between the headrests.

The child, who turned out to be Magick, was turned over to the Nebraska Health and Human Services System, and the assigned social worker safeguarded her in a foster home until the constables arrived.

"I told them not to interview her." Deavers slid Jinx a sideways glance. "Told them you said you'd bring your own detective. So they've got her in foster care—get this—with the Fosters, so she's now part of a Foster family. Ain't that a kick?" He bellowed out a laugh that deteriorated into a rasping cough.

Raven's cell phone shrilled. She dug it out of her bag and answered with a chipper hello. In seconds, she slumped over against the door and reduced herself to a nose-running, eye-tearing, mucous-dripping heap.

Jinx said, "I'd be willing to bet that's her fiancé. He's been MIA the last few weeks."

"Ain't that the way it goes?" Sheriff Deavers shook his head. "The good ones are always taken. My ex-wife, Linda, she remarried. Made the best apple pie in three counties. Don't miss her, but I do miss coming home to the smell of apple pie."

They shared a laugh. Raven had all but disappeared below

the headrests, where she seemed to be carrying on a conversation with the back floorboard.

The Sheriff checked the rearview mirror. "How'd she get that partial eclipse under her eye?"

Jinx told him how she'd violated procedure, busting in on Joe Bright to get Cedric back. Then he turned the conversation back to Magick.

"What kind of condition was she in?"

Sheriff Deavers powered down the window and spit. "Let me put it this way: the social worker threw up while bathing her."

He spoke of greasy, matted hair, caked-on dirt and arms and legs eaten up with chigger bites. The way she had a knife strapped to her leg and a haunted look in her eyes when the Game Warden slipped up on them. At the Fosters, they discovered she didn't have on panties, and everyone speculated on what might've been going on out there.

"Of course no one talked to her, because you said not to," Deavers reminded him, almost accusingly.

Jinx thumbed at the back seat. "In Texas, you have to be careful with kid interviews. If you ask leading questions, the defense attorney can get the tape excluded. I just want to be careful. Nothing personal; I'm sure you've got great people."

He told Sheriff Deavers the story of Marina Rice; about how Raven, convinced Marina had been abducted by her non-custodial parent in a sleight-of-hand perpetrated on Judge Masterson, single-handedly tracked her down and brought her home. That he found it ironic how Evan Rainey, who'd represented the scheming father in the Marina Rice case, now represented the Hursts in an attempt to wrench Magick from the clutches of Fleck Standish and his lunatic mother.

Thinking of Rainey triggered thoughts of Sigrid Pierson.

She'd called five times since Monday; now he hoped she'd fade out of the picture.

Jinx checked his watch. Nine o'clock dark. The kid was probably asleep. Best thing to do would be to rent a room, get up early and interview her before they set out for home. Naturally, he'd put Raven and the kid on a different flight. It wouldn't do, having Standish and the girl on the same airplane.

But Raven, who'd revived herself after the spook's phone call, had her own plan. "Let's talk to her now, while the event's still fresh."

"You just don't want to stay overnight," Jinx said.

"That, too."

"You can leave after you interview the kid. Judge Masterson's faxing documents to the Nebraska court. Tonight, we're checking into a motel."

"You're getting me a separate room. And I don't want any connecting doors between us."

Putting an end to any horseplay he might've otherwise dreamed up.

Early Thursday morning, the social worker brought Magick to the NHHSS offices and made an interview room available for Raven to get Magick's statement on videotape. Before crashing another agency's domain, Raven observed the girl through a two-way mirror, exploring the room and examining the toys.

Magick bore little resemblance to the child in Marcy Hurst's photograph. Coal black hair appeared harsh next to her pale skin, even with a pink bow pinned to a section of hair. Raw, measle-like spots covered her arms, some of them bloody from fervent scratching. And when she walked the perimeter of the room and ended up with her hands and nose pressed against the mirror as if she sensed she was the guppy in the fish bowl, ghostly eyes shined under fluorescent lights.

Raven held a laundry bag of anatomically correct rag dolls—one adult male, one adult female, one male child, one female child. The child abuse unit had several sets on hand: dark-skinned dolls with dark hair, light-skinned dolls with light hair, light-skinned dolls with dark hair and even a set with red hair. She selected those bearing the closest resemblance to people in Magick's life.

She inhaled deeply, then walked inside to meet her new charge.

"Hi. I'm Raven." She strolled over to one of two beanbag chairs, plumped it up and nestled herself into it. "What's your name?"

She got a slow blink filled with mistrust.

She scanned the girl's outfit: purple shorts and a lime green tank top. Probably a last-minute choice, pulled from the rag bin. Magick's overalls, she'd been told, were filthy. Not surprising, since the Game Warden had to take Fleck Standish by the fire station for a hose-down before booking him into the Saline County jail. If the interview played out as she suspected it might, those clothes would turn out to be evidence.

"I like your shorts. Are they new?"

Slow nod.

"That's my favorite color." Raven flashed a little grin. "Too bad they're not my size, huh?"

Another eye blink.

The cameras rolled. So far, not much to go on.

"I brought some dolls," she said, emptying the cloth bag into her lap. "I thought we could take a look at them. What do you think?"

Another slow nod.

First things first.

Get the basics.

If I can't show she's qualified to testify in court, we're screwed.

"I want to talk to you about telling the truth and telling lies. Do you know the difference between telling the truth and telling a lie?"

Please, please, please—know the difference.

The child nodded.

Now you have to explain it to me.

"That's great. What does it mean to tell the truth?"

"To say what's real."

Yes!

She fought an enthusiastic head bob. Put on her poker face and willed herself to take slow breaths. "And what does it mean to tell a lie?"

"To say stuff that's not real. Like if you make it up, but it didn't happen."

Thank you, God.

"That's right." She kept her face carefully blank. "What happens when you tell a lie?"

"You get in trouble." Magick's lower lip protruded. She dropped her gaze and toed the carpet.

"What happens when you tell the truth?"

"You get in more trouble."

Poor, precious baby. What kind of life have you lived up 'til now?

"It's very important that we tell the truth in this room. Do you promise to do that—to only say what's real?"

"I promise."

"Why don't you sit next to me, so we can talk about these dolls?"

Where the microphones will pick up your voice better.

Magick took a tentative step.

"I think we should call this one Raven. That's me." She

rifled through the bag. Held up the girl doll. "This can be you. What's your name?"

"My old name, or my new name?"

Big shock. "What's your new name?"

"Buddy." Said softly and to the toes of her Keds. "Before I got my new name, Fleck called me Magick. But that's a secret."

Raven's heart thumped. She forced a smile. The child didn't call him Daddy; she called him by his given name. "Why's that a secret?"

" 'Cause Fleck says so. Me and Fleck, we have lots of secrets. Can I sit in your lap?" Magick scrambled across the bean bag chair, and snuggled close. A faint dirt ring circled her neck, but her hair smelled of coconut shampoo, and the hint of fabric softener floated up from her clothes. "Will you rub my tummy like Fleck does?"

The question jarred her.

"Does he rub you anywhere else?" Magick's gaze strayed to her crotch. Raven handed her the rag doll. "Use the Magick doll to show me."

Magick peeled off the dress and gently placed it on the bean bag chair. She pulled off the panties and tossed them aside. "You don't need no drawers," she said in an unusually low, gruff voice. "Just one more thing to take off."

"Who says that?"

"Fleck." She splayed the legs and pointed to the genitalia. "That's where he puts it."

Raven's heart hammered so loud she thought the audio might pick up the beats. "Do you have a name for that part of your body?"

"Fruit salad." Without prompting, the girl grabbed the adult male doll. She stripped off his clothes, examined the cloth penis, then tried to yank it off.

"What do you call that?" Raven asked.

"Banana." She flattened the male's hand between the female's legs. "Fleck rubs me here." Magick slid her a sideways glance. She lowered her gaze and spoke to the dolls. "But it's a secret. We have lots of secrets."

"Will you share those secrets with me?"

Slow nod.

"Tell me another secret."

The girl ground the male's head between the female's legs. "That's a big secret. You can't tell."

"What other secrets do you and Fleck have? Can you show me with the dolls?"

"Uh-huh." She slapped the male doll on top of the female. "When he puts his banana in my fruit salad," she said with a sigh. "That's a pretty big secret."

Raven steeled her nerves. She wanted to cry; to crush the girl's head until the memories of what Fleck Standish had done to rob her of a childhood would disintegrate. They had enough information to put the man away for sex crimes; but she also suspected Lyrica Prudhomme played a big part in the abuse.

She handed Magick the adult female. "Have any women ever done anything to you that you didn't like?"

A head bob.

"Who is this dolly?"

"Miss Lyrica." Magick stripped the doll clean.

Told you so, she signaled Jinx telepathically. *I told you she was bad news.*

Magick faced the female dolls inches from each other.

"Has Miss Lyrica ever done anything to make you feel uncomfortable?"

"Uh-huh."

"Can you show me what Miss Lyrica does to Magick?"

The girl forced the dolls together. Wrapped the larger one's arms around the small one in a hug.

Magick let go. The dolls went limp. "Sometimes she hugs me too tight."

"Does Miss Lyrica do anything else?"

"Dries my eyes when Fleck makes me cry."

"Has anyone else ever touched you in a way you didn't like?"

The child hung her head. "I'm not s'posed to tell."

"It's all right. You're safe here."

"I can show you," she said, "but you have to get a bunch more man dolls."

"How many?"

"Maybe eleven or twelve."

By the time the tape quit rolling, Raven was looking cross-eyed and wearing Magick like a belt. The only thing more therapeutic than making Exhibit A for the prosecution would be a set of brass knuckles and five minutes alone in the cell with Fleck Standish, one-upping Dorretha Bright.

Down the highway, Sheriff Deavers escorted Jinx through the Saline County jail, past the holding tank, to the block with Standish's cell.

Deavers stopped at the entrance and clapped him on the back. "Got your hooks?"

Jinx rattled a canvas bag. "Chubbs. Virtually unpickable."

He'd brought along a set of leg irons, too. And an oversized pair of cuffs large enough to snap around the telephone-pole-wristed Tongans that American Airlines hired to handle baggage at DFW Airport, just in case Fleck Standish had massive wrists. And a belly chain. But what he'd *really* wanted to bring was the vintage ball-and-chain with an iron collar to tighten around Standish's neck.

Deavers stopped halfway down a corridor of metal bars, in front of a cell not much bigger than a cage. A large man wearing stripes rested on a metal bed mounted to the wall. His hair seemed unnaturally dark for his fair complexion, and it trailed past his shoulders in matted, greasy sections. A scraggly, unkempt beard hung nearly to his chest. To Jinx, Fleck Standish didn't look much like a survivalist. Just a fat puke wallowing on a cot.

Sheriff Deavers cracked a smile. "Here's your boy." He barked orders at the prisoner. "Get those jail clothes off."

Standish fisted sleep from his eyes. Stared at them with a glazed expression. "Everything?"

"As the day you were born."

The inmate made no move to comply. Jinx removed a set of jail khakis with Tarrant County Jail stenciled on the back, shoved them through the bars and dropped them onto the floor.

Standish regarded them with a blank look.

"Judge Ronald Masterson sends his regards." Jinx lazily fanned away the gamy air with a copy of the arrest warrant. "And the District Attorney says *hi*. Now get up off your goat-smelling ass, turn around and put your hands against the wall."

Standish roused himself up on one elbow. "Who're you?"

"Constable Jinx Porter." He slid the warrant past the cell bars and flicked it in Standish's direction.

"Who?"

"All you need to know is I'm the one who's gonna make sure you spend the rest of your natural life in the pen, sitting on a one-piece, stainless-steel crapper, wearing Brogans and slides, dragging a cotton sack between your legs like a tail. You might've had help pulling this scam, but your little entourage ain't gonna be there to help you hoe crops in a hundred eighteen-degree heat."

Standish scoffed at the idea. He sat upright, bent over and picked up the warrant. As he unfurled the pages, his eyes drifted over each sheet. "I'll get me a lawyer."

Sheriff Deavers cut in with the cadence of a drill sergeant. "Get your clothes off, face the wall, do it now, you do not want my help."

Standish stood. Shucked right down to the tamale.

Deavers barked out orders. "Run your fingers through your hair. Fold your ears forward."

Jinx knew, on instinct, the Sheriff was inspecting for razor blades or anything else that could be used as a cutting tool.

Standish complied. Satisfied, Deavers said, "Open your mouth and lift your tongue." Nothing under there. "Turn around." Standish faced a metal grate that doubled as a view to the outdoors. "Spread your cheeks."

Jinx grimaced. He averted the sight before it could permanently scar him. He didn't want to start waking up in the middle of the night comparing Standish's ass to Rorschach inkblots.

"Turn around. Lift your balls."

Nothing hidden under the scrotum.

"Pick up your feet," Deavers snapped. "Put your traveling clothes on, put your property in the onion sack and leave our duds on the cot."

Jinx spoke in a deadpan baritone, running down what Standish could expect once he shrugged into his jail threads and went back home.

"Yessiree, you'll be trudging around the farm, carrying a hoe from dawn 'til dusk, picking cotton at the Ramsey Unit . . . hoeing cabbage at the Eastham Unit . . . rasslin' pigs down at the Ferguson Unit . . ." he said, drawing out the descriptions of manual labor to prolong the agony.

"Interference with Child Custody?" The inmate folded the warrant into a paper airplane and sailed it toward the seatless commode. It crashed into the cinder-block wall and fluttered to the concrete floor, six inches from the toilet. "Even if I have to do time, I guarantee I'll be out in less than five years."

"Don't be so sure. When we get back to Texas, I'm filing so many sex crimes charges against you the D.A.'ll have to give you your own file cabinet." He motioned for Deavers to unlock the cell.

"Never make it stick," Standish said with a headshake. "Magick won't testify, I guarantee."

Jinx wanted to ball up a fist and smear that smug grin across his prisoner's grizzled face.

Instead, he inflicted a dose of mental pain. "Let me give you a different kind of guarantee. Hardcore inmates don't kowtow to child molesters—don't think somebody won't put the word out. You won't make bail, either." He let out an Arizona chuckle, a kind of half-cough, half-laugh that he hoped conveyed an air of certainty. "By the time your case goes to trial, they'll be using your ass for a basketball hoop in the jail's rec area—"

Reality soured Standish's smirk.

"—and I guarantee by the time you get out of the joint, your butt'll be stretched as big as a hula hoop." Jinx mimicked Deavers' drill-sergeant cadence, delivering each word with an emphatic beat. "Now get your goat-smelling ass up, turn around, put your hands behind your back and don't give me a reason to dole out any frontier justice."

Chapter Twenty-Four

By the time Raven's plane touched down, Jinx had already booked Fleck Standish into the county jail Thursday afternoon, and was waiting at the airport with Garlon Harrier and the Channel Eighteen crew.

They sauntered up the jetway to camera flashes and directional lights. Magick clutched a Barbie doll and a cellophane pack of cookies in one fist; with the other hand, she held onto Raven.

One look at the crowd and Magick tightened her grip. "Are we in trouble?"

"No, sweetie. These people are happy to see us. You're about to be on TV. Give them a big smile?"

"Can I stay at your house?"

"You don't want to do that . . . you've got family here. They want to take you home with them."

Magick rooted her feet in place. "I don't wanna see Venita no more."

"Not Venita. Your mama's parents want you to come with them." An unpopular idea, judging by the kid's expression. God only knew what kind of brainwashing the Standishes had done to her. "Look, there's Jinx."

Magick shook loose.

Made a break in his direction.

With gangly legs flying, she scampered across the carpet with her arms outstretched. She apparently didn't notice the elderly couple standing off to one side, loaded down with gifts, but Raven recognized them from Jinx's description.

Bo and Marcy Hurst.

My work here is done.

Well, well, well. Would you look at that? Are those tears in Jinx Porter's eyes? Who said there's no crying in police work?

Garlon Harrier shoved the mike in Jinx's face. "How's she doing?"

Jinx's voice cracked. "Why don't you ask her?"

Magick whipped out the Barbie. "Lookie what Jinx bought me." She stuck out a bare arm and used the doll's head to point out the crusted-over bumps. "And ointment for my skeeter bites."

A look of discomfort settled over Jinx's face. Sweat glistened on his forehead. He caught Raven's eye and jutted his chin in a *Come on over* motion.

Raven shook her head. He deserved the limelight for himself. He'd done an outstanding job and should revel in it without having to share.

The Hursts hadn't seen their granddaughter in years, but she took to them like a cow to a salt lick.

At the courthouse, Judge Masterson granted temporary custody to the maternal grandparents until the outcome of Fleck Standish's criminal case. If the defendant asked for a jury trial, he might spend as long as a year cooling his hocks in the calaboose before his case popped up on the docket. By that time, Magick would have a new life, and the judge wouldn't be inclined to undo his ruling in the final order.

Getting to take Magick home after the hearing was tantamount to taking her home for good.

On the way out to Jinx's patrol car, Sigrid Pierson sidled up beside him. He got a trapped-badger look on his face and mumbled unintelligible comments under his breath.

"So that's how you do it, Jinx Porter?" Rainey's PI halted,

hand on hip. "Play 'Hump-me-dump-me' and don't return my calls?"

"Let's talk about this away from the courthouse." He keyed open the passenger door.

Anchored next to the vehicle, Raven waited for the drama to unfold.

"I'm talking to you now, mister." Sigrid scowled. "You think you can just get me drunk and take advantage of me?"

"You're a grown woman. Nobody put a gun to your head and made you swill down those chasers. You oiled and lubed yourself."

"I'm not talking about boozing it up, and you know it."

Raven arched an eyebrow.

"Get in." Jinx motioned her into the car, effectively giving Sigrid Pierson the brush-off. "Have a nice day. We're leaving."

They roared off in a cloud of blue smoke.

A block from the courthouse, Raven twisted in her seat. "You haven't changed a bit, Jinx Porter."

"Don't know what you mean." He barely lifted his haunches from the seat. Dug into his back pocket and fished out a tin of Copenhagen.

"You went to bed with that idiot, didn't you?"

"I ran into her at the Ancient Mariner, that's all. She was soused, so I took her home. That's all there was to it. Let that be a lesson to me: 'No good deed goes unpunished.' I can't help it if she wants me."

"Ha!" The word exploded as if fired from a revolver. "You think every woman wants you." She turned her face to the window. "You even think Agnes Loudermilk wants you."

"She does."

"You're so full of yourself."

"*You* don't want me."

"You've got that right, buddy."

But for Jinx, a seed of hope germinated: *So how come it's such a big deal who I bed down with?*

Raven sauntered into the Constable's Office a few minutes after five Thursday afternoon. Apparently, Georgia was manning the front desk when it should've been Dixie, because the grandmotherly woman was tossing orange peel remnants into the trash, and packing up her snack tote.

"Hi, Georgia. Any messages?"

Instead of answering, Georgia cut her eyes in the direction of Ivy's desk.

Cézanne and Duty were studying progressive grade school photos of Amos thumbtacked to a cork wallboard.

She lit up with delight. "Did you get my dress from Oklahoma?"

"Sure did, Miz Raven. It's so pretty. Only it has to be hemmed."

"Let's get it over to Bridal-Wise. They don't close until six."

An encrypted message passed between Cézanne and Duty. Raven interpreted it: *Don't say anything else.*

"What's going on?"

Cézanne affected a pleasant expression. "I think Georgia has something she wants to tell you—" the smile turned sour, "—don't you, Georgia?"

Georgia grimaced. "Honey, you're probably wondering why I'm working Dixie's shift."

"Do I want to know?"

The secretary spoke with the authority of a conspiracy theorist. "Dixie and Ivy figured out you were back when they heard your voice on the radio. They took off like a couple of F-16s. I guess I don't have to tell you they didn't pick up their dresses yesterday."

Raven stiffened. She eyed Georgia with the intensity of a cat, hiding in the barn rafters, on-point and patient, waiting to spring. "They don't have their gowns?"

"No, honey. They forgot."

Her voice spiraled up an octave. "Have they lost their minds? I'm getting married in two days. These people don't even know if their dresses will fit. It's bad enough I need to have my backup gown altered; for all I know, the seamstress'll be so busy working on their clothes she won't have time for mine."

Cézanne answered in slow, deliberate sound bytes. "We should go now."

"Ain't no hurry," Duty piped up.

Cézanne shot her a wicked glare.

"What do you mean by that?" Raven narrowed her eyes.

"It's nothing. Duty had a premonition, that's all."

"Wasn't no premonition. I had a vision—"

"That's enough." Cézanne administered her words with a guillotine-like chop of finality.

On the drive to Bridal-Wise, Raven recounted the arrest of Fleck Standish.

"We're friends, right? So I'm going to be a pal. I'm going to make your job easier by giving you a homicide tip in advance." Raven pulled down the visor and checked her shiner against the cosmetic mirror. Still purple, not quite as puffy; but the flesh-colored concealer stick she bought when Sheriff Deavers stopped for another pouch of Red Man seemed to be doing the job.

"You're about to confess to killing Miss Groseclose, aren't you?" Big sigh. "I knew you did it. You never had anything nice to say about her."

"Almost as good. If Fleck Standish doesn't get sentenced

to the maximum punishment allowed by law, I'm going to kill him. Justifiable homicide. Just so you know."

Duty, who'd been dozing, popped open her eyes. "Don't worry about him, Miz Raven. He'll rue the day he was born."

"How do you know?"

"Saw it in a dream." Duty grinned big. "By the way, Miz Raven, I been wantin' to axe you, how's Mista Jinx?"

"That asshole?"

Duty folded her arms across her flat chest, and cupped her elbows in her hands. "Hmmmm. Gonna have to check my spell—" Her eyes fluttered in astonishment. "Did I say spell? I meant spelling. I'm not supposed to be casting spells. I'm a terrible speller. Gonna have to work on my spelling. Yessum, soon as I get home."

Cézanne hit the brake and sucked air. "Oh, no." She slowed the car to a crawl.

Duty went into a panic. "I'm sorry, Miz Zan. I won't say any more about my premonitions. I know you think I'm crazy when I—"

"Stop rattling." Cézanne pointed at the horizon.

Raven shielded a hand to her forehead and squinted against the sun.

A plume of smoke rose above the roofline of the shopping center.

Neon orange traffic cones popped up in the oncoming lane. Sawhorses, striped with reflective paint, blocked the artery leading to Bridal-Wise. In the distance, *Quicksilver* and *Panther,* two of the Fort Worth Fire Department's fire engines, idled in the parking lot while sparkies in turnout gear charged their lines. Water spewed past the fog nozzles for a quick knockdown, sending a geyser of sparks into the black air like Hell's fireflies. Charred columns in front of the designer boutique jutted up like burned frankfurters. A yawning black hole replaced the plate glass window where the storefront's foyer used to be. The scorched metal awning outside the dress shop suddenly toppled over.

Dixie and Ivy stood near the fire trucks, gawking.

Random thoughts entered Raven's head, but her speech came out in clear, unwavering tones. "Ohmygod. They're hanging around like a couple of cloves on a ham. If I find out they don't have those dresses, I'm going to kill them."

"I could have it done for you." Duty.

Patrol cars cordoned off the arteries leading into the shopping center. Cézanne approached the police barricade. A uniformed officer standing near a blue-and-white directed traffic away from the scene. She downshifted into neutral, powered down the window and badged him with her gold panther shield.

He shook his head. "Sorry, Captain. You're gonna have to turn around."

"What the hell happened?"

"Hell's right, Captain. They had a two-alarm fire. Whole place is destroyed."

Cézanne did a double-take. "Everything?"

"I heard rumblings from the arson guys. Apparently the automatic sprinkler system failed to activate. One said they were off, in violation of city code. And the pyro-eaters brought in a cadaver dog, so something else may be going on."

"If what you say's true, then it'll be my case anyway." Cézanne snapped her badge case closed, dropped it in her lap and popped the gearshift into first.

"Captain, it's their fire."

"It's *my* body."

"No, ma'am, it's the *ME's* body."

"But it's *my* crime scene."

"It's *my* wedding." Without awaiting additional details, Raven unlocked her door. Sprinted across the parking lot with the cop commanding her to stop. Pounded the pavement in strappy sling-backs, with her gauzy, flower-print skirt flouncing up in back like a horsetail. Sprinting past Dixie and Ivy, she arrived at where the front door to the storefront should've been. She stepped inside a building heavily charged with smoke and heat, and held her badge aloft.

Acrid smoke tweaked her nostrils. Burned beams that resembled alligator hide stood where walls had once been. A couple of arson investigators crunched through the charred rubble. Watery soot rained down on their slickers like tear tracks of mascara, and each breath she took felt like a charcoal briquette stuck up each nostril.

"Stay back," one barked.

"But my bridesmaids' dresses are in here."

He chortled. "Not anymore."

The eerie cry of a rusty hinge pierced the soot-filled air. A fireman staggered out from the back of the building, pulling a metal rack of bagged dresses in his wake. Wheels screamed against a layer of debris piled up on the floor.

A strange exchange took place between arson investigators.

"What the hell?"

"Looks like these made it through the blaze."

"Impossible."

"Not really. These bags must be made of flame-retardant asbestos."

"Just because the protective covering made it doesn't mean what's inside did. Probably heated up like an oven. Open them."

Please, God, let these dresses belong to Dixie and Ivy.

The fireman pulled off his gloves and stuffed them in his

pocket. The metal zipper on the garment bag hissed as he tugged it open. He dislodged a fluff of fabric from its cocoon and exposed the first of a dozen bridesmaid gowns.

Cheap-ass, hot-coal-and-damnation rental dresses, of an orange so bright it could fry the wearer's retinas just by looking at it. How'd they survive the inferno?

But she knew. They'd booked the Concorde to the Earth's core in time for Hell's Prom, then returned from the crackling flames of the permanently damned to mock her and her entourage.

She reacted to the stress by doing something completely out of character: sat down on the curb and laughed. Cackled until tears streamed down her face. Knee-slapping, gut-wrenching guffaws that caused the arson investigators to look at her slitty-eyed. The *pop-pop-pop* of an automatic weapon caused everyone still standing to hit the deck.

She glanced around, baffled.

A drive-by? In the middle of the hands-down, worst day of her life?

Overhead beams snapped like chopsticks. Charred braces caved in, sending sparkies running for cover. The fire Captain hollered at the nozzle man to hit the crossbeams with a water-charged hose. Steam spewed into the air, creating a soupy fog.

Raven gradually became aware of Cézanne and Duty cozying up beside her.

Her maid of honor offered advice. "I'd stop the horse laughs if I were you. I'm pretty sure FD thinks you might be involved. Pyromaniacs like to watch fires, you know. It's a hobby."

Another charred brace gave way. Sparks showered the area, spitting and hissing. A fireman pulled two folds of two-and-a-half-inch hose, and knocked down the blaze like the

Jolly Green Giant pissing out a campfire.

"I heard noises like this before," Duty muttered to Cézanne, "when my gramma Mablene hauled me to a revival. But the people were under a spell and the preacher didn't want to wake 'em until after the rattlesnakes got put back in the sacks."

A visual that sparked another round of donkey brays out of Raven.

Cézanne grabbed Duty's hand and tugged her close. "Stop talking. Can't you see she's traumatized?"

"I'd wear one of those dresses. I think it would look nize with my skin. Can we take these with us?"

Raven stopped laughing. She regained her composure and mumbled, "They're satanic."

Duty said, "I think they been blessed by God. Imagine—all the beautiful, high-dollar dresses in the store goin' up in flames and here's just the right sizes to fit the fat sows in your wedding. How lucky is that?"

The arson investigator broke the spell. "The only way these dresses would look good is if you held a couple of flares in each hand and directed traffic around a major ten-fifty."

Speaking in the ten-code, police lingo for a fatal collision, brought Raven around faster than a nose full of smelling salts.

Dixie and Ivy eased up close.

Duty addressed a couple of firefighters. "Can we have these dresses? 'Cause I'm sure the lady would let us use them for Miz Raven's wedding Saturday, since the real dresses are gone."

Ivy rolled her amphibian eyes. She stared without blinking. "I'm not wearing that."

Dixie said, "Me neither."

Raven's lower lip quivered. "But I'm getting married in less than two days."

As if she'd anticipated the bride's next thought, Dixie piped up in her irritating soprano. "I'm done with shopping. This is it for me. I'm not traipsing down the aisle looking like a friggin' fireball with feet."

Ambling back to her car, Ivy called out over her shoulder. "Sorry, Raven, you're on your own."

Cézanne slipped an arm around her shoulder. "Screw 'em. You still have me, Georgia and Shiloh."

"But I have five groomsmen."

"Want me to fire two of them for you? We can get rid of the ugly ones."

"We could get rid of my cousin," Raven said, trancelike. "I'd planned to kill him before the wedding anyway."

"If you was to let me be a junior bridesmaid," Duty said, "you'd only have to fire one."

"What about the hem of my back-up dress?"

"I won't let you down, Raven." Cézanne gave her a gentle squeeze. "We'll do it tonight."

"You know how to sew?"

"No, but I'm hell with a staple gun. I mean, how hard could it be?"

The first useful idea of the evening flashed into mind. She knew a woman who made all of her grandkids' clothes.

Lola Askew.

Lola could help.

Chapter Twenty-Five

When Raven returned home from Bridal-Wise, she glimpsed Clem Askew rocking back and forth in the metal glider on his front porch, toying with a shoebox resting in his lap. With a curt wave, she keyed open the door and carried the Vera Wang into the house. She trundled upstairs and placed the beaded gown on the bed, then pulled the knob until it clicked shut behind her.

Downstairs, she poked her head into the laundry room. Jezebel and her kittens were snoring like a tuba quartet. She refilled the cat's food bowl with a can of sliced beef for finicky eaters, said, "Bye, babies," and headed for the Askews'.

The old man looked up from his shoebox. Shouted, "Say, girlie, lookie what I got."

Her instincts went on point. Too small for an alligator. Not big enough to hold a penis pump. Might actually be shoes?

She ventured out to the curb. Forced cheer into her tone. "Whatcha got?"

He hollered, "A present," and waved her over.

She narrowed her eyes. "What kind of present?"

"Gotcha something pink and furry."

Bunny slippers?

She looked both ways before crossing the street. At the porch, she glanced around. The Askews' garage door gaped open and the car was gone.

"Where's Mrs. Askew?"

Brows furrowed. His eyes went watery. "Been dead over twenty years."

"Not your mother. Your wife."

"I'm not married."

Here we go.

"What's in the box?"

Gnarled fingers pulled at the top. It fell away, exposing green Easter nesting with a wrinkled, retractable penis poking out of the center. The appendage rose to half-staff, listing from side to side.

Raven stared in disbelief.

"Pat the mousie," Mr. Askew said with a leer. "Make him spit."

She pivoted on one heel and headed for her house with the neighbor's cries echoing in her ears.

"You want some?"

Twenty minutes later, Lola returned home. With her silver hair strained back from her face in a bun and her shoulders hunched from the slight hump on her back, Lola plodded into the house weighted down by a huge handbag. She returned to the car, empty-handed, where Raven caught up to her unloading groceries from the back seat. She needed to disclose Mr. Askew's latest stunt. But she needed the dress hemmed, and Lola might not take kindly to Raven's suspicions that her husband had the onset of Alzheimer's. Some people enjoyed living in denial.

She decided to wait.

Lola agreed to bring over her sewing kit after dinner.

When she arrived at Raven's house later, her husband trailed her into the living room with his rubber-tipped cane prodding the floor and a hand-held steamer in hand. With downcast eyes, he followed the women upstairs. He placed the portable steamer on the bathroom countertop, then shuffled over to the bed. He glanced around, studying the details of the room as if this were his first visit.

"Isn't it just exquisite?" Lola lifted the beaded bodice to the light. "Run on home, Clem. And don't set anything on the stove."

"I can stay, Mother."

"Law me. Get over to the house. This is women's work. I'll be home directly."

Footfalls descended the steps. Raven knew he'd reached the first floor when the soles of his shoes squeaked against the hardwood. While Lola gushed over the Vera Wang, Raven stood at the landing with her ears pricked up for the sound of the front door snapping shut. She almost went downstairs to double-check, but returned to Lola's side when she heard the telltale click.

One could never be too paranoid with Yoruba Groseclose's murder unsolved and a killer on the loose.

The Libyans.

Her heart thudded. They had her picture. Maybe they'd gotten the wrong house?

Lola broke the spell. "Let's get us a chair. You can stand on it while I tack up the hem."

A mouthful of pins kept Lola working in silence. Without having to make small talk, Raven reviewed the past seven days.

Directly or indirectly, Yucatan Jay had brought misery and taint to everyone he'd come in contact with. Was this how it would be when she and Tommy had children? Always looking over one shoulder, wondering if the bag boy at the grocery store or the delivery guy from the pharmacy was stalking them for death? Suspecting anyone with Mediterranean skin or African lineage? Sleeping with one eye open?

By midnight, the ice pink gown hung in the closet and

Raven finally relaxed. She walked her neighbor across the street, said good night and promised her one of Jezebel's kittens.

Exhausted, she flicked off the light and flopped across the bed. Her lids grew heavy. Within seconds, she floated off into a deep sleep—

—and awakened to a calloused hand clapped over her mouth.

Every muscle in her body tightened. Fear gripped her heart.

Fight or flight.

She grappled for the Lady Smith resting beneath the pillow. The intruder flung himself on top of her, effectively pinning her in place. In an instant, her mind shifted into cop mode. If he let her live, she'd make sure to give an accurate description to the police, right down to his rangy, gamy smell.

"It's me babe. I'm home. For now."

"Tommy?"

He released her and rolled off to one side.

Raven sat bolt upright. Flung her arms around him and buried her face in his neck. Whiskers bristled against her cheek. "Are you hurt?"

"Me? No. Just a little scratch. Say . . . do we have a first aid kit?"

"Ohmygod, you *are* hurt. Turn on the light. I want to see you."

"No lights." His calloused palm scratched her face. "Y-Jay's injured."

"He's here? Good, I'll get my gun." She searched the shadows. "By the way, could you start me a grocery list? Jot down detergent with bleach alternative. I hear its harder to pin a murder charge on somebody if the blood spatter's been compromised. Now, where's that cretin cousin of mine?"

"Next door. The Victorian."

"You broke into Miss Groseclose's house? You can't go in there. It's a crime scene."

"You're telling me. The whole place is fucked up. Burglary?"

"No, it really is a crime scene. Old lady Groseclose was murdered last Friday."

He sucked a breath in through gritted teeth. "That makes it kind of bad."

"Bad? What do you mean *bad?*"

"When we were coming through the back gate, Y-Jay tripped over this little, short guy. Really, Raven—" he paused to lecture, "—how many times have I told you to get a lock?"

"Little, short guy? This little, short guy—what's he look like?"

"He has a groove in his head about this big around." She sensed him rounding his thumb and index finger into a circle. "Look, I don't want to worry you, but people are still after us."

"What people?"

"Don't ask."

"The little, short guy . . . is he a gypsy?"

"Gee, Rave, I didn't bother to ask."

"You don't have to get smart with me. Where is he?"

"We took him next door."

"To the murder house? You put him inside Miss Groseclose's Victorian?" Her voice crescendoed an octave.

With great patience, he stroked her hand. "No, Raven. We did not stash him in the house. We propped him up in the English garden and we're using him as a gnome."

She gulped in a fresh breath of air. "Is he dead?"

"Uh, let's see . . . big hole, weak pulse . . . I'm thinking if he isn't, he probably wishes he was."

"This sarcastic side of you I'm seeing—I don't much like it."

"Well this dumb act of yours—I'm not much liking that, either."

He didn't say what'd happened to the gnome in the garden. Only that they'd found him that way, next to her back gate, when they slipped in through the alley.

Her heart raced. "You didn't kill him, did you?"

It was a throat-constricting moment.

"Of course not."

"Thank God. Because I'd have to call the police, you guys would be arrested, we'd have to cancel the wedding . . ." Her mind played out a series of events, none of them pleasant, including viewing the Death Row lethal injection procedure through Plexiglas. "What'll you do now? Call an ambulance?"

"Since we can't stash him next door, we'll have to find another place."

"Hospital?"

"Or the morgue."

"What about me? You're leaving me again, aren't you?"

That went without saying.

A few minutes after Tommy took off, she received a distress call from Lola Askew.

"Honey come quick." Her voice vibrated through the earpiece. "Clem's wandered off."

Raven hurried across the street. With Libyans on the loose and Y-Jay and Tommy in the neighborhood, if Lola's husband were shuffling around lost, God only knew whether the old man would end up with a hole in his head, too.

In under ten minutes, three squad cars rolled up in front of the Askew house. While Lola gave the uniforms a description of her husband, Raven stood on their lawn with her arms braced, squinting at Miss Groseclose's flower garden for signs of a gnome. The only movement from that direction came when a raccoon waddled out. It froze long enough to take stock of the fanfare, then took off in the opposite direction. Raven shivered. The temperature had dropped. Moisture hung heavy in the air. The sweet scent of rain alarmed her; Openly Gay José had predicted a string of hot, sultry days free from weekend showers.

Headlights rounded the corner; an unmarked vehicle slid up to the curb. The driver's door opened and a leg swung out. Raven moved beneath the glow of the street lamp. It took a few seconds for her eyes to adjust to the light.

Cézanne trotted across the street. She pulled Raven beyond Lola Askew's earshot and spoke in low, even tones.

"We got a make on the latents from the Groseclose murder."

Raven knew better than to ask. When it came to dispensing information about pending investigations, Cézanne's explanations were as guarded as a Masonic handshake.

Her eyes shined ghostly blue. "It took longer than usual because the prints weren't in AFIS." She meant the Automated Fingerprint Index System. "He had no criminal record."

"So how'd you identify him?" Raven looked past Cézanne's shoulder at Yoruba Groseclose's darkened Victorian . . . and at her own house, lit up like an emergency flare.

"Through the military."

"Armed forces? Carswell Air Force Base?"

"Marine Corps. Retired." Cézanne got a missile-lock on her.

"The Askews are retired military. You should talk to them. They might know the guy."

"Maybe they do."

The silence stretched between them.

Seated in a glider, bathed in the incandescent glow of the porch light, Lola Askew tuned up crying. Her hands fluttered like white pigeons and her voice went shrill when she said, "Alzheimer's."

"I'm sorry, Cézanne, but I have to go to her. It's my fault—if I hadn't asked her to hem my dress, he wouldn't have wandered off."

Cézanne clutched Raven's shoulder hard enough to make her hunch. "Did you not hear a word I said?"

"I heard. You think Mr. Askew might know who killed Miss Groseclose." Raven shook her head, as if loosening the cobwebs would reveal the answer. "He won't make the most reliable witness. He has dementia."

"I'm pretty sure he'll remember this."

Raven scrunched her brow. Realization dawned. "Since when does a homicide detective conduct missing person interviews at this time of night?"

"When the missing person committed the homicide."

Chapter Twenty-Six

When Clem Askew still hadn't been located by one-thirty Friday morning, Cézanne tried calling in one of the K-9 officers to bring a scent canine. But the men with dogs on graveyard shift were at a warehouse working a Signal 9—burglary in-progress—and wouldn't go back in service until they flushed out the intruders.

Raven called it a night. The first thing she did when she arrived home was throw the deadbolts on every door. The digital display on the microwave oven clock flashed electric blue numbers, fixing the time at two o'clock. In seventeen hours, would Tommy show up at the rehearsal dinner?

Before heading upstairs, she ducked into the laundry room to check on Jezebel. The new mama squeezed her eyes and gave a silent meow. The bottom of Jezebel's food bowl gleamed; the three kittens had distended stomachs and were sleeping off the effects of a good meal.

"Nighty-night, babies. You're not staying," she reminded Jezebel.

Raven decided to forego a shower. Instead, she hiked up a pair of fresh cotton panties and slid a camisole overhead before climbing into bed. Sleep did not come easy. For the longest time, she stared at the ceiling.

What would make Clem Askew kill poor Miss Groseclose?

Her eyes flickered to the bathroom, to the oval of stained glass. Each morning when the sun hit the window, colors glowed with breathtaking beauty, staining the carpet in rich hues. Now, beacons from the police car's strobe lights glanced off the glass and brought it to life. Scarlet crescents of leaded glass appeared downright spooky. Each time the rotating strobes hit the crimson panes, it reminded her of a pulsing heart during cardiac surgery.

She closed her eyes and drew in a deep breath. Listened to the rush of air coming from the A/C vent. Thought of Tommy and how her life was about to change in a major way.

Mrs. Thomas Greenway.

Raven and Tommy.

The Greenways.

She drifted into uneasy slumber.

A phantom sound pricked up her ears. She slitted her eyes open. Carnal panic went through her head. Her lids fluttered in astonishment. She sat bolt upright, overcome with the skin-crawling sensation she had an intruder.

Tommy?

Libyans?

She slid her hand under the pillow. Tightened her fingers around the Pachmeyer grips of the Lady Smith. Slowly drew it to her side, making sure it stayed hidden beneath the covers. Her heart beat so hard, it echoed in her ears.

"Who's there?" Her voice faltered. "Tommy?"

She settled back into the pillows with the Smith pointed at the door. A sick feeling gripped the pit of her stomach. Fear set off a low-level hum in her ears.

She eased back the covers and lopped a leg out of bed. Made contact with the carpet and crept the rest of the way out with her gun lowered at her thigh. Maneuvered her way past the corner of the bed and worked her way, slew-footed, toward the closet.

If an intruder had hidden—

A whispered greeting came from behind.

"Hi, girlie."

Clem Askew.

The unmistakable swing of metal sliced the air. She didn't see him hit her, but the crack of his cane rang in her ears. The .38 went airborne onto the landing. It teetered a few seconds between the stairs and the railing, before disappearing from view. Her hand went numb. The sickening sound of stainless steel popped against the floor tiles below.

So this was where homicide detectives would draw the chalk outline: her coiled in a fetal position with her head bludgeoned into the Berber carpet.

Get up or die.

The room blurred. In a moment of disorientation, she suspected this must be how an aneurysm felt. She scrambled upright on shaky legs and stumbled to the bed with the silhouette of her neighbor reflected in the bathroom mirror. She hit the nearest wall switch, dimmed down low, and waited for her eyes to adjust to the low-light conditions.

He leaned jauntily on his cane, then rocked it back and forth like a putter. "I've seen what goes on in this house." Anger pinched the corners of his mouth.

A lance of terror went through her heart.

He took a step, dragging the cane behind him. The contours of his face hardened. He raised his cane. Swung so hard it whooshed through the air. She hunched on instinct. Drew her hands up to shield her face, stunned when it spliced the mattress, barely missing her head.

The cry she attempted came out a mere whimper. "Why're you doing this?"

If she could get to the Mossberg in the closet—

She considered her chances for success. The old man could cave in her skull from behind before she lunged for it.

He watched her, slitty-eyed, while ticking off her vices. "You had that man over here. I saw your silhouettes. You did things. I reckon we'll see what happens when you do those things to me."

She carefully modulated her voice to conceal her fear. "Tommy's my fiancé."

"Not him. The other one. That tow-headed fellow with the straw cowboy hat. I saw what he was doing—and you let him. You never let me do that." A look of outrage settled over his face.

She listened in stricken silence to his ravings, knowing what he was capable of, not daring to think about what he had in store for her. It should've been easy to get away, with Askew having the speed of a slug on a cold December morning. But tonight, ancient reflexes were in fine form and the adrenaline rush he seemed to be experiencing made him unusually strong and doubly dangerous.

Startled into terror, she said nice things. "Mr. Askew, you're married. Your wife's my friend. So are you. Put that down. Let's talk."

The neighbor was in a filthy mood. She could almost see the homicidal ideas flickering behind the cold depths of his eyes. Intakes of breaths came in excited waves.

"Get that shirt off."

She let the silence speak for her.

He drew back the cane and paused in mid-air.

Her heart leapt to her throat. "Mr. Askew, please think about what you're doing."

His face went red. Neck veins bulged. Metal hissed through the air, thudding against the covers. Raven rolled off the mattress, onto the floor and staggered to her feet.

"Drop your drawers."

"Whatever you want." She planned to agree with him as

long as she could so they wouldn't be arguing, him near the door and her cowering behind the bed. He had the thousand-yard stare going, making her wonder how many personalities had seized control of his mind. She forced the next words from her mouth. "I think about you a lot. You're a handsome man. But Lola's my friend."

"Lola?"

"You remember. The lady has a crush on you."

"I don't know anyone named Lola. Get your clothes off."

She started with the top button on the camisole. In a gut-cramping moment, she unfastened it.

"Speed it up. Lemme see what you've got under there." His hand moved to his crotch. Fumbling, he grated the zipper teeth the length of his fly.

Her skin went cold. Did she care? Not much. He'd already killed Yoruba Groseclose; given the choice, she'd get off light with sexual assault.

What am I thinking?

He's not gonna lay a finger on me.

Cornered in the far part of the room, her eyes darted around in the search of an escape hatch. Out of options, she settled on the bathroom. Took an invisible measurement of the distance and sent a message to her brain: *You can make it. Lock yourself inside and scream bloody murder for the cops.*

A thinner, more fragile inner reply stopped her.

That's nuts. Once you commit, there's nowhere to go. He can set fire to the place—get the Mossberg out of the closet; blow the door to smithereens—cut you in half.

"Two can play the game, Mr. Ask—Clem." With a quick glance-around, she inventoried items that could double as weapons. "*You* take off *your* clothes."

Now it was his turn to look flustered.

"Let's see what you've got."

Lamp. Within the lunge. An easy swing.

"What?"

End table. Bigger, sturdier. Would cost precious seconds lifting it.

"You're obviously proud of it. Whip it out and show it to me."

Slipper chair. Could wield it like a lion tamer. Toss it through the stained-glass and follow it out.

Her stomach went hollow. She loved that window.

Got no choice. Cops'll hear and barge in like the cavalry.

"You're a real spitfire." He pulled out his flaccid penis and massaged it. "Talk dirty to me," he said in a low growl. What started out as an unimpressive short arm suddenly grew into a testosterone-gorged hogleg.

Raven's mouth went desert-dry. She struggled to control the tremble in her voice. "I'll take off my top if you'll take off yours, Clem."

Her neighbor worked himself into an excited pant.

Put down the cane, you crazy sonofabitch . . . hope to God you get tangled up in that shirt . . .

"Don't try anything sneaky. I'll kill you deader'n Yoruba. She liked it, girlie . . . not at first. But after she took a wallop upside the head, she gave in."

"Liked it?" Raven asked. But she was thinking, *Are you insane?*

"Smiled when I put it in."

Before or after she died?

Raven unfastened the last button. "Your turn, Clem. Take off your shirt."

"Let me see them."

"You want these?" She opened the camisole, peek-a-boo, enough to show off her cleavage. "You first."

He propped the cane against the nightstand, suddenly

looking pretty vulnerable with his Black-Eyed Susan poking out from his boxers and his red tartan halfway undone.

Raven did a mental countdown, waiting for him to shrug out of the shirt. In her mind, it was the closest she'd come to a multi-second lead.

"You want me bad, don'tcha, girlie?"

Her chest heaved with great intakes of air.

An inner voice cried out: *Do it now.*

Opposing logic tried to trump instinct: *Not yet. Bad timing, and he'll kill you.*

Instinct won.

Now, dammit.

Raven snagged the lamp. Hurled it at him and made a run for the bathroom. Grabbed the back of the slipper chair and dragged it in behind her. Slammed the door and locked it.

Sorry about the window, Pawpaw. So very sorry.

Fists pounded the door. Threats and obscenities pierced the wooden barrier between them. As Askew's tirade evolved into a frenzy, she made out the word "shotgun" and yanked open the shatterproof door to the shower.

Lifted the chair overhead.

Gave it a mighty swing.

An explosion of glass rocked the small space.

The window fell away. She scrambled to stick her head out.

"Somebody help me," she screamed. A half-dozen uniforms turned to look. "Askew's in my house." Behind her, the sharp crack of splintering wood echoed off the tile like broken bones.

She hoisted herself up in a last-ditch effort to get out. Pulled her sticky red hands to her and wondered, entranced, why they didn't hurt. She straddled the jagged opening, mangling one thigh. Felt a tickle crawl down her leg and saw the first splatters of blood on the floor of the shower.

Orders squawked through a bullhorn pierced the night. They called on Askew to give up.

Raven inventoried the distance to the ground in a glance.

The bathroom door banged open.

The last thing she saw before sailing through the hole like a Hail Mary pass was the barrel of the Mossberg being leveled at Askew's hip, and the grenade-like blast as she took a header out the window.

Chapter Twenty-Seven

The Fort Worth police officer Raven landed on broke her fall.

For a moment, they stared at each other, dazed; her, half-undressed, and him wearing a windbreaker with Crime Scene stenciled onto the back in yellow block letters. Across the street, with a uniform posted at her side, Lola Askew wept into gnarled fingers.

It took an hour of intense negotiations to get Askew to surrender once the SWAT team rappelled up the rear balcony and stormed the second floor. Someone opened the front door and let her inside. She stood near the sofa as officers led Askew down the steps with his hands cuffed behind his back.

For a moment, he looked at her blank-faced. Then she saw a flicker of recognition. "Raven?" His voice quaked. "What're you doing here?"

"I live here."

He glanced around confused. "What am I doing here?"

Damned if I know.

Until the Crime Scene detective removed his jacket and swept it across her shoulders, Raven didn't realize she was shivering. Uniforms settled Clem Askew into the caged back seat of the nearest patrol car, where he sat wordlessly staring off into space.

In an unguarded moment, she slumped to the floor with her back to the wall. Voices buzzed around her in fragmented sentences.

". . . place is built like a fortress . . ."

". . . have to be neurotic to have this many locks—or involved in illegal activity . . ."

". . . so many deadbolts the Screaming Eagles couldn't get in . . ."

". . . lucky we got here when we did . . ."

"Miss?"

Raven stared up in a zombie-like trance. The crime scene detective offered a wet dishtowel from the kitchen. She blinked, unsure what to do with it.

"There's an ambulance on the way. You need those hands stitched."

"What?" Raw tissue glistened.

"Your palms. And your leg's messed up."

She took note of the laceration on her thigh, then quickly pressed the damp cloth over the gash.

The crime scene detective spoke at a speed that mimicked a record slowed to thirty-three-and-a-third.

"What?"

"I asked if there's someone you can stay with tonight."

She blinked.

Cézanne would be down at the PD. Shiloh and Kenny lived thirty miles away. Georgia's husband took chemotherapy treatments and didn't need the aggravation—and Dell?

Dell would be good.

"Jinx," she whispered. Realizing her mistake, she opened her mouth. The detective interrupted her before she could speak.

"Not Jinx Porter," he said, and she nodded. For her trouble, she got a *Hope you know what you're doing* look, which sort of resembled the *Gee, I'm so sorry* look, which was the first-cousin-once-removed to the *Are you stark-raving mad?* look. He pulled out a cell phone and thumbed the on-button.

"What's the number?" She recited it, slowly, as he punched out the exchange. The faint staccato of a dial tone filtered through the wireless. Jinx answered on the fifth ring.

The detective ran down the fiasco and caught him up to speed.

"He wants to talk to you."

Raven took the wireless. "Jinx?" At the sound of his voice, she fell apart.

"Don't cry, honey. I'm on the way."

Raven refused the ambulance, choosing to wait for Jinx. It took sixteen stitches to close the three wounds; by the time they arrived at the Château Du Roy, it was close to five in the morning. She still needed to give the police a statement, but Jinx made her an appointment for later that afternoon and gave her the day off to pull herself together.

He even volunteered to sleep on the leather love seat. But he looked so uncomfortable with his knees practically tucked under his chin, she stopped in the doorway on her way down the hall and told him to join her.

In the dark, flat on her side, she listened to him breathe. The Siamese should've been there, making a hard landing on the bed. She wondered if he was thinking about Caesar, too, but decided not to ask. Out in the courtyard, Glen Lee Spence and the Munsch brothers were halfway through their drunken countdown with "Forty-nine bottles of beer on the wall."

She rolled onto her back and spoke to the ceiling fan whirring overhead. "My life is circling the drain."

"You'll be fine." He gave her an unenthusiastic pat on the behind. "You're getting married in one day."

"My great-grandmother made that window. When Pawpaw built our house, he had a bricklayer cut a custom-made hole to fit it."

"It was pretty, what I saw of it."

"I always wanted it. He said I could have it when he died. Now it's gone."

"Have it fixed."

"There are some things that can't be mended."

Kind of like us.

He rolled over and draped an arm across her ribcage like old times. He pulled her close, and when he pressed a kiss into her hair, she didn't balk.

"I miss the cat," he said softly. "Hell, I miss *us* . . . the way we used to be before I screwed things up with Lucille."

Coming from him, it was as close to an apology as she could expect.

Poor Jinx. He'd used up the last of his nine lives boffing Evan Rainey's gumshoe—she didn't need to be in the same bed with them to know what happened; she'd seen the betrayal in Sigrid Pierson's eyes when the play-detective bushwhacked him at the courthouse. That's just the way Jinx operated. Once he grew bored with a woman, he left her in the bosom of the scorched Earth. A tear slid into the corner of one eye and dropped onto the pillow. "I know you try to be good, Jinx. You just can't seem to pull it off."

"I could change, Raven, I really could."

"I still love you. On some level, I probably always will."

He bolted upright. "Does that mean you still plan to marry the spook?"

"Now more than ever."

Chapter Twenty-Eight

The Novocain doctors used to stitch Raven's gashes wore off around nine Friday morning. At ten o'clock, she took a laundry bag outside to pick up sections of stained glass from the broken window. She'd already reclaimed more than half of the pieces, pausing intermittently to look for fracture lines, when a huge black man with a face as big around as a chocolate cake chugged into her driveway in a rusted-out pickup and cut the engine. The door swung open with an eerie squeak and he slung out a leg that seemed too large to fit in the space hollowed out for the driver.

Huge feet hit the ground. Dust shimmered up and landed on the tops of his shoes. He angled over in threadbare overalls, with a tool kit swaying to his gait.

"Miz Zan sent me."

"Pardon?" Raven squinted into the sun.

"Yo' window need fixin'." He pointed a frankfurter-sized finger, thick with calluses, at the hole where the oval window had been. "If I was to cut some plywood to fit, you could take yo' time puttin' the pieces back together." Meaty lips split into a grin. "Miz Zan said a man blew a hole in yo' wall big enough to push a cow through. Don't much look like a rough neighborhood to me, but I reckon white folks got problems, too." He stuck out a ham-hock hand. "Leviticus Devilrow at yo' service. Descendant of the Shreveport Devereaus." He shoved a finger into his bib pocket and fished out a laminated newspaper article, yellowed with age, then waved it close enough to read the caption beneath the photo: *Senator Devereau denies ancestors kept slaves.*

"You're Deuteronomy's uncle?"

"Yessum. She say she gonna be in yo' weddin'. Ain't that nize?"

Remains to be seen.

"Why're you here?"

"Miz Zan say you gotta get that hole patched, and there's a busted door need fixin' around back."

"How much is this going to cost?"

"Don't rightly know. Lotta work ahead and Miz Zan say you'd be wantin' it finished before dusk. I'm thinking maybe if I was to work real fast, you'd see fit to gimme three hundred dollars."

"Three hundred dollars?" Her voice shot up an octave. She excused herself and went inside to call her maid of honor.

When she returned, she put him on notice. "Cézanne already paid you."

Devilrow looked everywhere but straight at her. "Miz Zan's a cheapskate. She don't know the value of craftsmanship. Now, I took note of the damage and I'm gonna need at least two hundred more."

Lacking patience, she said, "Hit the road."

"One hundred."

"Not even fifty."

"Okay, I'll do it for an extra twenty-five."

"Deal." Devilrow's bartering had blurred her irritation. "But you're furnishing the lumber."

With a wary headshake, the handyman unleashed the three-man crew moving about in the pickup bed like slobbery, dancing Rottweilers.

As long as there were workmen around, she'd be confined to the house.

She made a couple of frantic phone calls to ensure last-minute details stayed on schedule.

The florist had bad news.

He delivered it in effeminate tones that started out calm, but background noises hinting of urban demolition wrecked his composure.

His strident voice vibrated through the earpiece. "The Birds of Paradise were supposed to arrive at DFW. Sadly, they went to Dallas Love Field by mistake."

Raven sighed. "That's correctable." She expelled a nervous giggle. "I mean . . . it isn't like they went to El Paso. You can go get them."

"Easy for you to say. I think we should discuss carnations. White carnations with baby's breath and a few stems of purple statis. Doesn't that sound pleasing?"

"It's a lousy hour-and-a-half drive to the airport and back." She stiffened. "We have a contract."

"This is true. Only the dogs ate them. We call that *force majeuer*."

"What?"

"That's the provision that holds us harmless for acts of God. A *bona fide* reason why we're excused from delivering the Birds. The dogs ate the Birds."

"What dogs?"

"Drug dogs." A huffy sigh filtered through the earpiece. "I understand they were German Shepherds."

Her heart thunked. Words came out slow and deliberate, as if restating the problem would make it go away. "Drug dogs ate my Birds of Paradise?"

"Like a tropical salad."

"I don't understand." She blinked hard. Her speech carried the sluggish, dull measure of someone on opium. Involuntary panting forced oxygen-infused blood through her veins. "How could this happen?"

"I'm thinking they opened their mouths and took big bites."

"Don't get smart with me. You have no idea what I've been through."

Raven shook her head, unwilling and unable to process this latest development. A crash of metal made her hunch involuntarily. The florist screamed, *"Watch out, idiot*—not you, dear. I'm talking to these—*big galoots in steel-toed boots, ransacking my shop! I've got a lawyer nicknamed the Sledgehammer and when we get through with you—"*

"Focus." Raven pictured him in a garden-green apron, mincing about the shop with the cordless phone pressed to his ear. She shouted to get his attention. "I need you to focus."

"You were saying? Ah, yes—Birds of Paradise. You're not getting them."

"What the hell happened?"

As if explaining to a tourist of foreign extraction, he spoke in slow, deliberate terms. "It seems our Hawaiian distributor tried to smuggle in a kilo of cocaine with the order—*don't make me come over there and hurt you!*"

Raven held the phone aloft. The yelling stopped and the calamity faded to a din. Wincing in anticipation, she drew in the receiver. The shop owner returned, mainlining soothing explanations into her ear canal.

"I'm sorry, I seem to have inadvertently come under the scrutiny of the DEA. They sent the Gestapo in to question me about the coke, which I know nothing about. Now where were we? Oh, yes . . . so I have lots of carnations. I know you think carnations are *bourgeois,* dear, but I could do an exquisite arrangement—"

Echoes of shattered glass, tinkling to the floor like sour

notes on a xylophone, filtered through the line.

"Scratch the carnations. We still have two buckets of lavender-blue gladioli in the cooler . . ." A sharp intake of breath came through the line, followed by, "*Don't do that! You bastards'll have to pay for that!*

"Never mind, Raven. 'X' the gladioli. *Frickin' storm troopers just stepped on them!*" Sounds went muffled, as if he'd covered the mouthpiece with his hand. *"Yes I'm talking to you. Is there anyone else around? Stupid jerk."*

She heard him crystal-clear.

"How about making an *avant garde* statement with your wedding? I have chrysanthemums. They're in pots, Raven, but don't give me any static . . . we can remove the foil wrappers and group them together in clumps where nobody can tell. What are your colors again, dear? Because these mums are kind of a burnt orange and maroon combination and they won't work with everything . . ."

Mums from Hell.

In a color from Hell.

Thoughts of Geneva Anjou's Ugly Dress Rack popped into mind.

She hung up on him. Leafed through her address book and punched out the number for the bakery. A tone purred and she got a response.

"I'm checking to see if you have my cake ready."

A Hispanic woman spoke in broken English. "You order? I help you."

"Yes, I ordered a wedding cake."

"I get the pen. What you want?"

"I already ordered it. It's a five-tiered Italian cream cake with lavender flowers on it. Only now I have to change the color. They need to be pale pink."

"We gotta yellow or black to put the name on it. Or *rojo*.

We can make red for the name."

"I don't want any writing on it. It's a wedding cake."

"It's free. Spell your name, I write it down."

"It isn't supposed to have anything on it except the flowers."

"This *panadaría*. You want flower-chop for *flores. Adiós y buena suerte.*"

She hoped like hell the woman hadn't just wished her luck and slammed the phone in her ear. Luck didn't hold. Raven pressed redial. The same attendant answered in a thick-tongued accent.

"Let me speak to the manager."

"He no here. I get the pen. What you want?"

"My wedding cake."

"How many?"

"A five-tiered Italian cream cake with pale pink flowers on it. And a chocolate groom's cake with strawberries dipped in dark chocolate, with white chocolate, so they look like little tuxedos."

"¿Qué?"

"Put somebody else on the phone."

"You need the phone?"

"I don't *need* the phone. I'm *on* the phone. Let me speak to your boss. *El jefe.*"

"Everybody baking. You want order?"

"Don't make me come down there."

"Okay. You come down. We open 'til five. *Hasta luego.* Bye-bye."

A dead connection hummed in her ear. Furious, she pressed redial.

Same lady, same problem.

"If you hang up on me again, I'll have you killed."

"I get the pen. What you want?"

"A wedding cake. I want my big-ass, five-tiered wedding cake with pink frickin' roses made of icing. And if I don't get it, I'm going to show up there and hold your head underwater until the frickin' bubbles stop coming up, and then I'll walk away quietly."

For a moment, only the staccato sounds of background Spanish hung in her ears.

"*Lo siento.* Sorry. I have to put the phone down for the bathroom. You wait. I gonna watch my hands." The receiver banged down. Momentarily, running water hissed through the open line. It abruptly shut off with the woman's return. "I get the pen. What you want?"

"I want a lock of your hair and your shirt."

She severed the connection, convinced she should try back later.

At least she still had the caterer.

A young woman from "It's Greek to Me" answered the telephone in a fright-filled tone.

"Oh, thank God," she said before Raven could identify herself. "I didn't think we'd ever reach you. There's no easy way to say this . . ." Deep sigh. ". . . Bernard is dead."

Who the hell's Bernard?

Raven held the phone aloft. Stared at the mouthpiece and wondered if she'd misdialed.

"That's right. He was stabbed this morning, opening the store. The police think it was robbers, but I think we both know what really happened, don't we?"

"What?" She wondered if a confession hung by a tenuous, gossamer thread.

"Dewayne did it. I mean, we all knew they were getting it on in the back office ever since Xavier walked in on them—Ohgod, every time I think about him recounting that story, I get the ugliest visual of Bernard, naked, and Dewayne making monkey sounds underneath that stupid gorilla suit. Anyway, it was either Dewayne that killed him . . . or *you.*"

"Me?"

"Well, sugar, you both had motive. Nobody really believed you didn't know your husband was queer for Dewayne. We all figured the marriage was a business arrangement more than anything else. Not that we won't miss Bernard. But he *was* a real bastard the last time you showed up and demanded to see the books."

I'm starring in a soap opera. No—worse: I'm the lamp on the table in the scenery of the soap opera.

Raven pulled up a chair and sank into it. Outside, Leviticus Devilrow moved past her rolling eye carrying a sheet of plywood past the window. He shot her a look of utter disgust.

She returned her attention to the phone fiasco. "Who's going to oversee the catering?"

"Are you kidding? There's nobody left to run this sinking ship. We're all taking the day off to tie one on—except for Dewayne, who's down at the police department talking to Fort Worth's finest."

An unintended squeal came out of Raven's mouth. "You can't take the day off. The Greenway wedding is tomorrow."

"Fuck the Greenways. We're going out to celebrate." The jubilant mood turned sassy. "You know, if you weren't such a goody-goody you'd come with us. If I were you, I'd go out and buy me a new hat . . . with big fruit or lots of feathers on it. Make it pink. Anything but black."

Raven snarled out a reminder. "The Greenways have a contract."

"Not my problem. Besides, I haven't been paid in two weeks, so if they lock Dewayne up you'll need to come down and do payroll. Are you meeting us at the bar, or not?"

"The Greenways can sue, if you don't follow through."

"No they can't."

"Yes they can. And Mr. Greenway's in the CIA. He could probably have you killed."

What started out as a belly laugh degenerated into the rasping cough of a two-pack-a-day smoker. "He'll have to find me first. I'll be the one wearing Jackie O sunglasses, lounging in a hammock under a mosquito net outside a thatched hut, with a big-assed Mai Tai in my hand."

Raven's voice spiraled upward. "You can't bail on the Greenways."

"*Force majeuer,* hon. Means it's out of our control. Tough-titty for the Greenways but that's life. May they live happily ever after. At least they woke up on this side of the dirt today. Which is more than I can say for Bernard . . . dumb bastard."

Cézanne, leg-ironed to her desk at the police department, sounded harried when she took Raven's call.

"Working a new murder?"

Long sigh. "Really, Raven, you know I can't talk about on-going investigations."

Should've known I'd run up against a wall of blue ice. Cézanne never gives away details unless you convince her you know more than she does and play, "I'll tell you, if you'll tell me."

"You working a case on somebody named Bernard?"

"Bernard Waxworth, of Waxworth and Kippering, Inc., also known as one of the owners of 'It's Greek to Me' caterers. What do you know about it? You didn't kill him, did you? Because I'd like to wrap up this case in time for your wedding."

"He's really dead?"

"Deader'n Hogan's goat." Stated matter-of-factly.

"He was my caterer."

"Oh, honey, no," Cézanne said, injecting the right touch of dread into her tone.

"Oh, honey, yes."

"Then perhaps we should refer to him as the late Mr. Waxworth, since he won't be showing up tomorrow."

"Are you always this calm?"

"It's the Zoloft talking. Without it I'd be a screaming Mimi," Cézanne said, full of sugar, the way she did when she wanted Raven to know she was pulling her foot.

"I don't suppose you have any extra?"

"Oh, honey, no. That would be illegal."

"You don't suppose your girl Duty might be working her black magic on me, do you?"

"Don't even say that as a joke. Duty scares the shit outta me."

"This Bernard guy—can you tell me what happened to him?" Raven got a visual of her maid of honor lounging back in her government-issue chair, looking down at the Trinity River from her fourth-floor office, taking a load off her high-dollar shoes.

"Mr. Waxworth's at the ME's, leaking like a sieve. A hundred and one stab wounds—overkill—and we both know what that suggests: *homosexual frenzy*. I'm taking a suspect's statement right now, so I'll need to get back with you."

"Dewayne?"

"Dewayne Kippering. How'd you know?"

"Psychic." A long pause of dead air stretched between them. "Maybe I can make your life easier." She recounted the conversation with the employee, capping it off with a suggestion to interview the wife.

"Thanks for making my job harder. Are you sure you didn't do it? Because if you tell me you did, I could probably work it out for you to turn yourself in after the honeymoon."

The distant sound of shattered glass sheared Raven's attention. "By the way, thanks for the handyman. I think he just broke a window."

"That's him. Never leave him alone or you'll come back and find him naked in your pool. God knows if he's taking a bath or using it as a commode. Don't give him a key to your house, either. He has this unpleasant hobby inventorying other people's refrigerators."

"Tell me again why you sent him?"

"To alleviate your stress. Don't thank me."

"I won't." She watched Devilrow through the window, loafing. "He brought his helpers."

"Good. That should speed things up."

"They're obnoxious. They're gathered in the back yard, farting like a free-fire zone in Vietnam. It's like they've got some sort of contest going. By the way, we have no flowers."

"No Birds of Paradise?"

She heard the spring in Cézanne's chair go *sprong,* and figured she'd removed her feet from the desk and planted them on the floor. "You could say the Birds went to the dogs."

"I don't even want to know what that means. Look, sweetie, give me a couple more hours to finish up here and I'll figure something out. There are scads of florists in this town. Maybe I can call in a favor. We're still good on the cakes, right?"

"It's a question mark."

No Birds of Paradise, a big black hole on the cakes and no catered meal because a disgruntled employee chose that morning to do in the boss. Thoughts of a foodless, flowerless wedding sent her straight to the liquor cabinet. She poured a shot glass of Cape Horn rainwater and belted it back, wincing at the burn.

Get a grip—after last night, she was lucky to even be here.

Her brain did a double-take.

Who was she kidding?

If she'd *really* gotten lucky, Clem Askew would've killed her deader than a wedge and she wouldn't *have* to worry about the absence of flowers or how to feed seventy-five people, since everyone would bring covered dishes and wreaths to the wake.

She spent the next twenty minutes nibbling on leftover Quiche Florentine and forking rosemary chicken from the French take-out place down the street.

By dropping a bag of sawdust into the Jacuzzi, Leviticus Devilrow invented a cheap ploy to clean the pool before leaving. But Raven heeded Cézanne's warning. She saw him off as soon as he boarded up the hole in the bathroom wall and brushed the last coat of paint onto the new molding around the French doors.

A little after four, Tommy called. The airliner found Yucatan Jay's luggage and they needed to pick up his suitcases at baggage claim. After that, they'd stop off at Aunt Wren and Uncle Jack's hotel and dress for the rehearsal dinner.

Raven's heart ached.

Deep down, she wanted to spend the next three hours alone with the man who'd blitzkrieged her into loving him. Instead, she stopped by the PD and gave detective Teddy Vaughn her written statement, then drove to Cézanne's to get the latest on Clem Askew.

On the ride over, Tommy delivered more bad news. Something unexpected had come up with Y-Jay.

"What does that mean?"

"I'd rather not say. It'll only stress you out more than you already are."

"If you're not going to say, then allow me to alleviate my stress. He's fired."

"What?" The brandy smoothness went out of Tommy's voice. "You can't fire him. He's a groomsman. I don't go around firing your bridesmaids."

"That's because two of the rats already jumped ship. Besides, I'm having a gun concealed in my bouquet, so if anything goes wrong. . . ." She took a deep breath and let it out slowly. "Don't even think about not showing up."

Her mind raced a mile a minute. She hardly realized she was standing on Cézanne's porch, jittery as gelatin, until Duty opened the door.

"Come on in, Miz Raven. Miz Zan told me what happened." Maroon eyes narrowed. Duty grabbed hold of her wrist and tugged her inside. "Seen Mista Porter lately?"

"This morning."

"Uh-huh." Her head bobbed. "I thought so."

"What does that mean?"

"Nothin'." But the girl moved close enough to pluck a loose thread from Raven's sleeve. "I'll just take that off yo' hands. Got anything on you that might belong to Mista Porter? No, I don't expect so."

"What?"

"Never mind. Be right back." Duty left her standing in the living room, where a Harlequin Great Dane with a look of intelligence took up the better part of a sofa. She returned with a hairbrush and motioned Raven into a chair. "I'm gonna help you get ready. By the time you leave this house, all you'll need is to slip into yo' dress. What kind of outfit you got for the rehearsal dinner tonight? Me? I'll be wearing Miz Zan's turquoise chemise with spaghetti straps and a cocktail-length skirt. I also got *peau de soie* shoes dyed to match. That's French for silk. Miz Zan taught me."

"Where's Cézanne?"

"Called a minute ago to say she'd be late. Got a little

problem down at the office. Something about a special assignment. She didn't sound too happy about it." And then, "Think you could leave yo' shirt with me tonight?"

Chapter Twenty-Nine

Dusk melted away in pink and purple swirls, as if God used the horizon to put his stamp of approval of the bride's new colors.

While the rest of the wedding party milled around inside Shiva's Palace, Raven paced beneath the overhang outside the heavy wooden doors, waiting for Tommy. Foo dogs, symbolizing luck, prosperity and safety, guarded the entrance to the upscale Thai restaurant. Woven bamboo blades on ceiling fans spun lazily overhead; porcelain garden seats depicting an elephant parade lined the length of the front porch. Five minutes went by. When Tommy didn't show, she wandered over to the koi pond. Bamboo canes, filled with wax to form candles, floated next to water lilies and speckled orange fish.

She wondered what was taking so long. God forbid he had second thoughts. Strolling through the garden, she passed a kneeling Shiva made of reconstituted stone and wondered if it would do any good to make a wish on it. She decided to try.

Please make Tommy's love for me true.

Near a hedge of azaleas, a metal sphere the size of a gazing ball sat on a bronze and verdigris pedestal; upon closer inspection, Raven recognized it as a Zen fountain, where water gurgled up and bathed the orb before disappearing into the base, where a recirculating pump forced it back out.

Ten minutes passed without any sign of the groom.

To make matters worse, Shiloh and her husband went AWOL.

An Oriental voice called her name over the intercom, instructing her to pick up the nearest phone. Shiloh wasn't coming. Kenny brought home a virus making the rounds at his workplace and they were both throwing up their toenails. With any luck, Shiloh said, death would prevent her from having to clean up the bathroom.

"You're not just trying to get out of being my matron of honor, are you?"

"Let me put it to you this way: our house smells of imminent death and decay. When the Budget Casket ad came on in the middle of daytime programming, I picked one out from the showroom floor."

Disappointed to the point of devastation, Raven cut through the bar on the way back inside, past thatch umbrellas sticking out of teak patio furniture. A handcrafted bamboo screen set in a box filled with smooth stones formed a sculpture that acted as a room divider, shielding patrons from the glare of a brilliant sunset. She charged a Bellini to her table, and drank it half-down.

Still no Tommy.

Inside, she passed a Thai princess statue in the traditional greeting pose, standing in the vestibule.

Her stomach clenched.

Tommy wasn't coming.

Her mind reeled back to Sabina Balogh, Princess of the Gypsies, pointing that gnarled, yellowed finger in her face. Sabina's scathing hex danced between her ears.

You'll not marry. I curse you.

With a cobweb throat, Raven headed for the private dining room on lead feet, anesthetized to indignity.

Her eyes glistened. White noise filled her head. What would she say to her guests?

Dell's broad-shouldered back blocked her view. He was

talking to Jinx. A look passed between them—a kind of sad resignation—and Dell stepped aside.

Background conversations degenerated to a numbing din.

With nerves steeled, she glided in with a fixed, unpleasant smile.

Activity faltered. For no reason other than instinct, she supposed, the guests turned her way, waiting expectantly for an update on what had become of the groom.

A stout, bald man with azure blue eyes that usually sparkled like star sapphires now had a look of desperation on his face. He hung up a nearby house phone and moved toward her in slow motion.

Uncle Jack.

The sick feeling, which started in her stomach, sent a sharp pain to her heart. In her mind, she heard the remnants of extreme anxiety in Tommy's voice, the night he went away.

Uncle Jack—if Uncle Jack shows up on your doorstep and says I'm dead, maybe *you can believe it. Or the President.*

Her uncle's lips moved but it was Tommy speaking inside her head.

Something's come up with Y-Jay . . . I'd rather not say . . . it'll just stress you out.

She listened in stricken silence, held captive by her intuition.

"Raven, honey, I'm really sorry—"

No, no, no, no, no.

"—to be the one who breaks the bad news—"

Libyans found them.

The strangled-cat sound that started in her belly came out her throat.

"—but Tommy and Y-Jay—"

The room tilted. Smears of color from her friends' clothes slid past.

Jinx and Dell each grabbed an arm and hoisted her erect.

"—will be about an hour late. Unless the tuxedo shop in Dallas can outfit your cousin, he's dropping out of the wedding."

Pulled from the jowls of a conniption fit, Raven instructed the restaurant staff to serve the guests, with or without the groom. She sat to the right of Tommy's empty seat at the head of the table, with Cézanne at her side and Duty in the next chair. Dell and Jinx seated themselves across from her, followed by Uncle Jack and Aunt Wren, leaving Dixie and Georgia, and their respective husbands, and Ivy to fill in the rest of the chairs. Waiters in formal dress swarmed the banquet room, whisking away salad plates, replacing them with platters of crispy whole fish with maraschino cherry eyes, bowls of fresh shellfish and rice.

Halfway through the choreographed food ballet, a scruffy-looking man appeared in the doorway. He gave her a slow stare. Raven took him in—the faded jeans, the dark beard and mustache, the unpolished boots—in one dismissive glance. She nudged Cézanne to pass her the nearest wine bottle.

A waiter breezed by and she buttonholed him. "That guy's obviously lost. Would you please tell him this is a private party? He makes me nervous."

The employee bustled off with purpose in his step. Raven returned her attention to Jinx and Dell, studying the cherry-eyed fish heads with great intensity.

"Do they serve anything else here?" Jinx pushed his plate away.

Raven snipped off her words like nail clippers. "If y'all want a steak, order one."

"What kind do they have?"

"Oh, for God's sake, do I have to do everything around

here?" She craned her neck past Cézanne to catch Duty's attention. "Tell the waiter to bring two rib eyes and a couple of baked potatoes." She whiffed the air. "What's that smell?"

Cézanne rolled her eyes. "Duty has a little—how shall I put this?—a *gris gris* bag. A kind of charm. She wears it around her neck. I don't know what's in it and I don't want to know. It's like a punch in the face, but if it keeps the boys away, I'm all for it."

Raven eyed the doorway again. The uninvited man still loomed large. Lacking patience, she shot him a look of utter disgust.

He winked.

Even, white teeth sucked the breath out of her.

Tommy.

She pushed back from the table with such force the flatware clanked and the wine glasses rippled. Crying his name, she flew at him with outstretched arms.

In that timeless moment, there was no rehearsal dinner. No wedding guests. Only herself and the guy she loved, impersonating one of the Ayatollah's men. It only mattered that he'd returned with all ten fingers and all ten toes, and a tongue capable of doing magical things . . .

. . . like it was doing right now.

A collective "Ahhhhhhhh," resounded throughout the room. The drone of applause followed. Tommy lifted her off her feet. Squeezed her so tight his hug left her breathless.

He pressed his lips to her ear, hard and insistent. "How's my girl?"

She managed to croak out how she'd almost gone stark-raving mad without him. That if he ever left her again—the only exception being death—she'd have to kill him herself.

Tommy's mouth tightened. "There's something I have to tell you." He wore the expression of someone who's realized too late the zoo's locked him in and left the door to the python cage open, or discovered they were about to renege on a promise.

"You don't want to marry me." Her stomach rolled over.

"Nothing like that. No, it's just that . . ." He must've snapped to her panic because he said, "You know, Rave, it can wait."

"You're not married to somebody else, are you?"

"Stop guessing. Everything's fine. The wedding's on."

Just like that, the room came back to life, buzzing with conversation, clinking glasses and clattering flatware. She pulled him to his spot at the head of the table, not giving a damn that Y-Jay was conspicuously absent.

"Isn't your cousin supposed to be in the wedding party." Cézanne to Raven.

Tommy swallowed hard. A strange look passed between him and Uncle Jack. A cloth napkin, folded into a swan, rested in the middle of his plate. He shook it out and spread it across his lap. "Y-Jay's either out at the bar trying to convince people he's the Czar of Prussia or he's still by the koi pond making wireless calls."

He recounted the harrowing landing at DFW. Told them how the pilot hammered the plane so hard into the tarmac it felt like they'd been shot down.

Starting with Jezebel and the gown, Raven wrapped up the wedding debacle with stories about the flowers, and the caterer's death.

"I'll handle it in the morning," was all Tommy said. He ate all of three bites when the muted shrill of a telephone cut through the lull. His eyes flickered to Uncle Jack. They exchanged guarded expressions. As if by mutual agreement, Tommy excused himself from the table.

Duty looked up from her plate and shot him a knifelike

look meant to cut him dead.

When he didn't return after a few minutes, Raven dispatched Dell to look for him. Ten minutes later, Dell came back alone.

"Where's Tommy?"

Jinx reclined against his chair back. He rested his hands on his stomach like a happy Buddha.

"Probably went to the bathroom and climbed out the window." He appeared vaguely resentful when Tommy returned with a box of long-stemmed roses.

"These are for you." They pulled up an extra chair and set the flowers on the seat. "By tomorrow, you'll have so many roses, the scent'll probably make you woozy."

Outwardly, Raven smiled. Inwardly, she was still torturing herself with the most unpleasant of thoughts.

Sometimes Jinx annoyed her with his mind-reading.

Tommy invited Jinx and Dell to the bachelor party back at Uncle Jack's hotel, but Jinx wanted no part of it. He even tried to sneak out before dessert was served. He couldn't take another minute of Raven and her starry-eyed gaze, gulping champagne and speeding courage into her system.

As he made a beeline for the door, his ex-girlfriend charged up like a horse out of a paddock. She held onto a wine bottle as if it were a Molotov cocktail.

"Where do you think you're going?" She threaded her fingers through his. Got him in a vise grip and squeezed.

"Home."

"No, you're not." Brimming with playfulness, she gave him a hip check that pushed him back into the banquet room. "You and Dell have to go to the bachelor party."

"Is that so?"

"Yes, that's so." With a quick head toss, billowy dark hair

slid back over her shoulders. She studied him a moment, then seemed to realize she was pouring her energy down an empty hole. "At least let me walk you out."

She looked so pretty with her cheeks aglow and her eyes sparkling. And the slinky, low-back dress she had on that dipped so deep he half-expected to see a magnificent display of butt cleavage. Every head in the restaurant turned when she glided past. Judging from the envious looks of men dining with unremarkable ladies, they'd pegged him for a lucky dog. But the women—Raven had the most amazing effect on other females—like dominoes tumbling, a dozen compacts snapped open as they checked their reflections and made touch-ups in the presence of their companions.

"I wish you'd at least try to make friends with him. He's new in town and he's giving up his job for me. You might even grow to like him. Even if you don't, I do. So, if you respect me, you'll make an effort as a favor to me."

He let out a brittle chuckle. "Don't push your luck, Raven. It's enough I'm coming to the wedding. I'll even bring a gift." He shook free of her hand.

She sidestepped back into the trajectory of his path. "I don't want your gift. I want you, Dell and Tommy to be friends."

"Not gonna happen."

"Why?"

"Let it go." When she didn't move, he took her by the shoulders, lifted her up on tiptoes and set her out of his way.

He ducked out through the Tiki bar and walked around the side of the building.

Duty bolted from the koi pond yelling his name. As soon as she linked arms with him, a stout-smelling odor reached his nose. A strange little pouch dangled from a leather thong around her neck.

"Where-ya goin', Mista Jinx?"

"Anywhere but here. What's that?" He thumbed at the *gris-gris* bag.

She lifted it enough for a quick stare. "This? It's just a little somethin' I whipped up for Miz Raven's wedding."

"Like *'Something old, something new, something borrowed, something blue'?* "

"Kinda. Only this is *None of the above.*"

"You're not gonna tell me, are you?"

"Cain't. If I did, it wouldn't work." They reached the side gate leading to the parking lot. Duty's hand dropped away. "I know yo' sad, Mista Jinx, but everything's gonna work out for the best, I just know it."

"How can you tell?"

"Just remember, Mista Jinx." The girl looked at him with cold scrutiny. "Sittin' in a henhouse don't make you a chicken. And wearing a wedding dress in church don't make you a bride."

He hit the freeway and didn't stop until he ended up in front of Lyrica Prudhomme's townhouse.

House dark, shades pulled.

His heart raced. It took a moment to screw up his courage. As an afterthought, he fished out the cellophaned fortune cookie he'd tucked in his pocket, tore open the wrapper and snapped the cookie in half. He opened the car door and held the shred of paper up to the dome light.

Happiness is right in front of you.

He thumbed the key remote, heard the locks snap shut and listened for the telltale chirp. Undaunted, he navigated the length of sidewalk to the witch's front door with a head full of bees. The air around him felt thick and heavy, even after he loosened his tie and unbuttoned his collar.

Halfway to the awning above the porch, he reconsidered.

Still time to turn around and go home.

Two gas sconces flanking the front door beckoned him with an eerie flicker. The pull of the doorbell claimed him. He lifted his finger and pressed.

When the witch didn't answer after the fourth chime, he gave up and headed back to the car. A playful voice called out his name.

Lyrica Prudhomme strolled down the long expanse of drive with a determined expression on her pale, marble face. She wore a long, black cape and flowers in her loosely-pinned hair.

"Lovely night, Constable."

"Going out?" He looked past her shoulder to the raised door on the garage. The rear end of a Cadillac, as black and shiny as her pupils, gleamed from within.

"It's the summer solstice. A night of celebration."

The moon reflected the sun's glow like a shiny silver platter. Stars winked like a thousand sparklers.

"We got Magick back."

"I heard, Mr. Porter. It's all over the TV. Congratulations. I hope you're satisfied I had nothing to do with what happened. I would've told you if I'd heard from Fleck."

Her intoxicating fragrance snaked up his nose.

"Then again, I guess maybe you already know that, since I did hear from him. Imagine me, sitting in my office, watching a conversation take place on the instant messaging system. You're very lucky, Mr. Porter, that I didn't tip him off. You're even luckier I have no plans to contact the District Attorney's Office, since I doubt you got permission from the court to hack into my computer."

Every muscle in his body tensed. "It's okay if you want to call me Jinx."

"Wiccans don't hurt people, Jinx. By befriending Fleck, I

had at least some control over what happened to Magick at these rituals. You may not know this, but I turned him in to Child Protective Services—anonymously, of course—at least three times."

A tip he intended to verify as soon as he got to work Monday morning.

"Would you like to come with me?"

"To your witches' coven?"

She gave him a sly wink. "No, Jinx. Not to my witches' coven."

She glided toward him. Stopped a few inches away. Lace gloves, with the fingers cut off at the second knuckle, graced her hands. She reached for him. This time, he didn't pull back.

A shot of heat went straight to his head, harpooning his brain, as her delicate fingers caressed him through the trousers of his tux. And when she slid his zipper down and forced the flap of his briefs aside, he half-expected to pass out from blood loss. Icy fingertips maneuvered him free. Beneath the pale moonlight, he closed his lids and surrendered to her touch.

At the rustle of material, he opened his eyes. She removed one glove, lifted her bare hand to her mouth and licked the inside of it.

He thrust himself into the curve of her palm.

The second stroke took his breath away.

To hell with it. I've already lost Raven. To hell with everything.

Lyrica Prudhomme couldn't have done better if he'd given her personal instructions.

On the fifth stroke, he groaned.

"Let's go inside. This isn't a one-way street."

Like a trick pony, he followed her into the townhouse, uncaring what kind of devil's trade she expected him to make. He only knew that tonight, falling into her bed, letting himself be swept into a labyrinth of seduction, would lessen the gnawing pain of losing Raven tomorrow.

In the privacy of her bedroom, the witch's clothes melted off her. Lighted wicks from a dozen candles filled the air with the strong smell of sulphur. As shadows lapped the walls of Hell's meat-locker, the enchantress pressed the button on a remote control. An instrumental version of "Hotel California" played in the background. Sinewy specters coiled up from the flames, dancing to the music's rhythm like cavorting demons. Lyrica Prudhomme unfastened her hair. It flowed past her shoulders, framing her ghost-white face.

Made him want to check his hole card.

Instead, he checked his watch.

She won't get married for another twenty hours.

What am I doing here?

When the witch took his hands and cupped them to her breasts . . . tilted her face to his . . . he knew.

He found himself at a moral crossroad.

He *could* change his behavior, really he could.

And if he proved he'd changed his womanizing ways, Raven would take him back.

Succumbing to the sorceress's spell, he called Raven's name and sank into Lyrica Prudhomme's softness, prepared for damnation.

Hours later, he wheeled his car in the Château Du Roy parking lot. Glen Lee Spence and the Munsch brothers were sitting in the back of a pickup truck, having a tailgate party complete with beer cooler and chips. With a dismissive wave, Jinx headed up the sidewalk.

Agnes Loudermilk was at her usual post, puffing on a cigarette.

"How's it hangin'?" she yelled, then doubled over and let out an extended cackle, as if she thought this was uproariously funny.

He paused at the bottom of the stairs. "I don't think that's appropriate for you to be saying stuff like that."

Her eyes thinned. Like that, she turned on him.

Hackles raised, she squared her shoulders and flicked her cigarette over the railing, missing him by a foot.

Her voice pitched to incredulity. "Well I already called the police and they say they can't do anything until you expose yourself to me."

"What?"

"That's right." She punctuated her comment with a nod. "You have to actually show it to me before they can lock you up."

He averted her gaze and plodded up the steps.

"Is it hard enough to cut diamonds?"

Jinx refused the bait.

"I've seen 'em bigger than that before." Agnes tried again.

She was still hurling insults when he reached the door and shoved the key in the lock.

Then it hit him.

The reason he couldn't stand the old woman.

The flaws I see in Agnes are the same flaws I have in me.

Chapter Thirty

Raven knew it was Saturday because she woke up in a cold sweat.

The plywood board Leviticus Devilrow temporarily installed over the hole in the bathroom wall darkened the room to the point of morbidity. She snatched up the remote and flipped on the TV, flooding the room with color. Standing before a Doppler radar map of the Metroplex, Openly Gay José called for sunshine as bright as his canary yellow suit and matching polka-dot bow tie. But after slapping down the hall in flip-flops with her fingers "X"ed behind her back, Raven stepped out onto the back balcony, took one look outside, and sucked in a sharp intake of air.

The bottom was about to fall out of the sky.

A few minutes before nine o'clock, a couple of Jehovah's Witnesses dropped by. Unable to shoo them off with diplomacy, she resorted to lies.

"Does your church use rattlesnakes as part of your service? Mine does." She opened the door wider and thumbed at the laundry sack full of leaded glass on the living room floor. "I could let you hold one to prove your faith in the Lord, if you like."

They declined. When they pushed a copy of *The Watchtower* on her and invited her to their services, she said, "Pray for me," and shut the door in their faces.

Instead of dropping the propaganda into the recycle can, she hatched a foolproof idea to prevent annoying solicitors from bothering her. At ten-thirty, when a couple of Mormons on bicycles showed up and rang the doorbell, she thrust the Jehovah's Witness publication in their faces.

"I'm tickled pink you're here. I never have anyone I can share the Word with. Do you have a few hours to spare?"

They left.

Around eleven o'clock, after she put in a couple of desperate, last-minute phone calls to the caterer and the bakery, the doorbell chimed. On the way to the door, she popped a couple of antacid tablets off the roll and crunched them like peppermints. This time, she considered representing the wounds on her hand as evidence of stigmata and prepared to offer the uninvited caller an opportunity to glimpse the face of Jesus on the bottom of her swimming pool.

Instead, she snatched *The Watchtower* off the crocheted doily.

The door-to-door salesman turned out to be the crime scene detective she'd fallen on top of. With hair the color of cinnamon and a big smile bracketed by laugh lines, he stood on the porch dressed in civilian clothes, with his arm in a sling.

"I stopped by on a welfare check. How're you getting along?"

"Better than you, apparently." She dropped the pamphlet onto the lamp table and patted a small yawn. Threatening clouds the color of steel wool hung in the distance.

He reintroduced himself.

"Slash Vaughn," he said, offering his injured fingers by way of a handshake. He stared, unblinking, through compelling turquoise eyes, seemingly waiting to be invited inside.

"I'm getting married today, but I have time to make you a cup of coffee. After all, if you hadn't been there to break my fall . . ." She turned her back on him, headed for the kitchen and listened for the authoritative clunk of the door shutting. "You take milk and sugar?" she called over her shoulder.

"Black."

Jezebel padded into the room long enough to bray in rebuke. Raven came up with a reasonable translation: *You're loud. I have babies asleep.*

"Want a kitten? They should be ready to go home in six weeks. You can have your pick."

"You're talking to a dog man." A thin shaft of sunlight slanted through the plantation shutters in the dining room. It hit the crystal chandelier, casting rainbows of color across Slash's face.

He trailed her into the kitchen, where the smell of warm cinnamon rolls filled the air.

"I'm here about the fire at Bridal-Wise. We think it's an insurance deal. I thought you might've remembered something that could help us, especially since you seemed so emphatic about picking up your bridesmaids' dresses before the fire."

"Mrs. Anjou said Wednesday. She drilled it into us. I can't help it if I picked a schizophrenic and two bipolars to be in my wedding. You should ask her about that."

"We would, but it appears she may've been involuntarily cremated."

The news sucked the air out of Raven's lungs. "Mrs. Anjou's dead?"

The detective gave her a slow nod. "In the fire. What I'm about to tell you doesn't leave this room—the arson guys said whoever did it used a time-delay device."

"But if she was inside the building, why wouldn't she run out?"

"Exactly. Cézanne Martin's assigned the investigation. We're waiting for the ME to post the body."

Two cinnamon rolls and two cups of coffee later, Raven sent the detective packing.

At three o'clock, on the way to her hair and nail appointment, she drove past Thistle Hill.

She hadn't planned to stop in at the reception hall to check on the cake and decorations, since Dixie, Ivy and Georgia promised to take care of the last-minute details. But the sense of foreboding she felt watching the two-story, red brick Georgian recede in her rearview mirror made her turn around and go back.

Inside, she found the women standing around a table, staring at a five-tiered cake.

At the sound of her footfalls, they turned and greeted her with ghastly facial expressions.

"What?" She halted in her tracks. "What's wrong? The cake's here. That's a good thing, right?"

The wedding cake—a replica of the Leaning Tower of Pisa—had *Over the Hill; Happy 50th* written across the top in black script.

Raven rushed the table. "Ohmygod. This isn't happening."

"Honey, have you given any thought to postponing the wedding?" Georgia reached out and gave her wrist a squeeze.

Ivy volunteered one of her tasteless, white trash ideas. "We could buy tubes of ready-made icing at the grocery store and scribble a bunch of swirly things on top. We could do psychedelic colors and make it like a tie-dyed wedding cake and just tell everybody it's a seventies theme. When were you born?"

Raven fought the urge to thrash her.

Dixie came up with a solution. "I can run by the market and pick up a couple of pounds of plump strawberries. If we cut them up and pile them on top at the last minute, maybe it'll look like it was supposed to come out that way."

"Perhaps you hadn't noticed," Raven wailed, "but it's about to fall over."

"I can fix that, too." Dixie shouted to the janitorial staff push-brooming the hardwoods. "Hey-you! Bring me a couple of bricks." To Raven, she explained in her maddening, sing-song soprano. "Don't worry, I'm not going to smash it. I'll wedge them under this lopsided part to shore it up. Then I'll arrange some nice flowers around the brick—nobody'll ever suspect."

She left Thistle Hill fighting hysteria. The church was on the same street as the hair and nail salon, but city workers in reflective gear were out in full force, setting up orange-striped barricades and blocking off arteries. The side street they re-routed her to took her past the block-printed message on the church marquee.

Raven took it as a sign.

Don't give up. Moses was once a basket case.

After the stylist finished Raven's hair, she passed her off to the Vietnamese girls for a manicure and pedicure. Two women of indeterminate age hunkered over her feet, pointing. As if she didn't exist, one forced her hands into a bowl of milky water and spoke to the other in their native tongue.

Whatever the woman said evoked a wild cackle from her colleague.

Words flew in staccato tones, followed by knee-slapping hoots.

"What's wrong? Is something wrong?"

More sing-song staccato, trailed by high-pitched guffaws.

Raven narrowed her eyes. "Are you laughing at me? *Ouch!*" She yanked her hand from the grasp of a woman with nail clippers. She shook the sting out of her hand. "Be careful. I'm getting married in two hours."

Words erupted from their mouths like automatic gunfire. The nail tech with the fingernail clippers shoved her hands back into the water bowl and the two Orientals doubled over.

Fits of laughter degenerated into gasps for air.

"You pick color," said the woman performing the pedicure. Raven showed her the bottle of pink nail polish she'd brought along to match her gown. The tech held it up to the light, said something in Vietnamese and the other girl hooted.

"What did you just say? You don't like this shade?"

"It very light. Very light. You no want." She marched over to a rack, where dozens of bottles in festive colors lined the wall. She traded Raven's choice for one of her own, a lime green with a touch of glitter.

"This better."

"I'm not wearing that."

"This better."

"No."

They settled on purple.

What the hell? She and Tommy could share a good laugh on the honeymoon. Maybe even role-play the part of *Vietnamese whore,* to his *G.I. Number-One.*

The nail technicians exchanged words, then had a rollicking good time at her expense.

In a last act of defiance, she decided not to tip them.

It wasn't until a man in a Ram truck rolled up beside her at a red light, pointed a finger at her vehicle and mouthed *Tire,* that she realized impending disaster loomed large.

She pulled off the road, got out and circled the BMW.

Now she knew the nature of that big crash coming from the bed of Leviticus Devilrow's pickup. He'd dumped a box of roofing nails onto the driveway and managed to retrieve all but the one in her steel-belted radial.

Chapter Thirty-One

By the time Raven rode her car home on the rim, the clock on the dash read five-thirty.

The only person in the neighborhood who would've cheerily fixed the flat tire for her was also the one being held on a two-hundred-thousand-dollar bond for the murder of Yoruba Groseclose. As she killed the engine, the first splats of rain pelted the windshield. Sprinting to the porch, Raven tilted her face to the storm clouds, feeling the rain like God's sneeze on her cheeks.

At the front door, she found a note Cézanne looped through the brass knocker. She slitted open the envelope and read:

Raven,

Good news, bad news.

Good news. Nobody got killed last night, unless you know something I don't know.

Bad news. Every officer has been called in on special assignment. It seems some big shot dignitary's arriving in Cowtown this afternoon and anyone who's not on life support has to pull guard duty. I'll be at the wedding on time—Slash swore he'd cover my post—but I may still be in uniform.

I'm so sorry, sweetie, but it can't be helped.

Stopped by to see if you needed anything but you weren't here. I take that as a no.

Love, Cézanne

Upstairs, Raven managed to save her hair, fluffing it with a pick and a blow dryer. Dell could drive her to the church, but Dell didn't answer the phone. It didn't seem proper to filch a ride from Lola Askew, and Jinx wasn't picking up either. Cézanne had been scratched from the lineup of "People to contact in the event of disaster," and she'd rather have a monkey with diarrhea running loose in the house than call Ivy, Dixie or Georgia.

That left a taxi.

The clock was closing in on six, and the cabbie was late. Instead of bagging her petal-pink gown and putting on the finishing touches at church, Raven dressed at home. When the Pakistani driver didn't pull up to the curb until six-fifteen, she'd already scrolled through the mental list of people she knew well enough to ask for a ride, and realized the only ones left didn't get invited to the wedding.

The chapel train that looked perfect when she first saw the dress now seemed as long as a parachute. She gathered the folds of silk and hiked them, knee-high, to prevent the hem from skimming the ground. From the back seat of the taxi, she encouraged the foreigner to floor it.

"I do not wish to receive a ticket."

"I'll pay the ticket."

"This I do not know for certain."

"I'll give you a hundred dollars."

"It is done."

The hair-raising ride began.

A mile from the church, near the entrance to Trinity Park, the driver pulled off the road and skidded to a stop. Raven looked at the rearview mirror and locked gazes with the droopy-eyed driver.

"What's wrong?"

He pointed.

In the distance, barricades striped in reflective paint closed off the Seventh Street artery that led downtown. At the Henderson Street intersection near the First United Methodist Church, uniformed policemen worked crowd control.

"It appears we cannot get much closer," he said to the mirror. "Traffic has backed up."

It was true. A quarter-mile up the road, a lone officer appeared to be redirecting traffic at an alarming rate. Cars completed mid-block U-turns as fast as he could perform the hand motions.

Her head had that bursting-thermometer feel. Bleary-eyed, she made a calculated decision.

Bottleneck be damned; if the cab driver couldn't talk the policeman into letting them through, she'd get out and walk.

Caesar knew he'd been missing for eight days. In people-to-cat ratio, that meant four months. He'd pretty much given up on ever finding Jinx.

He walked near the banks of the Trinity River where the feral cats drank. Caesar tried to lick off the dust, but realized that by doing so, he was removing the last of Jinx's scent from his rangy coat.

The winds abruptly changed.

The girl's scent hit his nose.

The girl always splashed herself with that smell. He'd never known anyone else with that same scent and he assumed this belonged only to the girl. Even though the aroma only lasted for a moment, he recognized it and followed the direction of the breeze it floated in on.

Each step brought a stronger smell. Heart racing, the cheetah came out in him. He stretched his body to great lengths, pounding the earth with his paws. He pulled in the girl's scent with each hard landing. In the distance, a human form took shape. Cars sped by, churning out fumes and blocking his view.

A familiar tone reached his ears. He recognized the sentiment behind the voice, and whiffed the stink of fear coming out of her skin.

"Ohmygod. Caesar? Is that you, Caesar?"

He trotted toward the sound with yowls of ecstasy hanging in the air.

Good to see you.

Where's Jinx?

Take me home.

Now!

Yowls of ecstasy turned into howls of rebuke.

Where's my bowl?

Why'd you leave me?

You're going to pay.

What about that nap?

Pick me up.

Hate you guys.

Chapter Thirty-Two

The traveling dignitary Cézanne referred to in the note turned out to be the reason for the traffic jam. By the time Raven reached Henderson Street, a steady gathering of people had grown so thick it took the PD's Mounted Patrol to work crowd control.

Her pleas to cross the street fell on deaf ears. The motorcade had rounded the last corner and was moving toward them like a sleek anaconda. Raven spotted a colleague on horseback and flagged him down.

"I'm getting married and I'm supposed to be at the church right now." She pointed across the street.

"Congratulations. Who's the lucky guy?"

"Nobody from around here. Look, we need to get through."

"Tough break. We can't let you cross until the motorcade passes."

"Who's the big shot?"

"The President."

"Of the United States? What's he doing here?" Fucking up her life, that's what.

She surveyed the throng of people and wondered how she'd ever get past the congestion.

Several feet away, a fistfight broke out.

The officer parted the crowd and dismounted.

A crow-in-heat screech that could only have come from Glen Lee Spence pierced the air. He was decked out in a red cocktail dress with rhinestones and spaghetti straps, sporting a disposable camera in one hand and a five o'clock shadow above his carefully lined, crimson lips. As part of the entourage, the Munsch brothers dressed in second-skin, sequined gowns, like back-up singers for the Supremes.

"Apparently, you do *not* understand," Glen Lee shrieked, his strawberry blond hair made limp by the humidity, "I have a wedding to attend. If I am not there, the bride will never forgive me."

"Back off, buddy. Nobody gets across."

Raven shrank into the crowd to keep Glen Lee from spotting her. She pulled in great gulps of air so thick each breath had a bad taste. The odor of fresh manure snaked up her nostrils. When she checked the sidewalk to see if she'd stepped in it, her hundred-eighty-degree turn put her face to face with her acquaintance's big brown Bay.

She kept reminding herself she didn't steal the horse from the Mounted Patrol officer—merely borrowed it long enough to neck-rein her way two blocks down the street. By the time they galloped into the parking lot of the First United Methodist Church, her wedding gown was speckled with mud and her veil fluttered in the trees like a wayward kite. She dismounted in front of the huge Gothic doors, looped the reins through the hood ornament of a Mercedes Benz, gathered her muddy skirt and took the steps in twos.

Throwing herself into the red-carpeted foyer, she ran, smack-dab into Jinx.

"You're thirty minutes late," he said in a voice laced with impatience. "The tension's so thick you can knead it like bread dough. People are so bored they're playing driver's license poker and some are even checking the organ donor boxes on the backs of their licenses. Not me, though. I thought maybe you were suffering from a case of rabbit fever, in which case I win the office pool."

They set up an office pool?

"You think I'd run out on Tommy?" A laughable idea at best.

The contours of his face hardened. "What can I say? When you hear a stampede, don't expect to see butterflies."

"What the heck is that supposed to mean?"

"Means listen to your heart."

She spoke in a string of breathless whispers, laying it out for him like a losing hand of Five-Card Stud. "Like it or lump it, this wedding's taking place."

"Just as well. I understand the wedding announcements for the Sunday newspaper go in on Thursday. At this point, if this fiasco doesn't go off, trying to get that write-up out of tomorrow's edition would be like asking Moses to chisel off the Eighth Commandment."

"Anything else?"

"Yeah. Dell had to go to the rectory and wake up the preacher. He's down with the flu, but he arranged for a friend to perform the service. You'll like him. He's a happy drunk."

"He's intoxicated?"

"Three sheets to the wind. But hey, you just missed the worst of it. Somebody clogged up the commode in the ladies' restroom and the toilet overflowed. Caused a massive line to the men's room. Kind of reminded me of the toilet paper lines back in Soviet Russia. The singer's pretty good, though."

"I don't have a singer. Just an organist."

But according to Jinx, Emma-Jewel Houston showed up and broke into an old spiritual that was so well received, she started taking requests. If he could be believed, the jail matron wasn't half-bad.

"My Uncle Jack's missing from the hotel. You're giving me away."

"Can't do it." Jinx locked her in his unblinking stare.

"I'm not taking any guff off you today, Jinx Porter." She balled her fist and showed it to him. If he wanted a fight, she was booted and spurred. "You're walking me down the aisle—"

"Gangplank—"

"—and that's the end of it. I've been through Hell and high water for you."

"It was all I could do to drag myself out of bed today. I only showed up to see if you'd quit taking leave of your senses." His gaze swept her from head to toe. "I'll give you this much: I don't think I've ever seen you looking more beautiful."

She glanced past his shoulder, through the double doors, to a church full of open-mouthed guests craning their necks to get a better take on the problem.

"Does it feel hot in here to you?" She fanned the air in front of her face. "Because, if you ask me, the temperature's more suitable to an oven."

"Get used to the heat. You're about to board the direct flight to Hell."

"Listen to me, and listen good." She unclenched her fist, grabbed his wrist and tightened her grip. "Caesar's on his way."

His eyes doubled in size behind the tick lenses of his wire-rims. Hostility drained from his face and his voice crackled with amazement. "You found my cat?"

"I had to slip the cab driver a hundred bucks, but he'll be along just as soon as he can find an alternate route. I told him you'd pay him an extra hundred, once you get the cat back."

He wore the expression of a man contemplating ditching her.

"I have to see if I can get any of this mud off my dress, Jinx.

You just be here when I get back." For a second, she thought he might keel over. "Pull yourself together. For God's sake, you'd think it was you getting married."

She sauntered off on aching feet, to a room the church designated as the bridesmaids' dressing area. When she flung open the door, the suck of indrawn breaths filled the room.

Deuteronomy Devilrow summed up the sight for all of them. "Lordy, Miz Raven, what the hell? Who did this to you?"

"My thoughts exactly." Raven narrowed her eyes. "Take off that dress."

"This dress?" She fanned out the skirt, making it look even uglier.

"Yes. The dress from Hell. Get it off and give it to me."

"Here, take mine." Cézanne contorted her arm in an effort to reach the invisible zipper.

"Don't you dare take that off. You're my maid of honor and you're, by God, gonna walk down that aisle with or without clothes."

"My dress will fit you better."

This called for a snap decision. "Fine. Duty, you're still in the wedding. Cézanne, gimme that dress."

While Duty helped Cézanne out of her gown, Dixie gave Raven's hair a bit of last-minute attention.

Cézanne re-dressed in a blue cocktail dress she brought for the reception. After fluffing out the fishtail train on the periwinkle dress, she nudged Raven out the door, into the hall.

Duty followed, giddy with excitement.

Paused in the foyer, Raven took stock of the church.

The organist's hands were poised above the keys. Cézanne gave the woman the high sign on her way down to the front pew.

Duty stepped off to the first strains of the wedding march.

Jinx Porter stood near the exit. With his face buried in cat fur, he was in no position to walk Raven down the aisle and she knew it.

Pawpaw would've told her if she wanted the job done right, she should by-golly do it her herself. With an air of new-found confidence, she squared her shoulders and glided over to Jinx.

"You love the Siamese more than you ever loved me, Jinx Porter." She glanced at Caesar's profile, cold-nosing Jinx through an eternal smile. His throat vibrated like a tuning fork. "Stay or go. It's up to you. I'll be fine."

"Raven, wait—"

The quake in his voice made her heart clench. "Don't say anything, Jinx. I value our friendship too much to hear this."

They shared an unspoken moment, Jinx, Caesar and Raven. Then the wedding march went from *pianissimo* to *fuerzo,* and a roomful of guests rose from their seats. At the front of the church, Deuteronomy Devilrow stood off to one side. Cézanne stepped up beside her.

Raven's pulse did a little tap dance.

I wish you were here to see this, Pawpaw. You're probably doing a one-and-a-half-gainer in your grave.

Chapter Thirty-Three

Raven had traveled halfway down the aisle before she realized the man standing next to Tommy was the President of the United States.

The groom gave her a wink. His broad smile lit up the room.

Then he glanced past her, to the double doors.

For a moment, she expected him to bolt and run. But he flashed a reassuring grin and she returned it. A few feet shy of the altar, she passed Georgia, Dixie, Ivy and Cézanne. Ivy had on an eggplant-colored pantsuit that showcased every body flaw and a tumbleweed hairdo capable of blocking the screen for three rows of moviegoers. Georgia wore a sea green knit suit that accentuated the bulges, and Dixie's hot pink silk dress matched her newly-dyed hair. Only Cézanne looked normal. When the maid of honor flashed a subtle "OK" sign meant to boost her confidence, Raven got a little shiver. Things might turn out all right in spite of the hurling confusion from the past eight days.

Tommy cut his eyes to the door and back.

She joined him near the pulpit. He took her hand and helped her up the first plateau of steps. The preacher, an elderly man who looked five minutes away from disintegrating, reeked of communion wine.

Raven shoved her bouquet at Duty. She mouthed, "I'm giving myself away," and he gave a head-bob of understanding.

Tommy greeted her in a brandy-smooth voice. "You're beautiful."

Her chest swelled with sheer happiness. "So're you."

Arm in arm, they ascended a trio of steps. The wedding promenade faded into silence.

The preacher cleared his throat. Alcohol fumes invaded their shared space. "Dearly beloved—"

Tommy glanced at the door and back.

"—we are gathered here today to unite this couple in holy wedlock . . ."

Raven barely heard the rest. She studied the contours of his strong jaw. The way his blue eyes twinkled—

—when they weren't riveted on the double doors at the entrance to the church.

Probably expecting Yucatan Jay to bust in and knock Dell out of the Best Man slot.

Moved to distraction, the preacher's words dissolved before they reached Raven's ears.

". . . if anyone knows of any reason why this couple should not be married, let them speak now or forever hold their peace."

Raven's breath caught in her throat. She held Tommy in her gaze and listened to her heart pound. She didn't need any drama from Jinx or Dell. Or women rocketing from their pews like pop-up targets, declaring their undying love for her man.

Tommy cut his eyes to the door.

"The rings, please."

Tommy refocused his attention. He dug into his pocket, pulled out the diamond-encrusted band from Tiffany's and stuck it on his little finger.

Raven turned to Duty, who appeared to be daydreaming. "The ring," she hissed.

"Say what?"

She mouthed, "The ring," and watched Duty's face pale to an interesting shade of watered-down chocolate.

" 'Nigma has it."

"What?" In a stage whisper.

" 'Nigma. Don't be mad, Miz Raven, but I put the ribbon on his neck and strapped Mr. Tommy's ring around him like dog tags to see how they'd look, and I forgot to take it back. Miz Zan made me tie 'Nigma outside under a tree, so I expect if yo' want Mr. Tommy's ring, we oughta send somebody outside to get it."

From the gray depths of her eyes, Raven mustered her fiercest glare. Between gritted teeth, she spoke in a ventriloquist's voice. "*You* get it."

Titters erupted from the guests.

Raven pleaded with the preacher through widened eyes. Duty made a break for the side door.

Nobody said anything, but everyone tracked her movements with great interest.

The preacher whispered, "I suppose we ought to tell them what's going on."

"Do you have something you can read while we're waiting?" Tommy, cool and composed.

The preacher flipped through his Bible. His finger moved down the page and stopped on a familiar passage. He lifted his chin and addressed the people in a melodramatic voice.

Something having to do with love being kind, not boastful.

But he could've been reciting the multiplication tables, for all Raven cared.

Tommy whispered, "It'll be fine."

The side door jiggled. Clearly, Duty was locked out. Raven rolled her eyes at the bobbing shadow rushing past the stained-glass windows. Momentarily, the girl sprinted up the aisle like the backdraft in a four-alarm blaze.

She held Tommy's ring aloft. "Got it!" Nervous laughter rumbled through the onlookers. "Here you go, Miz Raven. 'Nigma got dog slime on it, trying to swallow it, but I pulled it from his jaws and if you just spit on it and polish it against yo' dress, it'll come right off."

Acoustics amplified the giggles. Dixie and Georgia huddled together, heaving with silent laughter. Even Dell's cement-eagle face cracked.

"Raven, repeat after me . . ."

She slipped the gold band on Tommy's finger and stared, misty-eyed.

It was happening.

Really happening.

Her chest constricted.

Almost over now. Thank God. One more minute and I'm Mrs. Tommy Greenway.

The preacher prompted her. "I, Raven . . . take you, Tommy . . ."

"I Raven . . ." But Tommy wasn't listening. He was checking out the doors again. ". . . take you, Tommy . . ." For no reason other than instinct, she tracked the trajectory of his gaze.

Yucatan Jay!

Even though she hadn't laid eyes on him in years, she recognized him on sight. The devil wore cowboy boots and blue jeans. Standing at the entrance with his gaze deadlocked on the groom, he tapped his watch crystal. Jutted his chin at the outdoors, *Let's go.*

Her stomach roiled to think what might be coming.

". . . to be my lawfully wedded husband . . ."

". . . To be my . . ." The rest of the words slid back down her throat.

The preacher gave her another cue.

Tommy affected the countenance of a cornered wolverine. Frantic, Raven glanced over her shoulder at Yucatan Jay, now holding his upright fist in a militant salute and tapping his watch in a cruel game of charades.

Breaths came in shallow gasps.

Tommy whispered, "Raven, hurry up. That's what I tried to tell you last night—we have to go."

"Where're we going?"

He gave an almost imperceptible headshake.

Words impacted her like an anvil dropped from a cliff. He didn't mean *she* and Tommy had to go; he meant himself and Yucatan Jay. *Tommy never intended to leave the CIA.* Yucatan Jay made sure of that. Pawpaw had that psycho-bastard, emotionally-bankrupt daredevil pegged from the get-go.

The preacher prompted her to finish.

People twisted in their seats, craning their necks to get a good look at the disruption.

"What're you doing, Tommy?" Her eyes rimmed. Her composure tanked.

His velvet voice was anything but soothing. "Just say the words, so we can get outta here."

"Wait—you're leaving with *him?*" She felt a drop in blood pressure.

"I have to. It'll be the last time. I promise."

Thunderstruck, she stared at Yucatan Jay.

Heard PawPaw's voice resounding in her head. *That boy may not've thrown in with the Devil, but he's driving the official pace car down the highway to Hell.*

"You promised me. The last time was the last time." She experienced a lightheaded rush, finally seeing where all this was heading.

Desperation flickered in the groom's eyes. He was running short on time and she knew it.

"We'll straighten it out when I get back."

"Get back from where?" As if she had a plan.

"Libya."

The preacher intervened. He addressed the couple in a voice meant only for them. "Do we need to take a moment?"

"No." Tommy whirled his finger in the universal, *Speed it up* gesture. "Please continue." He pulled Raven's hand to him and slipped on her diamond band.

"Wait!"

The ultrasonic explosion came from her own mouth. With a head full of static, she looked over at Dell, solid and dependable in his tux. Words spoken in earnest at the Greenwood Grocery came back to haunt her.

It should be one of us, Raven.

She scanned the faces in the room and landed on Dixie, digging into her purse for a tissue. She passed it to Georgia, who had put her hand to her bosom and clutched. Ivy, overmedicated and inert as a car stalled on the side of the road, had either passed out or fallen asleep. Dixie dug through her bag a second time and whipped out a canister of pepper mace.

Raven glimpsed Jinx, snuggled in the back pew, cuddling Caesar-the-Siamese beneath his chin. She heard his advice lolling around in her head, as clear as if he were piping it directly into her ear.

When you hear a stampede, don't expect to see butterflies.

On the brink of tears, she glanced at Cézanne for support. The maid of honor's arrested breath had flushed her cheeks beet red.

The danger alert she'd experienced on that country afternoon went off inside Raven's head.

I almost got hit by a train. I almost got hit by a train.

Wedding be damned, this was plain fucked-up.

She squared her shoulders. Fury invaded her body.

Tommy lied—she'd never make a CIA wife. With a church full of people holding their collective breaths, she summoned the courage to speak.

"Just go."

A combined gasp that sounded like airbrakes on a fleet of eighteen-wheelers filled the room.

Tommy squeezed her hand. "Come on, Rave." He moved within inches of her face. "There's still time. We can be done with it, and I'll see you when I get back."

Be done with it?

"I don't think so."

"We agreed to be married."

"You love the job more than me."

The preacher sliced his hand through the air, in the direction of an anteroom off to one side of the church. "Perhaps we should take a moment."

Tommy revved up another finger-twirl. "No. Let's get the show on the road."

Her lips went numb.

At least with Jinx, she had Loose-Wheel Lucille to be mad at. How could she direct her anger at an entire agency that wouldn't even admit its employees existed, especially when the burners were cranked up high, and flames were licking at their operatives' haunches?

She gave her man a bland smile and did her own dirty work.

"I can't marry you." Her throat tried to close around the words. "You're already married—to your eff-ing job." She shot the preacher a frantic look. "Can I go to Hell for saying that in church?"

Dell passed a meaty hand across his brow, flinging invisible sweat.

The President of the United States turned to the deputy. "I'll be damned," he growled out of the side of his mouth. "She dumped him."

Dell returned a sphinx-like smile. "Texas women know when to pick up their brass."

Dixie popped the cap off the pepper spray, gave it a brisk shake and lay in wait with her finger poised atop the pressure valve and the stream-hole pointed toward the aisle.

Dumb broad.

Didn't she know that stuff didn't work on drunks and psychos?

Tommy Greenway and Yucatan Jay were out the door like a stampede of shorthorns.

The President faded out a side exit with his entourage, emptying out half of the church.

For no good reason, Deuteronomy Devilrow threw the bridal bouquet on the floor. In *voce fuerzo,* she summed up the disaster in a sentence.

"Bucked from the bronco of love."

Undertones of grave explanation resounded in the preacher's words, but inside Raven's head, the announcement took on all the characteristics of radio squawk. She took a deep breath and wished for a meteor screaming to earth.

Dell took her by the arm and pulled her aside. "I know the Limón brothers. Want me to call 'em? They oughta be out of the pen by now."

"Can we at least get out of church before we start talking about hit men? Besides, Cézanne's overworked. I don't want her put-out with me."

"I know this is unorthodox, Raven, but look around." He gave the guests a furtive glance. "Most of these people are our friends. The reception's paid for. I'll marry you right now, if you'll have me. The only thing missing is my kids—and I can explain when the time comes."

She blinked in the hurling confusion.

"You heard me. I'm offering to stand in as your groom."

Jinx and the Siamese couldn't get to the front of the church fast enough.

He said, "Marry me." The cat hissed. His paw shot out as a warning to Dell and let out a yowl that sounded like the skirl of a bagpipe. Then he tried to bloody up the deputy in earnest.

"I'd reconsider marrying anyone who'd have this kind of luck," Raven announced to the candidates at large.

Behind her, Duty called out in a stage whisper, "See Miz Zan? I told you it works. All she needed was a little help."

Cézanne drew in a sharp intake of air. "Are you claiming credit for this?"

Duty toed the floor and affected a coy head-tilt. "Well, I don't like to brag . . ." A rose petal from Raven's bouquet lay on the red carpet like a huge snowflake. When the girl bent over to retrieve it, Cézanne's stern warning and dagger-eyed glare stopped her.

"Don't do it."

"I spent ten thousand dollars on this wedding." Raven scanned the faces in the room. Everyone returned blank stares. Deep down, she hoped Tommy would come sauntering back in. Seduced by the location, she added in spite of herself, "I ought to be marrying *somebody* today."

Cézanne motioned her over and whispered out of Duty's earshot. "You don't have to marry anybody today, if you don't want to."

The preacher frowned, bewildered. He'd been nipping at the communion wine and couldn't have cared less. "Pick one or the other," he said, and then belched out a fireball.

Caesar let out a chopping meow.

Duty returned Raven's bouquet. Raven passed it to the detective, and sandwiched Dell's hand between hers. "You're amazing. I never thought I'd have a friend as good as you. I love you, Dell . . . but not the way you want me to. You deserve someone who'll worship the ground you walk on. I can't marry you." She let go and his hand slipped away.

"And Jinx—can you honestly say you're ready to commit to one person? That you're ready to settle down and make me your number one priority?"

"Absolutely. I can do that." He trailed off and looked at her hopefully, but his face said, *Not hardly*.

"It's always been you, Jinx." She opened her arms to him, glorying in his embrace. "But you broke my heart." Letting go, she appealed to his sense of decency. "How could I ever trust you?"

"I promise to be faithful to you."

Cézanne grabbed her by the wrist. Yanked her close and imparted advice based on instincts that had been tempered in a hotter furnace than hers. "Don't you see what's happening? This is the *rebound*. You're a ticking time bomb waiting to go off in his arms. You don't need a serial groom, or one who couldn't be faithful if doctors tattooed the Seventh Commandment on his dick, and administered Depo Provera. Pick somebody who'll take these vows seriously."

"Pick Mista Jinx. Pick Mista Jinx," Duty mouthed, eyes scrunched tight and her fingers "X"ed at her sides. Goosebumps broke out over her arms. Her lids popped open and the mantra came to an abrupt halt. Her eyes went wide. "Uh-oh. Here comes trouble."

Lyrica Prudhomme and Sigrid Pierson stood silhouetted in the doorway. If Loose-Wheel Lucille stumbled in moldy from the grave with her false teeth clattering around in a highball glass, it wouldn't surprise Raven. Worse, the party crashers seemed to be networking, getting angrier by the minute. Getting Jinx out of the church in one piece would be like trying to pluck a wildebeest from a lion attack.

The dismal sight was enough to take the angle right out of the man.

And enough to reaffirm Raven's faith in the bad behavior of men.

World-weary, she mimed a smile. Inwardly, she vowed to keep her voice light and convincing, even as she swallowed a lump back down her throat.

"The party's still on at Thistle Hill. Come help me eat cake and God-knows-what other kind of food we came up with at the last minute. I think there's a band setting up, so let's all go have a good time." On that note, she lifted her skirt enough to skim the steps without falling flat on her face. "Now if you'll excuse me, I'm on my way to the bathrooms to make sure nobody commemorated this life-altering event with dirty limericks."

She swished up the aisle with thoughts of freedom vibrating off the top of her head.

Ivy awakened, bleating like a tethered sheep. "What happened? Is it over? Did I miss anything?" She blinked away sleep. "Where's the groom?"

"If you were any dumber," Dixie said, "you'd qualify for a service-canine."

"Oh, yeah? Well, your cologne reeks worse than cat pee."

"Look who's talking. You couldn't find a corpse in your car until it started to stink."

Hair-pulling commenced on the spot.

When Raven reached the foyer, the policeman whose horse she borrowed waited by the door, arms braced.

"Are you going to arrest me for borrowing your mount?"

"Nope. I'm here to save you. There must be a thousand

gypsies from all over the United States waiting for you in the parking lot—"

She gave him her best *So what?* look.

"—and the one with his head wrapped in gauze has a produce crate of rotten fruit."

Chapter Thirty-Four

After recovering from their collective shock, guests from Tommy and Raven's nuptials arrived at Thistle Hill to a brilliant explosion of Birds of Paradise and Tiger Lilies, accented with fern fronds. For a moment it seemed Tommy *could* work miracles. Still raw and aching from the church fiasco, Raven bit her lip. She had to admit getting dumped for a job hurt worse than getting dumped for another woman.

As for the rest of the drama, Tommy might as well have lifted his hind leg on her.

Her friends found her sitting on the top step at the service entry—a mere husk of the bride who'd arrived earlier at the church—with tears cutting tracks down her face, her shoes paired together near her swollen feet, a half-guzzled bottle of Dom Perignon and a head full of white noise from the guests gathering inside.

Cézanne lopped an arm around Raven's shoulder and dropped down beside her. "You did the right thing. I respect you for it."

She didn't trust herself to speak.

The detective broached another hot potato. "I hate to tell you this . . . none of the servers showed."

Raven gave a brittle chuckle. "What else is new?"

"Well . . . I didn't want to say, but the photographer forgot to bring film for the camera."

"No wedding pictures?"

"None."

"Best news I've had all day." She took another slug of champagne.

Duty trotted out and joined them. "Channel Eighteen's out front, Miz Raven. They wanna know if you'll give 'em a quote. If I was you, I'd talk to 'em. *Star Search* could be watchin'. You might get discovered."

Raven's gut clenched. "After all that's happened the past eight days, they'd have to edit a mile of footage just to make me look sane."

"I think you're a smart cookie." Cézanne, doubling as spin-doctor. "If you want, I could go talk to Harrier for you. He's actually starting to grow on me in a sleazy sort of way."

Raven flopped her head against the detective's shoulder. "When I was little and got sick," she said airily, "my mother would rub my tummy. It made me feel better."

"Want me to call her for you?" Duty.

Dixie bustled up with her take on the matter. In the fading light, she ran down the list of reasons not to be married. "I think your man has a deep-seated fear of intimacy and commitment. Then there's that bigamy problem, since he's *married to his job*. Not to mention—and, mind you, I'm not saying this to hurt you—but he's mouth-wateringly handsome, and that means you could've spent a lifetime going to restaurants where he's the only one at the table who gets waited on. Really, Raven, the only place to find a committed man is in the nuthouse."

On that stunning observation, Cézanne said, "Don't you have cake to serve?"

The part-time secretary ricocheted off Ivy and Georgia coming through the back door.

Ivy brandished a dessert fork with a couple of strawberries speared through the tines. "Guess this goes to show the hen never cackles 'til the egg is laid."

Duty plucked at a loose hair from Ivy's sleeve and got a live one.

"Ouch. What the hell's wrong with you?"

Duty pocketed the talisman. "You can't have much fun in a body cast, sister."

"Whatever that means," Ivy snarled.

Except for Georgia, the rest of the women kind of already knew.

Georgia scrunched her face. Troweled-on make-up cracked around her eyes and mouth. "Honey, do you want to break something? Sometimes when I feel bad, I break things. Usually it's my husband's stuff. Still, I find that pulverizing things empowers me."

Everyone paused to take her own personal inventory.

"I can have him killed for you," Duty volunteered. "I got a quick-acting spell, can put him in the ground before this time next week."

Cézanne fixed her with a squint. "Don't make work for me. Clean your room before you make any more work for me."

Ivy handed Raven a note. "Gil's sorry his brother didn't have your wedding gown cleaned in time. But he said to give you this." The deputy tendered a hand-scrawled IOU good for ten boxing classes.

She crumpled the paper and stuffed it down her cleavage.

Shiloh Willette slipped up from behind them on wobbly legs, carrying a barf bag strategically poised beneath her ghostly pale face. She spoke in the woozy way of someone who'd chug-a-lugged cough syrup. "Hey, Raven. I'm so sorry. Would you like Kenny to kill him?"

"What's with you people?" Cézanne glanced around, baffled. "Look, Raven, do you need a blubbery cry? Maybe go someplace where you can scream at the top of your lungs?"

She shook her head. The move had a dizzying effect. "I'm fine. Really. I hope everybody has a good time."

"Poor brave thing." Cézanne took her hand. "Come on, sweetie. Let's go inside."

"You go. And bring me back some cake. I'll take the top tier." Cézanne got to her feet. Raven looked up expectantly. "And make sure the little bride and groom are on it, so I can do bad things to the groom."

Duty's face lit up. "I got an idea—"

"You've caused enough mischief for one day." Cézanne, pouring another cup of guidance down an empty hole. "Raven, sweetie, I felt a raindrop. This is no place to hide out."

Raven moaned. Gave them a vehement headshake and felt sick. Words tumbled out in an upward spiral. "I can't go in there. All my friends are in there."

"You have to go in," Cézanne insisted. "All your friends are in there."

Shiloh knelt beside her. "You're not the first person to have an aborted wedding. I married Jinx, remember?" This triggered an eye roll. "When the preacher asked the deal-breaker question—the one where you're supposed to speak now or forever hold your peace—my maid of honor, a skank who tended bar at the place I waited tables, whipped out a Polaroid taken the night before of herself gobbling Jinx's goober and handed it to me."

Duty visibly paled.

Raven's mind replayed a short film clip of Loose-Wheel Lucille under Jinx's sheets, choking the ferret. "I know the feeling."

"Jinx hired a fellow to videotape the ceremony. My old boyfriend busted through the door, jumped on the chapel train of my dress and screamed, 'For the love of God, woman, don't do it!' My brother lifted him up by the belt loops and pitched him out—but only after calling him a few choice cuss words.

"A day or two before I filed for divorce, I tried aversion therapy. I put that dress on—the shoeprints are still there—and sat in front of the TV with the remote control in my hand, rewinding the part where Jinx vowed to love, honor and cherish me. Each time I played it back, I thought of the snapshot my maid of honor handed me." Shiloh squeezed her hand. "Don't feel sorry for me, Raven. The road to a good relationship is long and hard."

Raven blinked back tears. "I reckon that makes me a relationship cul-de-sac."

"The point is that I went through the ceremony knowing the truth. You figured it out before it was too late. You're not a relationship cul-de-sac . . . maybe a detour."

Grim nods, all around.

Shiloh's wedding took the prize. "How'd you like to be on your honeymoon when your husband tells you he doesn't really love you, after all? Oh, hell. Why'm I telling you this? I only wanted to make you feel better. Maybe Cézanne'll loan you her Mercedes and you can park it on top of him. Matter of fact—" she pointed, "—I see Jinx made it to the reception, so you and I could carpool. You flatten Tommy, I'll cream Jinx."

Cézanne linked arms with the jilted bride. "C'mon, sweetie, let's go get ourselves on the ten o'clock news. Here's your opportunity to save the world from bad manners."

Raven squeezed her sore feet back into her shoes.

Shiloh grasped her free hand. "Actually, you're lucky."

"How do you figure?"

They strolled toward the TV cameras, to where Garlon Harrier waited with the news crew.

"You don't have to send out wedding cancellation notices. All the guests are here. You'll save on postage because they can take their presents back home with them."

Duty went wide-eyed. "You mean she cain't keep the loot?"

"These aren't spoils of war, Deuteronomy." Cézanne turned to Raven and continued to count her blessings for her. "You've got great friends, honey. And you still have two good men still willing to marry you."

"One." Shiloh. "Jinx is a bum."

Duty's eyes glittered. "Miz Raven, did you know that Motown guy's here?"

"Who?"

"The record guy."

"Must be somebody Tommy invited."

The silky pipes of LeAnn Rimes filtered out on the breeze. Raven did a double take. "LeAnn Rimes is singing at my wedding reception?"

Shiloh nodded. "Either that, or she's a look-alike with a tour bus parked on the other side of the building."

Duty gathered her skirt and petticoat and bolted indoors.

"It doesn't have to remind you of a wake." Cézanne smoothed a lock of hair from Raven's face. "It's okay if you have a good time."

After the interview with Harrier ended, strains of "Big Deal" filled Raven's ears. She gave Cézanne a funny look. "Is that Duty singing?"

The police captain strained to hear. "Holy cow. It is. We've gotta get inside before she starts pulling threads and yanking out hairs."

"She's pretty good, don't you think?"

"Next thing you know, she'll be pandering for a recording contract."

Emma-Jewel Houston bounded outside with such enthusiasm the door sucked shut behind her. Basking in the incandescent glow of the wall sconces mounted just above her head, she said, "Girl, this party's unbelievable."

"You seem awful happy." Raven cocked an eyebrow. "Did you get laid?"

"Even better. I got my old job back. A couple of dumb bastards from the Warrant Division screwed up big-time and one of 'em's taking my place. Ain't that a bitch?"

"It is for them."

"From here on out, I'll be riding around in a patrol car."

"Congratulations."

"Same to you, girl. You don't know it yet, but you dodged a bullet today."

The headlight beacons of a police Crime Scene van swept the parking lot. Cézanne grabbed Raven's arm and pulled her to a stop. She squinted fiercely and shielded her eyes against the brights. Slash Vaughn motioned her over with a wave.

"Be right back." After a lively discussion that included hand gestures, headshakes and finally culminated with Cézanne turning her back on him, she returned to Raven's side. "He wants to talk to you."

"He's not going to arrest me for burning down Bridal-Wise, is he? Because you know I didn't do it."

"He wants to ask you out. I know you're still hurt over what happened tonight, but I think you should go. Slash may be the last of the good guys, Raven."

"This, coming from the rebound expert?" Raven started toward the van thinking, *When does it all end?*

The blacktop steamed under the first drops of evening rain. Raven reached the driver's window as a wall of water moved in from the west.

Slash lowered the glass halfway. "Get inside."

Rain sluiced down the windshield. On shaky legs, she skirted the front of the vehicle to the beat and swish of the wipers, not really caring if her curls unwound or her mascara ran down her face in rivulets. She hiked up her skirt enough to climb into the passenger seat, with her hair wet against her neck and face.

She pulled the door to her until she heard an audible click. "Cézanne said you wanted to talk to me. Am I in trouble?"

"There are still a few women out there who might think so." He gave her a cagey grin. "Zan told me what happened."

Raven gave him the *Yeah, well that's life,* head bob.

"I didn't really stop by this morning to talk to you about the fire." The silence stretched a couple of beats. "Don't you want to know why?"

"You wanted to talk to me about Mr. Askew?"

"No."

"You found my prints in Yoruba Groseclose's house and you're here to pin the caper on me?"

"No." He gave her a slow stare.

"I give up."

He looked through the windshield, past the clunking wipers, as if by doing so, it would make the words come easier.

"I'm sorry about your wedding. But I'm glad, too."

What?

"I'm glad because that means you're not off the market. And when you fell on me the other night, I took it as a sign we might become friends. Maybe even good friends. But when I asked about you, Cézanne said you were off-limits because you were getting married. Only now you're not. So even though my arm still hurts, I'm feeling kind of lucky."

His words caught her off-guard.

"I was wondering if—when the sting goes out of this—you

might consider going out to dinner with me?"

"Let me get this straight: you want to date me?"

"Very much."

"And you're aware I have a gypsy curse on me?"

"Doesn't matter."

She wasn't sure she should be going out with the kind of people who wanted to date her. But the chances of finding a decent man were slim, and none; and Slim just left town. She'd have better odds matching all six numbers in the State lottery. Then again . . .

She flashed her best beauty pageant smile. "I'm supposed to be suntanning in Cozumel tomorrow. Maybe I'll see you when I get back."

He twisted in his seat, relaxing his back against the door. "Isn't that interesting. Tomorrow happens to be my day off. What if I went along?"

Epilogue

For Raven, coming home to Jezebel and her kittens eased the sting of getting dumped.

At least she didn't have to spend the night in an empty house. And she'd have an automatic support system beside her when she got up and read her wedding announcement in the society section of the Sunday newspaper. At least she wouldn't be around to take congratulatory phone calls from people who weren't there to watch the Shakespearean drama unfold or hadn't heard the news.

And if the President's visit didn't merit a couple of columns in Monday's edition, she'd ask the features editor to print a correction when she returned from Cozumel.

She kicked off her shoes. Pitched an envelope containing a generous gift certificate from The Sharper Image onto the sofa—a present from the President and First Lady. Deadbolted every lock on the door and thought of ways to spend it as she dragged herself upstairs on aching feet.

In the sanctuary of her bedroom, she flicked on the stereo and selected a couple of Enya CDs, then shrugged out of Cézanne's dress and turned on the shower. Moments later, with hot water misting the tiles and Enya's pipes filtering through loud and clear, she closed the door to her own steam room.

Half of her tension ran down the drain.

She stared at the three-carat diamond and wondered if she should return it, sell it or break it into smaller diamonds, then considered waiting a few days to decide, when she could think clear-headed.

All in all, she threw a damned good party.

Duty got to sing with LeAnn Rimes, and the Motown king gave her his business card; Glen Lee Spence and the Munsch brothers called in a couple of gay waiter-friends who were willing to serve cake; Ivy put in a phone call to her part-time job at the brewery and a couple of beer trucks rolled up with enough suds to float a battleship. Jinx and Dell even shared the first dance with her—

Was that ever weird, being sandwiched between two rivals?

—and Cézanne pressed the warring heifers into service, slicing fruit and salami and making finger sandwiches with pimento cheese and meat products Shiloh and Kenny hauled in from the supermarket.

The hot water ran out.

Raven cranked off the faucets. Tomorrow she'd board the flight to Cozumel. Maybe pick up a few treasures from beach boutiques and set fire to her wedding dress while belting down umbrella drinks at the Tiki bar.

With the promise of fresh hope in the air—Cézanne promised to feed Jezebel, and Slash agreed to pick her up at noon and drive her to the airport—she sailed out of the shower and capsized into a watery grave of trouble.

The last thing she expected to see was a western-booted, Wrangler-wearing cowboy seated on her bed.

She assessed her chances of taking him. Six feet tall—that would give him an edge—one-ninety; who could tell with his clothes still on whether he pumped iron . . .

. . . but she knew.

And she knew better than to get him on the same level—say, the bed—to equalize his brawny advantage.

Her eyes flickered to the pink diamond, still on her left hand.

"Surely you're not thinking of using jewelry as a weapon." The intruder taunted her with his brandy-smooth voice. He unbuttoned his shirt, exposing a buff chest and killer abs.

New plan.

"You're probably thinking, *Maybe if I use sex as a weapon . . .*"

How does he do that . . . read my mind?

He peeled off his shirt and dropped it on the floor. Went for his belt buckle and unzipped his fly.

She flinched, seeing where all this was heading. Standing on the bathmat, shivering, her voice warbled with the effort of speech. "Let me get dressed."

"I warn you, clothes won't help in a situation like this. Honestly, Raven, putting on clothes just makes me have to do more work taking them off."

She moved uneasily under his intent regard. "What're you doing here?"

"I got as far as Atlanta." His eyes glistened. "I thought, *What am I doing? Yucatan Jay can handle this alone. I made a promise I wouldn't leave her. If my word's no good to the one person I love more than anything else, then* I'm *no good.* So I caught the next direct flight home."

Honestly, the man should have scaffolding and DANGER—DO NOT CROSS tape around him.

Cool air from the A/C whispered over her face.

"Come on over, Rave." His blue eyes were sparkling. "Give Big Tom some sugar."

Goosebumps popped up on her arms and legs.

He thought he could wear down her resistance.

That she was a ticking time bomb, waiting to go off in his arms.

They spent the next two hours making love in the sweetly-scented light of a candle. With her head cradled against his chest, and a thin snore coming from Tommy's mouth, Raven made herself a promise.

Tomorrow, things would be different.

The tickets to Cozumel were still good.

And Cézanne had been right about Slash—there *were* good men out there, even if the odds of finding one were like hitting the lotto.

But people win the lotto every day.

And everybody knows if you don't play, you can't win.

She drifted off to sleep in Tommy's arms, feeling God's kiss on her self-esteem and a recurring thought, piped into her head from the spirit world.

Thank God I got off the track today.

I almost got hit by a train.

About the Author

Laurie Moore, Edgar-nominated author of *Constable's Apprehension,* was born and reared in the Great State of Texas, where she developed a flair for foreign languages. She's traveled to forty-nine U.S. states, most of the Canadian provinces, Mexico and Spain.

She majored in Spanish at the University of Texas at Austin, where she received her Bachelor of Arts degree in Spanish, English and Elementary and Secondary Education. Instead of using her teaching certificate, she entered into a career in law enforcement in 1979. After six years of patrol work and a year in criminal investigations, she was promoted to the rank of Sergeant, and worked as a District Attorney investigator for several DAs in the Central Texas area over the next seven years.

In 1992, she moved to Fort Worth and graduated from Texas Wesleyan University School of Law, where she received her Juris Doctor in 1995. She is currently in private practice in "Cowtown," and has a daughter who graduated from Rhodes, a destructive Siamese cat and a sneaky Welsh Corgi. She is still a licensed, commissioned peace officer.

Laurie has been a member of the DFW Writers Workshop since 1992, and an office holder on the DFWWW Board of Directors for the past four years. She is the author of four published novels: *Constable's Run* (2002), *The Lady Godiva Murder* (2002), *Constable's Apprehension* (2003) and *The Wild Orchid Society* (2004); four short stories: "A Mother's Day

Gift for my Sister" (*Haunted Encounters*), "Brad's Story" (*Haunted Encounters*), "His Name Is Howard" (*Heroes for Humanity*) and "Hero in Blue" (*Heroes for Humanity*); and two juvenile/young adult novels in the Deuteronomy Devilrow Mystery series: *Simmering Secrets of Weeping Mary—A Deuteronomy Devilrow Mystery* (2005) and *Delivering Dauphine—A Deuteronomy Devilrow Mystery* (2006), written under her pseudonym, Merry Hassell Frels. Writing is her passion. Contact Laurie through her website at www.LaurieMooreMysteries.com.